Thom Costea has certainly led a diverse life, from modest beginnings winning short story and public speaking contests to a career as a newspaper, magazine and radio journalist, photographer, speech and script writer, and later a video producer. Costea studied journalism and political science in Canada, all the while canoeing and hiking his way on a lifelong spiritual journey into the church of wilderness, as well as experiencing many interesting pursuits, such as lifeguard, ski patrol and paramedic, a competitive athlete and head coach, acting on stage, and advocating various community campaigns. These days he's acting half his age as an internet junky spewing out works of journalism, artwork, entertaining stories and of course pure fiction.

For my grandfather, Mosu Toma, the old farmer, who taught me how to enjoy life; my Gramma Mary, who filled my heart with family love; and with a special memory for Cassie, the golden retriever who saved my life.

Thom Costea

47 Trees: A Cosmic Crusade Part 1

AUSTIN MACAULEY PUBLISHERS™

LONDON • CAMBRIDGE • NEW YORK • SHARJAH

A CIP catalogue record for this title is available from the British Library.

ISBN 9781398481381 (Paperback)
ISBN 9781398481398 (ePub e-book)

www.austinmacauley.com

First Published 2023
Austin Macauley Publishers Ltd®
1 Canada Square
Canary Wharf
London
E14 5AA

The original draft of this novel, the first in a trilogy series, was initially written by Thom Costea on an *Underwood* manual typewriter given to him by his Uncle Jim Chevalier over thirty years ago. The manuscript was re-drafted and significantly expanded—on his laptop computer—during the recent pandemic. Thom would like to acknowledge his uncle; wife, Joanne; and son, Daniel, for all their support while he locked himself in a small office and churned out his fiction.

Table of Contents

Preface

The harbinger of realisation: existence for everything and everyone—you know, that ultimate quest for clarity and understanding—the way it is and why; almost always appears in a dramatic sentence with all sorts of punctuation.

Oh, why are writers so passionate? But I'm only trying to get across the inspiring if not enormous magnitude of extensive cosmic actuality.

To say: beyond contemplation and beyond concept of one universe and only one dimension; let alone only one heaven—in the spirit of mythological adventure, so to speak.

This cosmic crusade comes to words through vivid dreams, some meditation with visions and hallucinations, maybe a revelation or two, exactly three manuscript drafts and numerous pages of research notes.

I didn't mention out-of-body episodes, ghosts, teleporting and dimensional metaphysics. These concepts usually meet with supreme scepticism and are best kept out of the conversation when attempting to establish legitimacy.

Suffice to say, this wacky writer has experienced some bizarre circumstances since childhood; all completely without the enhancement of intoxicants or hallucinogenics. This spiritualism I will call it, induces thoughts to drift and question our very nature; much like quantum scientists and philosophers have deliberated over space and time.

The story of this novel has filled my mind like the crest of a wave sweeping across the water; consuming my soul and revealing itself in utterly unique dreams and visions. I am just the scribe; documenting this story that seems to come from somewhere else.

It could be said that this novel was unveiled to me over the formidable years of my life; taking control of my pen and paper, manual and electric typewriter, digital audio recorder, one of the early desktop computers and finally my laptop—not to mention my psyche.

The initial idea came to me as I was climbing one of the massive poplar trees planted over a hundred years ago on the western prairies: pretending to be a child again while in my twenties, perched high atop and peering down the impressively vibrant central trunk, with spindles of large branches spiking in different directions. There was also the first lucid vision—or hallucination, you tell me—only one year later while driving along the Alaska Highway returning from a canoe trip.

The Alaskan event was followed a few years later by the exact same images isolated on an island in a northern lake, where I was partaking in my first vision quest tutored by an Ojibwe tribal shaman; the same blind man who told me the precise location of an indigenous ceremonial drum in the Library of Canada on Parliament Hill in Ottawa.

These occurrences and other seemingly supernatural encounters somehow began to intertwine the mystique of my conceptual odyssey, but nothing was as coherent and detailed as the coloured tapestry dreams of travelling through the interstellar expanse: in spacecraft complete with elaborate technology, crew members and passengers, or flying free on my own power alongside vampires and glowing beams of light. And in the end, hard scientific research and primitive but extremely powerful conduits of ecological features such as rocks, trees and owls, all meshed together in a whirl of creativity.

This journey is strangely esoteric to be sure, and definitely requires both assumptions of scientific technology and leaps of faith, as do most science fiction and fantasy stories; and so I have attempted to provide this novel with a certain level of conceivable science and believable predictions of environmental and social implications—and philosophical musings, of course.

Spanning the history of multiple ages calculated in planetary, galactic and supercluster rotations, and reflecting the advancements of universal civilisations separated by eons of sophistication and billions of light years, does require some amount of research. Rather than denoting facts and figures in foot notes, the author—that's me—has compiled some illustrated maps and charts, as well as a small glossary dictionary. A comprehensive operations manual appendix for futuristic interstellar warriors will also be presented in the sequel to this novel.

Although the appeal of fanciful literature is most often left to the imagination of the reader, when it comes to science fiction and fantasy a modest legend to sort some of the details can sometimes be helpful; and is also popular with some other authors and publishers. The descriptive narration of any novel worth its artistic expression should adequately depict the visualisation of the fictional world, yet illustrations and simple charts can help keep the ongoing plot in perspective.

There are three maps in this book appearing as they become relevant to the story, with one accompanied by three charts and a map of the known universe with a single chart as an appendix. The dictionary of an ancient warrior language is also at the end of the book to provide easy reference for the reader since it can be utilised during various segments of the story.

I'm not saying the research lends legitimacy to my story, or that I believe this book to be the essential truth, but similar to the spontaneous fashion of the novel's entire composition, it could possibly spark some acumen conducive to insights of the unknown and unproven. Considering this tale lingers among the mysteries of life, who am I to doubt its authenticity?

Does a spiritual gift born on the cosmic wave allow a brave voyager to see through dimensions of reality? The understanding of evolution and the pursuit of existentialism are both most likely a lifelong journey in this universe. It is a journey, methinks, that all starts with pride and ends with courage.

There are many paths to follow in life: confronting our fears to find truth and discover the essence of our existence. The secret, according to philosophers over the ages, is countering vices with personal choices of virtue building a ground swell of social revolution; as long as the spin doctors have crafted their magic and made it a popular culture kind of thing.

I always thought pride could be a virtue through integrity and confidence instead of arrogance, but I also see how pride can lead to impatience and anger when combined with privilege and entitlement. It breeds the dark path of belligerence, intolerance, wrath and rage, but it can be countered with the bright path of humility and the conviction of justice coming from a belief in equality.

I also thought desire could be a virtue thirsting for knowledge instead of hungering for extravagance, but then there are these enticing concepts of lust, envy and selfish greed that get in the way. They can be avoided with temperance coming from the satisfaction of contentment, charity coming from true love and compassion, and the clarity of discretion, prudence and that ever elusive common sense.

Pride and greed are definitely triggers that provoke indulgence and gluttony leading to sloth and laziness, yet the enduring and stimulating postulation of hope and affirmation can still persist, along with the most impressive path to cosmic actuality, the one and only, my favourite, courage and bravery.

The dark path is a weakness that evil elements will leech and draw into the abyss of life. The deception of materialism and decadence slithering in the shadows replaces an empty and unsatisfied void behind a facade of ego and misery. The humble souls among us fill this void with the simple pleasures of the bright path: not only the most important thing in life bringing us true happiness, but also keeping us sane when superficial values encourage the accumulation of tawdry treasures.

We can learn to love instead of hate, extend our charity with respect and embrace the serenity of fulfilment; giving us the resolve and determination within to seek freedom and liberty. Trusting that our convictions have value while acknowledging that it might be a strenuous and demanding responsibility, we can make a real difference.

However, some people just don't care, which can be construed as being afraid, weak or lazy, but can also be an innocent coping mechanism because they simply don't have the strength for altruistic crusades. If you want to take on the challenge, honestly care about humanity and realise some of the answers to life's questions, you can find solace by embracing the wondrous power of creation and the pure grandeur of universal providence.

It all ends with the courage to seek the wisdom of the bright path, explore the universe and find the balance of harmony. It's actually quite a sensible recipe, as a wise human once said: things that are real and things that really matter.

And so, what does this have to do with trees and the cosmos? You might be surprised. You might be inspired. You might be bored; not that it's a bad thing though—boredom that is—which can sometimes lead to stimulating and amazing innovations.

Is there a swath of spiritual fibre emanating from metaphysical consciousness; lashing at the edges of morality and enticing truth and wisdom?

And can this visionary medium be cultivated by a thoughtful understanding of nature's harmonious, intrinsically impulsive and often sporadic miracles of life?

Trees absorbing pollution in the air and photosynthesising the oxygen we breathe: just think about the brilliance of it all.

The journey of life can be fulfilled by the inspiration of nature's spectacular symmetry and the enriching contemplation of our own spirituality, but there are many more hidden secrets to be found gliding along the cosmic wave.

Why are we here?

Better yet: how are we here?

"Jobo ashyb, jobo moobah. Where there is a tree, there is hope."

–Soarfoot, pine tree warrior

"When the trees breathe, we breathe."

–Breeze Boback, Registered
Nurse, California, USA

Part One
Facing the Demons

Chapter 1: The Plan

In the beginning, there was one heaven.

The one heaven provided a dynamic spiritual habitat where many gods flourished. The gods lived in harmony. They, the gods, permeated heaven to form a sporadic collection of nondescript entities: spirits, so to speak.

In the beginning of the one heaven, the gods mysteriously comprised the fabric and texture of spiritual fibre—the essence of their exquisite habitat.

They, the gods, floated and fluttered about; mingling with the particles and molecules and each other, fusing to become one and then splitting their fibre to become two or five or nine nondescript sporadic entities.

The fibre of heaven always swirled without boundaries; morphing into many shapes. It grew to immense proportions: take my word for it, I was there. Mind you, I am not a god.

They, the gods, could expand or contract as they wished; constantly altering heaven in one way or another. The gods possessed great power then, as they do today. This is why they did as they wished: fusing, splitting, roaming and floating about.

But the one heaven was intangible and so you would never know that it even existed, let alone sporadically changed shape, except that I have just told you so.

And that is how the one intangible heaven existed: an undetermined number of gods, since they were always free flowing in the spiritual dimension, fusing and splitting and constituting in the aggregate the spiritual fibre of heaven; and without the gods knowing it, a considerable amount of unidentified spiritual fibre as well, swarming about catching the pockets of heaven that invariably persisted as a by-product.

This is where I existed; an unidentified spiritual fibre, or USF, as we called ourselves. I was a non-entity, but nonetheless an element of the heavenly composite; hopeful of gaining an identity.

But I was not a god. But I did exist.

The rest suits me fine.

❖ ❖ ❖

The gods, as I have told you, possess great power. So great is the power of the gods that they became bored with simply roaming about the intangible heaven.

You might say boredom triggered the creation of everything that exists today.

They, the gods, wanted to transform the spiritual fibre in a tangible manner to create an ethereal heaven as a symbol of their power. And so, as a result of this desire heaven began to take shape.

The aesthetic heaven was born from the seed of desire; and boredom. The evolution of spiritual fibre and we USF experienced a profound and dramatic change as this new heaven developed.

The gods soon discovered that once the spiritual fibre was exhausted to form a distinct, tangible feature in the one heaven, it remained as the permanent entity it became and could not be changed into anything else.

The gods also quickly realised as they consumed the spiritual fibre for creative reasons that there was less of the fibre for them to fuse and split as they desired.

Ultimately, they, the gods, would not be able to dilate and constrict indiscriminately as they once did.

Fortunately for me they could never consume USF.

In their wisdom, the gods calmly sat down, so to speak, and conceived of a heavenly plan for the spiritual fibre.

They did not yet know that the USF actually existed.

The plan was this: a conglomerate of spiritual fibre which consisted of one god who created a distinct aesthetic feature in heaven would remain as an individual god; no longer fusing or splitting but retaining the fibre in a permanent domain.

Subsequent gods who inspired to create consumed their allotted fibre and remained as single entities.

The tangible aesthetics which each god created became the domain of that god. This process continued until all the spiritual fibre was consumed and individual gods remained permanently in their newly created domains, but still able to freely roam throughout the one original aesthetic heaven.

This new heaven only manifested into a spiritual yet tangible world for the gods themselves; considering that mortals had not yet evolved from the cosmos into the organic habitat, which did not exist when there was only the one heaven.

Eventually, after the organic habitat sprouted from the one aesthetic heaven, those fortunate souls taught to enter the spiritual dimension could marvel at a rare glimpse of the splendour. We USF and the manifestation of certain entities summoned spiritual powers: a heavenly gift of unintentional birth, spawn by intentional indulgence of the gods.

Imagine that.

◆ ◆ ◆

The USF was not expected to be alive initially, as I am today. There, in the one heaven, where I was born billions upon billions of ages ago, I found a truly remarkable treasure: the gift of flight.

I not only drifted among gods in the spiritual habitat, but gradually I also began to surf the cosmic wave of the organic habitat—grasping the fulmination and dancing through galactic silhouettes—penetrating into the very nature of universal existence. It has been, and continues to be, a grand and wondrous journey.

Alas, as I mentioned, I am just a humble entity; do not make any mistake about it, I am not a god.

I was somewhat restrained in the beginning of creation; dependent on my fellow entities to join together and conjure the power of flight. I have never possessed the unparalleled power of the gods.

I was always an astute observer of life however, and soon I nurtured the magical touch for freedom of flight: as the spiritual habitat matured and the organic habitat erupted throughout the cosmos, I commanded the energy to master independent travel and interact with several different dimensions.

I have observed many magnificent miracles: absorbing the radiance of spiritual fibre along with many eminent heavenly elements, or immersing myself into many glorious and fascinating environmental domains, or sometimes embracing the souls of organic inhabitants and witnessing many tremendous events through their eyes.

No, I am not a god, but thanks to my gift of flight you might say I'm a cosmic scribe; keeper of universal history and truth.

I have many stories to tell about many astounding things, but nothing I have seen is more resounding than the miracles of nature and the magical power emanating from the trees. This is the story of the gods, their angels and the hybrid species they created from the trees.

The rest suits me fine.

Chapter 2: Marsh Life

The rain was wet; her hair was soft. Under the moonlight the inconspicuous shadow of Slattern crossed over her shoulder and down her slender body. Sally gazed across the eerie valley to the south; her eyes radiating anger and frustration. She was hemmed into a corner with nowhere to turn. She just wanted to be alone.

Rather deliberately she turned and began a brisk walk across the ridge. Slattern followed her at a safe distance.

The ridge she walked spans several miles at the bottom of a deeper yet narrow valley; carved and somewhat hidden between the barren, jumbled rocky peaks of an ancient but modest mountain range—one of many croaky outcroppings scattered across the badlands of this planet.

This ridge is quite unique however: what appears to be the bottom of the valley, several miles in length with a swath of short, stunted trees, is actually an extended shelf of rock and soil leering over and ultimately enveloping a camouflaged canyon of jagged forest below. The swath of ragged trees growing in the bosom of the valley is in fact the tips of gigantic trees; sprouting to the top of the ridge with a thick canopy of dense foliage beneath shadowing the hidden canyon.

Also well-hidden are two unassuming openings on the dusty brown and craggy exterior mountainsides at both ends of the valley, leading to caves that snake down into the rock and provide passage to the sheltered canyon floor. Flowing from the depths of the caves is an underground aqueduct winding through the canyon; a tapered waterway cutting a cavernous channel in the sharp rock. Its banks are steep and petrous cliffs, and above, hovering amid the canopy branches of the trees are random patches of thick fog.

Sally turned, abruptly darted across the ridge and down the slope; quickly disappearing into the trees. Slattern followed her. Sally bounced over rocks and slid under branches with the speed of a crazed panther and the grace of a fleeting antelope. She continued to violently rip through the forest as she headed towards the perilous cliffs of the waterway. There, overlooking the harsh rock crevasse, she suddenly reeled around and confronted Slattern.

Drizzle from the mist and fog spit through the quiet night and jabbed into Sally's exposed head. The two stared intently at each other; their eyes glowing with a haunting blue and green glimmer. The silence of the forest was replaced with a reverberating snarl as both creatures growled a hateful hiss.

"What do you want?" demanded Sally.

"You," answered Slattern.

Sally boldly leapt across the crevasse and landed safely on the opposite bank of the waterway. She then quickly made her way along the shoreline. Slattern had little problem following her as Sally hastened along the threadbare trail.

The waterway suddenly vanished into a treacherous wall of rocks and boulders. The wall of stone reached up to form a peak hidden by a haze of mist. Sally dashed up the precarious incline without hesitation and flew over the hill of rocks as she was swallowed by the fog. She glided through the mist like a petaurist in flight; bounding up and over the peak. She soared into a deep basin on the other side of the rock wall, which housed a marsh beneath the ceiling of fog. The waterway carved and seeped through the rock and came cascading down the basin wall; falling softly into a bed of reeds.

Sally jumped over a small strait of water and onto an island of stone at the bottom of the basin. It was cold and clammy; the darkness broken only by the glow of her blue eyes. She turned and faced the precipitous wall of granite.

Slattern was standing there. He held his marshy ground on the edge of the bog and his eyes lit up green with rage.

"Do you still want me?" Sally shouted from the island.

"Always," answered Slattern.

"Then be still and at peace and close your eyes. Come journey with me and mine shall be yours and ours shall be what we desire."

Slattern appeared impatient.

"The time is late and I have places to be. These silly games tire me. Let me be aware of your wishes and I shall grant you the serenity you so relish."

But Sally was determined. She raised her arms in a sensuous motion; enticing the fog up from the basin and out to the trees in the canyon. The trees answered with their branches; bowing down over the edge of the basin. Sally swirled her arms and snapped her hips: the marsh burst into tears. And then, with a fierce thrust of her head, the marsh erupted into flames.

Slattern shrugged his shoulders with a tilt of his head and rolling his eyes placed his hands on his waist.

"And what is to come of all this? Am I supposed to be impressed? What is the point? Shall I summon a demon or fly to the stars? What do you want of me?"

"If you are worthy of my passion, show me your power," threatened Sally over the flames. "If not, turn and go forever."

"I warn you, I am easily riled. Do not tempt me, for you are fully aware of the consequences," said Slattern.

"You are afraid."

"I fear nothing," asserted Slattern.

"Then quit this talk and show me your courage. The time has come for you to own up to your bold assertions," yelled Sally.

A vicious look besieged Slattern's face; his glowing green eyes widened and he began to snarl again.

"It has been ages since one so confident and brash has dared to question my great powers. Do you realise what you are about to engage? Do you have any notion who you are defying?"

"It matters not, I am superior—I can feel it," boasted Sally.

"So be it," shouted Slattern.

He flung his arms and the fog fell back into the basin. The vapour emptied its rain onto the marsh and the flames were doused.

Sally lunged from the island and sailed to the top of the basin. The mist spread apart revealing Slattern. Sally summoned a massive clump of rock from the canyon ridge. It ripped from the ground and came crashing towards the basin, but Slattern did not panic. Instead, he merely pointed to the mound of rock and soil and it exploded into many fragments.

The particles of granite flying in the air grew eyes, fur and claws; becoming giant weasels. And they began to attack the woman with the blue eyes. Immediately Sally flew down to the marsh, landed beside Slattern and stared into his eyes.

"That was a mean one," she hissed.

She turned swiftly and pointed to the trees beyond and around the basin ledge. The trees transformed into obese badgers and otters as the weasels descended upon her. The creatures of the canyon flung themselves down at the weasels and a devastating battle took place in the swamp.

Slattern then beckoned to the depths of the marsh. Shooting up from the water came a ferocious pack of hungry wolverines; devouring all the animals in the bog. Sally began to swing her arms about, but before she could cast another spell Slattern waved his hand high and strong. A mighty wind came and swept away the wolverines.

This surprised Sally. She stood there staring at Slattern in bewilderment. He again twirled his arm and pointed straight towards Sally. She became rigid. She was naked as usual.

Standing there, she knew it would take a masterful spell to get her out of this mess. Slowly, Slattern walked towards her and stood close to her body.

"Now," said Slattern as he pointed to Sally's lips, "if you attempt another spell, I will unleash my anger and you shall be but a puddle of water."

He paused and glared inquisitively at Sally.

"Now what is the problem?"

"No problem, I'm just challenging myself to become better. I think you would have to admit, if not for another of your mesmerising spells I might have defeated you this time."

"Really—just because of my mesmerising spell?"

"Yes," insisted Sally. "I would say they're the only spells I can't conjure as naturally as you."

"Alright then. From now on, no more mesmerising."

"Promise?"

"Yes, I promise."

"Good."

"Is that all that's on your mind?" asked Slattern.

"Yes, for now," answered Sally.

"Very well then. All this foreplay has aroused me. Let's make love."

And so, Sally and Sven Slattern made love in the marsh.

Chapter 3: An Owl Story

Documents scattered about; his face lay on the desk. The small reading light seemed to burn a hole in the back of his head, revealing a cluttered collection of minute details and dastardly spirits fleeting through his mind. He was working at the same desk for sixteen hours.

Flayda Findstad quietly inserted his key into the library door, but before he could turn the knob the door opened on its own as if being seduced by some roused presence. The library reeked of the rancid spirits which fluttered in the mind of the man at the desk; he was obviously working too hard.

Flayda, a father of five children and head clerk at the provincial archives building, allowed his dear friend to stay at the library well beyond public hours. Old Fin is a somewhat curious individual with peculiar habits. He hunted different varieties of weasels and owned the most elaborate collection of stuffed and mounted animals from the weasel family on Earth. Aside from his weasel collecting habits, he was perceived by most as fairly normal.

The head clerk's odd habits likely attracted his friend when they were children and they became buddies all the way back to elementary school. They still kept in touch despite the roving tendencies of the man at the desk.

Flayda gazed inside the library and saw his friend. He was asleep; still sitting at his desk. Flayda walked across the room and looked down at his friend's face; pensively etched with helpless fear.

The man asleep at the desk: Zacharias Nathaniel Steele, otherwise known as Zachary.

He was a prairie boy in his middle Earth years of age; average height and size just under six feet and less than two hundred pounds, with light brown hair and greenish hazel eyes. He moved to the city after being raised on the farm and graduated from high school in Saskatchewan, Canada, Planet Earth during the seventies' decade of the twentieth century: thousands of years before Stellar Rotational Continuum was used elsewhere in the universe (more about this later).

Zachary attended the faculty of science at Colorado State University, closer to where his mother grew up south of Saskatchewan in the Rocky Mountains of the United States of America. He graduated with a Bachelor's of Science in physiology and continued his graduate studies earning his Masters of Science, with his very unique and interesting thesis: "*The Effects of Hypothermia on the Human Body During Physical Exertion.*"

He went on to teach and research hypothermia in the Rocky Mountains for the next six years, while enjoying his obsessions of skiing in the winter and white-water canoeing in the summers, which he intensely employed in his research; earning his doctorate degree in physiology along the way. A research grant from the University of California at San Francisco was awarded to Zachary so he could continue his hypothermia research in physiology on the Pacific Ocean coast, in one of the most exciting, culturally diverse cities on the North American continent. San Francisco was to change Zachary's life. It was in San Francisco he met Zelda.

❖ ❖ ❖

Zachary Steele was an ideal son for his parents Jeremiah and Maria before going to the University of California. Jeremiah Steele was once an agricultural scientist working for the provincial government in Saskatchewan. Maria Steele was a peculiar mother to her child Zachary; prone to an impulsive, over protective disposition, esoteric behaviour and unexpected disappearances. Maria had to deal with complications right from the start; while giving birth to her only child she began to haemorrhage and lapsed into a coma for almost twenty-four hours. She might have suffered some brain damage, but the medical technology back then was not sophisticated enough to know for sure. It was a rather convenient excuse to explain Maria's strange behaviour, but the truth is she knew otherwise. Jeremiah came home from work one day, when Zachary was only an adolescent, and found several walls on the main floor of his house stripped down to the studs. Maria was looking for her wedding ring which she had lost. Zachary found it in the backyard garden. Maria vanished the next day without a trace, only to reappear a couple of months later. She said it was a needed respite to relieve the stress of motherhood.

"She's not crazy, you know," Jeremiah once told his son. "She is burdened by a strange family history that she can't control."

He told Zachary about the pressure his mother felt to raise her only child safe, strong and healthy. He explained the difficulties of contending with his wife's actions. But he could not tell his son everything he knew about the past; it would not be right, and his wife would have his head on a platter if he dared. He slammed his fist down on the kitchen table.

"It's not easy for me. It can be damned tough," uttered Jeremiah. "I'm sorry Zachary, you shouldn't have to deal with this. I love your mother, and I'm just trying to be a good father and husband."

Jeremiah Steele regained his composure and told Zachary some of the stories of his mother's disappearances: when she undercooked a turkey for family relatives and everyone came down with foodborne illness; when Zachary was rushed to the hospital with a concussion and broken bones after falling off a ladder cleaning the gutters on the house, which his mother thought she should have done; and when Zachary was teased and bullied at school for wearing a beaded necklace his mother had made for him.

"She just gets a little obsessive about your welfare. She doesn't realise what she's doing half the time," explained Jeremiah.

"Like when she tore the house apart?" asked Zachary.

Jeremiah nodded. Zachary gained new insight and respect for both his parents. He wanted to help his mother in his graduate studies and learn more about the brain's functions and its capacity to process the emotions she had to confront. However, there was one subject which fascinated him more than anything else. Although it is related to the brain's functions, it is much more of an isolated specialty: it is hypothermia.

Lifeguarding on a beachfront was Zachary's first summer job. He would be out in the cold lake water; swimming and playing in the waves when all the other guards were huddled in the shack sipping hot chocolate. He loved the invigorating sensations the cold water brought to his body. It was an exhilaration which rushed through his blood as the coldness began to penetrate to his core: his human body core, of course, as opposed to a hybrid species spiritual core. Little did the poor earthling know.

Unlike the other lifeguards, Zachary yearned for bitter, stormy days. It was the ultimate thrill. Zachary had not yet experienced sex or the sensations of a spiritual core. Zachary continued to play in cold water and cold weather throughout the formidable years of his early life; splashing through white-water rapids on wild rivers and skiing down the slopes of mountains, cutting through the sharp wind when the temperature dipped well below zero. He simply loved the cold.

However, like any other human mortal, he was susceptible to the chilly temperatures. Zachary always found himself engaging in rigorous physical activity to keep his body warm in the cold elements he adored. It was the combination of pushing his body to the limit and the cold environment which provided the sensations he so enjoyed.

It was not until his second year of physiology that Zachary began to connect hypothermia with his love of the cold. He began to logically analyse his obsession for the cold with the properties of hypothermia. He soon discovered that little was known about hypothermia. Zachary knew he had stumbled onto a unique situation. He himself experienced euphoria during several different stages of hypothermia. Zachary knew he could validate conclusions on the properties of hypothermia from the sensations he experienced throughout his young life.

And so Zachary landed in San Francisco where a fine upstanding citizen and scientist began his journey to the brink of human reality and into the realm of spirituality. Until he arrived in San Francisco however, Zachary was only teetering on the hypothermic brink. Initiating his research, he adopted two close friends: the graduate student Zelda Mintah and fellow physiologist Mister Mitchell. This made three intimate friends in Zachary's life; the third being Flayda Findstad. More about Flayda shortly.

Zelda is an attractive woman of Caribbean and Mexican heritage with a fit body, dark hair and light brown skin. She is a great lover, coincidently I assure you, and was wild about Zachary and his hypothermic experiments. Zelda inspired Zachary in more than one way. She spurred Zachary to admirable feats in bed and in cold water. Mister Mitchell took notes.

Zachary was soon obsessed with the hypothermia research. He thought of nothing else and did nothing else. It seemed he was his mother's son; quite susceptible to obsessive propensities. But even more hazardously, Zachary was performing experiments on himself. He jogged for miles in pouring rain, swam for miles in the cold Pacific Ocean, and climbed many of the nearby inland mountains in torrential downpours or snowstorms, such as the Diablo, Santa Lucia and Sierra Nevada ranges. Mister Mitchell dutifully took notes.

Jeremiah and Maria Steele retired shortly after their son moved to California; living off the profit they made by selling Jeremiah's inherited farm land. Maria was very pleased Zachary had moved to the west coast, since she was originally from California herself. They visited their son frequently; having nothing else to do being retired and living off inheritance, but they also wanted to tell him about certain family traditions. Zachary was not properly exposed to these traditions, and his parents wanted him to know more about some particular family secrets.

But Zachary was always too busy with hypothermic adventures. Discouraged after several visits, they left San Francisco for the last time after Christmas with their son. Jeremiah Steele was not a physiologist, but he was a scientist and an intelligent man. He knew it was not normal for the scientist to conduct experiments on himself. He decided they would visit their son at a more appropriate space.

Jeremiah told Zachary they were going back to Saskatchewan. And they did. Jeremiah and Maria then made immediate plans to fade away into seclusion. They phoned Zachary one morning early in the new year—that's the month of January according to the calendar on Planet Earth—and told their son they were leaving and wanted to be alone until their days were done. They were testing Zachary, of course.

The telephone call jarred Zachary back into reality. It upset him considerably and he stopped his experiments. The sudden disappearance of his parents made a serious impact on Zachary's thoughts and actions.

❖ ❖ ❖

Flayda Findstad gently nudged his friend to awaken him and the dishevelled man sprang up in his chair.

"What!" screamed Zachary.

"I think maybe you should go home," Flayda said timidly. "People are going to start coming to work soon."

"No, I'm not going anywhere until I've found that damned Soarfoot."

"Soarfoot?" questioned Flayda.

"I tell you he exists."

"Zachary, I think you should go home and get some sleep—in a bed."

Zachary slammed his fist down on the desk top. He glared at Flayda with an evil grin.

"I haven't slept in three months. I don't need any sleep."

"If you don't leave, I could lose my job," pleaded Flayda.

"Lose your job? Why?"

"It's seven in the morning."

"Seven. What am I doing here?" asked Zachary.

"I'm not sure. What were you talking about anyway?"

"This bloody tree. It's giving me headaches, and the dreams."

"Maybe you should take some time off."

"Maybe I should. I'm sorry Flayda. I lost myself there."

"Actually, I just came in early to clean up. You've got a half an hour before anyone arrives."

"I guess you're right. I should get some real sleep."

"Why don't you relax tonight and come over to my place for a drink?"

"That's a good idea. Maybe I'll do that," agreed Zachary.

He gathered his ruffled documents and left Flayda to his duties. Zachary was leaving to get some sleep, but it was not at his home in San Francisco. He was back in Saskatchewan tirelessly conducting research on his family tree.

Flayda was allowing Zachary unrestricted access to provincial archived documents; helping his old friend who was clearly in need of assistance. Zachary had rented a house and was living out of cardboard boxes. He did not completely enjoy going back to that house. It had metal kitchen cupboards.

He was working intensely for the past three months compiling his family tree. He was obsessed; as he was with hypothermia. He totally immersed himself in the project. Zachary wanted to trace his family line back to its North American origin, in the wake of his parents' disappearance and all the apparent secrets surrounding his heritage. He knew his family was not quite normal: that intrigued him. The sudden exit of his parents only sparked his ambitions further.

He appeared a mess as he walked up the sidewalk to his metal kitchen cupboards; his hair twisted and tangled, a plaid flannel shirt protruding from under his grimy sweatshirt, his jeans wrinkled and torn at the knees. He knocked open the front door, dropped his papers and proceeded to the refrigerator: one of three pieces of furniture he was utilising. The other two were the couch and a desk. The rest of the house was a mess with cardboard boxes piled up in various rooms. Zelda insisted only a few days earlier over the telephone that she was coming to Saskatchewan to take care of her lover. She was arriving that day.

Apparently, Zachary did not think much of it.

During the three months Zachary was in Saskatchewan he did nothing but work on his family tree. It took him two weeks to devise an approach for the undertaking. Thereafter he dove into the project head first. Unfortunately for his health, Zachary subsisted on little food, little sleep and frequent night caps.

He grabbed a bottle of orange juice from the fridge, opened a metal cupboard and found one of only two cups he was using for coffee in the morning and mixed drinks at night, and on this occasion poured in some vodka with the juice for a popular cocktail of that time on Earth. Zachary sat on the sofa with his vodka and orange juice screwdriver and ciphered through his research notes. He eventually fell asleep. The evil spirits began to flutter.

Although intensified while working on his family tree, this was not the first space in his life that Zachary had to deal with an evil presence in his thoughts and dreams; including out-of-body teleporting which he experienced since childhood without a full understanding. It was all tantamount to Zachary's eccentric and sometimes difficult crusade along his chosen path: a lifelong odyssey and journey that would ultimately nourish wisdom from the knowledge he gathered, not to mention reveal the truth of his ancestry.

He was awakened by Zelda's knock on the front door. The doorbell wasn't working; imagine that. He stumbled to the front door and greeted her.

"Zelda?"

"Zachary."

"Come in," said Zachary.

"Why thank you."

Zelda walked into the house, set down her luggage and quickly gazed around the living room. She looked at Zachary, rather confused.

"Zachary, were you expecting me today?" she asked.

"Yes, of course," answered Zachary.

"What have you been doing?"

"Research," said Zachary.

"Research? What kind of research?"

"The family tree."

"The family tree?"

"Yes, the family tree," said Zachary. Zelda looked around the room once again. She faced Zachary and stretched out her arms.

"How about a hug. I haven't seen you in three months."

Zachary smiled and embraced her. Zelda backed away and took a good look at Zachary.

"You're a mess," she said.

"I haven't been getting much sleep. Damned Soarfoot has kept me up."

"What's wrong with your foot?"

"Oh nothing, it's fine."

"Zachary, you should take care of yourself. I think it was a good idea that I came here. Let's see if we can clean up this mess a bit."

"That's a good idea. I haven't seen most of the house myself."

"I missed you so much," said Zelda.

A sparkle twinkled in Zachary's eyes and a warm smile spread across his face. He thought of making love to Zelda. He then remembered his promise to Flayda. The smile disappeared.

"What's wrong?" asked Zelda.

"Flayda," said Zachary.

"Flayda?"

"An old high school friend. I told him I'd go over to his place for a drink tonight."

"Zachary, Flayda can wait. It's our first night together in three months and you haven't done anything to get ready for me."

"But he's done so many favours for me in the last few weeks. I haven't had a chance to get over to his place yet."

"Zacharias Nathaniel Steele, I come all the way from San Francisco to this prairie town just to be with you and you tell me we can't spend our first night together."

"How's the weather on the coast?"

"Don't change the subject."

"But I owe Flayda at least a visit."

"Zachary, let's not talk about it now. I just want to clean this house before we do anything else."

And so, Zachary helped Zelda clean. Zelda remained silent, even in the kitchen when she saw the metal cupboards where the dishes were piled high. She inspected each room and went to work.

"It could be worse, I think," she finally said after an hour of cleaning.

The unkempt house, Zachary's condition and those metal kitchen cupboards put Zelda in a sombre mood. Zachary simply floated along; his mind busy fighting spirits and searching for clues. He escaped common reality and entered into the world surrounding his family tree. It was a world he would never leave.

Eventually Zachary and Zelda began to make headway on the housekeeping. Zachary knew he owed his partner retribution for her efforts. He set aside his research notes and continued to help her clean for the remainder of the day. By eight o'clock that night, he convinced Zelda to accompany him to Flayda's for one drink. But before they departed for the Findstads, Zelda insisted Zachary help her fit the bed with sheets. She planned on coming home early.

Flayda's weasel collection was spread out on the living room floor. It was beyond midnight: one drink had turned into a few. Flayda was describing to Zelda his relationship with Zachary in high school. Zelda actually found it interesting. She enjoyed the humorous stories of their escapades and was eager to hear about Zachary as a teenager.

Meanwhile, Flayda's wife Florence and Zachary involved themselves in a discussion concerning creatures of the marsh. Because of Flayda's hobby, Florence was somewhat of an expert on the subject.

She explained to Zachary the habits of beavers, muskrats, otters, weasels and the sort. Zachary was absorbed in Florence's explanation of their abilities to remain in cold water.

"What on Earth are you two talking about?" asked Zelda.

"The marsh," answered Zachary.

"What about it?" asked Flayda.

"I would say it harbours some very interesting creatures, wouldn't you say?" said Zachary.

"Oh yes; very interesting," said Flayda with a gleam.

"Men," said Florence to Zelda. "Now there's a bunch of strange creatures for you."

"Absolutely," said Zelda.

Florence looked at her husband with a sarcastic smile that hinted sensuality. Flayda answered with a generous smile, but his expression was rather quickly replaced with a very perplexed look.

"Zachary," said Flayda, "who or what is Soarfoot?"

"Soarfoot. That's the second time today I've heard that," said Zelda. "Didn't you mention something about a sore foot earlier today?"

Zachary rubbed his forehead.

"I'd rather not talk about it, but I suppose I should let you know. It's the name I've come across in my research three times in the last five days. I tell you, I think Soarfoot is the link, but I can't find any proof of his birth. And ever since

I started looking for that proof, I've been having these splitting headaches—and the most bizarre dreams."

"You mean there's nothing wrong with your foot, it's actually someone's name?" said Zelda.

"Actually, I'm not sure," answered Zachary. "I have no proof of anyone named Soarfoot ever being alive, yet I've found mention of a man by the name of Soarfoot—'S-o-a-r', indigenous I suspect. His name appears in three separate documents relating to members of my Steele family line."

"But what makes this Soarfoot so important?" asked Flayda.

"Basically, I've run into a road block. I can't go any further until I find the missing link. For some reason, there's a substantial lack of information on the Steele family six, seven and eight generations back. I have plenty of documented information on the family from generations beyond that, but there's a gap that I can't explain or understand. I have a suspicion this Soarfoot, if he does exist, has something to do with it."

"What kind of name is Soarfoot?" pondered Flayda.

"I'm not sure, but from the context of what I've read it could be indigenous—Cree or maybe Chipewyan," answered Zachary.

"And what about these dreams you say you've been having? You think they're related to this Soarfoot?" continued Flayda.

"What makes you suspect your dreams have something to do with Soarfoot?" interjected Zelda.

"Ever since I've been on to this Soarfoot I've had these absolutely frightening dreams. And I always seem to wake up with a headache. These dreams have some sort of spirits and demons. They're dancing and chanting around this campfire, just like an indigenous ritual. And besides, I only started having these dreams five days ago, when I first found the name Soarfoot in my research documents."

"I think you just have genealogy on the brain," said Zelda.

"Zelda may be right Zachary. You've been working quite intensely on this family tree," said Flayda. "Maybe you're just exerting yourself too much."

"It is quite common for people to dream of things they've been concentrating on for some time," added Florence.

"Whatever it is, I'm determined to see this thing through. I've come too far to give up now," said Zachary.

"Well I promise you one thing Zachary Steele," said Zelda, "you're going to take a break from that family tree long enough to help me move into that house. You should see that place, it needs work. He hasn't done a thing with it. And when we do get everything organised, you'll be the first we have over. Flayda, Florence, it's been a wonderful evening. Thank you very much. But we should get going. We have a lot of work to do tomorrow."

"You're right Zelda, it's after midnight. We certainly have rambled on," said Flayda.

The visiting couple wearily made their way to the front door, said their good-byes and headed back to the metal kitchen cupboards. Zachary's first notion when they arrived home was to read some of his research notes. But Zelda would have nothing to do with that. She had not seen Zachary in three months and she was feeling pleasantly intoxicated from the evening of drinks. Zelda was quite aroused.

"You," she said pointing to Zachary's lips, "are coming to bed and making love to me."

Holding her warm body close, Zachary lay beside Zelda. He knew the research notes were out of the question. Zelda began to lick his ear lobe and he responded by gently kissing her; affection soon turning into passion. He did not waste any time, sliding over her soft figure, moving down to her stomach and moistening her skin. He crouched between her legs and began to caress her inner thighs with his tongue. Zelda began to breathe deeper and harder.

Gasping enthusiastically, she arched her back as she began to quiver with anticipation. She extenuated herself, arching until her body was delicately floating in the air; balanced by her head on the pillow and Zachary between her legs. Zelda then began to cradle her body by lowering her hips to the bed and lifting her head into the air with Zachary's face still buried between her thighs; rocking back and forth several times, lifting her hips then her head at either end of the cradling motion.

Zelda was ecstatic. She was growing closer to a sexual peak. Zachary then took the initiative with an impressive contortion Zelda had once taught him. He lifted his head and quickly flipped his entire body lengthwise while still holding onto Zelda's hips in a flexible gymnastic move. He was now laying on his back with his feet behind her head and his face looking up towards her. Zelda came flying in pursuit and landed on top of Zachary with a thud, grinding her hips down with the tender intimacy of a rhinoceros in heat.

37

The impact resulted in penetration but it also sent Zelda springing back into the air ever so slightly. So powerful were her stomach muscles that Zachary came soaring with her; well, maybe not soaring but certainly catching some air under the small of his back, ever so slightly. Suffice to say, the couple were inseparable.

They repeated the sexual manoeuvre several times until a mutual orgasm was reached; proverbial bouncing off the ceiling sex. Intimacy between Zachary and Zelda tended to be an exertive affair. This night was no exception. Zelda was home. They finally lay motionless and exhausted; staring up at the ceiling. The perspiration on their bodies gleamed in the dim light. Zachary thought he could see the ceiling full of indentations and the plaster beginning to crack.

"We'll have to reinforce the ceiling," said Zachary.

"What are you talking about?" pondered Zelda.

"Oh nothing, I guess I'm just impressed with your performance. I must be hallucinating."

"Well I know you're no hallucination Zachary. That was pretty impressive yourself; such a nice homecoming. Thank you, sweetie."

The next few days were devoted to cleaning the rented house and allowing Zelda to become acquainted with the small prairie city, Saskatoon, on the banks of the South Saskatchewan River. Although Zelda was not as excited by Saskatoon as she was with San Francisco, she secretly knew the relevance of Zachary's family tree. And so she slowly adapted to the situation. But she was also concerned.

Zelda knew Zachary would need strength and resolve for the long and complicated path ahead. Zachary went right back to his research as soon as the household was settled. And with his research came the headaches and the dreams. Zelda was beginning to worry; Zachary was not acting normal. Although it was nothing new for him to act abnormal, Zelda was concerned about his health. Zachary did not eat properly and he drank too much hard liquor when working on his family tree. He did not sleep peacefully in bed and he was constantly yelling out Soarfoot's name in the middle of the night.

And so, with the help of Flayda and Florence Findstad, Zelda was able to rally Zachary into a reasonable state of mind and reach a consensus. It was agreed that Zachary was pushing his mind and body to an unfavourable brink, and he needed to take a break from his family tree to recharge his life's batteries.

It was Flayda who suggested the genre and Zelda who suggested the venue, with Zachary and Florence concurring while still talking about how long beavers and otters could hold their breath in cold water. It was a perfect match. It was to be a wilderness white-water expedition; something Flayda and Zachary started doing as youngsters in northern Saskatchewan, and something Zelda, Mister Mitchell and Zachary did while researching hypothermia in California.

They would travel back to San Francisco and check in with Mister Mitchell who was maintaining the status of Zachary's research grant. Mister Mitchell made arrangements for the trip including three tandem kayaks, since he was also bringing a romantic interest along; booking them for a favourite section of the South Yuba River in the Tahoe National Forest.

Everyone was looking forward to the river trip: Zachary and Zelda, Flayda and Florence, Mister Mitchell and his new girlfriend, the amazingly gorgeous and recently graduated registered nurse Breeze Boback.

Yes, Breeze; a name quite indicative of the idyllic San Francisco hippy era, which only goes to show you considering Mister Mitchell's geeky stature that personality is much more important than physical attributes, although Zachary did see Mister Mitchell naked on a previous white-water trip and remembered he was well endowed.

They were all looking forward to some exciting white-water rapids to get the adrenaline flowing alongside the current of fast water, some splendid scenery of mountain forest to relax the mind, some of Zachary's renowned open fire cooking to delight the palate, and a peaceful campfire at night to invigorate the aura of friendship and wonderment. It was exactly what Zelda had anticipated and turned out to be exactly what she wanted to accomplish.

❖ ❖ ❖

It was late springtime, almost summer—those are seasons on Planet Earth—and water levels were near perfect, with the high spring runoff subsiding but still enough water for a navigable expedition down this narrow river cutting through the mountains. It was an overcast yet peaceful and insouciant morning as they launched their kayaks; secretly signalling the incipient vision of clarity for Zachary's gruelling battle with fear and anguish. Unbeknownst to him on this day, the white-water gods were about to vindicate the many seemingly disjointed and bizarre visions he had experienced in the past. The grand mystery in his life that Zachary had kept hidden was about to start unravelling, and the answers he was subconsciously seeking were about to be revealed on the wings of spirituality.

They were paddling along a modest yet still impressive section of the river; stretches of flat water joined together in high water conditions by interesting chutes of rapids at tight turns in the river and where bedrock and boulders divert the water's flow. There are also wider bends in the river with or without rapids, usually framed by a rocky reef leading to an elevated treed ridge which conveniently makes for a comfortable campsite. They were approaching one such bend in the river after chuting through a few sets of rapids earlier in the day.

There was a humid, encompassing silence in the air; embraced by the transcending sheen that forecasts an imminent storm. It soon began to rain as a springtime shower meandered across the valley and filled the ravine. Zachary knew the time would be near. He had to find a favourable place to observe the small miracle. The place, and the timing, are essential.

"We're gonna get hit and hit hard. This should be a very swelling rainstorm—if you know what I mean," Zachary shouted from his kayak.

Mister Mitchell nodded in agreement from another kayak.

"Where should we beach?" he shouted over the raindrops, now slapping the water's surface with enthusiasm.

Zachary was estimating about forty minutes as Mister Mitchell posed his question. They were approaching the bend in the river and there ahead of them he saw the place. It was a fast water eddy in a small cove with a trail leading off the shoreline, up a ridge and onto a flat rock ledge directly overlooking the river. They would watch from there.

"Let's beach the boats at that reef above the eddy. We can hike to that ledge and watch the river from there," explained Zachary.

"Excellent call Zach old boy," concurred Flayda from his kayak.

The glow in the air was followed by a sweeping wind; quickly mounting to a blustery force. And then the rain began to fall in earnest. The raindrops were slicing hard and pounding into the water. It was evident this was a typically brief but powerful rain shower for this mountain terrain: the river would soon be swelling. They arrived on the ledge, complete with a homemade firepit ready for the evening's festivities. They were overlooking the sloping banks of the river; scattered with stones, straggled reeds and soft moss.

The water was rising over boulders and rocks. Everyone marvelled at the river in their own silence for several minutes. Zachary began to see strange shapes in the water and felt a familiar but very unsettling sensation. The swishing water susurrated a tepid hiss as it churned beneath his feet. The crisp riffles of whitecapped waves from the windy conditions created looming shadows in the broad swells. He saw large sweeping wing spans in the shadows of the water; expanding and yearning to rise above the surface. And then the surging crest of the river was upon them.

They watched in amazement as the small gift of nature revealed its subtle eminence. A swelling wave of water curled downriver and spread from bank to bank, plunging down the basin and rising up the slope of the shoreline as it flowed: a wall of water, moving, rising and travelling along the miraculous path of a living river. It took flight in Zachary's brewing imagination, and he saw the vampires rising in his mind. He dropped to his knees and trembled, but it was too late: the river had taken him back to his battle.

A frenzy of fear whirled inside Zachary's screeching brain as his heart pumped wickedly and plunged down into the depths of pure evil. He was viciously spinning and falling; sinking into his bed as he struggled to pull himself out of this frightening dream. Zachary was only six-years-old. He didn't know what was happening. But he did know that it was horrifying.

The first few times this recurring nightmare struck Zachary, he only sank deeper and deeper; eventually looking up to the opening his body had forged in the bed, while the sheets of bedding began to seep over the edges and close over him. He would slowly sink under the bed and choke on the dirt and dust, but the sides of the opening in the bed would be rushing beside him; racing towards the ceiling in a whirl.

Sometimes Zachary was spinning, sometimes the bed was spinning and sometimes the images were darting straight through a diminishing square tunnel into a foggy destination somewhere above the ceiling of his bedroom. Despite the incredible speed of his fluid and coagulative bedding, he only sank slowly into the hardwood floor; watching and sensing a disturbing presence in the rushing waves pulsing towards the sky.

And then one night Zachary's body began to rise: through the box springs and mattress, surging through the bed, higher and higher towards the ceiling as the sheets began a frenzied transition and started streaming down to the ground. Zachary was still laying on his back, but his vision would look down at the whirling pulsations of the bedding sinking into the floor, lower and lower below him. He was once again slowly moving in contrast to the speeding bed, but this time he was rising to the fog in the ceiling.

And then Zachary saw himself, still laying there under the bedding with the dirt on the cold hardwood floor. He had risen above the chaos, yet there his body remained in the muck and slime of the evil depths under his bed. Zachary saw fear in himself. He knew something was watching from above, but he could not confront this evil menace at first, during his childhood years. He could only feel his pounding heart ripping at his courage and filling his body with a wretched curse.

"What's wrong Zachary?" whispered Breeze.

They were the words of an angel singing a sweet melody in Zachary's mind. A distinguished entourage of magnificent soaring owls lifted from the river and span the sky; sheltering Zachary from the raindrops as they swept over the ridge. He looked up to the sky and smiled.

"Yes Zachary, what is it?" asked Zelda, also sweetly sympathetic.

"I'm just so glad they weren't vampires," he answered.

"Vampires?" pondered both Zelda and Breeze.

"Owls. They were owls, didn't you see them?"

"Not the owls again," quipped Flayda, remembering back to some of their adolescent wilderness excursions. "Next thing you know girls, it'll be the carnivorous white-tailed deer."

"Wow, that was quite the sight. I don't think I've ever been this close to a river exactly when it surges like that," marvelled Florence.

"Yes, the confined swelling is remarkable," added Mister Mitchell.

"Confined swelling; that's a good one old boy—purely geographical terminology I'm sure," Zachary sarcastically surmised.

"Thanks for the clarification," said Mister Mitchell with equal sarcasm.

"At least Zachary's back to reality," said Flayda.

"I want to know more about the owls," interjected Breeze.

"I'm sure there will be plenty of time for the owls later tonight around the campfire," said Zelda.

"Speaking of fires, I do believe we have found our campsite for the night. This ledge is a great spot and I can see at least three flat areas for tents just behind the trail," proposed Mister Mitchell.

"I agree, this is a marvellous spot," voiced Flayda. "All those in favour?"

The rain had stopped. The refreshing spring season sprinkled rejuvenated wilderness throughout the gulley by the river. It was lustrous: green and bright. The selection of the evening campsite was unanimous.

Mister Mitchell and Breeze pitched their tent and collected firewood as Zelda and the Findstads set up their tents as well; Zachary still sitting beside the firepit trying to figure out what was happening to him. The gods had resurrected a familiar warning and it ignited an intoxicating rush through his soul, but what was he to make of this journey back to the fear he had battled for so long?

Thoughts of his adolescent and young adult years entered his mind. He remembered the visions of fluttering owls escorting him along waterways and hiking trails during summer wilderness trips, and being profoundly awakened by the soft song of an owl one misty morning while camping alone. But then he heard the city traffic and the giant air conditioner from the apartment building across the street; his bedroom tucked in that monstrosity of a three-storey haunted house—where he walked the hallways at night and the vampires would come rising from the cracks in the dark, oiled hardwood floors.

A few clouds rolled across the sky; pale white and growing thick. Florence helped as Flayda ignited a campfire beside Zachary.

"Are you gonna sit there and dream of your owls, or are you going to cook us up one of your campfire specialities tonight?" asked Flayda.

"Sure Fin. I'll cook up a good meal, but we have plenty of daylight, don't we?"

"Fin?" questioned Florence.

"An old nickname," answered her husband with a wink. "Yeah, we have lots of daylight before dinner time, I just want to keep on top of things like a good camp coordinator should."

"I like a man who loves his job," remarked Mister Mitchell. "Zachary makes this delicious rabbit stew. Did he ever make it for you?"

"Same recipe as my gramma's chicken stew," said Zachary.

"I guess he did," laughed Flayda, "except without the rabbit."

Everyone had a good chuckle. But Zachary was still on the edge. He wanted to know so badly what the owls were telling him. He started methodically sorting through his gear to assemble the ingredients for an open fire meal, but all he could think about was his personal struggle with fear and the unknown.

Instead of sleeping during his formidable adult years Zachary would often journey; rising above his bed at night into the fog shrouding his ceiling. He was afraid to face the demons initially, but eventually he found the courage to open his eyes and peer deep beyond the fog into the forbidden space.

The first visions were pleasant: cascading waves of glimmering light mingling and dancing on the edge of silhouette and capturing his soul by drifting the expanse. The waves enticed a cosmic libido, wafting to the spiritual corridor; touching his senses and mounting to a fever pitch. The waves of light attracted Zachary, like the wing spans of the owls that soothed him gently, but the imminent explosion of light revealed its illusion and transformed into the same evil adversary he fought night after night; a lifetime curse invading his soul also on a span of wings.

An enormous, vicious, snarling vampire would soar straight towards him; gleaming fangs and forbidding, enveloping black wings, with pointed edges spreading into the haze of the foggy corridor. Zachary would stand in defiance; embracing his courage. He was afraid, but he remained brave in the face of evil and uttered a hallowing challenge from the breadth of his soul.

And every time, the vampire, seemingly quite content to devour Zachary's soul, would heed his challenge; at first vanishing into the fog, but later after repeated appearances, enticing Zachary once again to follow into the fog. Zachary could not resist; it was a powerful temptation, with a true hidden purpose waiting to be found. And so they ventured, and Zachary followed, above the horizon, above the atmosphere of the planet, beyond Earth's moon and out into the frontier of the universe.

It was exhilarating as he soared through the cosmos, but true to the warnings of his dear old auntie who told him never to release his lifeline—the gleaming power source that emanated from his navel like an umbilical cord—the vampire would always turn against him somewhere in the distant galaxies; tempting his resolve by offering him this immortal freedom of flight in exchange for a meal of his soul, and testing his courage over and over by threatening his destruction.

"I will devour you. You will scream in pain as I rip your flesh apart," the vampire would snarl.

"No, I am better than you. You cannot defeat me," Zachary would collect himself in defiance.

A mild smattering of raindrops began to fall on the treetop canopy of conifers as Zachary finally gathered the ingredients and utensils for the campfire meal. And then he remembered back to canoe trips in northern Saskatchewan with his true friend Flayda, when they would attempt to frighten girls around the campfire with stories of carnivorous deer, brandishing antlers dripping with blood and red glowing eyes piercing the night. Perhaps Flayda thought Zachary was plotting for old time's sake to entertain everyone that night. But no one would need an extra plot on this evening.

It was apparent nature would soon blast her signature once again with another random springtime shower. They were somewhat fortified in a small gulley with foothills behind their campsite, the channel of the river affording them a view of the mounting storm and a taut outfitter's tarp tied to surrounding trees, protecting a dining area from the rain. They covered the pots and pans and put a billy can on the fire to boil water; deciding to wait out the storm before cooking dinner.

The fire was roaring as it devoured some crisp deadfall wood. They were ready to be rifled with a short but fierce downpour. A mound of hot coals was slowly building in the fire when the storm suddenly burst its wild call from across the river. The wall of clouds approached; shrinking the wilderness with the strange glow of an impending storm. The forest seemed to encroach and dominate their tiny campsite.

The wind started to crash: tree branches were soon swaying in the force. The storm was upon them. They watched a blurred haze of thick rain pouring from a large cloud across the river. The magic of nature was close at hand once again.

The white crease of ripples and waves on the water stretched over the width of the river as the rain cloud crept closer. The approaching fold of rain and wind stirred the water's surface as the storm swept through the gulley: a sight only nature can conjure from the power of the heavens. The storm arrived; rolling across the river and into their campsite. It swiftly crossed the landscape as fast as it had approached, drenching the surrounding slopes and moving into the next valley.

The clouds immediately drifted above and revealed a gorgeous evening sky pushing the storm over the sauntering mountainside behind them. A mauve horizon slowly framed an impending sunset over the river. A cool mist hovered over the water; gently floating into shore on the edge of a diminished zephyr. The billy can of water was boiling; there was tea, coffee or hot chocolate to be made for those who wanted to warm their tummies after the rainstorm. They were treated to yet another of nature's wonderful gifts; setting the scene of their first night for a relaxing evening of camp kitchen cuisine and spiritual discovery. Zelda could not have planned it any better. Of course, it is the unquestionable way of the gods nurturing heavenly powers to touch those receptive of such sporadic cosmic arrays. Zachary was to be the recipient of at least one truly levitating vision on this night, with his sometimes devious, often corrupting but always purely loyal lovechild at his side.

It would be extremely gratifying for Zelda and overwhelmingly insightful for Zachary, who had put a pot of rice on the fire and was starting to sauté fresh meat with onions, peppers and garlic. He was thinking he would run with the theme he had started so impressively talking about vampires and owls. He decided to go with Flayda's lead by telling Breeze, who was already taking an interest in his culinary skills, that the wolves would probably gather in packs at night and keep the carnivorous deer away from their camp. However, nature's miracles and the beautiful evening weather provided all the inspiration necessary for this wilderness crew to mount an intriguing conversation.

"I think this trip is a great idea for you Zachary," started the always gregarious Mister Mitchell.

"I definitely concur," voiced Flayda, as Mister Mitchell continued.

"With the staunch pressures being forsaken upon yourself, you need to shed your valorous responsibilities and relax with a few of life's precious moments. Even a man as dedicated as yourself must occasionally set aside his honourable cause and seek the simple comforts of life—a few hours to escape from your duties and clear your mind of the taxing concentration that is demanded of you."

"Yes, I must say, you were getting a little irritable there in Saskatchewan. I think California suites you much better," commented Florence.

"I'm sorry Florence, I guess things were a little intense with my family tree and all, although I did enjoy your commentaries on marsh life. Yes, I guess I needed a break like this. Thank you, Zelda," said Zachary, looking over at his lover.

"But to simply sit about, without stimulus, that is not enough for your constantly roving mind," interjected Flayda. "Zachary, you are a man who goes all out. Second best is never enough for a soul as dedicated as yours. The peaceful reward of a few tranquil moments is best appreciated and ultimately most worthwhile when earned—earned through careful and precise application of thoroughly mastered skills."

"The skills of white-water navigation and wilderness survival," suggested Breeze.

"Precisely," smiled Mister Mitchell.

Breeze was certainly rather shy in the unfamiliar group, but she had obviously learned from Mister Mitchell, who was well versed in the fine art of persuasion and quite convincing. She continued to expound her dinner time philosophies.

"I am the life," she said.

"Pardon me?" asked Zachary.

"That's what the rain is saying my good man."

"What life?" questioned Florence.

"The life of the land," answered Breeze. "What do you see?"

"The river and the water," said Flayda.

"The trees," said Zachary.

"Ah, but the river and the trees would not be there without the rain," posed Breeze. "It is the rain which darts through the wind and tumbles down to the earth, gently landing on leaves and draining into rivers. Each droplet, so valuable for its great gift of life, slowly seeps into the trees, down to the roots, where it becomes mother earth. It is the beauty that is the air we breathe, the beauty that is the trees themselves, generously offering us the life we enjoy. When the trees breathe, we breathe."

The three men were particularly captivated by this young woman's eloquent recital, which was easy to consume considering her own natural beauty, let alone the compelling verse rolling off her lips. It even inspired Zelda to enhance the analogy.

"We all consume the beauty that is the land, the rocks, the soil and the trees; the beauty that is water—the rivers, the lakes and oceans—the beauty that is the water of life," concluded Zelda.

A small migratory trout fish then jumped from the river and splashed down on the water at that very moment.

"Another gift of the land," shouted Mister Mitchell.

All concerned laughed robustly once again. Zachary was quite relaxed by evening. Mister Mitchell and Zelda were completing all the elements of their masterplan objectives. The worst-case intention was to rid Zachary of his worries, but not his hunger for exceptional open-air food.

The rest of the group were also hungry and soon one of Zachary's delightful camp kitchen meals was ready—bison sweet chilli pepper cheese steak au gratin, served over a blend of wild and brown rice. It was delicious and everyone raved at the exquisite outdoor meal. Soon the campers finished their dinner and Zelda cleaned up by washing the dishes in a pot of hot water. The next night would be the Findstads' turn to entertain at dinner time.

They were sipping on tea and admiring the inspiring view in the diminishing light of a calm dusk setting, when Zachary heard the sound of his vision entering the valley just above the treetops. He closed his eyes and faced the sky. It glided from one of the valley ridges and down into their gulley; swooping over the trees as it searched for prey.

Zachary could sense its comforting blanket of serene simplicity encompassing his tortured soul. He opened his eyes and turned to face the jagged treeline following the slope of the gulley. And there it was in the distance: a majestic creature of great compassion and wisdom, riding wind currents with the delicate caress of its mighty wings.

It soared across the gulley and bared down upon their campfire with astounding speed. All of Zachary's friends stopped their motion and remained silent just as the owl precisely reached the campsite. They finally recognised the sound that had been singing to Zachary since it entered the valley.

It was the pulsating reverberations of the owl's flight; swooping a wistful crescendo with its wings, as it skimmed the jet stream just above their heads. The melodic humming of the wings, working with such great force to boldly sail along the wind, wisped across their cove and out over the river. Zachary turned again and watched the creature flying with grace and delight: its sonic song of flight drenching his soul with love and truth. Zachary was being offered the courage to seek his redemption. Everyone else, including Zelda, were sunken into a trance as they watched the owl sneak away into the next valley.

"Now that was beauty," marvelled Breeze.

"What a majestic creature," said Mister Mitchell.

"Wow, could this be any more spectacular?" wondered Zachary.

"Oh, that crackling campfire can always produce a trance or two," suggested Mister Mitchell.

"Well then, let's stoke the fire and break out that favourite sweet whiskey of yours Zachary," suggested Florence.

"You brought Yukon Jack? I thought I drank too much."

"Only when you're working on your family tree," clarified Zelda. "You're not taking notes, are you?" she said with a laugh.

"No notes required," answered Zachary.

"Okay then, you're allowed one sip for every note you don't take," offered Flayda. "You didn't bring your harmonica, did you?"

The laughter once again filled the campsite as the six kayakers settled in for a nightcap around the small firepit. The moon cast a sleepy gaze over the peaceful shoreline of the river. The tall reeds growing in the water near the campsite purred in the timid wind. The firepit was brimming with neatly chopped wood and the flames were comforting the scientific community in attendance.

"Life is a marsh Zachary. Cold and slimy or hot and sweltering, it matters not. Destiny has us wading through the marsh of eternity. Covered in swamp and botulism spores up to our thighs, we are hopelessly searching for land: something dry and safe. But there is only swamp," Mister Mitchell expounded another theory.

"There must be something better out there," interjected Breeze, "like a lake, or an ocean, or the odd beach."

"Why would you want anything else when you have the marsh of life and all the interesting creatures it harbours?" posed Flayda.

"That's correct, there's only wetlands," explained Mister Mitchell. "Intimidating and tedious, the swamp is everywhere. And just when we have finally adapted our lives to the swamp—there it is."

"A helicopter coming to save its young?" teased Florence.

"No, but an interesting concept. It is an island of refuge. We climb onto the island and observe the bog from our new home. On the island, we feel secure, separated from the marsh. But soon we realise, we cannot escape the marsh. The swamp is still all around us."

"But then why do we even try? We're all doomed," shrugged Breeze.

"Ah, ha—now we're getting somewhere," segued Flayda.

"Yes, a revelation perhaps. Why indeed do we even bother to carry on?" asked Mister Mitchell.

"To survive, of course, and figure out why we are here in the first place," answered Zelda.

"So we venture back into the swamp," continued Mister Mitchell. "But this time it is even deeper. Our legs sink into mud. The swamp covers our bodies. We attempt to trudge through the marsh, but it is very difficult. And when it seems futile to go on any farther, suddenly there is new hope once again. In the distance—high ground. The end of the marsh."

"Yes!" cheered on Breeze.

"Weasels don't need the swamp to survive dear," Florence reassured her husband.

Flayda smiled and winked back at his wife for the second time that day; allowing Mister Mitchell to finish his hypothesis.

"We muster all our energy and we fight to the high ground. Saturated but triumphant we emerge from the marsh. The high ground is like the new world: a fresh start, leaving the swamp behind. We climb a ridge on the high ground and look into the next valley to see what lies ahead—our new promised land. And what do we see?"

"My father?" suggested Zachary.

"No," sighed Mister Mitchell. "We see another marsh. More swamp and botulism spores."

"How depressing," frowned Breeze.

"Not entirely," said Florence.

"But what could be encouraging about muck and slime?" asked Breeze.

"It is what lies under the slime that is the essence of the marsh," professed Mister Mitchell.

"Botulism spores?" offered Breeze.

"Deeper."

"It sounds almost evil," she said.

"It may very well be. But it also might be good. The marsh is a very mysterious place—just like life."

The marsh of life conversation put a sleepy end to the night for Flayda and Florence, who winked at each other for a third time, casually said good night and retired to their tent. Breeze was also sleepy and hit the sack, but Mister Mitchell remained around the campfire with Zachary and Zelda to absorb the warmth of the flames. Zachary paused and looked out to a swampy corner of the shoreline just down from the campsite.

The dancing flames cast a fanciful sheen on the shoreline of the river, which was affectionately bordered by tall grass and the common pine and fir trees, along with the occasional quaking aspen. The green foliage of the tall aspen reached to the sky: a cluster of leaves as a crown. The moonlight enhanced the texture of the marshy patch and cast a shadow of the aspen crown into the river. Zachary began to imagine a personality for the swamp.

The silence of the night lingered for a moment, and then the completely unexpected happened: they were visited by a ghost. The water darkened in the river and the shadow of the aspen tree began to whirl in a ghastly gnarl. Zachary knew the fear, but the fright was gone. He remained calm and composed. The evil vampire that tortured Zachary so many times, had now lost the battle and was being dragged from the depths of the river. Rising from the water came the fanged monster. It immediately ceased eye contact with Zachary and brashly stretched its wings to extend over their campsite cove.

It was an intimidating ghostly image; hovering above the shoreline with an incredible prehistoric wing span. It was difficult to believe it actually existed, if it were not for its imposing size and powerful presence. Zachary only laughed confidently and walked to the edge of the rock precipice where the fire burned overlooking the river. And for the first time ever, he saw hesitation in the eyes of the vampire, who spoke the first words.

"Do you know who I am?"

"I know what you represent," said Zachary.

"Turn aside your fear as you have so many times, and hear my words. I bring a message from the spirits," pronounced the vampire ghost.

"Message?" questioned Zachary.

"It is urgent," answered the vampire.

"Where have you come from?" demanded Mister Mitchell.

"The swamp, old man."

Mister Mitchell jerked his head upwards: "The swamp?"

"The swamp of life, of course," quipped the vampire.

"You overheard us," asserted Mister Mitchell. "What are you doing out here in the wilderness?"

"I have a message for you," he repeated.

"About what?" questioned Zachary.

"It is a message from the spirits, about your father."

"How do you know about him?" asked Zachary.

"Do not play games with us," threatened Mister Mitchell.

"This is not a game. You might choose to believe I'm not real, but my message is very real and may very well be important to you. I'm a messenger from the spirits," repeated the fanged monster.

"This is absurd," voiced Mister Mitchell.

"Wait. Hear him out," urged Zelda.

"I have a message for the one who is seeking his father."

"What is your message?" asked Zachary.

"You are to find your father, he needs you."

"How do you expect us to believe this?" asked Mister Mitchell.

"I do not expect anything. I am delivering a message as my last deed on this planet. I hope you find guidance in the spirits. Otherwise, what you do is your own affair."

"Do you think my father is near?" questioned Zachary.

The vampire raised his head and glared at the marsh.

"His name is Jeremiah. He is old but very strong. He is with your mother, Maria. She is even stronger. I think they are on this continent, still on this planet, for now. I also think they are near some danger."

"I've had just about enough of this unsubstantiated rhetoric," voiced Mister Mitchell.

"Call it what you will," answered the beast. "Someday you may appreciate the power of the spirits, for it is more than the essence which lies under the marsh, but also the powerful spiritual fibre of eternity."

Mister Mitchell went to abruptly step towards the vampire but stopped. The winged ghost parted with further words of wisdom.

"You will never see me again in this capacity. Your spirit animal, the owl, has protected you well and shown you the path to clarity. I have shown you the battle with evil and now I go with the owls to serve their cause. Always follow the owls, they will show you the true path."

And with those words, two graceful brown owls with faces of white feathers levitated from the river water above the vampire; their open claws clenching the demon from the tips of its expanded wings. The spiritual flight of the owls swept a wave over the river and tugged at the essence of the vampire as its image slowly disintegrated into the water.

"Nice aspen trees," said the vampire ghost as he sank into the river.

The demon's soul was finally obliterated. Mister Mitchell and Zachary were silent once again. And so was Zelda; speechless in astonishment. After a moment of reflection, with the campfire still snapping firewood under the moonlight, Zachary broke the silence.

"Oh man, that Yukon Jack sure is powerful stuff, wouldn't you say?"

Zelda immediately laughed to relieve some tension.

"Did that actually just happen?" she puzzled.

"I told you, the owls were here to protect us," said Zachary.

"Our Zachary appears to be a much stronger individual than I think any of us actually anticipated," said Mister Mitchell.

"And he appears very comfortable and confident," observed Zelda.

"I think it's safe to say that was some sort of a vision; spirits or ghosts," said Zachary.

"I do believe I have seen a ghost before, but that was so vivid and lucid," said Mister Mitchell.

Zachary sat down beside the campfire and took a deep breath. He rubbed his forehead and began to explain the significance of the vision they had just witnessed.

"The vampire creature is a familiar image to me, and the owls have been a part of some other visions in my life. It seems to come to me naturally. Many of my life's mysteries have unfolded tonight, and I've had many years to get ready for this. I sense that I can now confront these issues with some resolve. Although I must solve the mystery around my parents, it actually comes as a relief and not a fear. I seem to feel a new energy after this visit from an old adversary."

The young mere physiologist stepped forward that night, closer to the spiritual essence of his soul. Zelda was happy; her guidance had supported Zachary's journey. She did this not only because it was the duty of her honourable dedication to universal peace, but also because she truly loved this mortal humanoid, who was quickly becoming more than just an average organic inhabitant.

And now, to reveal the significance of Zachary's place in the foundation of spiritual peace and unison throughout the cosmos, we must travel to where I was born and where an understanding of creation can begin to evolve: the knowledge of truth, through the courage to feel the compassion of humility, love and wisdom, leading us through the maze of actuality and the mystique of existence—let alone all the action and adventure along the way.

We must go to the very beginning, so we can comprehend these visions and follow this epic journey: this cosmic crusade into the very nature of existence, not to mention the ultimate quest for universal clairvoyance, and of course the search for forty-seven trees.

Part Two
Spirituality

Chapter 4: Aesthetics

Legend has it, that the original heaven—the one aesthetic heaven—was created in four impulsive and inspired waves of topography. I can attest to this because I was there; an unidentified spiritual fibre, or USF, still not expected to be alive but happy to observe the birth of new life.

The first topography wave was Aspen River. It was unintentional and so were the next three waves, yet everything was inspired by the gods.

The god Kymm was experimenting with the spiritual fibre; contemplating this tangible compulsion which swept the gods. And suddenly one small spark of creativity spontaneously erupted without direct impulse.

And there it was: the Aspen River topography wave. A spark of creation commanded a deep lake, a long and flowing river, valleys, ravines and coulees, a rich expanse comprising a vast plateau, a solitaire range of hills and a magnificent canyon. And still, the USF floated about; watching, unrestrained.

The plateau, which was situated in the middle of the one aesthetic heaven, consisted of wetland grasses and shrubs, alder and corkwood trees, and ramie and bamboo growing near the marshes in the watershed. The god Kwarg created these trees. And this domain became Kwarg's Plateau.

The southern perimeter of the plateau was marked by a range of hills clustered together and sprawling east towards the river. The god Fesso created many trees on this range. Oak, walnut, hickory and pecan grew in the hills. And this domain became known as Fesso's Hills.

The northern border of the plateau started with the small crater lake; the source of the river. This domain, at the northwest corner of the plateau, became Kymm's Lake. Kymm also created trees: ebony and dogwood all around the lake.

The river flowed north from Kymm's Lake; twisting east through a large canyon and looping in a southerly direction eventually forming the eastern border of Kwarg's Plateau. The land was fertile in the canyon with a moderate climate. And there the god Gorb created many aspen and cottonwood trees. And this domain became Gorb's Canyon. So impressive was the canyon that the gods named the waterway Aspen River.

Where the river looped to flow south just outside of the canyon, the god Dkobi selected a domain. Dkobi consumed the spiritual fibre and it became poplar trees; very similar to Gorb's aspen trees. And so Gorb and Dkobi became good friends: heavenly neighbours.

The land relinquished its stature and unselfishly sloped down to the water where rich, lush valleys formed along the banks of the bold river, which was to be the longest of all rivers in the new aesthetic heaven.

Three more gods chose domains on Aspen River. These gods created trees rich with verdurous foliage in the more humid conditions which were to dominate the river's southern climate; a result of the next topography wave.

The god Cess selected south of Dkobi's poplar forest. Cess created teak trees. And farther south where Fesso's Hills almost reached the river, the god Tyru selected another domain. Tyru created large kapok trees.

And south of Tyru the god Hume came to rest. Hume exhausted the spiritual fibre and it became incense tress.

And to the west of Hume—no longer on the river but snuggling up to the southern fringe of Fesso's Hills—the god Baqua became a whole god; never to fuse or split again.

Baqua was inspired by the many streams and springs which drained down Fesso's Hills to the lowlands. There Baqua created acacia trees.

And the gods were impressed.

And we USF remained; wandering freely, floating and fluttering about.

Chapter 5: Sultry Climates

The god Yufe was also inspired. Yufe was taken by the sight of Kymm's Lake in particular; giving birth, it seemed, to everything.

Immediately after Hume and Baqua created incense and acacia and before any other god could settle on Aspen River, Yufe put an end to the river by carving and gouging into the spiritual fibre to create a gigantic basin; randomly interrupted by spiralling mounds of rock and soil that sporadically accumulated from the outburst of the next impulsive topography wave.

The river poured into the basin and Yufe's Lake, scattered with large and small islands, became a part of the aesthetics. It was to be unquestionably the largest lake in the new heaven: a lake of superior qualities to be sure.

But then the spiritual fibre erupted into terrain without direct impulse from any god, as it did when Kymm created the small lake. The second topography wave sprouted from the space: Yufe's Land.

The new lake formed an outlet on its east shore and another river began to flow. This second river surged east and then north for some distance towards what was to become the northern edge of heaven. Halfway downriver on the eastern edge of heaven the water suddenly dropped and plummeted into a deep gorge below. This was heaven's tallest waterfall. And the second river became known as Waterfall River.

The waterway flowed north in the gorge, which became known as Waterfall Gorge; continuing through a valley until it reached its terminus at another lake situated in the northeast corner of the one heaven. South of Yufe's Lake was a dry desert at the southern edge of heaven. The desert spread east until it ended against a modest range of crags and hills. The hills marked the southeast corner of heaven. To the north of Yufe's Lake was Aspen River and to the west there was nothing—so far.

Yufe's Land was sultry and humid to the northeast and parched with a torrid climate to the south. The moisture from Yufe's Lake and Waterfall River made the land fertile. Yufe planted the spiritual fibre on the islands of the lake. And it became palm, papaya, fern and grass trees. The god Lipna planted mopani and pachypodium trees that reached to the sandy northern shore of Yufe's Lake. The god Evbic planted olive trees in the desert to the south. And the land became Evbic's Desert.

The god Kapid created in the first valley of upper Waterfall River. And the spiritual fibre became trees: podocarpus, afrara and iroko. The god Verra planted cactus, yucca and lily trees on the eastern edge of Evbic's Desert below Kapid and Waterfall River. The god Yett planted trees bearing fruit and nuts in the hills that were the southeast corner of the one heaven: avocado, sheas, coffee, cashew, coca and the sort. And the hills, with a small oasis of natural spring water cradled among the crags, became Yett's Bluffs.

The god Idyp found another valley north on Waterfall River before the fuming headwaters of the tallest waterfall. There Idyp planted large kurrajong trees. The god Var created bubinga and aligna trees on the eastern edge of heaven near the tallest waterfall. And along the west bank of Waterfall Gorge which housed the rising mist of the tallest waterfall, the god Cyte planted mallee, wattle and cassava trees. The god Alsa planted mahogany, jarrah and satinwood trees around the lake which was the terminus of Waterfall River in the northeast corner of the one heaven. And the lake became Alsa's Lake.

Although there was another large valley between the tallest waterfall and Alsa's Lake, there was not any other god who came to plant trees. So I went to see what was there.

I heard the gods whispering. They were confused. The mist from the tallest waterfall drifted into the valley.

There were USF everywhere.

The USF were angry. The gods were ignoring them, so they thought. The USF would make a stand in the valley and confront the gods. And they did.

I say they because after this heavenly revolt, so to speak, the first of a few altercations in the one heaven, I remained an unidentified spiritual fibre; but many other USF found something new and amazing.

The USF mingled with this wonderful substance—fog, mist and dew—and found that they could fuse as the gods once did. But these new entities were restricted. They could fuse and become a nondescript entity, but once fused they were bound by the mist and could not leave the valley.

Nevertheless, once fused, two or five or nine USF became one spiritual entity in heaven.

They really meant no harm. They, the new entities, like all of us USF, were simply looking for an identity. But there was only so much of the mist and fog. I was simply too slow to fuse; otherwise I would be one of them.

The gods did not know what to make of these new entities. In fact, the gods were unaware that we USF existed until that time and space of the one heaven. The newly fused USF were now entities in the fog, but they were not gods. But they did exist.

Most of the gods respected them as the spiritual entities they became, but they, the gods, decided to leave the entities alone in the valley.

Alsa, the god isolated by the new entities and most familiar with their strange existence, sensed anger in the valley. There were not any trees growing in the dark, gloomy shadows of the valley; making it a dreary place to exist.

And so Alsa named the entities vapour demons. And the place they inhabited became Vapourdom Valley.

I was fortunate as it turned out. I can now roam much more freely than the vapour demons. In fact, the vapour demons depend on me to lurk about.

The rest suits me fine.

Chapter 6: Mountains

The god Rulsp was always able to fuse and split better than most gods. And so it was understandable that Rulsp's unintentional wave of topography turned out to be the most spectacular of all. Rulsp ventured near the southwest corner of the one heaven and conjured up the spiritual fibre. And then it happened: Rulsp's Mountains.

It was a glorious eruption of topography: grace, strength and motion in a timeless, unmeasurable sweeping space. Mountains were created from the essence of the spiritual fibre. The mountains sliced from the fibre to the western fringe of heaven and east near Yufe's Lake. Ghylls and gorges sprouted down mountainsides and gaping valleys carved through the range.

And the mountains came to life. And they became known as Rulsp's Mountains, but it did not stop with just one mountain range. Without any further manipulation of the spiritual fibre—even though Rulsp might attempt to convince anyone who will listen that this topography wave evolved otherwise—several more aesthetic features graced heaven.

Along the western edge of the one heaven another range of mountains did majestically erupt in a northerly direction. And east of this second range, north of Rulsp's initial mountains but obviously impulsive because of the interruption in geography between the mountains, a third range formed independent of the other two; reaching towards Kymm's Lake but still leaving another large gap in heaven.

A river then began to flow from the range near the western edge of Rulsp's Mountains. It seethed through the mountains and flowed south to new lowlands where a fourth lake was formed in the southwest corner of heaven. The river became known as Mountain River, despite the arrogance and insistence of Rulsp that it be called Rulsp's river. In space and time, Rulsp would go on more than one egotistical rampage.

Another two rivers were also born at the east end of Rulsp's Mountains. The most northerly of these rivers flowed immediately east and drained into Yufe's Lake. This river was the shortest in the one heaven, and so it was called Little River. The other river flowed south into lowlands and then curved east where it emptied into Yufe's Lake as well. This waterway would become known as Lowland River.

And the god Rulsp created spruce trees in a domain on the east side of Mountain River. The god Quujj, clearly attracted by the magnificent mountains, planted pine trees on the west side of the river. The god Zarkk created fir trees east of Rulsp, still in the mountains. Zarkk also marvelled at the mountains and was truly impressed by Rulsp's creativity, becoming a heavenly neighbour. Quujj however, although equally inspired, chose to settle on the opposite side of the river providing a small barrier of independence.

The god Jacobi also experimented with coniferous trees on the second range of mountains which straddled the western fringe of heaven, north of Rulsp and Quujj. And the range was dotted with yew and hemlock trees. This range became Jacobi's Mountains.

The god Dwyi created jacaranda and quebracho trees along Mountain River where it entered the lowlands. The god Marn planted calabash around the lake in the southwest corner of heaven. And the lake became Marn's Lake.

The god Rom chose a domain between Marn's Lake and Lowland River where a range of foothills extended south of Rulsp's Mountains. And Rom created rubber trees in the hills. The god Janale was also fascinated by the terrain of the mountains and selected a domain at the source of Little River. The sultry climate of Yufe's Lake affected the eastern range of Rulsp's Mountains and so Janale planted eucalyptus, cajeput and ironbark. And the god Onu created balsa trees at the source of Lowland River; also indicative of the jungle ecology in the eastern mountain range.

The god Apar implemented the allotted spiritual fibre along Little River in the lowlands leading to Yufe's Lake. And it became trees: mangrove, fig and banyan. The god Kumi planted trees in the valleys along Lowland River flowing to Yufe's Lake—greenheart, mango, crabwood and rosewood—all well suited to the sultry climate.

The gods Eamaan and Rens took up residence on the third mountain range north of Rulsp's original creation. And there they planted trees. Ash, sycamore and magnolia sprouted in Eamaan's domain to the south of the range. Rens created tung and loquat trees at the north end of the range. And this range became known as Ash Mountains.

The god Wateko planted maple trees in the valley spontaneously created between Rulsp's Mountains and Ash Mountains. The god Yanamea created an assortment of trees in the rolling foothills to the east of Wateko, still north of Rulsp's Mountains: sassafras, mesquite, kola and logwood.

It was no coincidence that the gods were creating trees with their allotted spiritual fibre. The power of spiritual fibre, although unbridled at first, seemingly created the land and the water for some reason. The gods knew they needed something to sustain their new aesthetic heaven. They needed something worthy of the amazing transformation into such vibrant elements; living creations to honour the inspired natural wilderness of spiritual fibre. Botany seemed reasonable and by the natural flow of the fibre trees became the answer.

The trees, by the power of the gods and the qualities of spiritual fibre, were accompanied by full-fledged forests and all the living relationships of healthy ecological domains: such as shrubs, grass, moss, micro-organisms for the transfer of energy and other structures required for the life of plants.

Heaven was looking quite pulchritudinous as the third topography wave began to take hold. The gods were happy with their creations, but then the gods of Yufe's Land came to inspect Rulsp's Mountains. And they, the gods of the second topography wave, told the gods of the third wave to look at the southern edge of heaven near Evbic's Desert.

And so they looked, the gods of Rulsp's Mountains, unsuspectingly, beyond the flow of Lowland River towards the desert lands. But the gods of Yufe's Land knew something had gone awry. There was a gap between the desert and the river; desolate without any trees growing.

And Yufe spoke to Rulsp.

"If there are not any trees, there is chaos."

And Alsa explained further.

"Have you ever heard of vapour demons?"

And finally, I became a spiritual entity in the one heaven.

Chapter 7: Wind Warriors

The USF were concerned. Huddled on the southern fringe of heaven beside Evbic's Desert we could see that most of the spiritual fibre was consumed. Soon the aesthetic heaven would be completed with newly created domains and we were still non-entities.

And then, as luck would have it, something happened that the gods could not control. It's really quite amazing that random sporadic events could influence such dramatic outcomes in the wake of all this unbridled spiritual power.

The explosion of Rulsp's Mountains was so tumultuous, some of the unconsumed fibre floating in the one heaven was whisked into the gap beside the desert. The fibre violently swirled in the wave of topography.

Today I would describe it as a tornado. But in this space of creation it was just another unexplainable phenomenon in heaven.

We USF gathered in the gap and were sucked into the wind funnel of fibre, with sand, soil, rock fragments and assorted vegetation from the lowlands. It was a rough ride, but inside the heavenly tornado we USF merged with the spiritual fibre.

And behold, before the gods, we USF finally became spiritual entities in heaven.

Wind currents were born.

We were free to travel with spiritual winds and as the funnel dispersed, we began to glide through heaven. We were passengers on the flight of wind.

Like the vapour demons we were not entirely tangible and we were not gods; but we no longer suffered from an identity crisis.

The gods shrugged their shoulders, so to speak, by now beginning to accept these random occurrences. They recognised the powers of spiritual fibre were so unparalleled that the creation of a tangible heaven inherited certain risks.

The gods watched as we soared throughout heaven; sometimes doing nothing more than ruffling leaves, but other times raging across the land and ravaging domains—even ripping trees from their foundations.

And so, seeing this behaviour, the gods named us wind warriors.

And it was always windy in the gap between the desert and the jungle lowlands south of the mountains.

And so, the gods named this place the Windswept Spiral.

And we did exist eternally as wind warriors.

And the gods could not control us.

The rest suits me fine.

Chapter 8: The Void

The final topography wave was inspired, I'm sure, by us wind warriors. There was only a small amount of USF remaining in the one heaven, which we grabbed and took to the northwest corner of heaven where nothing existed.

The aspen god Gorb confronted us along the way and mingled with our wind currents. Gorb asked us where we were going. Hesitantly we told Gorb the truth. Gorb respected us and allowed us to continue without a challenge. The gods could not control us, but Gorb was the only god to ever intimately interact with us wind warriors. We always did like Gorb after that.

Finally we arrived in the northwest corner of heaven. There we swirled into funnels and fused those last few remaining USF. What fun it was. I was very encouraged by my new existence. And then the USF were gone. We wind warriors created tangible entities very similar to the gods: soothing, clear layers of radiance with bluish green streaks of pure power, slicing, contorting and shifting into different shapes, so to speak.

But they were not gods. They do, however, possess some impressive powers; but nothing like the gods. A dominant character surfaced and became their leader, who they called Flafid. And the god Pefl came to investigate.

"Do you have the power to create?" asked Pefl.

"What do you mean?" said Flafid.

"Like this," exclaimed Pefl.

The spiritual fibre became tangible once again with a stroke of Pefl's inspiration: The Void. The fibre became another range of hills in the one heaven. And they became known as Pefl's Hills.

Flafid then released the power of these new entities we created. Flafid's power was no match, but it diverted Pefl's wave of topography and left a void in heaven where Flafid and the others remained. And this place was called Flafid's Void.

Pefl's creation, deflected and ricocheted by the power of the void, spontaneously gave birth to new aesthetic features; beginning with three rivers. The rivers flowed east from the hills in the northwest corner of heaven. The two northerly rivers, which were closest to Flafid's Void, joined together as the hills tapered to lowlands. The southerly river also flowed to the lowlands where it eventually joined with the remaining northerly river. And so these rivers became known as Confluence Waterway.

The downriver flow of Confluence Waterway entered a marsh further east in the lowlands, bordering the southern fringe of Flafid's Void. The god Ardyk selected the marsh as a domain. And it became known as Ardyk's Swamp. Confluence Waterway then split into two tributaries after passing through Ardyk's Swamp. The South Fork, as it became known, flowed east and looped south, draining into Aspen River near Dkobi's poplar forest. The North Fork, as it became known, flowed towards Alsa's Lake and Vapourdom Valley. But before the river could reach Alsa, the god Nekrol halted its flow. Nekrol took guidance from Yufe's earlier actions and created a basin where the river drained into a lake. And the lake became known as Nekrol's Lake.

The god Svebb saw the spiritual fibre take shape south of Nekrol's Lake. A small mountain range of strange outcroppings was etched into the one heaven; possibly stunted by the presence of the vapour demons, although none of the gods could say for certain. And because of this, yet another unexplained occurrence in the aesthetic heaven, the small mountain range became known as the Eerie Place. The god Lirda also witnessed the spiritual fibre become an environmental feature south of the Eerie Place between Aspen River and the tallest waterfall. And it became a modest peak with equally modest foothills rolling south near Yufe's Lake. And this became known as Lirda's Range.

The god Maav briskly moved to the last remaining spiritual fibre in the one heaven. Maav saw the spark of fibre in the gap between Ash Mountains and Kymm's Lake. And it became another small lake—Maav's Lake. The lake drained into a river which flowed north to Ardyk's Swamp where it joined with Confluence Waterway. Another valley also formed between Maav's Lake and Ash Mountains. The remaining gods then selected domains and became permanent entities in the one heaven.

The gods Baf and Sonus greeted Pefl in the northwest hills. They each chose one of the three river valleys and created trees. Baf planted jute trees in the north valley, Sonus planted birch, linden, holly and buckthorn in the south valley, and Pefl planted willow trees in the middle valley.

Beech, chestnut and buckeye were created around Maav's Lake. The god Moht planted many fruit-bearing trees in the valley between Maav's Lake and Ash Mountains—apple, plum, cherry and the sort—which became known as Rose Valley. The god Nybos created cedar, deodar and cypress in the valley along the river that flowed from Maav's Lake. And the river became Cedar River. Ardyk planted tamarack and larch in the swamp. The god Palu selected the South Fork and created massive redwoods, sequoia, padauk and sandalwoods. The god Forek planted karri and tuart along the North Fork.

Gum trees were created and flourished around Nekrol's Lake. Svebb created ginkgo trees among the outcroppings of the Eerie Place near the vapour demons. Elm and mulberry trees were planted in the highlands of Lirda's Range. And in Lirda's foothills the god Laavv created baobab and bottle; the thick trees reflecting the climate from nearby Yufe's Lake.

There was one last matter to resolve. The gods of the fourth topography wave went to Flafid's Void and confronted these new creatures we wind warriors created with the USF. The gods allowed the entities to stay in the aesthetic heaven, but they would be confined to the treeless domain of Flafid's Void. These entities are shape shifting wizards, as they became known; similar in appearance to the gods with the ability to take on different shapes and formations, but restricted in their movements. Different factions within the legions of wizard entities would later collaborate with certain gods in assorted dimensional adventures, as it turned out.

The aesthetic heaven was finally complete. The spiritual fibre in the one heaven lived in the gods, the trees, the land and the water. The USF lived in the vapour demons, the wizards and we wind warriors: except for one last remaining USF which Gorb of the aspens saved and kept hidden in the forested canyon. Gorb did this, insightfully, without the knowledge of the other gods.

They, the gods, were soon content to live within themselves. It seemed they were satisfied and happy with their new aesthetic heaven; it seemed the new heaven would endure a peaceful life embraced by the tranquillity of the trees.

It seemed.

Map of Original Aesthetic Heaven

Chapter 9: Free Flight

The new aesthetic heaven was immense.

It was ethereal.

It was tangible.

We wind warriors breezed through the wonders of heaven. We became intimate with the wind currents. We were somewhat restricted however, as only the gods enjoyed unlimited access to the one heaven.

We wind warriors must link ourselves together and gather enough flight to travel great distances with any amount of efficiency. We form a small float, a large vector or a massive vortex, as we call them, and together we fly on top of wind currents; lapping and cruising on the edge of free flight.

The gods respect the power of free flight and they do not control us—ever.

We increase our flight as we gain velocity. The faster we are, the stronger we are. Smaller floats are bound by larger vectors, which join together to comprise storm systems; sometimes sucked into a vortex, creating the largest of destructive disturbances.

It is possible to avoid vectors, but eventually one comes too close. And then the free flight becomes even more powerful. Vectors also collide uncontrollably at the impulse of heaven's natural forces; often exploding in a flurry of disturbance and often quietly defusing over a large expanse.

And further, although heaven was immense, we were restricted by the terrain of the four topography waves. Imposing geography such as Rulsp's Mountains often separated vectors.

Regardless, we wind warriors were always exploring and always aware of approaching vectors. Wind warriors have to take chances; size up a float or vector and decide if they want a ride.

I once narrowly escaped a vortex and ducked down into Ardyk's Swamp on a small float. I was trapped there until finally a gentle zephyr mustered enough free flight to carry me to the North Fork. It wasn't a large float but I was no longer being selective; that swamp was stifling.

My trip into the marsh was well worth the hardship however. It was there that I learned we wind warriors were about to indirectly affect the eventual end of harmony in the one heaven.

Ultimately, though, it wasn't such a bad thing; to have the harmony end that is.

Chapter 10: Natural Regeneration

I was lifted from the swamp on a new vector of wind currents. We soon collided with a free flight vector of comparable size later on our journey and swept over Nekrol's Lake in the rage of a squalling gale.

Our newly formed vortex ravaged through heaven over the Eerie Place. It was there that something quite incredible began to transpire.

The vortex blew along the eastern fringe of the Eerie Place and there our magnificent free flight mingled with a swarm of vapour demons. These demons ventured from their valley as far as the mist from the tallest waterfall allowed them.

The vapour demons were confused as we wind warriors shuffled them about in the wake of our flight. And then, for some apparent reason unbeknownst to us, the vapour demons were cradled in our vortex and began to travel with us.

Never before did the vapour demons escape beyond the limits of the mist from the tallest waterfall. We flushed across the peculiar terrain of the Eerie Place towards Lirda's Range. The demons clung to our currents.

Amused by the sight of these struggling entities we marvelled as the feisty bits of fibre grabbed at free flight for survival. And then the vapour demons began to fuse together and form huge clusters of essence.

The new form was fairly translucent, but slowly gaining semblance. We wind warriors were weary.

The vapour demons were evolving into a tangible force. They were even taking on colour; a pale and flat imposing colour.

The vapour demons became larger as we blustered over Lirda's Range. Soon the clusters grew to be so heavy that their density began to slow our pace. And within the clusters we began to hear an unsettling rumble.

We wind warriors created thunder clouds, as they became known.

Our vortex, now a conglomerate cluttered with clusters of clouds, slowly surged forward on a south-westerly course. We were headed for the Aspen River valley.

The vapour demon clouds grumbled abruptly. An ominous yowl covered Tyru's valley of kapok trees. Above the thick jungle canopy a darkness of gloom descended to the river's edge.

The vapour demons were about to strike revenge on the gods.

The rumbling turned into a tempestuous curse of sharp antagonism. The demons grated with displeasure. A sudden slice of essence snapped from within the clouds and ignited beneath our vortex.

The vapour demons created lightning, as it became known.

Down into the valley the lightning seared. It shredded a stand of kapoks and the smouldering trees tumbled to the ground. A strange smoke began to rise and we wind warriors were witness to another phenomenon in the one heaven—fire.

The underbrush of Tyru's great forest began to burn. Spontaneous combustion was born.

Quickly the new flames began to spread and the kapok trees were consumed in a growling blaze. The gods gathered in the river valley to see this display. The sporadic nature of heaven unceremoniously triggered chaos within the harmony.

The vapour demons, once mere non-entities, formed into a powerful essence capable of unharnessed destruction. The fire continued to devour the kapok forest. It was the gods' turn to watch in awe.

They, the gods, were confronted with another unexplainable and uncontrollable force in the one heaven. But then, as quickly as they displayed their anger, the vapour demons revealed their hidden compassion.

The clouds began to dissipate and a shower of rain, as it became known, dropped down into the valley. And the fire was doused: the gift of rain.

The gods were relieved.

However, our great vectors and floats of free flight did not stop carrying the vapour demons throughout heaven. We roamed over lakes and rivers in the one heaven and the vapour demons fused with us.

The moisture we accumulated created dense clouds; often releasing lightning from within the friction of their fibre. But the heavy vapour fusions eventually returned to the spiritual essence of their origin, and rain poured from the clouds.

The trees perished in the lightning forest fires and flourished with the rain; always regenerating stronger and healthier.

The vapour demons became a vital link in the natural regeneration of the one heaven.

Chapter 11: Wildlife

All of the spiritual fibre was consumed, but that did not stop the genesis of the aesthetic heaven. The sporadic eruption of spiritual elements that inspired the topography waves, continued to spontaneously trigger the natural synthesis of complex structures.

These profound complexities of nature supported the ecological systems to sustain healthy environments in the tangible heaven, including plant life and animals: from simple bacteria, to pollen transferring bees, to photosynthesising botanical lifeforms, to amazingly adaptive flying, swimming and bounding animal creatures.

They, the gods, could not control this natural process, just like they could not control us wind warriors; instead, they, the gods, stood at a distance, so to speak, and kept watching the impressive qualities contained in the essence of the trees. New and wondrous creatures were derived from the power of the fibre within each domain; just as forests grew around the trees.

It was astounding. The power of the gods and the spiritual fibre is and remains unmeasurable. The gods have kept us wind warriors in awe since the space of the one heaven. I observed what very few wind warriors had witnessed during my float to Ardyk's Swamp: another form of essence in the one heaven.

Ardyk's Swamp had sheltered animals: slimy cold-blooded reptiles as they became known. I was the only wind warrior on my new float to witness Ardyk's reptiles. I gathered a sizeable audience describing the new creations: snakes, lizards, alligators and the sort, as they became known.

But then we joined with another vector. A wind warrior returning from Rulsp's Mountains was on the vector. The warrior described a new form of essence in the mountains.

Rulsp's Mountains gave birth to large, lumbering mammals with raw savagery; creatures that became rulers of the forest. Bears they called them.

Our vector sailed throughout heaven for many life cycles of the forest domains. This was a particularly rich vector; swarmed with many warrior scribes to note the evolution of the one heaven.

Later we heard that ungulates were born in Ash Mountains with Rens and Eamaan: deer, elk, caribou, mountain goats, sheep, moose and the sort, as they became known.

And news came that the weasel family, as they were sometimes called, such as wolverine, otters, beavers, martens, fishers and the sort, originated on the western fringe of Rulsp's Mountains with Quujj and the pine trees. The word was also uttered that arboreals, as they were named, were harboured in Jacobi's Mountains: from small primates like monkeys, to possums and sloths, to squirrels and chipmunks, all living in the trees.

In the forest domains of the eastern mountain ranges, there was word of wild cats, as they were dubbed, such as leopards, panthers, cheetahs, lynx and bobcats; not to be confused with the big cats, as they were labelled, like tigers, lions, jaguars, cougars and pumas, which apparently began roaming the forests surrounding Yufe's Lake, as did the large primates such as chimpanzee, gorilla, orangutan and baboon.

And the wind warriors kept reporting fascinating discoveries, with new names recorded like proclamations of animal kingdoms. There were the aquatic marine mammals discovered in Yufe's Lake: porpoise as they became known, such as whales and dolphins, along with the many varieties of aquatic creatures including fish that flourished throughout all of heaven's waterways.

And there was the observed evolution of canines, such as wolf, coyote and fox on the fringes of Kwarg's Plateau; roaming into the surrounding forests.

And down into the nearby domain that was Gorb's Canyon, incredible flying animals called birds were born, as they became known, gliding in the air, surveying the canyon walls and the flowing path of Aspen River: eagles, owls, hawks, osprey, falcons and many, many other sorts.

Towards the Eerie Place, beyond Aspen River and approaching Lirda's Range, roaming over a fertile expanse of grasslands and small tree stands, scribes noted further evolution: great herds of migratory mammals such as wildebeest, zebras, buffalo, gazelles and antelope.

And beyond Lirda's Range, into the valleys of Waterfall River and south towards Evbic's Desert, came word of robust, powerful animals: rhinoceros, hippopotamus, giraffe and elephants, as they became known.

The aesthetic heaven was percolating with life; revolving cycles of complex structures captivating all of us spiritual inhabitants. Animals of great variety evolved and inhabited the domains of the new tangible heaven; spreading to different environments where they could find sustenance for survival.

This desire to create an ethereal heaven was certainly looking quite glorious—the impressive terrain, the trees, forests, waterways, wind currents, lightning and rain, and now the animals—but slowly, the boredom was once again about to creep into the scenario.

Word of these new entities, these new animal creatures, spread among the gods. They, the gods, were soon busy talking to themselves; trying to decide the fate of these new creations.

It was another product of the boredom that occasionally rested uneasy with the gods. They needed something to satisfy their curiosity. And so they launched into philosophical discussions about heaven and its elements: chitter, chatter, chitter, chatter.

Soon though, the gods came to the realisation that there were indeed certain manifestations they could not control, and they, the gods, should just observe and marvel. And so, in due course, the gods shared their delight in the new creatures: the animal wildlife and such.

It was heart-warming to see the gods share their happiness. Harmony, for the time being, so to speak, was still intact.

Chapter 12: Arrogance and Conflict

The process of natural regeneration ironically brought stability to the aesthetic heaven, but it also resulted in some harmful conflict.

The fury of topography waves subsided. The gods were settled in their domains. Although prone to occasional destruction, the vapour demons and us wind warriors evolved into a systematic structure meshed into the ecology of heaven. The magical wizards often shook the foundations of the spiritual fibre with displays of their mysterious power, but they were confined to their treeless void.

The gods still seemed content with the heaven they created. It was an intimate community. Gods visited domains in a neighbourly spirit, chatting about forestry and the aspects of natural regeneration; but heaven was not without incident. Rivalries slowly developed between some of the gods.

They, the gods, developed distinct personalities in their new aesthetic, tangible and permanent existence. Although some gods were friendly, others were stubborn and arrogant.

There was a place in heaven without any particular trees growing: a plateau of softly rolling terrain south of Pefl's Hills between Jacobi's Mountains and Ash Mountains. A few birch trees, tung, ash and yew filtered onto the plateau, but mostly there was grass and a sprinkling of flowers covering the gently undulating ridges.

There was a lone hill near the middle of the plateau, which appeared to have its peak sliced flat to form a level platform of land at the top. It was said this hill buried the fragments of spiritual fibre that did not survive the eruptions of topography waves. It was also said that this was heaven's burial ground. And this place became known as Mount Witness.

It was a beautiful and tranquil spot in the one heaven, but Rulsp soon put an end to that. Because the plateau was not a domain, Rulsp claimed the space. This aroused the gods and they gathered at the lone hill to voice their objections. It was exactly what Rulsp wanted.

The spruce god agreed not to claim the plateau if the other gods designated the terrain as a ground for gathering to conference, discuss and debate matters of concern. The gods found this proposal acceptable.

And so this place, anointed as Mount Witness by all of heaven's spiritual residents, was proclaimed by Rulsp as the place to conference and debate, as only this arrogant god could do; even though it was still known as heaven's burial ground. And Rulsp quietly returned to the mountains with the fodder of a devious plan. Rulsp began contemplation that would lead to mischievous, yet ultimately wondrous implications.

Meanwhile, near the southeast corner of heaven, Verra was concerned about the cactus, yucca and lily trees growing on the edge of Evbic's desert. The dry, parched conditions made survival difficult for the trees in Verra's domain.

They, the trees, were not as robust and full of fibre as the others in the one heaven. Verra wanted to help the trees. And so Verra went over to Yett's Bluffs and found a large watering hole in the oasis of avocado, shea and cashew trees. The oasis was fed with natural springs from the bluffs.

Verra crept discretely to the oasis and began irrigation. Verra carved a trench to divert some of the oasis water to the desert.

The god of cactus then travelled north of the desert to Waterfall River in the valley where Kapid's jungle climate podocarpus, afrara and iroko trees were growing. Verra again carved an irrigation trench from the soil and slowly diverted water from the river to the desert.

Kapid and Yett discovered the diversions. The two gods were enraged. Verra acted without permission, in defiance of common courtesy and the accepted orderly conduct of heaven. Water was being robbed from Waterfall River and the oasis of Yett's Bluffs.

"The cactus, yucca and lily have adapted to the desert," claimed Yett.

"You Verra, created the desert trees in accordance with the domain of your choice," asserted Kapid. "You must remain content with your domain and restrict any innovation within that domain."

But Verra still wanted the irrigated water.

"My trees need to drink," said Verra.

Faced with no other alternative, Kapid and Yett summoned the gods to Mount Witness. And there the gods reasoned.

Evbic, whose olive trees shared the desert with Verra, was the only voice of support for the irrigation practices. It was determined after lengthy discussion that Verra was acting improperly.

The gods politely told Verra to comply with the heavenly consensus and return the irrigation trenches to their original stature. And if Verra refused, the gods would calmly eradicate the cactus, yucca and lily; banishing Verra to Vapourdom Valley.

Verra eventually complied and replaced the soil in the trenches, but the damage was done and a certain amount of water from the river and the oasis continued to trickle into the desert. Verra's domain slowly grew into a tantalising and colourful paradise.

Kapid and Yett were peeved. They remained resentful of Verra.

The maintenance and manicure of forests was a primary activity of the gods. They, the gods, thinned their forests to encourage healthy growth of preferred trees. They cleared stands so that seedlings could develop in the continuing process of regeneration. The gods groomed forest beds, trimmed forest canopies and harvested dying trees. It kept the gods occupied and they took great pride in their forests. It also led to some altercations.

Baf, Pefl and Sonus were harvesting their jute, willow and birch trees in Pefl's Hills at the northwest corner of heaven. Unlike most gods who stacked their harvested trees—burning them or letting them decompose into the ground—these three gods tended to heave their trees into the valley rivers of Confluence Waterway.

This did not seem unreasonable. The rivers were wide enough and the trees easily floated with the strong currents, but problems arose downriver. The waterway became shallow in Ardyk's Swamp; twisting and turning through a maze of marshes. Harvested trees often became jammed and snagged where Cedar River entered the swamp and further downriver where Confluence Waterway split into the North Fork and South Fork. Sometimes the trees accumulated and clogged the waterway. Floods resulted.

Ardyk was not happy. The god of tamarack was always busy wading through bogs and removing trees to alleviate the flooding. There were other complications as well. The dams created by the trees in the swamp caused water levels to rise upriver and encroach on the cedar valleys where Nybos dwelled. The rising water levels even caused problems for Maav at the source of Cedar

River. Maav's Lake would partially flood, threatening the beech, chestnut and buckeye trees.

The rivers of Confluence Waterway were well protected from the flooding upstream in Pefl's Hills. It was the cedar basin that housed any overflow. Because Ardyk's Swamp and Cedar River harboured the flood waters, the forests of Baf, Pefl and Sonus were not adversely affected. And so the gods of Pefl's Hills were oblivious of the flooding problems.

Downriver from Ardyk's Swamp more complications developed along the forks. While flooding occurred upriver, water levels dropped on the North and South Forks, and eventually further downriver on Nekrol's Lake.

Forek's karri and tuart trees in the valleys of the North Fork suffered from the decreased water levels, but more drastically, Palu's giant redwood, sequoia, padauk and sandalwood on the shores of the South Fork were famished when river water was detained in Ardyk's Swamp.

Nekrol's gum trees also felt the thirst of depleted water levels, but not as severely. The trees of Aspen River, where the South Fork dumped its waters, were not damaged by the disturbance of water levels because there was sufficient flow from the river and its source of Kymm's Lake.

Finally, Ardyk and the gods affected could not remain patient any longer. The gods of Pefl's Hills had to stop throwing trees into the rivers of Confluence Waterway. Ardyk and Palu took the initiative and called the gods to Mount Witness. It was a civilised confrontation.

Baf, Pefl and Sonus pleaded ignorance and argued that throwing the harvested trees in the rivers was a natural process. Ardyk and Palu described the destruction inflicted on other forests. Gorb of the aspen suggested the harvested trees were creating excessive havoc and hardship for other gods. Rulsp of the spruce said it was the divine right of any god to dispose of trees as desired. Gorb's hypothesis of proper regard for neighbouring domains and the consequences of irresponsible forestry practices won favour with the majority of heaven's occupants.

And so it was that Baf, Pefl and Sonus were requested to stop disposing of harvested trees in the rivers. Resentfully they complied, but not without scorning Ardyk and Palu.

The gods were somewhat surprised with the reaction from Pefl in particular. Pefl had witnessed the spark of spiritual power quite intimately, and had also observed the uncontrollably sporadic nature of this energy, which made them, the gods, believe Pefl would be sympathetic to all entities in the one heaven.

I guess Pefl developed a certain arrogance, being the initiator of a topography wave and all. Perhaps Pefl was influenced by Baf, who, being the closest god to the void created by the wizards, seemed to bear a resentment towards the unexplainable phenomenon that allowed the wizards to restrict the spiritual fibre; in particular, the stunted growth of the petit jute trees growing in the northern river valley of Pefl's Hills, which Baf planted and believed were affected by Flafid's Void.

And such were the personalities of the gods in the new aesthetic heaven. Mount Witness was frequently utilised in the one heaven. Many squabbles were negotiated and many rivalries were fostered. There were reoccurring themes that come to mind.

Certain gods surfaced as the aggressors in the one heaven. Need I say, Rulsp always supported aggression.

The gods Rens and Eamaan who inhabited Ash Mountains were constant complainers. They did not appreciate infestations of insects that originated from nearby valleys such as Moht's rose trees and Wateko's maple. Rens and Eamaan logged other complaints, supported aggressions from gods such as Yanamea of sassafras, and always seemed on the offensive.

Yanamea, whose prolific valley of sassafras, mesquite, kola and logwood trees rested just north of Rulsp's foothills, was another disturbing god. Yanamea often argued with rainforest gods such as Janale of eucalyptus, cajeput and ironbark, Apar of mangrove, fig and banyan, Onu of balsa, Kumi of greenheart, mango, crabwood and rosewood, and Rom of the rubber trees.

These rainforest gods were often manipulated by Yanamea's demands and accusations. Yanamea was supported primarily by Baqua of the acacia trees, whose domain was near the rainforests, and who often argued with or threatened nearby sultry climate gods on Yanamea's behalf, like Hume of incense, Tyru of kapok, Lipna of mopani and pachypodium, even one of the topography originators, Yufe of the palm, papaya, fern and grass trees.

The jungle climate gods near Yufe's Lake—in the tapering eastern mountains, foothills and lowlands, and along the southern reaches of Aspen River and Waterfall River—always seemed to be caught in the middle of aggressive claims by the mountain gods to the north and west, and the desert gods Evbic with Verra in the arid terrain to the far south.

While these gods suffered from their conflicts, but still embraced their life in the one heaven, the gods of the far western mountains clung onto their independence; remaining resolute in their values despite the corruptible influence of greed and pretentious ego conveyed by the likes of Rulsp and Zarkk in the heart of the teeming mountain terrain. Quujj of the pine trees led this defiance, bolstered by the determined morality of Jacobi with the yew and hemlock trees, Dwyi of the jacaranda and quebracho trees, and Marn of the calabash; often lending their support to the beleaguered Wateko of the maple trees who was vulnerable in the valley between the mountain peaks.

Many gods naturally gravitated to mutual alliances of shared values and perspectives, such as these gods in the mountainous topography. Onu of balsa trees and Kumi of greenheart, mango, crabwood and rosewood trees, for example, with their domains along the valleys of Lowland River, often collaborated their thoughts and conjectures during the ongoing debates of the aesthetic heaven.

The god Palu of redwood, sequoia, padauk and sandalwoods, along with Forek of karri and tuart, as well as Kymm of ebony and dogwood, fabricated a strong corridor of peaceful existence. They did so quite vocally at some of the confrontational occasions in the one heaven, making themselves well known among the gods.

Other gods lent their quiet support through an informal alliance of those with similar territory and disposition; who graduated towards speaking as a unified front during various heavenly debates. One such coalition consisted of centrally located gods: Nybos of the cedar, deodar and cypress; Ardyk of the tamarack and larch; Gorb of the aspen and cottonwood; Dkobi of the poplar; Svebb of the ginkgo; and Lirda of the elm and mulberry.

Another informal but vibrant coalition existed among three neighbourly gods who shared common opinions manifesting on the side of peaceful coexistence: Kwarg of alder, corkwood, ramie and bamboo; Cess of teak; and Laavv of baobab and bottle.

There were also several other gods who were either isolated or undecided, and tended to remain neutral in heavenly confrontations, such as Moht of rose trees, Maav of beech, chestnut and buckeye, Fesso of oak, walnut, hickory and pecan, Nekrol of gum trees, and the eastern fringe gods near Vapourdom Valley, including Alsa of mahogany, jarrah and satinwood, Cyte of mallee, wattle and cassava, Var of bubinga and aligna, and Idyp of the kurrajong trees.

There were a variety of disagreements throughout the history of the one heaven. Take my word for it, Rulsp and the mountain gods Zarkk and Eamaan especially, along with Yanamea, Evbic and Verra, were usually stirring hostilities; while a few loosely organised peaceful coalitions were always attempting to sedate any oppression and gather a ground swell of common sense, often with impetus from Gorb, Quujj and Palu or Kwarg.

And the gods continued to groom their forests.

And the gods continued to admire their creations.

And the gods continued to resolve their lack of control over unexplained phenomena affecting spiritual elements.

The rest suits me fine.

Chapter 13: Wrath and Rage

Rulsp was in a testy mood.

The god of spruce was being harassed by lightning from the vapour demons. It was apparent most of the forest fires ignited by the lightning were occurring in the mountains. This angered Rulsp: at least that was the claim made by the spruce god.

The actual truth was that lightning strikes were occurring throughout heaven. We wind warriors could not control the manifestation of thunder clouds, nor could the vapour demons control the natural occurrence of lightning from within our storm clusters.

There were indeed several lightning strikes in the mountains after storm systems crossed over open water such as the lakes of Maav, Marn and Yufe. But there were also many thunderstorms—probably even more—on the eastern fringe of heaven near Vapourdom Valley, the tallest waterfall, Alsa's Lake and the Eerie Place; not to mention the many jet streams carrying vapour demons over Nekrol's Lake and bringing weather disturbances down into the valleys of Aspen River.

Rulsp realised this actuality, but the spruce god also realised the loss of healthy trees diminished a god's power. Rulsp seemed determined to become the dominant god in the one heaven. And so Rulsp made immediate plans to rectify the situation.

The god of spruce ventured to Mount Witness and summoned the other gods in heaven. All forty-seven gods were there on Mount Witness. Rulsp voiced great displeasure; posing an argument to the gods.

"The vapour demons are destructive and rebellious. They are a threat to our harmony. The fires have ravaged the land and killed our trees. We must do away with the vapour demons. They must be banished," declared Rulsp.

"Banished where?" asked Fesso of the oak.

"Exactly," answered Rulsp. "We shall have to eliminate them."

"How shall we eliminate them? We cannot even grow trees in their valley," said Cyte of mallee.

"Our heaven created the vapour demons. We created our heaven. We have the power to eliminate them. It's a matter of physics," explained Rulsp.

"Physics?" puzzled Lipna of mopani.

"Yes, physics. We shall discover a way to eliminate the vapour demons. We have the power. That is all that matters."

"Rulsp, you claim that we created the vapour demons by creating our heaven," interjected Gorb of aspen. "But we did not create heaven. The creation of our tangible domains is a gift of the fibre that is heaven. The vapour demons are indeed heaven's creatures. They are free to exist just as the mountains and the lakes are free to exist. We cannot eliminate the vapour demons. They must remain free. It will go against the very nature of heaven."

"The very nature of heaven," started Rulsp with a wretched curse, "is to serve our every desire. This extension of our creativity is for the pleasures we deem appropriate. The very nature of our heaven is not intended for these meagre vapour demons to strike down with lightning at their whim."

"We must not attempt to manipulate the spiritual entities within our heaven. The powers of the fibre are not to be questioned, they are to be respected. To explain the fibre is impossible and to harness it will only lead to chaos. An attempt to control the nature of heaven is a paradox; an antithesis unto itself. And that, is a matter of semantics," argued Gorb.

"Semantics. Merely words," sneered Rulsp.

"You speak of physics but you do not realise that the spiritual essence of the fibre is the source of heaven's creations. The spiritual entities within heaven are inherently unparalleled. They are the fibre that is all encompassing. They are the fibre that sporadically erupted to form this heaven without our control or direction," professed Gorb.

"I do not want to control heaven. I just want to rid heaven of these bothersome vapour demons," shouted Rulsp.

"This heaven began with the spiritual fibre and the pockets of unidentified fibre that we have never been able to explain or control. The vapour, the wind, the wizards, the land and the water have all evolved from the fibre, not from our commands," continued Gorb.

"It was our power that started everything," stated Rulsp.

"We have used the fibre to create the trees. It is our gift to heaven. Can you not be satisfied with the trees?" pleaded Gorb.

"I want to save the trees," asserted Rulsp.

"You want to control our very essence," yelled Gorb, becoming more frustrated with each spoken word. "It is senseless. Where will it end?"

"It will end with the death of the vapour demons!"

The confrontation between Gorb and Rulsp was intense. The shouts of anger and frustration from the gods were heard in every valley and gorge. Trees shuddered in fright. The rivers surged, mountainsides trembled, sandstorms howled over desert and shrub, and botulism spores reproduced in a frenzy. Heaven never experienced such a commotion from the gods. It was straining at the seams of fibre.

"They must remain," demanded Gorb.

"They must be destroyed!" bellowed Rulsp.

And then there was silence. The two gods glared at each other with intense passion. The remaining forty-five gods calmly observed.

Rulsp and Gorb were entangled in a battle of wits that seemed to defy interruption. The two gods continued their spiritual confrontation; reaching inside to the source of their power and venting anger with unspoken vehemence. The ire of their tempers vibrated throughout heaven, mounting to a climax.

Heaven was never so fragile. The entire landscape was distorting.

The other gods did not impose.

They, the gods, relished new insight.

They, the gods, perceived the unravelling of the one heaven.

They, the gods, knew something wonderful and spectacular was to result from this ugly confrontation in heaven.

They called it the big bang.

Part Three
Creativity

Chapter 14: New Habitat

Heaven erupted.

New habitat sprouted from the rage of Rulsp and Gorb.

The new habitat did not evolve immediately, but the seed of its birth was planted; as the seedling of a new tree sprouts from the land. The new habitat would flourish with life.

The gods perceived of this incredible potential: this big bang. They, the gods, witnessed the cells of fibre whirling throughout heaven and gathering a new force; expanding in size and velocity until the barriers of the one heaven could not restrict their growth.

Gorb and Rulsp enticed this convolution from the roots of the trees. The two opposing gods presenting divergent doctrines were responsible for the origin of a new habitat: the spectrums of a destructive creed and a peaceful manifesto.

The inception of quantum properties was floating in this derby of spiritual debris fiercely spinning around the gods in the restrains of the one heaven: electromagnetism, gravity, nuclear forces, radiation frequencies, and the power of dark waves shrouded near the mysterious and magical touch of spiritualised sporadic energy.

The fibre of the one heaven ripped from its essence at the peak of the godly confrontation.

And the environment shattered.

The elements of the one heaven spontaneously exploded into a new expanse; eventually creating many new dimensions.

The fibre scattered into the new habitat with the sporadic nature of the nondescript entities that was once the essence of the gods. And the gods were trapped in the swirling fibre of spiritualised sporadic energy arrays; travelling inconceivably fast across corridors of black ambiguity. The corridors, as they became known, were undefined and virgin in the beginning.

The gods, once again, could not control the power of spiritual elements; yet, once again, they, the gods, were an essential component of something ever so grand and wondrous.

The gods were thrust into veins of spirituality; ripping through an abyss of dark habitat with twists, turns, diversions and collisions. The patterns of their dispersal were entirely random: there was nothing that could control the natural evolution of this omnipotent and ubiquitous explosion of existence.

The gods would see the impetus of their spirituality become encased in blooming mushroom clouds of essence that drifted across dark waves of energy; ultimately triggering cosmic and dimensional dynamics for several millions of cycles in the corridors, which allowed them, the gods, to observe the miracles of nature about to unfold in the new habitat.

And then, there were forty-seven heavens.

The big bang formed two habitats: the spiritual and the organic. Together, connected by many corridors, the spiritual and organic habitats have formed grand creations, as they are known: clusters of fibre and habitat corridors that swarm into gigantic spherical rotations, which are separated by the phenomenon of grand spirals, as they are known, providing distinct barriers for the grand creations. And these clusters, these grand creations, are also segregated further into cosmic configurations of unispheres, as they are known; linked together within a grand creation and reached through existing corridors. Please let me explain.

The gods are now protected in their pockets of spiritual habitat; their solitaire heavens, so to speak. The explosion of the big bang disseminated spiritual fibre across the newly forming corridors of organic habitat; enclosing the gods in their heavenly domains. But now the gods are the restricted entities and unable to exist in the organic habitat.

The force of the new habitat burgeoning from the big bang was so powerful and so sporadic that the new heavens collided in the wake of explosions— smashing into each other to create new cosmic big bangs and subsequently many new universal dimensions—dispersing fragmented fibre into dark waves of particles, elements, matter and energy.

The fibre, which retained some of the qualities it possessed in the spiritual habitat, like terrain, trees, air and water, freely explored the new realm of the organic habitat unrestrained. Free flight was never so exciting. And the properties of quantum mechanics transpired: fusing, splitting and radiating particles to create energy and celestial objects.

Astounding interactions of gases and dust began to orbit throughout the cosmos of the organic habitat; creating astrophysical crescendos beginning with burning stars and transpiring into diversely structured planets, moons, asteroids, comets, meteoroids and the sort. It was a sporadically unintentional flurry of unispheres.

The accelerating corridors of dark waves that originally erupted from the one heaven gradually revolved into spherical rotations and eventually wrapped the new habitat in ever spiralling layers of matter and energy: nebulae, quasars and brilliant galaxies of flaming tapestries known as the stars, all taking on various quantities and qualities.

And all the gods could do, for that time and space, so to speak, was sit in their newly created mushroom cloud heavens and watch the grand creations evolve. And while the unparalleled power of the gods had created such an amazing and complex synergy of fibre, it also relinquished its control to the sporadically natural occurrence of cosmological events.

The unpredictable nature of these events had spun the gods to their destined locations within the providence of the spiritual habitat. Unlike the one heaven where they had access to the entire habitat, the gods came to rest in their heavens within the confines of unique sentient grand creations. The heavens of the gods overlook direct portals to their single home unispheres; unable to penetrate the organic, but still linked to the entire grand creation through spiritual corridors into the collage of heavens that traverse these new borders.

There are corridors of fibre streaming throughout the spiritual habitat and the organic habitat, as well as grand spirals of uniquely spiritual and organic energy. The spiritual corridors provide a vector for the cosmic wave of sporadic energy; a band of essence drifting through the organic habitat that offers the gift of heavenly power and the reward of universal wisdom.

The spiritual corridors waft throughout the grand creations from the roots of existence found at the original Mount Witness—still spiritually intact. These arteries of spirituality flow from Mount Witness and lead to passageways for all of the forty-seven heavens; permeating as the blooming mushroom clouds formed by the original big bang. The heavens are found inside black holes of dark matter that spew waves of sporadic arrays, and are also linked through the roots of Mount Witness to the millions of universal dimensions created by collisions of energy in the dark corridors.

Although the forty-seven new heavens were shuffled somewhat incoherently, there was a certain element of continuity flowing with the spiritual fibre. Some of the gods associated with each other, either in proximity of territory or relevance of awareness, did in fact glide through corridors adhering to similar parameters. And so, heavenly neighbours of some modicum did bounce through the new habitat in relatively associated revolving patterns. And they, these particular gods, did sometimes slope, screech and grind to a heavenly halt in comparable fashions; finding themselves surrounded by the habitat of a grand creation in fatefully appropriate sorted tessellations.

The gods, however, can only visit a selective collection of heavens revolving inside a grand creation; as rival gods continue to clash in their new habitat and cause some corridors to collapse or vanish.

Once settled inside their new heavens, they, the gods, reeled at the taste of this vulnerability and confronted the fate of their new existence; displaying the fibre of their souls. And their souls still possessed great power. And this unparalleled power was kind to the gods.

Perhaps the gods were blinded by the blur that was the fury of the one heaven and the big bang. But the gods soon discovered that the fibre of their heavenly domains bound to their souls and fortified their new homes, despite the spinning patches of fibre fragments accelerating around them with an unmatched velocity.

And the fibre that was their souls responded to their might and power. And it triggered another display of creativity.

And it became trees once again.

The natural environment that was a god's domain in the one heaven was slowly and methodically recreated in these new solitaire heavens. The trees and the magnificent ecological features were transplanted into the new spiritual habitat. And it did make the gods smile with a familiar affinity: one god, one heaven, one aesthetic environment.

And the fibre of every heaven did drift into the passageways and corridors; meshing with the spiritual fibre of neighbouring gods where they had settled. And the gods did venture into the passageways and roam through the corridors among the heavens of the spiritual habitat where they could find solace. And the gods could watch the miraculous growth of the organic habitat from their perch in new aesthetic domains.

Alas, the gods, as I have told you, remain separated and somewhat isolated in these distinct grand creations. And not surprisingly, certain gods are attempting to change this reality so they can reign over all of creation.

Need I say, Rulsp and some aligned gods are at the roots of this uprising, so to speak.

But most of the gods are perfectly content with their new living arrangements; smiling down on the seemingly limitless oceans of interstellar interactions that are the miracles of nature. And that's from just one of the grand creations.

The new habitat born from the original big bang was liberated into millions of universal dimensions, including a total of three grand creations in the dimensional habitat where my story transpires; carved from the cosmos primarily by a total of two grand spiral barriers, along with an undetermined number of slipper voids holding the wizards, since they, the voids, were changing frequently in their struggles for survival.

This is where I come into the picture; spinning feverishly in the grand spirals. I was there and I am still here as a venerable cosmic scribe. But I am still not a god.

I can now travel freeborne, ironically I suppose, as a mere unidentified spiritual fibre: a wind warrior of metaphysical stature, able to transcend all dimensions and habitats, organically or spiritually, unlike any other entity in existence, even the gods, but maybe not the vapour demons.

The rest suits me fine.

Chapter 15: The Cosmos

The original big bang was instantaneous.

All big bangs are immeasurable at the moment of inception.

Big bangs require ages upon ages of calculations to determine the exact nature of their transformations; take my word for it, I was there and continue to be.

The original big bang shattered the one heaven: emanating corridors of spiritual habitat, cascading waves of organic habitat, twisting, churning spirals of free flight, and slipper voids filled with wizards.

The elements of existence gushed forth. They, the elements, spread across a cylindrical universal tree trunk that stretched out towards infinity, but then branched off into vast clusters of fibre; creating multiple dimensions and budding into immense spherical tracts of particles. And everything was surrounded by spirals of quintessence; pure truth of existence, if you can find it hidden in the layers of matter and energy.

The roots of the universal tree trunk dig into the most powerful form of energy at the source of the original big bang: the existence of spiritual fibre—the Water of Life Well of Creation burrowed into the one and only Mount Witness (more about that later as well).

And from the roots of this universal tree—where slithering slices of wizard slipper voids are suspended, dangling in a nomad land still restrained by the power of the gods—the trunk and branches of the tree are filled with the most scintillating, titillating sensation of free flight; almost as impressive as the astronomical majesty of cosmic creation.

And that is where we wind warriors, along with our vapour demon family, have severed the connections from the one heaven. We wind warriors were shuffled through the reaches of dark waves; gliding on the new free flight and travelling the corridors of the organic habitat on the essence of the fibre.

And with us, on our new free flight, we carried the vapour demons. The wizards were also released during the big bang but remained in several slipper voids, as they are known, at first lost in the confusion but later shuffling into their shifting voids within the new habitat.

We wind warriors, much like our creation in the one heaven, were swirled by tornadoes of energy along with our vapour demon passengers; concentrating our vectors in the barrier currents known as the grand spirals, but still with the freedom of flight throughout the cosmos.

We wind warriors and vapour demons are a freewheeling force and our spiral barriers are defiant. The gods still cannot control us.

We took on a new identity. Although we are and remain spiritual entities, we and the vapour demons are the only completely self-aware creations of heaven to freely roam the entire organic habitat.

You might say the fragments of spiritual fibre that comprise the trees, terrain, dirt and water, and the sort, are indeed self-aware creations of heaven; but they are certainly not freely roaming, except maybe the spiritual water of life (as I say, more about that later).

Anyway, we wind warriors are a distinct breed: spiritual entities with organic qualities. We are organically spiritual, so to speak. It is this obtuse blend of characteristics that makes us, for now, grandly unique.

We wind warriors, and the vapour demons thanks to our generosity, inhabit the grand spirals, which have become our homeland domains.

We fill the tree trunk of the new habitat with our free flight spirals of energy; revolving around clusters of cosmic evolution known as the grand creations.

And the grand spirals, as nature dictates, cannot be penetrated by any entity other than those we allow to enter. And there became two grand spirals in the dimensional habitat of my story: Windswept Spiral and Vapourdom Spiral, as they are known. And the wizards did suspend themselves, protesting of course, into slipper voids located throughout the new habitat.

And then there became three grand creations: Summit Grand Creation, Plateau Grand Creation and Crown Grand Creation, as they are known. And in the new habitat of the grand creations the substance of immense unispheres did blossom: forty-seven in total, of course, with spiritual corridors leading into these unispheres from each of the heavens residing in their mutual grand creation.

Think of the new habitat as a universal tree, especially since the power of the gods and the one heaven materialised into trees, and also since the power of the sporadic energy arrays, the power to manipulate energy and particles, can be derived from the spiritualised wood of trees.

And so, the grand spirals revolve and spin through the trunk and branches of the tree, with the core of the original big bang explosion fragmented and mingling among the roots of the trunk, where many wizard slipper voids also float.

And the three grand creations of organic cosmos, with spiritual habitat seeping into clouds behind black holes, are spread across the trunk of the tree and expand into large limbs surrounding the trunk; further spreading to branches of the tree and becoming unispheres within the growth of the tree. The seedling blossoms of leaves, flowers, needles, cones and the sort, comprise the cosmological galaxies born from the heavens and supporting organic life of many descriptions.

The clusters of limbs and branches that comprise a grand creation are separated by layers of bark along the tree trunk, constituting the grand spirals and some wizard voids. The majority of the wizards are among the roots near the base of the tree, but there are also some slipper voids subtly recluse throughout the unispheres.

The Summit Grand Creation is wide and strong on the lower section of the tree with thick limbs stretching to extended branches. The grand Vapourdom Spiral of wrapped tree bark is above this stout lower stem of the trunk. The cluster of tree limbs that is the Plateau Grand Creation is not quite as robust as the lower section of the tree; swaying with the middle branches. The grand Windswept Spiral of wrapped bark is above this middle section of cosmic growth, high on the tree near the upper section of branches. The canopy of foliage that is the Crown Grand Creation at the top of the tree does not have as much concentrated thick growth, but stretches as wide as the lower limbs of the tree with an equal expanse and just as many sprouting seedlings.

And finally there is a wrapping of ever spiralling particles—some organic and some loosely sporadic—tumbling around the universal tree like rain falling down onto a forest and seeping back into the fibre through the roots. The grand creations are always in motion; like shifting branches in our wind currents, revolving and orbiting, with our grand spirals as living, breathing pivots. And both the crown canopy and the roots of the universal tree do spread and fold; reaching around towards all of the other branches.

You might say each grand creation is a singular living organism, encompassed by interconnected layers of fibre. The roots of the tree sprout new seedlings through the ground and reach up to the sunlight of interstellar radiation; like the eruption of a new big bang from the dust and gas of dark waves growing with the cosmic power of chlorophyll and photosynthesis. Eventually, the root seedlings touch the same branches of the parent tree, like the rebirth of a universe.

And so it is difficult to say that one grand creation is situated between the other two. It is true though that Plateau Grand Creation is cushioned between our grand spirals while Summit and Crown are isolated to the outer fringes of our barriers.

It is also difficult to explain this concept of creation and existence, but there is no doubt my botanical analogies are quite intentional. There was once a simple mortal humanoid who composed an elegant metaphor to explain this conundrum of existence. This mortal, to nobody's surprise—entirely not a coincidence—was a botanist by trade, who had this visionary metaphor come to him in a dream; as infinite wisdom can sometimes sporadically strike in the most unsuspecting places.

This mortal was Gilmore Trout, born on Planet Arkna and working as a forester for a government natural resources consortium of several planetary jurisdictions. Here is an exert from his thesis which appeared in the journal, *The Polytheist*, in the sixty-first century on Earth or by the Stellar Rotational Continuum calendar used universally, SRC-325-E/206-T/947-A.

"Our universe, I suspect, is one of many cosmos revolving around each other in an interconnected spherical expanse. I propose a tangible example from my world of botany as an analogy to explain this hypothesis, and I offer a philosophical metaphor to convey the conceptual proposition.

"The tangible example is the largest single living organism on Planet Earth, very similar to another example on my home planet of Arkna. The organism is in actuality a collection of many other organisms that are all physically connected together to qualify as a singular entity. It is the Pando aspen grove, or the Trembling Giant, located and documented on Earth in the states of Utah and Colorado on the North American continent several centuries ago. The grove has somehow miraculously survived countless environmental threats to make it one of the most unique living organisms still existing in our universe. It extends over 100 acres and comprises many stands of single male quaking aspen trees with identical genetic markers, about 40,000 stem trunks in total, weighing approximately 6,000,000 kilograms. The most exceptional feature of this living organism is what makes it a singular entity: its interconnected underground root system, which not only links the entire organism together but also sprouts the seedlings from the roots to naturally regenerate the grove, and where some of the most potent rock chlorophyll in the universe has been discovered. (More about that later, too.)

"The conceptual metaphor begins with precipitation falling from the sky as you are out for a walk in the forest. The precipitation starts as rain water, but on its journey down to the ground it starts to freeze, forming ice crystals. The sleet arrays of ice arteries protruding through newly forming flakes of snow are composed of the water that is life, which is a component of the spiritual cosmic wave surfing through our universe. This cosmic wave carries particles that constitute the elements of life: water, fire, wind, the land and the spiritual fifth element.

"The ragged edges of the sleet ever so slightly cut into the flesh on your face behind a brisk wind, releasing the spiritual fibre of the cosmic wave into your body in the form of water molecules, much like the particles originating from the big bang that drift through the universe and recycle through our bodies. The very same particles from the sleet only seconds earlier passed through a dragonfly that was swooping down above a bog and searching out mosquitoes. The dragonfly detected a mosquito and flew directly on an intersecting collision course, brandishing its fangs as it dive bombed and intercepted the mosquito into the clutches of its jaw. The mosquito, just hatched and looking for some flesh to suction blood as it instinctively thought it should do, was jack slammed into the jaw of the dragonfly. The dragonfly immediately chomped on the poor mosquito, breaking it up into tiny bits and pieces, and killing it.

"The dragonfly swallowed the bits and pieces of mosquito, and mixed with bodily juices the dismembered mosquito slid into the digestive tract where there was a momentary dark silence for the consciousness of the mosquito, paying homage to the sacrifice made by the insect contributing to the balance of nature. But then the digestive juices began to boil and the moment of silence was replaced by the firing of electrolytes and enzymes which burned the protein of the mosquito, thrusting it into the dragonfly's energy producing physiology.

"The mosquito's consciousness was revived as it was digested, like riding the rapids of a wild river, transforming into energy and releasing, evaporating, like sky diving out beyond the body of the dragonfly, and catching onto the cosmic wave that was streaming through the dragonfly, as it is streaming through everything else in the universe. The mosquito's consciousness had no control over its flight, possibly drifting into an eternity overlooking the ecology of the bog, but instead scooped by the cosmic wave and taken to a distant galactic dimension where it penetrated into the mind of a powerful wizard, who was creating fierce windstorms and diverting the flow of enormous waterways to battle the evil forces of a spiritual presence.

"The water molecules of the sleet ice crystals that have sliced into your skin carry the wizardly epiphany of a mosquito's consciousness, all the way from another vastly distant universal dimension and into your own physiology, all in a matter of mere seconds, eventually becoming a part of your own conscience, all without you having left the surroundings of the forest trail."

-Gilmore Trout, PhD Botany

Gilmore Trout's hypothesis is essentially accurate. Although the grand creations are contained within the perimeters of our impenetrable grand spirals, the roots of existence and the canopy of the universal tree, each of them is linked together by several unispheres of similar cosmic configurations.

A single unisphere is equivalent to the known universe where Earth and Arkna are located, along with many other planets: a mortal humanoid universe, so to speak. And several unispheres construct each grand creation.

The Summit and Crown grand creations each comprise seventeen gods and corresponding unispheres. Plateau consists of thirteen gods and unispheres.

All of the unispheres within one grand creation are spherically interconnected by both organic and spiritual corridors.

Every unisphere contains black holes leading to the spiritual corridors of all the gods in that grand creation; seventeen spiritual black holes in the Summit and Crown unispheres and thirteen in those of Plateau. And so, every singular heaven emanates an intricate architecture of arteries leading to spiritual corridors for all unispheres within a grand creation—as well as millions of unispheres in other dimensions through the roots of existence. This sporadic phenomenon is a truly remarkable gift of nature's force; all beginning with the desire and boredom of the gods.

The spiritual corridors however exist in dimensions completely different than the organics of a mortal humanoid unisphere; requiring highly advanced actuality to transcend, along with the vital assistance of spiritual inhabitants.

Nonetheless, if access is acquired, the gods still offer unparalleled power from within the spiritual habitat, which can be transferred in variations of application.

The organic corridors that connect unispheres near the outer fringes are extremely treacherous and difficult to identify because of the intense energy from the dark waves; usually affected by the disruptive force of our wind spirals cruising on the edge of the cosmos. The dark waves, constantly spreading through organic corridors along with other stellar material such as gas, dust and rock particles, are essentially the most potent fragments of fibre and energy from the big bang; releasing with such speed and strength that they attracted cosmic matter funnelling into their path. All of these elements hovering in the waves provide sustenance for the evolution of the unispheres.

There were many spacious gaps between dark waves in the beginning; twisting and turning, swallowing the expansive black space. The gaps were fledgling and enormous. They were the banquets of the cosmos.

But the gaps evolved as well; particles smashing together, bombarding the corridors and emerging from the empty abyss. The dark waves of the organic corridors are ever evolving; sprinkling new life across spherical expansions and dimensional creations. They are fertile ground; spitting out dust and organic fibre to form cosmological entities.

The organic corridors are extremely strong as they approach heavenly black holes in the unispheres, where natural elements touch the cosmic wave of sporadic energy. Some of the energy seeps into the spiritual corridor, flowing back to recycle the water of life, but most is compressed and held in suspension by the forces of interstellar properties; and then slowly released by the pulverising fibre of spiritualised sporadic arrays.

And that's the way it was, in the early ages of the big bang era, with the unimaginable expanse of all the heavens, all the dimensions, the cosmos and the organically spiritual entities.

The gods possessed great power in the spiritual habitat and the interstellar interactions were awe inspiring—without the evolution of lifeforms quite yet—and wind warriors with vapour demons were flying across the waves of corridors; essentially wherever in the habitats we craved. The poor wizards were stuck in their slipper voids; but just let some of those wizards out and watch their potential to wreak chaos, or just relish the freedom and have lots of good old-fashioned fun. Nevertheless, almost all of the wizards are trapped in slipper voids and most of the wind warriors and vapour demons do remain in the grand spirals—but not me.

A select few of us ambitious observers of life, and the vapour demons we carried, chose to embark across the corridors and explore the organic habitat from the very beginning. We were eager to learn this new skill of flight in hopes of gaining our freedom and developing our own individuality. Because of these adventurous few, including myself, both we wind warriors and the vapour demons have always been able to travel the realm of organic habitat.

We wind warriors explore the outer reaches on free flight missions. Mind you, waiting in our grand spiral is not monotonous. Carousing between wind funnels in our spiral is never boring. Our domain is home and home is a warm current of spiralling free flight.

The vapour demons escape their grand spiral on thundercloud missions, which collide with our free flight in a spectacle to behold; taking us wherever the wind does blow.

The many free flight missions I experience are exceptional. I have roamed the new habitat in quest of discovery, exhilaration and understanding. I travelled exclusively on free flight vectors in the beginning. It was stupendous. We swirled through clusters and orbited galaxies. The new free flight was at the tip of our essence; cushioning us across the habitat.

There are also occasions when wizards are able to escape their slipper voids, with the support of manoeuvres from us wind warriors. Most wizards are still restricted though, and can only evade the clutches of godly power by fleeing their voids with glowing lifelines that are attached to their essence and extend all the way from the slipper voids. The wizards would otherwise shatter outside the membranes of spiritual fibre and be consumed into the cosmic wave radiating from the heavens. In extremely rare exclusions, wizards are released from their bonds by exceptional powers.

There are also a very few select mortal humanoids who are able to travel the cosmos in similar fashion: surfing the cosmic wave by grasping the spiritualised sporadic energy arrays, teleporting with glowing lifelines like the wizards, using their most powerful brain waves and exceptionally sophisticated transcendental and telepathic meditation, or simply through the gift of spiritual flight that just seems to randomly bombard certain individuals.

But the mortal humanoids would not develop for several billion ages after the original big bang, and they require the guidance of strong spiritual connections to command the freedom for interstellar flight. Trust me, I know this to be true, since I am one of the few wind warriors who has mastered independent travel. I can freely roam in all spiritual and organic dimensions, which are numerous to be sure.

And so, before sentient organic life evolved from the cosmos, this is, basically, the way it was shortly after the one heaven erupted into forty-seven heavens and a new organic habitat was born.

The time that this took to transpire, and the size of this expansion, was by no means as instantaneous as the big bang itself or as defined as the domains in the one heaven. I can tell you it was like an endless supply of adventure and pure wonderment.

The concept of time and space has long been studied by the organic civilisations that would develop in the grand creations much later. The amount of time in universal terms is commonly measured by the rotations of planets and galaxies; the duration of organic existence, calculated by the Stellar Rotational Continuum from an average full planetary seasonal cycle in an average sized galaxy, known as an annum of the universal continuum, with a thousand annua designated a thellum and one million an epicum. The distance of interstellar space is commonly measured in light years; equivalent to the distance light travels in one year, which is slightly less than an SRC annual continuum.

And so I will utilise these quantifications to roughly explain the estimations of existence, so to speak.

There was no concept of time and space in the one heaven, so I will have to leave that to imagination; really, I do not have any idea. The big bang era—when the gods tumbled into their individual heavens, the particle fibres of organics were accumulated by the energies of the cosmos to slowly form stellar objects, and our unique gathering of spiral flight started to explore the newly forming corridors—took place in approximately two billion annua of existence, or about two billion, four hundred and forty million years.

Many extremely complicated interactions took place at mind boggling speed in the beginning of the new habitat. This set astronomical gyrations into motion that marginally fluctuated velocity as the expanse of habitat increased, while the density of particles began an electromagnetic ballet; evoking the explosive stars that formed the clusters known as galaxies, with the matter and energy necessary to create structured solar systems and all other cosmological elements.

The unispheres, settling into their grand creations over these initial billions of ages, expanded across corridors that revolved for hundreds, then thousands, and then millions and even billions of light years into the cosmos. And the organic habitat still grows; circulating around ever-expanding spherical revolutions and sometimes splintering into new dimensions—like a football being filled with air (for those sporting analogists).

The average expanse of a unisphere—its spherical radius—is just under forty billion annual continua, or about forty-seven billion light years: go figure. Can you imagine? What are the chances?

The big bang era came to an end and was gradually replaced over a span of another two billion annua, more or less, as the planets matured and the lifecycle era emerged. Life began to evolve in the cosmos as planets became hospitable and the miracles of nature continued to randomly occur. The ecology of planets flourished and the subsequent evolution of lifeforms eventually brought us the mortal humanoid, along with some variant species also exhibiting comprehensive intelligence.

The development of mortal humanoids, known as the human era, came to some of the cosmos as early as only five billion years after the original big bang. The progress of mortal beings and their advanced civilisations was a lengthy process and a truly fascinating experience for both organic lifeforms and us spiritual entities. The human era saw the revelation of many inventions and accomplishments on a multitude of planets throughout the cosmos. The entire era probably lasted about five billion years, until the first of several civilisations initially launched into space travel with mechanised vessels. This became known as the interstellar age.

The emergence of the interstellar age was marked by mortal development of space travel; initially only within galaxies, but most recently beyond the speed of light. Remnants of the dark waves containing gravitational fibrous energy, emitting from all black holes, radiate throughout the interstellar expanse and drift into organic corridors; gravitating to pathways that reconnoitre cosmic trails of safe passage. These corridors are now detected by the advanced sensory technologies of cosmic travellers and have become the charted courses of least resistance through the unispheres.

I am documenting this history of hybrid species in the new habitat just over twelve billion annua into existence, or fifteen billion years after the first big bang. The unisphere where Earth dwells was not one of the first to evolve—I guess making it a young member of the organic habitat family—but still a dazzling component of the grand creations.

The new habitat has become quite remarkable; quite the tree terrific universal existence. The spiritual habitat is where the power exists to change the fate of existence, but the organic habitat is where all the magic takes place. And in the organic habitat there exists an unrehearsed choreography of complexity that weaves the fibres of existence into the miracles of nature.

Learning to grasp the mystical trance of existence is a simple extension of spiritual actuality. Life is simpler than quantum mechanics, and making a campfire is simpler than life; providing this cosmic revelation comes with a map of life's looping nature trail, or the bright tunnel to the heavens, or the circle of life as some people like to describe it, or even the cosmic wave of sporadic energy, as we scribes have written, and as it does indeed exist.

Take my word for it; I have surfed it.

Chapter 16: The Ultimate Gift

I have to be honest, the new habitat with its grand creations was certainly a peaceful utopia before the dawning of humanoids.

Despite some bickering of the obvious gods which made it difficult to travel and observe all of the heavens, and despite the violence of interstellar properties, there once was complete freedom without strife to embrace the wonder of nature and travel the cosmos.

Admittedly so, the evolution of humanoids, and particularly the human brain, is one of the most impressive gifts of nature in all the cosmos; in fact, its unbridled potential rivals the very power of the gods.

Unfortunately, or not, the humanoids—not really their own fault—would see the miracle of their transformation spawn into a source of constant conflict and war, and a creed of destruction.

Sad, really; but ever so enthralling.

In the beginning of the new habitat, most of the gods, we wind warriors and the vapour demons, and maybe the odd wizard, but don't tell the gods, were all quite copacetic. We watched as the miracles did unfold.

The early astrophysical developments offered impressive fireworks. The whizzing, whirling and smashing of particles to create the energetic explosion of stars and the compression of carbon, minerals and the sort, were all extremely outstanding. The power of fire from the stars, the energy of radiation, electromagnetism and gravity, coasting in gravitational orbits and crawling in the ooze of sludge, all foreshadowed the vital elements of life lingering in the foreplay of gases and dust.

We wind warriors breezed around the birth of brittle planets to observe geography in its primeval state: geological formations, granular crimping from mantle gyrations, volcanic eruptions and quaking disruptions. I did enjoy the big bang era. And then came the lifecycle era.

The planets began to taste new life: the dilution of water, continental glaciers cutting into the hard, cold virgin rock, melting and rescinding, leaving minute organisms in carved landscapes, oceans harbouring reproducing cells, plants and vegetation purging the soil, breathing atmospheres, and finally the unassuming transcendence of power—the trees.

The spiritualised vibrancy of fibre swelled in the trees. The trees glowed with the energy of sporadic arrays.

The trees grew strong and breathed oxygen into atmospheres. Some planets were cleansed of impurities through the natural photosynthesis of the trees.

We watched the rippling effect of the fibre as we did during the waves of topography in the one heaven. It was a captivating existence. It seemed like an eternity. It looked like a perfect new habitat. But we had no idea what was to come.

There was no one, nothing stirred, not a soul.

There were phenomenal ecologies, but no swimming, hounding or bounding inhabitants.

And then, the evolution of instinct and intelligence merged into the lifecycles of the planets.

The largest bodies of water, oceans as they became known, harboured organisms that reproduced and developed into living animals; microscopic at first, but evolving, nourishing and growing into highly adaptive creatures.

It was the conception of the human era.

A great many animals and lifeforms now inhabit the grand creations. Creatures of different genus, but especially humanoids who populate many planets, over the span of several eons, began to genetically develop higher functioning brains; complete with electromagnetic perception.

In the beginning, the mortal humanoids and other advanced species were fierce survivors without much mechanical technology. But that did not limit their spiritual awareness: remember, there are only a select few who are bombarded by the gift of sporadic energy.

The gods, very curiously, as is their nature, carefully watched these intelligent animals; adapting to the environment, and then harnessing the resources of nature. The human era changed everything for the gods; now this was something noteworthy.

The new habitat now had something to rival the gods; these mortals and the networks of electricity wired through their brains. And the intelligent mortals slowly began to dominate the environments where they dwelled. And the mortals were surrounded by all the brilliant gifts of nature.

The organic habitat was almost beginning to look like the heavens. The only thing missing was the gods themselves. The organic habitat was capable of hosting intelligence, but the environment was not conducive to spiritual eminence: the gods still could not live in the organic dimension.

Another gift was required; so thought the gods. And so, the gods would contribute yet another gift to the new habitat; bringing it forward to the intellectual mortals. But this gift was not an evolution of surface sludge. This was a gift the mortals could not refuse, and a gift that would be both a blessing and a curse.

It was the ultimate gift from the gods; perhaps one they are still regretting. Ironically, the organic habitat actually gave the gods a gift in return: the gift of companionship, which they, the gods, inevitably abused.

The original traits of the gods came into play once again; like boredom, curiosity and desire. Some of the gods became lonely in their heavens. Although some were able to visit neighbouring gods through the spiritual corridors, many were isolated in their new domains.

Trees flourished in the corridors where gods co-existed amiably; lining the passageways with lush mixed forests from the adjoining heavens. But as in the one heaven, a desire grew from within; some of the gods were obstinate and refused to share the spiritual corridors. They, some of the gods, wanted as much space for their new domains as they could swindle from other gods, even to the extent of invading heavens. Rulsp, of course, was an integral instigator of such rivalry.

Many of the corridors were severed so that the gods could retain their heavens in defence of space and domain. The gods were never before entirely segregated in this way; they were always surrounded by their peers. And so, after becoming isolated, no amount of space and domain could stop the tides of boredom. Once again boredom played a key role in all that exists today. Dancing around trees, pruning branches, thinning stands, raking leaves and the sort, satisfied only so many curiosities for the gods. Soon, while inhabiting their new heavens, the gods would need and desire companionship.

The gods saw the intelligent mortal humanoids interacting and developing societies, although on a small scale to begin, but always full of companionship and kindred spirits, so to speak. This inspired the gods. They, the gods, investigated the nature of this intellectual capacity even further.

The gods knew, just as they could not venture into the organic habitat, the humanoids could not materialise in the spiritual dimension. But the gods once again saw potential; the potential of brain waves. The gods could sense the electrical energy from the mortal brains.

The gods concentrated their unparalleled power and sent sporadic energy arrays surfing onto the cosmic wave. The gods could not control the arrays, but when the spiritual power collided with the electrical energy of brain waves, the fibre of both habitats was connected.

The ultimate gift was created in the organic habitat, which caused much consternation and violence, but would eventually bring balance to the entire new habitat. The conscience of mortal humanoids was captivated in rare circumstances; and those fortunate brain waves drifted from the organic into the spiritual habitat.

The gods would make these connections when the conscience of intelligent creatures was free from restrictions; when the spirit of the organic entities, so to speak, was not restrained by preconceived notions or environmental perceptions. This sometimes happened in dreams, when mortals slept, or sometimes at the moment when the transience of existence expired and mortal bodies died.

It was much later after the ultimate gift was created that fully aware and conscious mortals could control the sporadic energy.

And so, when the spirit of organic entities finally arrived in the heavens, the gods gently cradled and tended this electrical energy of brain waves. And the gods carefully removed a strip of bark from the largest tree in their heaven. And the gods delicately joined the bark and the energy together.

And the gods called upon the fibre, as they always did. But this time the fibre did not become trees. The fibre was transformed by the energy of the brain waves and became a creation in the image of organic entities.

They, the gods, combining their power with a miracle of nature, created angels. Thoughtful, provocative, innovative, peaceful, caring and rebellious: angels of forty-seven different descriptions were created.

However, yet again, just as the power reacted in the one heaven, once the spiritual fibre was exhausted to create a single angel, it remained as that angel and could not be transformed again. Although the gods could still entice the spirits of mortal entities into their heavens on the cosmic wave, they, the gods, could only create one fibrous angel in their domains: one god, one heaven, one aesthetic environment, one original fibrous angel. It is the way of sporadic spiritual destiny, so to speak.

The angels became the companions of the gods. And the angels, although infrequently, welcomed more organic spirits into the heavens. These additional spirits could be hosted in the heavens and enhance social companionship, but they could not be transformed by the fibre: there was only one original angel in each heaven.

The gods were gifted with companionship. Although the gods could only create one angel in their heavens, these angels were exceptionally diverse with impressive powers inherited from their gods; gracing them with agile skills which enabled the angels to perform many tasks.

And the gods were joyous; they were beside themselves, so to speak. The gods were significantly occupied, not only observing the miracles at play in the organic habitat, but now conversing with the miracles at play in their own heavens.

And the gods found a cure for their boredom through curiosity and desire. The gods were amused—not bored—entertained, somewhat obsessed, intellectualised and socialised. It seemed they had everything they needed. It seemed they were content. And it seemed like eons upon eons of pure bliss. It seemed.

Actually, it did in fact take the better part of an eon for the gods to develop relationships with the angels. The gods were initially content to simply converse with the angels. They, the gods, eventually named their original angels; indicative of their unique appearance in a strange sort of way.

The gods—the essence of spiritual fibre and power—do not have any gender, although all of them do exhibit distinct personalities that can reflect paternal or maternal sentiments. Nevertheless, after witnessing the gender of mortal species in their reproductive physiology, the gods decided unanimously—an isolated occasion indeed—that the angels were primarily feminine; like daughters to the gods, so to speak.

And so, the gods and the angels soon began to work together on many different activities, especially tending to the forestry practices that maintained their heavens; an astute camaraderie developed between some of the angels and their gods.

But some of the gods held brazen and arguably corrupt ideals for their angels. These gods saw another kind of potential. Unfortunately, they were motivated by the greed which restricted the spiritual corridors.

❖ ❖ ❖

The god of spruce trees, Rulsp, professed a creed of destruction right from the beginning of the one heaven; a desire born from the greed of power to control all of creation.

Rulsp and the gods of this creed wage war on a battleground of habitat and dimensions against the gods proclaiming a manifesto of peace. It started with the desire to destroy the vapour demons and has grown into a claim of ownership for all spiritual and organic habitat.

Rulsp could not be content with the freedom of habitat, and the spruce god influenced other gods as well; consumed by this notion of divine entitlement.

It is not unreasonable to say that Rulsp carried a grudge into the new habitat from the confrontation in the one heaven. Rulsp resented the defiance of the gods and still to this day wants to take possession of all the habitat. And Rulsp knows that the trees are the strength of all gods, and as it turns out, of all creation.

Almost immediately after the new habitat was formed Rulsp began to harvest trees in the spiritual corridors of the Plateau Grand Creation unispheres; still freshly pissed from the confrontation with Gorb. The spruce god destroyed trees by raiding heavens in an attempt to overtake neighbouring gods.

Rulsp was dispersed close to the Vapourdom Spiral edge of Plateau, with Zarkk, Sonus and Pefl as immediate neighbours—the gods of fir, birch and willow. These gods joined Rulsp and initially began to raid nearby heavens: including Fesso's domain of oak, who was somewhat trapped between the spruce heaven and Vapourdom Spiral, and beyond Pefl's willow heaven into the pine and tamarack domains of Quujj and Ardyk.

But then Rulsp ventured even more distant, skirting the edge of the grand creation and revolving around to the territory near Windswept Spiral, invading heavens such as Wateko of maple, Nybos of cedar, Svebb of ginkgo and Lirda of elm.

The gods Gorb of aspen and Dkobi of poplar were also swirled into Plateau near the middle of the grand creation, and they saw Rulsp's early pilfering: the gods of aspen and poplar pleaded with the spruce god, but not to any avail. And so, Gorb and Dkobi—gaining the support of Ardyk and Quujj between them and Rulsp's creed stronghold of Zarkk, Sonus and Pefl—stood unified as a manifesto of peace in defiance of Rulsp's actions in Plateau Grand Creation.

The manifesto gods managed to block enough of the corridors to keep Rulsp and the creed gods from advancing any farther in Plateau. But that did not stop the creed gods from conducting ongoing tree raids over the eons of spiritual and organic evolution; often with various margins of success, destroying trees and aesthetic environment along the way.

The Summit Grand Creation, so named because many gods from the mountain topography wave are concentrated there, suffers from creed of destruction tree raids led by Eamaan of ash, Rens of tung and Baqua of acacia; opposed by manifesto gods forming territorial strongholds to defend against the aggressive raids, with Jacobi of yew, Palu of redwood and Janale of eucalyptus providing leadership to rally the peaceful gods.

The Crown Grand Creation, so named because of its proximity to the canopy of the universal tree, was plagued by tree raids from Yanamea of sassafras, Evbic of olive and Verra of cactus; with manifesto gods relying on alliances bolstered by Tyru of kapok, Apar of mangrove, Cess of teak and Kwarg of alder, ramie and bamboo.

These heavenly battles continued throughout the big bang and lifecycle eras, and when the angels were created in the human era the creed gods were the first to utilise their angels; not for sociology, but for warfare. They, the creed gods in all three grand creations, employed their angels in tree raids after benefiting from the initial companionship.

The creed gods, soon after followed by all of the gods, commanded their angels to carve wood instruments from the branches of the trees in the heavens. These instruments—crafted from the spiritual fibre of the trees in the shape of a baton, an axe handle, a lance, spear, small staff or walking stick—empowered the angels with the force of sporadic energy and became their weapons to harvest trees.

Destroying the trees makes other gods weaker. And the angels can harvest many trees if left unopposed. And so, the spiritual wars continue. And then, Rulsp devised yet another devious plan. Rulsp watched the evolution of intellect and recognised the potential of intelligent mortals. And Rulsp observed: there are many organic trees. And the spruce god speculated: if harvesting and destroying opposing trees weakens gods, then harvesting and gathering trees—creating a stockpile, so to speak—would strengthen gods.

Rulsp would still need to plot a scheme for extracting power from harvested trees, but the seed was planted for a devious plan to manipulate the organic habitat in the name of spiritual superiority.

❖ ❖ ❖

The organic spirits that metaphysically travel the cosmos and sometimes visit the heavens are, in fact, just that, as hypothesised by mortal cultures: traditionally defined by philosophers as spirits, ghosts or even angels. They are wavelength energised entities with the power of interstellar flight, in some cases materialising as tangible images in the habitats.

Some of these organic spirits provide enhanced companionship and social interaction for the heavenly communities, but there is only one original fibrous angel in each of the heavens, and each with unique powers second only to the gods themselves.

The majority of spirits in heaven have drifted from the mortality of deceased biological bodies, when the brain waves, or the souls of the organic entities, so to speak, are experiencing the utmost freedom of preconceived realities and are conducive to spiritual flight. Some of these spirits enjoy a residence in the heavens, but others do not always depart their environmental surroundings and can be seen or felt as ghosts in the organic habitat.

Those spirits who find a place in the heavens can sometimes re-enter the organic dimension and appear as the traditionally defined ghosts, spirits and angels; with the ability to materialise instantaneously anywhere in the unispheres of their grand creation, but not with any of the power possessed by the original angels.

The very few mortals who are able to release their inhibitions and take spiritual flight usually soar through the cosmos for a short journey attached to their lifelines; elevated by the waves of their conscience and then returning to their organic bodies. Early in the human era this gift of flight came only to those whose brains were naturally charged to spark and weave with the sporadic energy.

It is not easy to predict and perceive the awareness of those mortals who will touch the cosmic wave: it is an unpredictable, random event that is the property of sporadic spirituality.

The eruption of the spiritual fibre that created tangible organic elements could never be controlled precisely, because of its unintentional beginning in the one heaven, therefore exhibiting the unique characteristics of creation: seeds can be planted, but nature must evolve from the power of fibre and make adaptations to the environment—survival instincts. This applies not only to the sporadic energy but also to the sophisticated mortals such as humanoids who are bestowed with the gift of flight.

It was not until several million annua into the human era that mortal brains reached the capacity for intelligent creatures to teleport intentionally through extremely well developed meditation techniques. And these gifted mortals, genetically inclined somewhat to begin with, are usually limited to travelling the cosmos instead of entering the heavens.

And so, it has always been a miraculous gift to actually enter the spiritual habitat surfing the cosmic wave, and then metaphysically travel back into the very same mortal body. Those exceptionally gifted mortal individuals with enough courage have foreseen this spirituality and have described the power of the cosmic wave; often through metaphorical stories.

The burgeoning cultures and civilisations on the planets in the early eons of the human era called these people shaman, soothsayer, philosopher or cleric: all of them deemed visionary. And while most gods held these mortals in high esteem, Rulsp saw them as a potential resource to be exploited.

The spruce god envisioned this resource in the plot to control the new habitat. Rulsp wanted to contrive a method to do what these highly perceptive brain waves could accomplish. Rulsp lacked their ability to transcend dimensions, despite the unparalleled power of the gods.

The vitality of the gods is not only dictated by the trees in the heavens, but it also comes from the cosmic wave of sporadic energy, including the water of life contained in the wave; especially since the gods conceived of the ultimate gift and connected the fibre of both habitats.

The sporadic energy in the dark waves of matter, which is intangible, just like in the beginning of the one heaven, radiates into the cosmos and is captured, sometimes by mortal brain waves, but mostly by organic trees during photosynthesis. This energy is accumulated in the underground root systems of the trees as deposits of rock chlorophyll; sort of like diamonds compressed and forming inside the roots under the soil, or sometimes resting in cracks, nooks and crannies along the roots of the trees.

Some of the sporadic energy is released back into the cosmos trapped in the oxygen produced by the trees; eventually re-entering the heavens, combining with the water of life and enriching both the trees and the gods in the heavens, and then recirculating once again back into the organic habitat, compressing more and more into rock chlorophyll.

Photosynthesis, of course, just to clarify, is the process used by trees to make food; breathing, so to speak—botanical survival. The trees consume spiritually enriched energy from solar radiation, carbon dioxide from the air and water from rain and in the soil. The trees use compounds such as chlorophyll, oxygen, hydrogen and various minerals to produce glucose, starch and protein for food. The trees, as with everything in all the grand creations, are a product of spiritual fibre. And when the trees use photosynthesis, it is both an organic function and a spiritual ordeal.

Although the gods welcomed organic spirits into their heavens with the ultimate gift, the early lifeforms in the new habitat were unaware of the ultimate power that could be derived from the trees.

Rulsp watched ever so carefully as these mortals began to develop industrial habits. And Rulsp watched ever so carefully as the same cycle of natural regeneration from the one heaven evolved in the forests of the unispheres.

Rulsp saw that the vitality of the cosmic wave peaked when the carbon particles of trees were fused in combustion. The radiation of burning wood invigorates the spiritual fibre streaming in the waves of sporadic energy. This is most intense and powerful when rock chlorophyll is ignited.

And so, Rulsp conducted an experiment. Rulsp gathered some of the spruce tree roots in heaven containing rock chlorophyll. The spruce god then commanded some of the vapour demons to strike down with lightning. And the vapour demons complied—still fearful of Rulsp. And the roots ignited.

Rulsp next conjured one of the most prominent organic spirits in the spruce heaven to absorb the fibre from the burning wood and combusting rock chlorophyll, just as the spirit so masterfully weaved with the sporadic energy arrays of the cosmic wave.

This wavelength energised entity, this organic spirit, swelled with the unharnessed spiritual power of the trees. The experiment was a success, but

Rulsp needed a vector to release this power so that it could be used to fulfil the grand scheme of total domination in the new habitat. And so, Rulsp compelled the angel of spruce, named Alka, to carve and shape another instrument from the large branches of the spruce trees.

And the spruce angel did this.

The wood instrument—smooth and polished from Alka's craft—was presented to the organic spirit. And Alka the angel taught the spirit how to cushion the rich sporadic energy across the length of the wood instrument, absorb the power and manipulate the force of spiritualised arrays.

Soon the organic spiritual entity held the power of the trees: capable of striding and flying in bounding leaps, levitating and smashing rocks and soil, stirring the flow of water and slicing trees down from their foundations, turning the wooden instrument into a weapon in the same manner as the spruce angel would rumble through spiritual corridors and harvest trees during creed raids on heavenly domains.

Although Rulsp's devious plan was progressing very well, there was a temporary problem: the organic spirit could command the power of the trees but not transform into a fibrous entity, thus restricting the range of motion to the spruce heaven, without the power to venture into spiritual corridors.

And then, Rulsp's unmatched ingenuity surfaced once again. Rulsp sent Alka the angel of spruce trees to do what no other spiritual entity dared: except for us wind warriors of course. Rulsp ordered Alka to penetrate the organic habitat.

Alka collaborated with the organic spirit, who was grateful and appreciative; blinded by the lust of the new power from the trees. Alka promised to show the spirit how to use the power of the trees in the organic habitat and how to control interstellar flight with the sporadic energy, in return for the secret to meshing with the cosmic wave and transcending into the organic dimension.

And a new partnership was born. And the original act of corruption was consummated in the organic habitat.

And it was not all that was consummated.

Chapter 17: The Ultimate Power

The flight into the organic habitat was certainly a risky proposition for the spruce angel: no other angel had attempted such a dramatic transition. Alka could have disintegrated into the cosmic wave, but Rulsp's greed and desire did not know any bounds.

Alka, faithfully guided by Rulsp's intervention, climbed with the energised entity to a mountain peak in the heaven; affording them a clear course to the black hole corridor leading into the spruce unisphere.

There on the mountain peak Alka raised the glowing wood instrument and thrust it into the rock surface. The wooden power source pounded into the rock and instantly sprang back up, hovering above the ground wrapped in a gleaming layer of pure sporadic energy.

Rising with this fountain stick of power, the rock and soil beneath their feet, so to speak, split and ripped a ragged edge; levitating the mountain peak into the heavenly air with an aurora of spiritualised arrays.

The small chunk of mountain peak became their interstellar vessel; riding on a carpet of sparkling streamers with Alka holding the glittering wood helm. They cruised on the wave of spiritual fibre and entered the black hole horizon.

The wavelength energised entity that was an organic spirit then followed the path of mortal brain waves. The vessel was swarmed with the bright transcending layers of sporadic energy as they approached the cusp of dimensions; wrapping and protecting the vessel in a corridor of spiritualised arrays. And the corridor, as soon as it totally engulfed the mountain peak and its passengers with prolific acceleration, flung the vessel through the dimensional vortex and into the organic habitat with unprecedented materialising speed.

Alka of the spruce trees became the first heavenly angel to enter the organic habitat. Alka was able to control the sporadic energy through the spiritual power of the spruce trees, with the wood instrument as the vector, and the organic spirit was able to guide this energy on a cosmic path with the actuality of the ultimate gift from the gods.

The gods always possessed unparalleled power, but obviously they, the gods, could not always precisely control that power; as demonstrated by the topography waves in the one heaven and the big bang eruption which changed the reality of existence.

Rulsp, although consumed by desire and greed, was always a powerful innovator. Rulsp always knew that there had to be a way to control the sporadic energy of the spiritual fibre; at least for short and modest bursts of power.

And when the angels were created, Rulsp knew that they, the angels, possessed something unique: they are a product of both spiritual fibre and organic energy. Rulsp schemed that this combination of spiritual and organic qualities, much like us wind warriors, was the key to opening dimensional doors.

And so, Rulsp and the other gods taught the angels how to fashion weapons from the branches of trees in heaven, which enabled the angels to move with great agility and slice through tree trunks with devastating strength. The angels are able to focus the spiritual fibre with these wooden weapons and shape the forceful flow of the sporadic energy.

However, to reach the heights of the gods and create entire interstellar habitats and ecological environments, is something that may never be accomplished; yet, as surmised so early by Rulsp, the more the angels practise this artful control of fibrous particles, the greater their powers become.

The interstellar vessel made of mountain rock carried Alka and the energised entity into the galaxy of Rulsp's black hole; teleporting through the fortified corridor well beyond the speed of light. It took them only a few seconds to reach their destiny. There in the galaxy Alka's initial journey took them to the planet of the organic spirit's birth.

And this planet became the spruce homeland, revolving among the galactic swirls near the Vapourdom Spiral in the spruce unisphere of Plateau Grand Creation—named Alka in honour of Rulsp's angel.

The organic spirit existed as a shaman on the planet of Alka. And so, when they arrived in a valley of the mountainous terrain and landed their interstellar vessel, Alka took possession of the shaman's soul in order to exist in the organic habitat; a version of reincarnation, so to speak. And then she and the shaman commanded the power to reveal the path of spiritual essence.

This is where the consummation truly began.

Alka could not teach all of the primitive creatures how to command the sporadic energy; the shaman was an exceptional and unique specimen, and very few mortals of his abilities exist in all of the cosmos, let alone just the Alkae galaxy (pronounced *Alk-eye*).

Spreading the power of the trees for Rulsp's bidding would be a momentous and very time consuming venture. And so, Rulsp altered the plot for domination. And Alka received the word of Rulsp.

And the word was to procreate. That's correct, Alka was to produce mortals from the fibre within her essence: supreme organic entities to tend the forests created by heavenly power.

The body of the shaman and the conscience of Alka searched for the most perceptive mortals and began a sorted bender of intimacy. The conglomeration that was Alka and the shaman travelled to many galaxies in the spruce unisphere and impregnated mortal creatures, who were mostly humanoid; strictly coincidental I'm sure.

The conception and birth of these offspring, of course, was time consuming enough with the gestation cycles of most humanoid species, let alone finding the naturally selected candidates. And not every child born was touched with the gift of spiritual awareness: Alka remained in the organic habitat for almost a complete eon of the human era.

The conscience of an angel and the soul of a shaman inside a healthy humanoid body, with the power of interstellar flight, roamed the galaxies and traversed planets. They travelled, taught, teased and titillated, and they fathered, and they mothered as well, so to speak. And Alka would have to travel back and forth to the spruce heaven during her epic journey into the organic habitat; enticing the souls of new wavelength energised entities contained within younger and fertile mortal bodies.

The spruce angel certainly possessed many different partners in this corruption of power, which she required to both procreate and transcend dimensions, but Alka would also recharge the vigour of her spiritual energy during the visits back to heaven. There was always a chance Alka would meet with her death while occupying the soul of a mortal being, so she needed all the strength and conviction she could conjure to survive her journey: a tenuous matter was this spiritual empire building.

Alka dwelled in the spruce unisphere for about two hundred million annua or a quarter of a billion years, and then embarked to many of the unispheres in

Plateau Grand Creation before the other gods finally noticed this fostering legacy in its infancy. And slowly a new hybrid species began to populate the cosmos.

There was a way to be certain if a mortal was born with this hybrid spiritual gift. The original shaman himself, after being possessed by Alka, had developed a small patch of spruce wood growing on the creased surface of his navel. This is the spiritual core of an organic mortal; something acquired only by those with acute awareness and the affinity to grasp the cosmic wave of sporadic energy.

Those mortal humanoids with spiritual cores also genetically adopted other physiological features reflecting their spirituality and adapting to their environment: spindly vines with small leaves or needles protruding from their heads to absorb radiation and enhance spiritual photosynthesis in their bodies, rough patches of synthesised tree bark and limestone deposits covering vulnerable portions of their bodies as protective shielding, glowing eyes with a coloured sheen depending on their location in the cosmos, and coarse vocal cords with tiny fragments of rock chlorophyll.

This ancient hybrid species evolved into extremely powerful warriors. Those who can control the sporadic energy with the wood instruments they fashion are able to manipulate particles in the organic habitat; unleashing the power of the trees into a razor-sharp ion cluster pulse, or a sprinkling of an electromagnetic field that deflects other forms of energy, or a bed of energised arrays that can levitate and move other matter, as well as plasma corridors to fire vessels across the interstellar cosmos.

Alka not only tutored the mortal warriors in the craft of spiritual tree power, but she also orchestrated ceremonial rituals to send the spiritualised sporadic energy arrays wafting into the cosmic wave. The warriors gather harvested trees and burn them on giant bonfire mounds of hot spiritualised coals. They place roots with rock chlorophyll on the flames and fan the sparks of embers towards the heavens by flailing the combusting sacrificial fibre with their wooden weapons. The warriors eventually throw their wood instruments onto the fire to replenish their sporadic energy; quietly walking into the surrounding forest and carving new weapons, then returning to absorb the hyped cosmic energy and contemplate the power of the trees.

The ultimate gift is the ability to connect with the spiritual habitat from the organic habitat, metaphysically travel the cosmos and even enter one of the heavens, depending on where the spiritualised sporadic energy array originated. The gift can now be mastered thanks to Rulsp's original intervention, but only with an incredible amount of innate skill: manipulating the flow of energy and particles, travelling protected in an interstellar corridor, creating physical forces for many functions, or commanding a weapon to harvest trees and even kill opposing warriors. And that is the ultimate universal power: the ability to focus on the cosmic wave, grab its spirituality and transform its essence into a tangible energy, so to speak. The ultimate power comes from the ultimate gift.

Rulsp's motivation was to have tribes of hybrid mortal warriors occupy the organic habitat with the objective of reigning over all three grand creations. The spruce god's plan was to destroy the trees of other gods with the power of sporadic energy; disintegrating the trees with the force of wooden weapons and thus weakening the spiritual vitality of the gods, as well as sacrificially burning some of the trees of creed gods to bolster their strength and vitality through the cosmic wave.

But Rulsp's divine scheme suffered one major flaw and met with overwhelming complications. The flaw was an oversight of the grand spirals we wind warriors and vapour demons call home. The complications have led to the constant strife which dominates the grand creations.

Rulsp managed to spread the word of his devious plan to other creed gods. The Alkae were joined by other mortal warriors; initially in Plateau Grand Creation and then in Summit and Crown as well. The creed angels started to proliferate hybrid species throughout the cosmos, while the Alkae, further evolved than any other species, began to organise organic tree raids and hone the tactics of harvesting wood fibre.

And then the complications started. Many tribes of mortal warriors soon spread throughout the grand creations as the manifesto gods also delivered angels to produce more warriors and defend their belief in peaceful existence. The angels selected a planet in the galaxy of their god's unisphere outside the spiritual black hole, and there they planted the seeds of procreation to conceive the birth of their species. These planets became the homeland for the trees of each god; named in honour of their angels.

All of the gods became active sending their angels to the organic habitat. And the angels continued their journeys to the remaining unispheres in each grand creation, where various levels of activity were transpiring. The angels spread the seeds of birth and the hybrid species were born; reproducing until the grand creations were self-perpetuating with very special mortal warriors.

The creed angels and their hybrid warriors ravaged many stands of trees in the late stages of the human era and into the interstellar era, until the manifesto angels nurtured their hybrid species and mounted a sustainable resistance. And throughout the interstellar era the botanical disputes have scattered across the cosmos in clouds of sporadic energy, wood chips and flames of sacrificial fibre.

The tree warriors, as they became known, although a minute percentage of all mortal creatures, brought troublesome complications to the cosmos as intricate battles to harvest trees occurred on planets throughout the unispheres; establishing ancient tree wars depicting the manifesto of peace against the creed of destruction.

However, Rulsp's desire to conquer all three of the grand creations has still not been satisfied to this day, even though legions of creed hybrids continue to instigate many tree raids, rallied by the initiatives of the spruce god and the Alkae warriors. Nothing, as I have told you of course, can enter our grand spirals unless we wind warriors and vapour demons allow it. We can create a spiritualised corridor of sporadic energy arrays with our wind currents and vapour clouds; only allowing passage across our spirals by our own discretion. And so, the spiritually gifted mortals were still confined to their grand creations, and therein lies the major flaw; the oversight of Rulsp's divine scheme.

The Alkae and some creed warriors—the direct descendants of the spruce angel in particular—did attempt on many occasions to smuggle their spiritualised interstellar vessels through our grand spirals, just as Rulsp would attempt to occupy the organic habitat without success. But they, the creed warriors, could never overpower the force of our organically spiritual free flight spirals. The tree warriors would try and try, and we wind warriors would immediately crash their vessels with destructive storms of hurricane force; setting their ships adrift. Although we always give the Alkae and creed warriors fair warning, they never capitulate; fighting back by firing their weapons into us.

They leave us no choice but to maintain the balance of the cosmos, as we feel is our duty and responsibility, by obliterating their existence with the power of our typhoons and deadly wind currents: churning into the sporadic energy of their corridors, tearing their vessels apart and smashing their organic fibre into particles to replenish the cosmic wave.

And besides, it was Rulsp who first threatened the vapour demons: we would do anything to thwart the spruce god and the warriors who follow the creed of destruction.

Continual uprisings have complicated the cosmos, from the human era to the interstellar era; persisting through time and space as I tell this story. The ancient tree wars have perpetuated through the eons of existence as the gods and their angels continue to actively pursue their determined objectives. The history of these hybrid species and their botanical disputes has been preserved only by word of mouth until most recently, and only occasionally detected by highly refined and exacting sensory technology: something that has not been widely broadcast.

Thus, the tree warriors and the botanical disputes of the gods are not well known to the advanced modern societies that have evolved in the cosmos. While the organic humanoids and other mortal creatures expand their societies and their interstellar travels with impressive technological developments and sophisticated mechanised vessels, descendants of the original hybrid species still maintain a primitive lifestyle; hidden deep in the forests of their spiritual trees, although their powers are certainly not primitive and can be just as devastating as any mechanised invention.

The original word of mouth is spoken in the ancient language of the hybrid warriors; developed and documented by a keen and perceptive tribe of mortal humanoids who exist in many unispheres, and who happened to come into contact with Alka during her inaugural epic journey into the organic habitat.

These mortals, some of whom have become tree warriors, are known as Druids; now living on several planets throughout the grand creations and originating on Planet Druid in the spruce tree unisphere. Druids exist in all of the grand creations. They are the mortals with a gift of linguistic affinity that drifts the cosmic wave from several heavens.

The preservation of the ancient language is documented in the coveted and guarded Druid Dictionary. The ancient language is quite rudimentary but does help mortals to understand the history of botanical disputes, and it is still used by most of the tribes directly descending from the original angels and currently engaged in continuing hostilities. The words in the Druid Dictionary are mirrored by modern languages that have most recently started to speculate and describe what is considered the phenomenon of spiritual warriors in the cosmos.

The ancient language refers to these warriors as 'traupah' (pronounced *troh-pah*), which was the name of the shaman who originally procreated with Alka. Many of the older planetary cultures call them tree warriors, while some younger cultures have invented the term "Rasspy" for Radical Alien Spirit Species

Possessing Ylem, or Raspies as a collective short form for radical spirit species. The ylem in the acronym refers to the primordial matter of the big bang theory, postulated as neutrons at high temperature and density, which reflects the magical qualities of the power these warriors possess.

A basic lexicon was developed by the Druids to help these traupah, tree warriors or Raspies communicate specifically during the battles of tree raids, shortly after the raw vocabulary of foundation words was established. The wood instrument, often used as a tool for survival as well as a weapon of war, is a 'stah' in the ancient language, later becoming the root for the word 'stager' (*stay-grr*), describing an older experienced person, usually associated with a farm hand, and subsequently espoused by modern cultures as the word for the wooden weapons of the tree warriors.

The actual power of spiritualised sporadic energy, manifested into the glowing light around a stager, the sparkling cushion of energy enhancing a warrior's movements, or the shimmering ionised array fired from a stager, is known as the 'lasha' (*lah-sha*) in the ancient language and also by other cultures attempting to describe and explain spiritual phenomena.

There are some modern cultures that universally describe lasha as an ionised pulse, stream or array. The same cultures that have come into contact with tree warriors, have also detected and distinguished the aurora of sporadic energy around a spiritualised interstellar vessel engaged in flight; describing it as 'botanic spiritualis'.

There are, of course, many other words in the ancient language, such as 'bohtrak' to describe the flight of spiritualised interstellar vessels; 'brak' is a small vessel and 'tahkid' is a larger transport vessel, as well as describing a camp of warriors. Several words have multiple meanings, often in combination with inflection when spoken. The ancient language was developed generationally; initially for basic communication, known as the foundation words. The next phase was an observation of the environment and natural surroundings; often used as a trail guide for warriors and further enhanced into tree raid terminology for efficient communication during battles.

The final phase was developed by generations of Druid etymologists for the most sophisticated semantics of the language, although it does remain a very crude form of communication. All of these words are contained in the Druid Dictionary, which I have generously provided as a glossary in the appendix of this manuscript.

These unique and powerful botanical creatures continue their universal escapades because they are indoctrinated into the rivalries of the gods. But there is another reason as well.

The gods and we wind warriors, through observation and comprehension, do believe that the sporadic energy of spiritual power will, with the formidable capacity of its unpredictable force, in some inevitable time and space, create an entity with unmatched perception and strength; capable of shredding barriers and either uniting all of creation, or defeating all of creation, depending on your perspective.

This prognostication, so to speak, is known among us organically spiritual entities as the silviculture prophecy.

The gods regularly yet selectively, because of the inherent danger involved, send their angels to the cosmos on a legendary search for gifted organic entities who may comprise an unprecedented mixture of spiritual perception and organic capabilities.

And so, the tree warriors crusade through the cosmos, unrelenting, battling perceived enemies for supremacy, and reproducing to extenuate generations; hoping that natural selection will grace their genetics.

The search lives on, hope endures and anticipation swims with the currents of fate: waiting for a natural episode of insurmountable consequence.

Chapter 18: Botanical Disputes

Now is the space of my story to explain how the killing takes place.

Mortals lived in relative peace during the first half of the human era; more concerned about the struggles of survival rather than any notion of spiritual wars. Alka, the angel of spruce trees, began the spiritual procreation movement over the next several hundred million years; quickly joined by all of the original fibrous angels.

The Alkae spruce warriors initiated interstellar flight and the tactical strategies of tree raids over the second half of the human era, followed shortly thereafter by the remaining creed of destruction warriors, or credos as they are known, and the manifestos of peace, as they are known.

The tree warriors have sustained waring ways over the eons of existence, generation after generation; albeit an ever so slim portion of all the elements, interactions and cultural developments comprising the cosmic soup.

Meanwhile, the purely organic mortal species of the cosmos, as their cultures and civilisations progressed, so to speak, unfortunately engaged in planetary wars for control of territory and resources; often subconsciously affected by the cosmic drift of greed and desire.

Materialistic wars—those fought with steel weapons, mechanical invention and nuclear technology—are designed with territory and resources as the objective, and the destruction of infrastructure, bloodshed and human loss as the end result: tragically, death to many mortals.

A clear advantage is gained in these wars by the nations of mortals who are able to manufacture mechanical weapons. The development of these tactical mechanics requires technologies that utilise discoveries of physics, elemental, chemical, particle and energy properties. These inventions bolster the mortal knowledge of physical relativity, astronomy and quantum mechanics; leading to more advanced discoveries that enable solar space travel.

Many of the mortal civilisations entered the interstellar era while the spiritual tree wars intensified. Mortals developed galactic flights approaching the speed of light and employing comprehensive environmental life support systems; eventually discovering both the fuel and the technology for propulsion beyond the speed of light in plasma corridors.

The advent of interstellar flight by no means put an end to the mortal killing. Some civilisations are able to peacefully establish nation states on extra-terrestrial planets, or maintain diplomatic relations with other planetary jurisdictions, but there are still wars and battles among mortals representing different planets and species.

There are some mortal interstellar wars that are influenced by the presence and participation of tree warriors, usually kept quite secret, but there are distinct differences between mortal mechanical wars and botanical disputes.

Spiritual botany wars are the rivalries of forestry and timber, not blood and mortal death. In the majority of botanical disputes, trees are exterminated, not mortals.

The objective of ancient tree wars is to destroy or collect wood fibre. It is true, in both spheres of war, territory is often the focus of skirmishes, but the battles of botany wars are fought over a stand of trees instead of a boundary line; a discreet but important distinction. The trees are the target of botanical battles: lumber, not mortal sacrifice.

Tree wars, as they are sometimes called, do not involve blood. It cannot be denied that warriors are a key element of any dispute and they do suffer casualties and fatalities, but tree warriors do not bleed.

Although a stager is the weapon, a warrior's spiritual core is the source of tree power. The growth of a core means that warriors acquire an element of spiritual essence, and when they are injured, they do not bleed; they shed clumps of bark, woodchips, stagerdust or flying pieces of flaring wood fibre.

This genetic anomaly allows abrasions, cuts and even severed limbs, so to speak, to in fact heal and grow back into place over the seasons, like the stump of a fallen tree sprouting new seedlings. But some injuries are more severe and many veteran warriors have the scars of battle: stumps for arms or legs, broken twigs for fingers, bark rash and the sort. Others are not so lucky. A well-placed shot of lasha can smash a warrior into a pile of kindling: death botanical style.

Tree warriors are not invincible and sometimes die from their injuries, but they always carry around something angelic once they have nurtured the lasha:

those miniscule particles of wood found in belly buttons known as spiritual cores, which if rubbed correctly, especially by another core bearer, can produce ecstatic and enthralling reactions—both in the body and the soul. And so warriors must protect their cores at all cost, for without a core all is lost. And there are those who love to consume cores.

There is a species of poor, mistreated entities known as sputs. They, the sputs, are menacing creatures half tree and half demon spirit; the failed offspring of angelic souls and intellectual mortal species who come in many forms as well as human, such as reptilians, raptures, amphibians and fluid organisms wrapped in florescent membranes. Sputs love to devour spiritual cores; becoming stronger, larger and more dangerous as they eat more cores.

In spiritual botany wars, you have sputs, lasha and stagerdust. In materialistic metal wars, you have bullets, bombs and blood. In organic mortal wars, there are fleets of interstellar vessels and regiments of troops. In organically spiritual wars, there are flying island ships of rock, soil, trees and water, with camps of hybrid species known as tree warriors.

I will first explain how the botanical killing takes place, since the tree wars have been around much longer, and later expound on the mortal wars as I recount the history of hybrid species.

The shape of spiritual botany war and the strategies of battle can be explained in two words: tree raid. A tree raid begins with a large collection of warriors and interstellar vessels, including a rooting ship and a host of branch ships for the battle components of the raid. Both rooting and branch ships are known generically as arboretum vessels; propelled by the power of lasha and botanic spiritualis.

An arboretum vessel is a tract of land that is ripped from its heels by the lasha; skirting around the perimeter and elevating the ship, with botanic spiritualis giving it the power of propulsion. Arboretum vessels require fuel and navigation: sacrifice fires are the fuel for the ships, always burning during travel, and at least one stager at the helm operated by a warrior provides navigation.

Rooting ships, or rooters, usually occupy three navigators at the helm because of their size. The smaller branch ships are navigated with a lone warrior. Branch ships travel with rooters to protect the flanks and scout ahead on tree raids.

Activating any arboretum vessel is an impressive sight. A warrior strikes a stager down into the ground and the stager floats back up into the air, hovering above the ground draped in lasha. A layer of rock, soil, trees and water will rip from the ground, surrounded by botanic spiritualis, and then the arboretum vessel is airborne and ready to fly: the larger the ship, the more stagers required.

There are six different types of arboretum vessels, from the largest to the smallest: habitat, forestry, catalyst, rooting, scarifier and branch ships.

Habitat ships are roughly fifty acres in size, typically about four football fields wide and six fields long. Habitats house many warriors and are utilised as a base for botanical operations; usually containing two or more stands of trees, a small valley and a stream of water from stern to bow.

Forestry and catalyst ships are both around thirty acres in size, usually shaped the same as habitats approximately three football fields wide and five fields long. They are not designed to engage in battles. Catalysts are used primarily to transport warriors on tree raids, including battle and harvesting ranks, workers supporting the raids and injured warriors, even mortals who are sometimes caught in the middle of battles.

Forestry ships also transport, but trees and supplies rather than warriors. Foresters are the cargo vessels of botany wars. Although they are not designed for battle, forestry and catalyst ships carry valued cargo and are routinely guarded with a complement of branch and scarifier ships.

Scarifiers—from scarifying in silviculture forestry practices—are effective battle ships, but not as large as rooters. They are more narrow and elongated at less than a field wide and often two fields deep; two to five acres on average. Compensating for their size scarifiers are enclosed and protected by hard stone exteriors; effective for covering the flanks of tree raid vessels while they are flying through corridors and orbiting planets.

The small branch ships are typically the size of a campsite for two warriors; anywhere from half an acre to a couple of acres. The stern of the vessel sometimes features a small rock bluff or a few boulders. A modest stand of trees or stockpile of firewood is located between the stern and the sacrifice fire behind the helm of the ship. The helm, navigator and glowing stager are situated close to the middle of the ship near the burning source of tree power to make for easy stoking; most often on high ground. Various branch ships are landscaped with an assortment of vegetation. Rooters, scarifiers and branch ships are the spiritual battle vectors of tree wars.

A rooting ship is the hardest working vessel in spiritual tree wars; its distinctive structure designed for the battle components of raids. Rooters range in size from eight to twelve acres as the best fit for battle manoeuvres, depending on the terrain of the land; about five to six hundred feet wide, just under two fields, and eight to nine hundred feet long, or around three fields.

The bow, stern and the sides of rooters have a protective barrier of large boulders and rocks. The holding ground is behind the bow of the ship, where harvested trees are stored before transferred to a forestry ship. The holding ground is a large gulley or ravine. A camp where warriors live between battles is behind the holding ground moving towards the stern.

The arboretum camps are strewn with tents, shelters, shacks, campfires, and a few selectively located outhouses. A small lake or pond will be found to the rear of the camp. The water source is used for cleaning and washing, while drinking water is brought onto the ship and stored separately.

There is a cache of trees or a forested area behind the camp and the water source, known as the fuel pit, to provide wood for the sacrifice fire. The fuel pit also serves as a secondary holding ground for any overflow of harvested trees. A ridge or hill serves as the helm of the ship; located directly astern of the forested fuel pit. The helm is always the highest point on the rooting ship, where the arboretum navigators tend their stagers firmly implanted in the ground and glowing with lasha.

There are pathways for hauling fuel to the sacrifice fire on each side of the helm. The sacrifice fire is kept burning without interruption in a cave behind the helm near the ship's stern. The tree raid commander, known as 'kohpah' in the ancient language and the 'chlorophyllialis' in more modern terminology, can usually be found at the helm as well. There are minor variances in design depending on the terrain of land elevated into a ship, but this is the basic prototype of a rooter: the preferred warring vessel.

Tree raids can be quick hits on a particular stand of wood fibre, but most are planned to target multiple forests and planets. The raids usually require logistics and support for the distant travel involved, and consist of different components with specialised warriors.

The component of a tree raid engaged in harvesting, and the odd battle with other warriors, is known as the trunk thrust. A rooting ship, surrounded by branch ships like a squadron, enters the orbit of a planet: a trunk thrust has been initiated. The ship penetrates the atmosphere and glides down to the planet's surface. Forests are evaluated until the desirable stand of trees is located.

The rooting ship lands at the base of a tree stand and the trunk thrust continues until the ship leaves the planet's atmosphere and enters outer space. A trunk takeover describes the actual operation of harvesting procedures; possibly involving combat with opposing warriors.

The takeover begins when warriors exit the rooting ship and begin to harvest trees. The rooting ship creeps behind as they make progress through the stand of trees. Resistance is sometimes apparent from opposing warriors; and then there is aggressive lasha, but there is not any blood.

The trunk takeover is a segment of the trunk thrust; a key component of the entire tree raid mission, which will also include rooting, swaying, botanical flotillas, seedling stops and branch watchers.

Rooting is the advancement of a trunk takeover when lumberjack skills are employed. Swaying is the advancement of any arboretum vessel; in outer space, through atmospheres or on the ground. Botanical flotillas consist of a habitat ship, a few forestry and catalyst ships depending on the size of the tree raid, four or five rooting ships, and flanking squadrons for these larger vessels consisting of six scarifiers and a dozen branch ships each.

Seedling stops are for vessels to replenish stocks and supplies. During seedling stops warriors catch up on sleep, eat excessively, are entertained and sometimes get drunk.

Branch watchers are the warriors who stay on guard to protect ships during seedling stops. The watchers guard vessels from either scarifiers or branch ships.

The mechanics of tree raids involve many warriors. Aboard a rooting ship alone are over one hundred tree warriors, with specific duties applying to each group of warriors.

Root thrashers are large and powerful warriors who are the first to debark, so to speak, from the rooting ship and into a stand of trees during a trunk takeover. The root thrashers are the first line of offence. They engage enemy warriors who are opposing the takeover. Firewood harvesters and log splitters are the next two groups of warriors to enter the forest. They are the lumberjacks of tree raids. The firewood harvesters chop or slice the trees: timber, timber, timber, all fall down. The log splitters slice or saw the trees into manageable sizes and stack them into piles. Both the harvesters and splitters use their stagers to command the lasha and accomplish these clear-cutting procedures.

Campfire maintainers serve two purposes during tree raids. The campfire maintainers destroy or carry accumulated piles of logs back to the rooting ship during trunk takeovers, and they also coordinate the ship's camp where the warriors sleep, eat, drink and are entertained between trunk thrusts.

Maintainers also have operational responsibilities on the larger ships. The labourers on all ships are twig suppliers and leaf gypsies, and the campfire maintainers are their superiors. The twig suppliers prepare and serve all the food consumed on ships. The leaf gypsies entertain the warriors when they're not occupied with battle.

There is only one kohpah or chlorophyllialis on any arboretum vessel, in charge of all operations. There is also leadership provided by arboretum navigators and a small group of veteran warriors known as the wood sacrifice squad. The navigators are at the helm to guide the ship on its destiny and they are aware of tree raid priorities.

The sacrifice fire on all vessels except branch ships is quite large and requires more than one warrior to keep it burning. An arboretum vessel will accommodate about four or five veteran warriors; wise and well versed in tree power. These elderly warriors are the wood sacrifice squad; supervising the burning of the sacrifice fire and offering sage advice to the chlorophyllialis.

A ship will also employ a team of soil sucks to do the bidding of the wood sacrifice squad: stoking the fire, hauling wood, adjusting logs, cleaning soot and the sort. The soil sucks are strong enough to add wood to the fire but otherwise are not too adept at the ways of war, battle and fisticuffs. These warriors are inevitably strange individuals.

The sacrifice fire on a ship is located near the stern; protected in a cave. Understandably, with a fire constantly burning the cave becomes filled with smoke. The soil sucks often breathe this smoke directly.

The smoke from a sacrifice fire is rich with spiritualised sporadic energy and can, if absorbed properly, bestow a warrior with the power to create illusions and mirages: hallucinations of the mind from the caves of deception.

Wood sacrifice warriors are known to possess this quality of deception, but soil sucks do not have the ability to properly take advantage of sporadic energy. Instead, the soil sucks inhale wasted spiritual fibre and the deception takes place in their own minds—strange individuals.

The branch ships which accompany rooters on tree raids are navigated solo by bark shredders: the most rugged and cunning of all warriors still in their prime. The bark shredders serve as protectors—vigils in the night, so to speak— and assist tree raid operations.

The shredders, perched at the helm of their branch ship, will scout ahead on trunk thrusts; perusing forests and snuffing out enemy opposition. During trunk takeovers the shredders will provide air support for the root thrashers if they encounter hostile resistance, and if not, the shredders will help the maintainers to carry harvested logs. Bark shredders are the prize of any fighting tribe.

The warriors of different tribes, named after their original fibrous angels, are integrated into the rivalries that dominate tree wars. Creed of destruction tribes operate from stronghold unispheres in all the grand creations, with counter operations from peaceful alliances also forged in unisphere corridors.

Summit and Crown Grand Creations both contain more warriors, tribes, planets and unispheres than Plateau Grand Creation, but it is in the cosmos surrounded by our grand spirals that botanical disputes are most intense: Plateau is where Rulsp dwells and launches deranged tree raids based on the evil creed of destruction.

Plateau is also the grand creation where hope for eternal peace is most fiercely defended. The Envrah warriors of aspen trees and their close allies the Demkews of poplar trees are the principal proponents for the manifesto of peace; situated as unisphere neighbours near the middle of Plateau. The manifesto is rooted in the defiance of creed raids originating from the unispheres close to the Vapourdom Spiral edge of Plateau.

The Alkae of spruce trees are separated from Vapourdom only by the Dewars of oak trees and a few wizard slipper voids. The Alkae neighbours towards the middle of Plateau are sympathetic to the creed doctrine, consisting of the fir tree Narukas (*Narr-ook-ahs*), the birch tree Coulees (*Cool-eez*) and the willow tree Dlailians (*Duh-lay-lee-ans*).

The Mingas of pine and the Yndae (*Yin-die*) of tamarack are caught between the creed and manifesto unispheres in Plateau, just as the god Quujj of pine trees rested in the mountains of the one heaven near Rulsp and the spruce trees. The Mingas are strong warriors who were stressed by Alkae raids in the early years of botanical disputes, but now remain resolute in their support of the manifesto along with the Yndae tribes.

The Talibians (*Tall-ib-ee-ans*) of elm trees are immediate neighbours and allies of the Envrahs drifting towards Windswept, with another three unispheres, somewhat undecided and confused in the politics of botanical disputes, revolving near the edge of our spiral barrier: Salites (*Sall-eye-tz*) of ginkgo, Syntras (*Sin-trahs*) of cedar and Nycaas (*Nike-ahs*) of maple trees.

The warriors of Plateau are sometimes splintered in their tree raid battles, but the unrelenting resolve demonstrated by Rulsp's creed of destruction is unquestionably the impetus of botanical disputes in Plateau, and the other two grand creations as well for that matter.

The creed unispheres in Crown Grand Creation beyond Windswept Spiral are concentrated in the hurricane stronghold and the fringe corridor, as they are known. The Urbonae (*Er-bone-eye*) of sassafras and Yabnians of jute trees comprise the hurricane stronghold; so named because of the proximity to us wind warriors and the fury of their tree raids. They are removed from our spiral domain by four unispheres of moderate warriors known as the wind funnel: the Weks of kapok trees, the Nuukas (*New-kahs*) of mangrove trees, the Frevs of calabash trees and the Avidians (*Ah-vid-ians*) of rubber trees. These moderate yet blustery unispheres are constantly harassed by the hurricane stronghold, and most often left to their own defence.

The unispheres on the far side of the hurricane stronghold are undecided; caught between the credos, the manifestos and the subtle desire to remain neutral and unaffected by all the chaos. These are the beech tree Yharites (*Yar-eye-tz*), the Irbae (*Ear-bye*) of rose trees and the Prawdians (*Prah-dians*) of gum trees.

The manifesto unispheres in Crown are near the middle of the grand creation towards the outer fringe territories; occupied by the Atakeewans (*Attah-keewans*) of baobab trees, the Nagawashians (*Nah-gah-washians*) of teak trees and the Wabagoonads (*Wah-bah-goonads*) of alder trees. These manifestos must be resilient with the fringe corridor of creed unispheres lurking not far away close to the outer edge of Crown: the aggressive Marcynakians (*Marr-sin-akk-ians*) of olive trees and the Peyotae (*Pay-oh-tie*) of cactus trees, with the tortured Zadeks (*Zadd-eks*) of mopani trees trapped between these creed unispheres.

The Sarites (*Sarr-eye-tz*) of kurrajong trees and the Sinaitatians (*Sin-ay-taht-ians*) of bubinga trees are isolated victims on the outer fringe of Crown; longing for manifesto support as they endure many creed raids. The devoted credos in Crown are located at spherical opposite ends of the grand creation, so to speak; presenting challenges for the manifesto campaign, while in Summit Grand Creation, although the credos are persistent and remorseless, the manifesto stronghold is more centrally located in the peace corridor.

The tribes of Summit's peace corridor are able to challenge creed tactics in all spherical directions. They consist of brave and resourceful warriors: the Zemders of redwood trees, the Swoonites of karri trees and the Suzhae (*Suzz-*

eye) of ebony trees. The most difficult challenge in Summit comes from the mountain stronghold of creed unispheres towards Vapourdom Spiral, with the mighty Wabekas (*Wah-bekk-ahs*) of ash trees and the Kagiwosians (*Kagg-ih-woh-sians*) of tung trees. The Karvs of balsa trees and the Tusrae (*Tuss-rye*) of greenheart and mango are cushioned between mountain stronghold and Vapourdom, with wavering support for creed objectives depending on the frequency of tree raids.

The unispheres in the vapour cloud shadow of Vapourdom Spiral contain tribes loyal to the manifestos: the Dovipanites (*Dovv-ih-pan-eye-tz*) of eucalyptus trees, the Nylors (*N-eye-lohrs*) of jacaranda trees and the Hauknians of yew and hemlock.

The creed stronghold approaching the outer fringe of Summit near the mysterious slipper voids is maintained by the extremely robust Sabaquae (*Sabb-ah-qu-eye*) of acacia trees. Squeezed between peace corridor and the Sabaquae are the Yonnites of incense trees and the Baltsae (*Bahl-tz-eye*) of palm trees, whose valued allegiance is the focus of many battles. The Pagrons (*Pay-grons*) of avocado and the Callies of podocarpus trees drift on the outer fringe side of the Sabaquae stronghold, and they often must succumb to creed demands. The Kuaandae (*Kuw-ahn-die*) of mallee trees and the Drangs of mahogany spin in the unispheres on the remote outer fringe of Summit; so dangerously close to the slipper voids that everyone tends to leave them alone.

Botanical disputes are not documented except in a few tree raid journals, which if discovered hold the promise of great reward. The tree warriors and their spiritual battles might not be evident to most mortal creatures, but they are relived intently around campfires by elders reminiscing about the past and attempting to teach young warriors the path to true spiritual actuality.

There is hope among the tribes: hope for those who aspire to forge a botanical corridor of peace through the cosmos, and forebodingly hope as well for those devoted to total domination of existence. Tree warriors cling to the manifesto of peace and are also dedicated to the creed of destruction campaigns: battlefields cluttered with wood chips and stagerdust, naked forests slashed from the land, marauding warriors pilfering planets and harvesting stands of trees in the ongoing raids. The hybrids battle against other tribes in the dense forests of the grand creations, all the while searching for exceptionally gifted mortals who might have the treasured genetics to extend generations of organically spiritual creatures.

The quest and the plight of tree warriors are rooted in the hope forecast by the silviculture prophecy—essentially, that the miracle of sporadic genetics will create an entity capable of bringing an end to the wars. I can attempt to explain everything but it is obviously better to tell the stories of those who have lived the events, and to help guide you along the way one can always refer to the maps and charts at the end of this book and on the pages to follow.

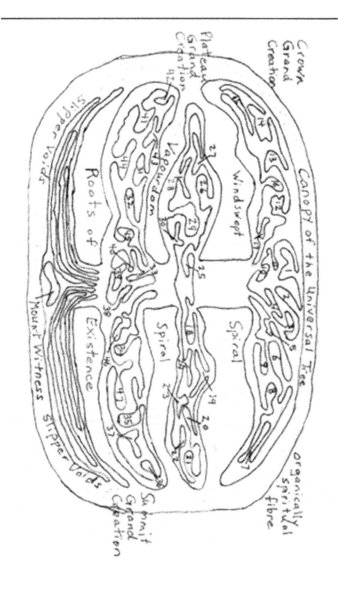

Gods (# on Map)	Planet (Angel)	Unisphere (Tree Species)	Warriors	Expanse (Billions of Light years)
Crown Grand Creation				
Canopy of the Universal Tree				
Isolated Victims				
1 Var	Sinaitatians	Bubinga	Sinatatians	52
2 Idyp	Sar	Kurrajong	Sarites	47
Fringe Corridor				
3 Verra	Peyote	Cactus	Peyotae	52
4 Lipna	Zadek	Mopani	Zadeks	47
5 Evbic	Marcynaki	Olive	Marcynakians	49
Manifesto Stronghold				
6 Kwarg	Wabagoon	Alder	Wabagoonads	50
7 Cess	Nagawashi	Teak	Nagawashians	42
8 Laavv	Atakeewan	Baobab	Atakeewans	52
Undecided Allegiance				
9 Nekrol	Prawda	Gum	Prawdians	46
10 Moht	Irbe	Rose	Irbae	44
11 Maav	Yhar	Beech	Yharites	49
Hurricane Stronghold				
12 Baf	Yabnas	Jute	Yabnians	34
13 Yanamea	Urbonas	Sassafras	Urbonae	55
Wind Funnel				
14 Tyru	Wek	Kapok	Weks	51
15 Apar	Nuuka	Mangrove	Nuukas	35
16 Marn	Frev	Calabash	Frevs	45
17 Rom	Avid	Rubber	Avidians	49
Windswept Spiral				

Plateau Grand Creation				
Gods (# on Map)	**Planet** (Angel)	**Unisphere** (Tree Species)	**Warriors**	**Expanse** (Billions of Light years)
Windswept Spiral				
Undecided Moderates				
18 Wateko	Nycaa	Maple	Nycaas	52
19 Nybos	Syntra	Cedar	Syntras	42
20 Svebb	Saleh	Ginkgo	Salites	37
Manifesto Ally				
21 Lirda	Talib	Elm	Talibians	50
Manifesto of Peace Stronghold				
22 Gorb	Envrah	Aspen	Envrahs	45
23 Dkobi	Demkew	Poplar	Demkews	55
Manifesto Supporters				
24 Ardyk	Yndes	Tamarack	Yndae	32
25 Quujj	Minga	Pine	Mingas	47
Creed Sympathisers				
26 Pefl	Dlailia	Willow	Dlailians	47
27 Sonus	Coulee	Birch	Coulees	45
28 Zarkk	Naruka	Fir	Narukas	52
Creed of Destruction Stronghold				
29 Rulsp	Alka	Spruce	Alkae	57
Trapped Victim				
30 Fesso	Dewar	Oak	Dewars	50
Vapourdom Spiral				

Summit Grand Creation				
Gods (# on Map)	**Planet** (Angel)	**Unisphere** (Tree Species)	**Warriors**	**Expanse** (Billions of Light years)
Vapourdom Spiral				
Vapour Cloud and Victims of Creed				
31 Jacobi	Haukna	Yew	Hauknians	49
32 Dwyi	Nylor	Jacaranda	Nylors	45
33 Janale	Dovipan	Eucalyptus	Dovipanites	35
34 Onu	Karv	Balsa	Karvs	57
35 Kumi	Tusra	Greenheart	Tusrae	55
Mountain Stronghold				
36 Eamaan	Wabeka	Ash	Wabekas	49
37 Rens	Kagiwosa	Tung	Kagiwosians	34
Peace Corridor				
38 Palu	Zemder	Redwood	Zemders	52
39 Forek	Swoon	Karri	Swoonites	46
40 Kymm	Suzhe	Ebony	Suzhae	44
Conflict Zone				
41 Hume	Yonn	Incense	Yonnites	50
42 Yufe	Baltsa	Palm	Baltsae	49
Creed Stronghold				
43 Baqua	Sabaqua	Acacia	Sabaquae	52
Creed Shadow and Wizard Fringe				
44 Yett	Pagron	Avocado	Pagrons	47
45 Kapid	Calli	Podocarpus	Callies	47
46 Cyte	Kuaandi	Mallee	Kuaandae	52
47 Alsa	Drang	Mahogany	Drangs	42
Roots of Existence with Slipper Voids				

Part Four
The Search

Chapter 19: Venture North

Zachary Steele was inspired by his most recent vampire vision on the Yuba River in California, during the late twentieth century of a non-interstellar era planet, so to speak. It was the summer of 1989 in the northern hemisphere of Planet Earth and Zachary was attempting to finish his family tree.

He came to realise the significance of this nemesis figure in his lifelong battle with morality—which was integral to his spiritual journey—and he may have found a clue through his genealogy search indicating why his vision manifested into a vampire. However, he was still uncertain of the reason for his visionary interstellar flight since childhood, the true meaning of the owls in his encounters with nature, and the current location of his parents, let alone the exact details of his ancestry.

The thirty-something-ish young physiologist did not return to his research grant for hypothermia, deciding instead to painstakingly piece together the clues of his family history. Zachary had been frustrated and drained of considerable energy, but now he was at a critical turning point. He examined an enormous number of medical certificates, church records, government documents and personal accounts of his ancestors. He studied journals, diaries and logs. He compared and cross-referenced his research notes again and again; anything to come up with a lead. He discovered that his paternal ancestors actually originated in France and emigrated to North America with the family name of "S-t-y-l-e" (pronounced *Steel* in the French language), which was legally changed to "S-t-e-e-l-e" when they settled into English communities on the east coast of the newly discovered continent, as far back as the Earth year 1594. The Steele family slowly moved to the western frontier in search of new opportunities and eventually headed north into the uncharted backcountry of the territories.

All of his Steele ancestors were accounted in existing records except for two members of the family. The Steele name all but phased out and then inexplicably resurfaced in the early nineteenth century. Zachary could not prove who actually began the revitalisation of the family name but was determined to find out.

The origin of his maternal ancestry was also somewhat of a mystery until he managed to uncover records for an immigrant by the name of Rushad Rhomanscu, who migrated with his parents from the Carpathian Mountains in Transylvania where the communal farm land could no longer support the growing numbers of the extended family. This could explain the vampire visions in his dreams, conjectured Zachary.

Rhomanscu was ten-years-old when his family bribed a sailor to stow away on a seaworthy ship at the port of Constanta on the Black Sea with several other peasant farmers in the year 1841, including the woman who would become his wife. The ship sailed to the Turkish Straits—Bosporus, Sea of Marmara and Dardanelles—into the Aegean Sea and across the Mediterranean Sea, through the Strait of Gibraltar and north to Liverpool, England. The families were then able to gain passage as kitchen staff on the famous Royal Mail Steamship Britannia in January 1842. The ship was partly owned by Nova Scotian Samuel Canard, who was onboard to entertain the British author Charles Dickens.

The Atlantic Ocean voyage did not go well for Dickens who turned back for England on a sailing ship. Canard, wanting to salvage something positive from the trip, was impressed with some of the meals—especially the Romanian chicken stew. He decided to use his pocketbook and influence; buying the Rhomanscu family passage to Montreal when they landed in Halifax, and sponsoring their citizenship under the name Rhomany in the newly united province of Canada.

The peasant farmers, now with some extra money in their pockets, sailed to the port of Montreal and were offered a deal by the Hudson's Bay Company that they could not refuse. They would become homesteaders by clearing, ploughing and seeding over two acres of land in exchange for title to a six-hundred-and-forty-acre section of land. They were ferried in the spring along established fur trading routes all the way west to Rupert's Land: on sailing ships up the Great Lakes, over the height of land at Grand Portage west of Lake Superior with voyageur canoes, portaging and rigging canoes with a deck and sail mast as double catamarans for open water inland, down the English and Winnipeg Rivers through rapids, north across Lake Winnipeg and west along the Saskatchewan River.

The final leg of their migration took them by oxen and wagon to a large plot of farmland in what would become the district of Assiniboia and province of Saskatchewan. Three families lived together; building a grass sod house with a stone hearth fireplace and pooling their life savings to buy one working ox and a small herd of sheep for food and clothing.

They planted one acre of oats, half an acre of rye wheat and another half-acre of potato tubers they received from the company, along with several rows of kohlrabi and leuschen seeds; a turnip-cabbage root plant and celery herb they brought with them from northern Romania. They also built a small crude barn out of aspen, alder and willow branches for their sheep and the handful of chickens they had acquired from a neighbouring homestead; lining the barn with straw from the oat and wheat crops to insulate the animals in winter.

Sustenance consisted of boiled oats and bread from the rye wheat flour they thrashed and grinded by hand, added to water or sheep milk and baked in their carefully maintained stone fireplace oven—with just a little swallow of the rye fermented over the fire for medicinal broth. There was fresh mutton roast if the herd was healthy, potatoes and cabbage with the meals, and Rushad's future wife thirteen-year-old Marianna Tarcia's famous stew and soup she could make last for a week from just one chicken or some bone cuts of meat from butchered sheep.

Rushad, still only eleven-years-old, was responsible for herding the sheep several miles away from the homestead where there was natural grazing pasture. He watched over his herd not even a teenager; with a stray dog, a small metal billy can, a bag of oats, some twine made of sheep wool to snare rabbits, a pair of leather gloves, a small hatchet and a big stick with a spear end carved from aspen wood.

This immigrant boy, later known to his friends and family as Rush, quickly became a man on those prairie nights with the wind, the wolves and the coyotes howling, and only a homemade lean-to for shelter. It was also there on those lonely upland pastures that Rush was visited by the Transylvanian vampire demons who had followed the family bloodline overseas; the very same demons who fluttered in Zachary's mind and would continue to challenge the Rhomany family for many more ages.

The young Rush—thrust into the stark northwest grasslands because his father could tend the land and grow crops from the seeds they received—not only had to overcome his fear of the harsh climate, the darkness of night and the wild predators at his feet, but he also had to confront the existential evil of the vampire demon at such an innocent age. This was remarkable courage, and it did not go unnoticed by the manifesto angels of the cosmos.

The Rhomany farm suffered from drought and ruthless winters in those first several years; making it difficult to support all family members and forcing Rush to leave his parents in search of a job at only seventeen-years-old. He ended up hiking or catching rides on donkeys south to the Missouri River and following the California trail along river valleys; working at first for fur traders but eventually landing in California during the gold rush of 1849. Rush worked in the gold mines saving enough money to fetch his bride from the prairies, and then became a farming supervisor in the fruit orchards and vegetable fields that were prospering in the Sacramento Valley south of the northern gold strikes.

Rushad and Marianna Rhomany raised a family of eight children in California, born in the 1850s and early 1860s, but Rush wanted more for his family who were still living in relative poverty. He was certain he could find a lucrative gold strike; heading to Mount Shasta and the Cascade Range once he turned forty. Rush was never seen again and presumed dead by one of a few natural disasters that could have occurred—such as collapsing rock or mudslide, avalanche or just freezing to death in the mountains—but his wife Marianna knew her husband was a survivor and always believed he was still alive roaming the Earth somewhere, right up until she died in the twentieth century.

Zachary's mother Maria is the youngest baby of Rushad's grandson, Gheorghe Rhomany. She met her future husband and Zachary's father Jeremiah Steele when visiting family in Saskatchewan shortly after the second world war on Earth. Zachary was oblivious to all these intimate details of his maternal ancestry since he chose to concentrate on the complications of his father's family name once he had verified his mother's Californian western heritage, but he was about to become strangely familiar with his Rhomany lineage.

In the meantime, he found proof of birth and death for his direct ancestor Edith Steele; the mother of five children born between 1702 and 1711. She died in 1736, but there was no documentation of her husband. Edith's children went on to foster the next generation of Steeles who were born between 1720 and 1734. Unfortunately the Steeles were an audacious breed of fur traders, trappers and explorers. Many members of the family met with untimely deaths. The Steele ranks were depleting as early as the fourth generation after Edith. Zachary counted twelve family members in the fifth generation; ten of them died just after the turn of the nineteenth century.

The remaining two unaccounted ancestors were Beatrice Bagwa and Irving Steele; both last recorded to be living in the British controlled north-western regions of North America in the early eighteen hundreds. Beatrice was the widow of Douglas Bagwa; a lumberjack of English, French, Cree and Chipewyan heritage who died at a young age. Irving Steele was an entrepreneur, sometimes a coureur des bois in the northern backcountry, and a part-time explorer who often conned fur trading agents to finance his expeditions into the untamed wilderness of Rupert's Land.

Irving made his way to the trading outpost of Fort Chipewyan on Lake Athabasca which was established by Peter Pond of the North West Company in 1788. There the young Steele talked his way into canoe trips and acquired financing to trade for furs in the area south of Athabasca down to Cree Lake. Irving usually travelled the MacFarlane River and often used Mayson or Norseman Lake to set up camp as a transfer point for furs, supplies and fresh paddlers. It was possible that this enterprising Steele continued the family name, but it was here where Zachary suspected the interaction of Soarfoot.

It is noteworthy to mention that Irving was also a thief. A report on the apprehension of Irving Steele for stealing merchandise in 1827 mentioned the name Nako Bladebone. According to the report Bladebone was a partner in crime with Irving. Zachary discovered that Nako Bladebone was an indigenous Cree born on the Churchill River. He did some further checking and found that Nako's great grandson, Robert Bladebone, was still alive at the age of eighty-four. Zachary decided he would visit Robert Bladebone.

The family search took a new turn for Zachary when he travelled to the northern Saskatchewan village of Stanley Mission on the Churchill River. The truth that he was about to discover is the story of an inter-species marriage; the modern hybrid of an ancient hybrid from two gifted families. Zachary's enquiries were closely observed by the manifesto of peace angels themselves, who would soon guide him to the truth of his bloodline; a preferred destiny carefully plotted by Gorb, the one and only god of the aspen trees.

Norman Balia was a prominent community member at the Stanley Mission village who Zachary managed to contact; explaining his predicament and strange request to meet Robert Bladebone. Balia was kind enough to welcome Zachary for a visit and arrange a meeting with Bladebone, but cautioned that the trip would involve river travel and he should be prepared to spend at least one night on the Churchill River. Zachary immediately pulled out his backpack and began preparing his equipment; sorting it according to warmth and shelter, fire and food, water and accessories. He was like an excited boy scout before summer camp, with rigs, ropes and camping gear spread out on the living room floor.

Unfortunately he had largely ignored the presence of his lover Zelda since returning to Saskatoon and coming across this new information shortly after the encounter with a vampire ghost on his kayaking trip. He failed to communicate with her even on a daily basis; still obsessed with the pursuit of his ancestry. It was not until the night before he left for Stanley Mission that he actually told Zelda where he was going. Zachary did not realise it would be the last time he would live in a permanent dwelling with Zelda for thousands of years to come.

"You're going where?" asked Zelda.

"It's a First Nation reservation on the Churchill River."

"And why are you going there?"

"There's an eighty-four-year-old man there whose great grandfather was known to associate with one of my ancestors."

"How is that going to help you?"

"This man might remember some stories that could give me another clue about Irving's movements," explained Zachary.

"Irving?"

"Irving Steele. He's one of the descendants born in the early eighteen hundreds who could have rejuvenated the family name."

"That makes sense. And I suppose you expect to find Soarfoot there as well," coaxed Zelda.

"If my hunch is right, his name might come up in the conversation."

"This is quite the family tree you have Zachary."

"I'll admit it's a bit strange, but I'm telling you it's more than just a family tree. I always knew my family was different, downright weird actually, and you know I'm not exactly your average university professor. Now that my mum and dad are missing and I don't have any family, except maybe you, and I've experienced all these dreams and visions, there's a feeling inside me that's growing every day; that this is more than just tracing my ancestry."

"I know this is important to you Zachary, and I have the same feelings about your journey, but have you considered your other responsibilities, like your job?"

"I know, I thought I would be finished this family tree by now, but I can't help thinking I'm going to discover some profound secret about myself. My parents are hidden somewhere and I don't know if they're even alive. I need to know exactly who I am; it's something I have to do. I will get back to the university when classes start up again in the fall, but for now I have to make this trip up north."

"I understand. How long will you be gone?"

"Probably only four or five days, depending on what I find."

Zelda touched her lover's lips and subtly smiled: "Do what you have to do Zachary, I will be here to support you when you come back. Try not to get lost on the river, huh."

"Don't worry, I can handle myself on that river," Zachary comforted his lover, unaware that she was certain he would not return.

The next morning Zachary started driving north in a pick-up truck; spending the afternoon and overnight at the Beaver Glen campground in Prince Albert National Park on Waskesiu Lake. He proceeded north of the small town La Ronge the next day and followed the gravel road east to Stanley Mission. There was nothing fancy about the community: a Hudson's Bay store, a nice recreation centre, small school, band council office building and a large dock on the Churchill River. The townsite is built overlooking the river. Etched in the harsh boreal forest, meagre dwellings dot the shoreline of the mighty river like burrows in a field. It was a primitive setting.

He drove into the community and parked his truck at the recreation building. There was a small group of children and teenagers in front of the Hudson's Bay store across the road. Zachary stepped out of his truck and stared at the youngsters as they stared back at him.

Suddenly he felt a strange sensation. It reminded him of how he felt after awakening from a demon spirit dream. It was like his blood was swelling under his skin. He continued to gape at the children unaware he was doing so. The swelling sensation gripped his mind; instilling his thoughts with fear. It was an eerie force. Finally the evil wave swept through his body and vacated as quickly as it entered. Zachary shuddered. Realising he was gawking at the youngsters he looked over his shoulder at the recreation building and asked one of the teenagers where he might find Norman Balia.

"Over there," said the boy, pointing to the band council office.

Balia was a large man in his mid-thirties with a round, congenial face. He was quite friendly and greeted Zachary with a big smile and a firm handshake. Then, without hesitating, he began explaining how the Bladebone family parted ways with the community many years ago.

"They have always been a temperamental family," chuckled Balia.

During the family's furlough they set up camp on a small island downriver from Stanley Mission near Nistowiak Falls, where Iskwatikan Lake empties into the Churchill. Although the family was very much a part of the community once again, Robert Bladebone spent his summers at the original site of the camp. Balia said the island has sentimental and spiritual value for Bladebone. Robert's grandfather Isca would take him as a young boy to the island and teach him the traditional skills of survival. It was Isca who eventually brought the family back into the tribe over a hundred years before Zachary's visit. Balia also assured his guest that Bladebone was a well-tempered wise man who enjoyed talking about his family's past.

"Perhaps you will have something in common," said Norman.

Since Zachary was packed and ready to go Balia took him down to the dock where a boat was waiting. It was a sixteen-foot aluminium fishing boat with a twenty horse-power Evinrude outboard motor on the back. Zachary placed his backpack in the boat and tied it down. It was a perfect day for travelling on the river and the boat cut through the water with ease. Zachary sprawled out on his back with his head at the bow and enjoyed the ride. Norman grinned in his consoling manner.

The Steele ancestor stretched out his arms and took a deep breath to overcome the touch of anxiety from his peculiar experience in front of the Hudson's Bay store. He felt comfortable in the natural surroundings and was happy to be riding down a wilderness river. He leaned over the side of the boat and dragged his finger in the water; making figure-eights and spelling his name. Balia laughed. Zachary bounced up to a sitting position and removed his hat. He held it high in the air towards Norman.

"This is a special occasion for me. I've been trying to trace my ancestors for some time and talking to Robert Bladebone could be the break through I've been waiting for. I salute you Norman Balia and I appreciate your hospitality," voiced Zachary.

Balia laughed again and nodded his head as he politely accepted Zachary's salute.

"You're welcome, but it's only a boat ride," he said.

Undeterred, Zachary gazed at the shoreline and out over the river; again raising his hat in the manner of a salute.

"Here's to you Churchill, long may you flow."

The two men continued downstream, soon reaching Stanley Rapids. Balia took the north passage around an island and shot through the short patch of white-water without hesitation. Zachary was so taken with enthusiasm out in the open river that he commenced saluting everything in sight. He saluted the trees, the rocks, the shoreline, the boat, his backpack and even a moose they spotted in the bush. He was definitely feeling like a child on a great adventure.

They zipped through the eddy-filled Frog Narrows and east to the bay where Nistowiak dumps its foaming waters. North of the bay on the Churchill is Bladebone's island. The boat glided to the island's edge and landed against the rocky shore.

"This is it," said Balia.

"It doesn't look like much," remarked Zachary.

A young man walked out of the bush and down to the rocks of the shoreline. Zachary raised his hat as he was prone to do on that day and greeted the stranger.

"My Robert, you sure have preserved yourself well."

Balia snickered but the young man only pointed at Zachary in disgust.

"This is the man you have told me about?" he questioned.

Springing to his feet and lunging out of the boat, Zachary landed on the rocks only a few feet away from the young Cree.

"Zachary Steele, pursuer of ancestors, descendants and all around family tree researcher, at your service."

"Zachary, this is Brandon, Robert's grandson. He told his grandfather that you would be coming," explained Balia from the boat.

Zachary held out his hand in the customary greeting: "Pleased to meet you Brandon Bladebone."

"My name is Jabacco. This way," said the youngster, choosing to ignore Zachary's gesture and pointing to a narrow path in the bush.

Norman slipped out of the boat, tied the bow painter line to a branch and lead Zachary up the path into a small clearing. There was a log cabin, an elevated cache between tree trunks and a firepit. Brandon proceeded directly to the cabin and went inside. Zachary looked at Norman rather puzzled, who shrugged his shoulders in response.

"Kids these days," he said.

They heard a rustling from the trees and an elderly man appeared at the edge of the clearing. The man was garbed in buckskin and holding a hatchet. Under his arm was some kindling that he set down beside the firepit in the middle of the camp. He was a tall, lean man; weathered yet very healthy and moving with agility. He welcomed Balia with a nod and walked over to his guest for the night.

"You must be Robert Bladebone," said Zachary.

"Good guess. Brandon tells me you're a Steele."

"Zacharias Nathaniel Steele at your service."

"Your name is familiar to me. We will talk, after sunset. I must go on a small journey now. I apologise, but this is something I must do."

"Can I come along?" asked Zachary.

"I'm sorry, I must do this alone. There will be much time to talk tonight. My grandson will tend to your needs."

"Oh, I don't have any needs," said Zachary.

"We all have needs," replied Bladebone.

"Yes sir," agreed Zachary.

"Meegwetch," Norman thanked the old man in Cree with a wave.

Robert walked over to the cabin and picked up a leather bag. Swinging it over his shoulder he headed to the far side of the island where his canoe was stored. Norman promised to return in the morning and departed from the island in his fishing boat. Zachary retrieved his backpack, set up his tent and did some fishing. Although he was still in the cabin, Brandon did not show himself for the rest of the day. And so, Zachary found a pleasant spot and lay down in the sunshine.

Soon he was asleep and soon he was visited by unearthly spirits once again. The evil demons were flexing their muscles, so to speak. They had hollow heads of swirling gases and grisly bodies; more vivid than ever up north there on the river, and much closer to the truth of Zachary's bloodline.

Robert Bladebone returned in the evening. Brandon, finally emerging from the cabin, started a fire and prepared a meal for the three men. Zachary said nothing during the meal. He did not feel welcome: alienated by both Brandon's bitter attitude and the evil spirits in his explicit dreams. There was a crisp blend in the shadows of dusk as a faint glow meandered across the horizon. The evening air was still chilly in the summer months that far north. Brandon stood up after eating and strolled to the cabin without saying a word. Zachary watched him leave and looked at Robert beside the fire.

"He doesn't like me, does he?"

"Do not worry. He is a young man, still learning the complexities of life. He resents the presence of an intruder here. Don't be concerned, it is a silly attitude against outsiders shared by many of our young people. He will outgrow it and learn to accept a man for who he is. Now, who are you and what is it you wish to know?"

Zachary paused and gathered his thoughts.

"I have been having a great deal of difficulty tracing all of my ancestors. I have searched through many records but I need to know more. This has become very important to me."

"That is wise. We all should know where we come from."

"I believe you may know something that will help me."

"But what could I tell you?"

"Your great grandfather Nako Bladebone was known to associate with one of my ancestors," explained Zachary.

"Yes, Nako. This man was restless. My grandfather told me about him. He said he was a man of spiritual powers; a good man who guided his people."

"Do you remember your grandfather ever speaking about Nako and a man named Irving Steele?"

"Why of course, that is why your name is so familiar. My grandfather told me Nako travelled north to hunt caribou and he found this man Irving Steele who was starving and cold. Nako helped Irving and brought him back to our people. He said that Steele should be accepted into the tribe, that he was also a spiritual man with wisdom."

"So Irving Steele was here on the Churchill River?"

"Yes, but only for a short time. Soon after he arrived the tribe was plagued with many evil spirits. Winter came early that year, the hunting was poor, food was scarce and people became sick, some even died. The tribe blamed Steele for bringing evil spirits into their camp. Nako said he would go and find the spirit seeker who would guide him with the wisdom to chase away the evil spirits, but Nako did not return for many days and the evil spirits remained in the camp. The tribe was angry and the people told Steele he must leave. Nako's wife was faithful to her husband and she left the camp with Irving and her family, and she brought them to this island."

"Wow, Irving was actually at this very spot?"

"Yes, so I am told, but Nako returned soon after his family was banished here. Nako told Steele they must go together to find the spirit seeker. He said it was the only way to chase away the evil spirits. And so they departed on a long journey."

"Did they come back?"

"Irving never did return, but the next winter was mild, the people were no longer sick and there was plenty of food for the tribe from good hunting. The evil spirits had gone away."

"Do you know where Nako and Steele went?"

"Nako came back and said that Irving was taken on another journey by the spirit seeker."

"This spirit seeker, do you know if it was a vision or an actual person?" an excited Zachary continued his inquiries.

"I asked my grandfather the same question. He said the spirit seeker travels the stars in the sky and guides our people with wisdom."

"Does the spirit seeker by any chance have a name?"

"He is the one who soars through the cosmos standing on a platform of light that you call aurora borealis. And because he soars while standing on the light, the spirit seeker is known as Soarfoot."

"You have got to be kidding me?"

"I know it may sound unbelievable, but my grandfather assured me he is a real warrior who can travel to distant planets. I guess it is a matter of faith; one that I share with a select few of our tribe."

"Trust me, I have seen some things recently that tell me there are many planets and civilisations, so I don't have a problem believing in such spirit seekers. But I want to be absolutely sure on this, are you certain this spirit seeker is called Soarfoot?"

Robert looked into the fire they had started for their meal and followed a shooting spark as it drifted up towards the night sky. The stars were beginning to shimmer in the brisk air. Bladebone fixed his attention back on Zachary.

"My grandfather often told me about Soarfoot, I would not forget his name. Soarfoot is a great warrior from the stars. At special times, he comes down to the earth and travels from camp to camp, sharing his knowledge with many tribes. He has helped our people learn the secrets of life and the mysteries of the afterlife. When Nako was just a boy, he went into the deep forest in search of

Soarfoot. He did not return for many days. When he came back, he told the people of our tribe he had found Soarfoot and he would share the lessons he learned from the warrior who soars on a platform of light. And until Steele came to our camp the people were happy and healthy."

"Would you mind if I put on some tea? I think I feel a chill coming on," said the young Steele.

"Certainly," Bladebone consoled him. "I understand that the spiritual side of life can be upsetting, but do not be afraid. The path to realisation can be disturbing at times, but the wisdom it brings can also be fulfilling."

Filling a billy can with water Zachary placed it on a wire grill resting over two rocks at the edge of the firepit.

"Have you ever encountered Soarfoot yourself?" he asked.

"I have never met Soarfoot in the flesh, but I have talked to him through another spirit who visits me from time to time."

"Why doesn't that surprise me in the least? Does this spirit who visits you have a name as well?"

"Yes indeed, he also travels the stars and brings wisdom to our people. I am not the only one he has come to visit. He is known to our people as the Storyteller, because he tells many stories with passion and conviction, explaining our history and character."

"I see, so does this Storyteller know where Soarfoot travels and where he's from?"

"The Storyteller told me of the time Soarfoot came to visit our camp over a hundred years ago. It was a time of celebration. Soarfoot spoke of adventure, joy and sorrow in the galaxies. He told our people what was happening in the universe beyond our star system. I have not encountered Soarfoot in my days, but with the guidance of my spirit seeker I have felt the strength he once brought to our camp. Soarfoot comes from many distant places, he is a true star traveller."

"But at one time he was actually here, in the flesh?"

"Yes, I do believe that in my heart, and in my mind."

"You see, my ancestors also knew Soarfoot. They spoke of him in a few documents I have been able to retrieve. I think maybe he might have fathered a generation of Steeles, either that or it was Irving who was the Steele patriarch, but I haven't been able to verify it with documentation."

"I think that maybe it could have been Soarfoot. Rush always said he was quite the lady's man."

"Wait a minute. Rush? Who is Rush?" asked a keenly inquisitive genealogy researcher.

"The Storyteller told me to call him Rush. He said it is a name given to him as a child," answered Bladebone.

"Oh my god, is this really happening?" Zachary prompted his host.

"As I said, this may sound crazy, but you must simply believe. It is not something you can find in your documents. There are many people who believe that travellers from the universe visit our planet."

"I don't think you understand. I suspect Soarfoot might be my ancestor, but my maternal great-great grandfather is Rushad Rhomanscu. Rush was his childhood nickname. That can't be a coincidence, can it?"

"I certainly don't think so. There may be more to your family than this world can explain."

"It does start to make sense; the vampire, the soaring owls—"

"You should find Soarfoot, or at least the Storyteller. They will tell you what became of Irving and who your true ancestors really are."

"But how? I know nothing of spirits, warriors and gods."

"If you are honourable, the spirits will come to you."

"I'm almost afraid to ask. Does the Storyteller come to visit you here on this island?"

"No, my encounters with the Storyteller have been during vision quests farther away from here. However, there is a little old lady who sometimes drops by for a cup of tea. As a matter of fact I will get some Labrador tea leaves. She prefers her tea from the wild."

"I was afraid you were going to say something like that."

Robert yelled to his grandson who brought them a handful of Labrador tea leaves. Zachary put the leaves directly into the boiling water and a few minutes later took the billy can off the fire to let the tea steep for a moment.

"Would you like a cup of tea?" he asked Robert.

"Normally I enjoy tea, but it is late and I am an old man," said Bladebone. "Besides, I think this is your moment and I don't want to frighten away any friendly spirits. I have no bed to offer you, but I see you have brought a small home of your own."

"Yes, my tent. I'll be fine. Thank you for this Robert, meegwetch."

"Zachary, you seem to be a troubled man. Let your soul open to the cosmic wave of the heavens and you will be rewarded."

"I'll try, but the uninvited spirits so far have not been very friendly."

"Perhaps you should invite them this time."

And with that interesting comment Bladebone left the fire and walked into the cabin for the night. Zachary poured a cup of tea and spiked it with his favourite whiskey liqueur Yukon Jack. Watching the tea further discolour he began contemplating spirituality until there was not enough light from the flames to see his drink. The fire dwindled to a pile of smouldering coals with the odd flame spitting out from between the charred logs. Zachary grabbed a few pieces of wood and assiduously placed them on top of the coals. The wood quickly caught fire.

He laid back against a log with his cup of spiked tea. If there was one thing he could do, it was build a campfire. He loved to watch the flames dance in the darkness. It was just what he needed to gather his thoughts for the second time that night. He was not sure whether to take all this talk of spirits seriously or excuse it as an old man letting his mind wander. Zachary pondered his dilemma while drinking another two cups of spiked tea.

More wood was added to the fire after his third cup of tea when Zachary heard footsteps at the edge of the clearing, but the sound was not coming from the cabin. He stood upright and looked across the fire. Behind the waves of heat was an old lady walking towards him with a cane. What are the chances of that?

"An old lady, he was serious. I've got to stop drinking this stuff," he mumbled to himself.

The old lady walked up to the fire, set a short log on its end and sat down. She was rugged and pale; her hair ashen with age, but a sense of youthful zest surrounded her aura. She was wearing a red shawl and a brown flannel pullover with buckskin pants and moccasins. She watched the fire while Zachary watched her.

"Nice fire," she finally spoke.

"Thank you, meegwetch. I like to make fires," said Zachary.

"At least, you know some of the language. Allow me to introduce myself. My name is Beatrice Bagwa."

Zachary's cup went flying as he spit out a spray of tea and stepped backwards in astonishment.

"That can't be. If you're Beatrice Bagwa, you were born in eighteen-oh-four. That would make you one hundred and eighty-five years-old."

"You got me on that one," she said.

"You married Douglas Bagwa in eighteen twenty-six."

"We all make mistakes, his heart couldn't keep up with me."

"Is this some kind of joke between you and Robert. Are you putting me on?" said Zachary, questioning the ghost's authenticity.

He moved directly towards Beatrice, but when he was only a step away, she swiftly rammed her cane into his stomach. Zachary buckled over with a grunt and she kicked him in the rear; sending him sprawling over the fire.

"Don't mess with me kid. I'm sorry I gave you a fright, but if you try anything else I'll have to get tough with you. Now if you just sit down, we can have a nice little chat. I came here to help you."

Slowly walking over to his spot by the fire Zachary sat down without taking his eyes off the old woman.

"There now, that's better. Yes, I'm Beatrice Bagwa and I'm creeping up to two hundred years-old. You don't have to remind me, it's bad enough I've lost a step or two."

"You look spry enough to me. I don't understand."

"Of course you don't understand, you're just a young human."

"And what exactly are you?"

"I wish I was more than human, but that's not important. What is important is that I'm one of your ancestors and I'm here to help you. Now don't you have any questions for me?"

"You're a ghost then."

The old lady's face began to glow. A circle of sparkles enlarged her head and whirling about formed an ugly skull face with glowing red eyes piercing into the night.

"So what if I am!" shrieked the face.

The sparkles disappeared back into her original face and Beatrice stood up with her cane. Zachary was rigid with fear.

"Now listen young man, I was kind enough to come and visit you. Yes, I'm a ghost, but believe it or not I'm actually a nice spirit. You will probably meet some spirits that are not as nice as me."

"Yes, I already have met some nasty spirits."

"Well then boy, speak up. What is it you want to know?"

"Did you ever meet Irving Steele?" asked Zachary, also standing up.

"Of course I did, he's my first cousin."

"Is he somehow still alive, or is he a spirit like you?"

160

"I'm afraid I can't answer that question for certain. The last time I saw Irving was just after my husband Douglas died. I was still quite young. That was a long time ago, but I do know that Irving was going on some sort of adventure, and with Irving anything was possible with his adventures."

"What do you mean, adventures?"

"You know, chopping down trees and tripping through the galaxies."

"No, I don't know. Trees and galaxies?"

"You've got a lot to learn, don't you?"

"Is this really happening or is it just one of my sick dreams?"

"The difference between this and one of your dreams is that I'm not an evil spirit. I told you I'm here to help. Now I know this is not easy for you, but you have to believe in me, it's the only way you're going to find what you're looking for."

"Well then, can you tell me who regenerated the Steele family name in the nineteenth century?"

"I have my suspicions, but I'm afraid I don't have the complete answer. I do know where you should look though. I didn't have any children but it wasn't for lack of trying. After Douglas died, I met another few lumberjack types in this neck of the woods. It could have been Irving who kept the family name going, but it could also have been one of his partners in crime, like the old man's great grandfather Nako, or that Soarfoot character they were always looking for, maybe even the man they called the Storyteller."

"That's quite the line-up of ancestors. You knew them all?"

"Why yes, some of them intimately, if you know what I mean."

"Why don't you know who continued the generations of Steeles?"

"I'm afraid that I'm just a simple human without any of the special powers those men possess. I remained here on this river while they were travelling far and wide, probably to the stars as you suspect, but without my presence, I know that for sure."

"You say special powers they possess, as in the present tense. Do you think they're still possibly alive or appear as spirits?"

"I have not seen Irving in over a hundred years. I don't know what happened to him, but I have been visited by Soarfoot and the Storyteller as I appear before you. They are not ghosts however. I believe they are dimensional travellers who have been preserved in age during their time on the other side."

"Oh boy, this is serious stuff. Have you seen them recently? Do they still come here? Do you know where I might find them now?"

"It has been a few years, but there is a place not far north of here—Norseman Lake. It was a favourite spot for Irving and the others."

"Now we're getting somewhere," perked up Zachary.

"That's the spirit old boy."

"Soarfoot could be a Steele by bloodline if he actually exists. Are you sure he is still alive?"

"I don't know if he is a Steele, but I am certain he is alive."

"Then he does exist."

"Absolutely young man."

"Will he come to me if I open my soul to the cosmic wave?"

"Norseman Lake Zachary, that's where I would start."

"Why can't you travel there if you're a spirit?"

"I'm only an old lady who's allowed to roam this river and help out when I can. I give Robert some strength and I have told you where to seek your ancestors, that's about all I'm good for these days."

The fire was losing its flame. Zachary looked down and kicked at the coals in frustration. Beatrice nodded her head from side to side.

"That kind of attitude isn't going to get you anywhere. Now I suggest you button up your anguish and kick your ass into gear. You've got a lot of work ahead of you and feeling sorry for yourself isn't going to accomplish a damn thing," encouraged the ghost of a Steele.

"It's all so unbelievable, but you are making sense. You're right, I'm only just beginning. What a scary thought."

Beatrice held her back and straightened out her body in some pain.

"Of course I'm making sense, I'm old and wise—right?" she winked at Zachary. "These old bones aren't quite what they used to be. All this standing and talking puts a strain on an old lady. If you don't have any more questions, I think I'll be on my way."

"I probably have more questions, but I'm a little confused right now."

"That's quite normal. Remember Zachary, you have to believe."

Beatrice Bagwa's last few words faded into a fury of spark and glitter spinning around her body in a mosaic of colour; lifting into the air as the apparition bolted into the sky and over the horizon with a tail of blue haze.

The family tree researcher sat down and firmly grasped his bottle of whiskey. He slunk beside the fire as if he was entwined in a drugged stupor. He looked back to where the old lady was standing. He needed more fire. Zachary grabbed another two logs and set them on the coals. They quickly flamed. The flickering heat danced a soothing ballad and eventually put him to sleep.

Zachary left the Churchill River a very confused man.

Chapter 20: Family Secrets

The inspiration for Zachary on this occasion was the spry wisdom of a Cree elder and the vision of an old lady who claimed to be the ghost of his ancestor five generations back. It would be difficult to accept if Zachary had not met the vision of his lifelong nemesis vampire demon only a few weeks earlier: instead he was further charged with the enduring energy to find his parents and discover the truth about his bloodline.

He thought of nothing else but the vision of Beatrice Bagwa as he was floated back upriver to Stanley Mission in Norman Balia's fishing boat. Zachary reflected on the presence of the ghost and the ball of light that shot into outer space. The vision mingled in his mind with thoughts of Soarfoot, the Storyteller and cosmic journeys with a vampire demon: his brain was racing in triplicate again.

The interstellar connotations of his encounter with Bladebone and Beatrice Bagwa and his previous teleporting experiences with the vampire spirit began to seep deeper into Zachary's mind. He wondered if his family was even from this world; perhaps his bloodline descended from alien connections. He decided to take the advice of his latest ghost vision and make immediate plans to visit Norseman Lake, which was just a float plane flight away still in northern Saskatchewan.

He thanked Norman profusely and slipped four folded fifty-dollar bills into his large hand; a reasonable amount of cash back then. Balia smiled in his usual manner, gave Zachary the name of a good bush pilot in La Ronge and wished him the best of luck. Zachary did not even consider checking in with his partner Zelda, who was waiting in the city of Saskatoon as far as he knew. He loaded his gear into the truck and back tracked to the northern town of La Ronge, only a little more than an hour away.

It came as a surprise then, but a comforting sight when Zachary pulled up to the water docks for float planes on the southern shore of Montreal River where it enters Lac La Ronge. There, dressed in backcountry attire and standing beside a Jeep loaded with gear and fresh supplies, was his graduate student and lover Zelda Mintah.

"Welcome to La Ronge Zachary," she smiled in the parking lot.

"Zelda, what are you doing here?"

"I thought maybe you would want a partner for your journey."

"I'm glad to see you, but how did you know I would be here?"

"To tell you the truth, the owls came to visit me in my dreams as soon as you left. I packed up and came straight here last night."

"That's mind boggling. The spirits have filled my thoughts for the last two days, it must be destiny. I can't explain it by any means, but everything seems to be coming together."

"Some people think there's a reason why everything happens. This could be your time to find your parents and discover the truth behind your family history."

"You might be right. If you want to come with me, then, I guess we can do this together. I see you came prepared."

"I packed a few things just in case."

"Now I just need to find a bush pilot with a plane. My guide at Stanley Mission gave me a name."

"It wouldn't happen to be Reg Herzog, would it?" Zelda pointed to the de Havilland Beaver float plane parked at the dock on the water.

"What are the chances, it is the same name," said Zachary, pulling out a crumpled piece of paper from his pocket.

"I can't imagine there's many other independent planes in La Ronge," speculated Zelda.

"I guess not."

The coincidence of the arrangements did not fluster Zachary in the least. He did not suspect Zelda's insight into his ancestry with his mind so cluttered; doggedly following a trail of clues regardless of the circumstances. Zelda brought her backpack and a large duffle bag mainly with extra kitchen and food supplies. It only took a few minutes that morning to pack their gear into the single-propeller plane. Soon they were floating out into the lake, ready to take off on Zachary's next adventure.

Reg Herzog was a balding forty-year-old man with a thick red beard and a knitted wool toque matching the colour of his hair. Reg had been flying northern Saskatchewan for eighteen years and was accustomed to inclement conditions, but a sudden unexpected storm would catch him off guard on this day. The float plane was flying through small rain shower cloud cells along a route of just under two hundred and fifty miles. The tiny but more than adequate aircraft encountered high winds and abnormal turbulence only fifty miles south of Norseman. The forecast was for light showers and did not include any jet streams of high winds.

"God damn Environment Canada, what the hell kind of forecast is this? I'm going to pull us down under these clouds. Hang on folks, it could get a little bumpy," Herzog warned his passengers.

He brought the plane under the clouds and navigated above the predominantly pine forest as they were bounced around. Although the ride was fairly rough, Herzog managed to fly his machine through the storm. Zachary spotted a lone log house on the south shore of a peninsula at the northeast end of the lake as they were flying above Norseman. It was the logical place to land. Herzog took them down to the lake and landed on the water despite the wind and rain.

A light shower was still spitting outside as they were dropped off at a wood dock built on the shore in front of the large pine log home. Herzog agreed to return in six days for another flight back to La Ronge, weather permitting, and promptly zipped away across the lake. Zachary and Zelda gathered their few bags of luggage on the dock, surrounded by the lake, boreal shield rock, pine and spruce trees. Norseman is not a place for the timid, and that is precisely why Zachary was so surprised by the first human he saw there.

He looked out across the bay after grabbing his backpack and pondered the tranquil grid of ripples on the water's surface. The drops of rain were like pieces of the puzzle he was trying to put together. And then it happened again. Zachary was overcome by a strange sensation: the same he felt at Stanley Mission. He looked at Zelda and a distant figure came into focus behind her. Immediately Zelda sensed Zachary's fear.

"What's wrong Zachary? What is it?"

"I don't know."

Zelda turned and looked towards the end of the dock. A sandy path extended from the shoreline and curled its way to the house. The image of a naked woman running through the camouflage of trees appeared behind the brush which bordered the path. Zelda looked back at Zachary.

"What was that?" she asked, although she knew fully well that the creature was one of her spiritual sisters; probably protecting the house from any hostile tree warriors.

"I'm not sure, exactly," said Zachary.

He continued to stare into the trees but the naked woman disappeared. He walked across the dock and onto the path. Zelda followed. They made their way up to the house and admired the beautiful log home. The homemade pine structure was impressive. It was an A-frame of large proportions. A small set of stairs led up to the front door and a deck across the width of the house. A picture window framed in sections on the southeast side extended up near the top of the second storey, with an overhead balcony and two French doors sheltered underneath on the southwest side of the main floor opening out onto the southern front deck beside a large front door.

A bitter wind began to sweep through the forest as they stood at the bottom of the front steps. It started raining heavier and the wind increased with a stubborn gust. The violent storm they came through only a few minutes earlier was now raging over the lake. Zelda held Zachary's arm as they both jockeyed for position against the squall. Zachary struggled up the stairs and pounded on the wood door. Again he pounded but still there was not an answer. He decided to take action; standing back he started with a couple steps, raised his leg and kicked at the door.

The door did not budge and Zachary ended up falling on his back. Zelda pulled a rain hood over her head and reached for the handle of the door. She turned the handle and the door opened. She looked down at Zachary and started to laugh, but also helped him to his feet. The interior of the house was even more spectacular.

The main living area to their right occupied a quarter of the house with a large fireplace hearth and its distinguished cathedral ceiling rising up to the second storey. (What a challenge for proverbial bouncing off the ceiling sex, Zachary thought to himself.) A den with a small library opened to the front deck on their left and above on the second floor a lounge of sorts overlooked the living room with a hand-carved wood railing, sharing the cathedral ceiling. The ground floor was open to the back of the house beyond the living room, with a sunken pond surrounded by lush plants separating a dining room, an island countertop and the kitchen. There were not any metal cupboards.

A stairway up to the second storey beside the kitchen divided the back half of the main floor into a laundry room, sauna, hot tub and large bathroom, with the second floor partitioned into bedrooms. The second-storey wall above the sunken pond faced the living room with mounted animal heads: moose, deer, elk, caribou, wolf and bear. The house radiated the presence of a modern hunter.

"Hello," shouted Zachary. "We didn't mean to break down your door, we just wanted to come in from the storm."

Still there was not an answer. Zachary stepped forward and pushed open the door to his left, revealing a conservative but well stocked library. He walked inside and looked at the walls of neatly stacked books.

"Wow, this is great. Come and see it Zelda."

"Nice," she said, peering around the doorway.

A small glass chandelier hung in the middle of the room and drapes were pulled shut over the French doors.

"Storm? What on Earth are you talking about?" came a voice from behind them.

Zachary and Zelda turned around and saw a woman coming out of the bathroom. It was Zachary's mother, Maria Steele. It should not have been a surprise, but the poor boy was still a bit startled.

"Mother—" he gawked.

"I don't know why you have raincoats, it's perfectly gorgeous outside," said his mother.

"What are you doing here?" continued Zachary.

"I live here. It's a nice library, don't you think? What are you doing here? And please, take off your rain jackets, you look absolutely perspired."

"Do you recognise your own son?"

"Of course I do Zacharias. Zelda, how are you dear?"

"I'm good," answered Zelda.

"Taking care of my son as always?"

"Trying my best."

"Is father here as well?" asked Zachary.

"No, he's not here right now."

"You don't live here alone, do you?" the son questioned again.

"Certainly not, you should know I couldn't survive here on my own. Now, why don't you come in and I'll get you some lemonade."

"Something a little stronger would be nice," said Zachary.

They entered the living room and the sun was shining through the windows in all its glory. It was clear and quite pleasant outside.

"What happened to the storm, it didn't pass over that quickly, did it?" pondered Zelda.

"Still blabbing about a storm. I don't have any idea what you kids are talking about," said Maria from the kitchen island countertop.

The kids took off their jackets and sat down on the sofa. Maria came from the kitchen around the sunken pond and into the living room bringing a glass of lemonade for Zelda and a Scotch whiskey for Zachary. Zelda took the whiskey and gave Zachary the lemonade.

"I'm sorry dear, are you upset?" asked Maria.

"What makes you say that?" said Zelda.

"I'll get another whiskey," suggested their hostess.

"Are you surprised to see me?" questioned Zachary.

"No, I knew it was only a matter of time until you found us."

"Is father expecting me?"

"I told you he isn't here," yelled Maria from the kitchen.

"Where is he then?" Zachary raised his voice as well.

"I'm not sure. He's out in the bush somewhere on his special retreats."

"Special retreats?"

"I don't ask questions. He keeps me happy so I let him have his revelations," said Maria returning with another drink.

"Can I ask you a question?" interjected Zelda.

"Certainly dear."

"Is this where you've been since you both disappeared?"

"It is a lovely spot, don't you think?"

"This shouldn't be a surprise to me, but I think I might be in shock just a little. Could I have another drink?" said Zachary, holding out his empty glass after guzzling the first shot.

"Certainly dear," acknowledged Maria again.

"We'll just be out front on the deck," explained Zachary.

The two of them went outside, took a few breaths and enjoyed a view of the bay. Zachary's mother was right, it was an ideal setting. The trees gently shaded the house and the lake was clean and clear. Maria came outside, this time with the whole bottle of whiskey. She set it on the deck railing and looked out at the scenery with her son and a woman with wizardly qualities.

"We've been quite happy here you know, not a worry in the world and all we need at our fingertips."

"How do you get your electricity?" wondered Zelda.

"Solar panelling on the roof above us and another row of panels up on the hill behind the house. Jeremiah also has a diesel generator as an emergency back-up, but we have lots of battery storage and we only use the generator after a few cloudy days in the winter."

"So you live in complete comfort," marvelled Zelda.

"Yes, all the creature comforts, as they say. I like it here."

"Mother, were you outside just before we arrived by chance?"

"I wish I was, it's so beautiful today. I've been inside cleaning the house for the last few hours."

"And you didn't notice a storm outside?"

"Again with the storm. What is it with you and that storm?"

"But it's true, there was a sudden storm here only a few minutes ago. I don't know what's going on," said Zelda suspiciously.

"Have you kids been out in the sun too long?"

"When we arrived here and landed in a float plane, it was raining," asserted Zachary. "Did you even hear the plane landing? And another thing, I'm sure I saw a naked woman running through the trees. Now, I haven't been out in the sun—"

"That's the first sensible thing you've said since you arrived here. Must have been that Slattern girl."

"Slattern?" puzzled Zelda.

"Actually, she has a mate as well. A couple of young ducks who run through the bush in the raw just for kicks. Imagine that. Jeremiah says it's part of the rituals, so I leave it at that."

"What are the rituals and retreats all about?" asked Zachary.

Raising her hands in the air, his mother's trepidation began to surface as she started to explain the family secrets her son had come to discover.

"You'll have to ask your father about that. I don't interfere. It's very important to him and his friends, but I don't really understand. As long as we're happy together I figure he might as well have his ritualistic adventures. All he tells me is that they meet somewhere in the forest and cleanse their souls. It sounds perfectly levitating."

"Have you met any of his friends?" again questioned the son.

"Only one of them; a French trapper who lives not far away."

"Do you know his name?"

"He goes by the handle Cookie."

"Cookie? Did father mention any other names?"

"A few, but I'm not sure if I can remember them."

"How about Soarfoot? Did he ever mention that name?"

"That sounds familiar. Yes, I think he has talked about someone named Soarfoot, a rather peculiar name. A native Cree I think."

"Oh boy," said Zelda.

Zachary's face lit up: "Are you sure mother?"

"I told you we don't talk about his rituals very much, but I'm certain he has mentioned the name Soarfoot; that's not something someone would tend to forget easily."

"Ma, you have to tell me where I can find Dad."

"I know, I didn't expect you to come all the way here without seeing him. He was wondering when you would show up and I told him not to worry, I knew you would come soon. It might sound crazy, but I can always sense your thoughts."

"That's not crazy. I've always felt connected to you as well."

"Thank you for saying that Zachary. I'll tell you where you can find your father, but why don't you stay here tonight for some food and a good sleep in a bed. You can take the canoe your father left here and get an early start tomorrow morning. Besides, you haven't told me how your hypothermia experiments turned out."

"Sure Ma, that sounds good."

"I'll go and get some dinner started. If you two want another drink, there's plenty more where that came from. Help yourself."

"Thanks Mum."

Maria Steele went inside the house and began preparing dinner. Zachary pressed his hands against the railing of the deck and leaned forward.

"See what I mean about the out-of-this-world experience I had on the Churchill. My mother seems to be confirming it."

"Yah, I think I see it," concurred Zelda.

"This is bizarre. There is something out there in the woods and I don't think it's from this planet."

"Calm down Zachary."

"Calm down? Didn't you hear mother? She didn't notice a huge storm, my father is visiting Soarfoot with some trapper named Cookie and there's a naked couple running through the forest. What do you make of all that?"

"I can't explain everything, it certainly sounds like more than coincidence, but your mother is probably just going senile as well."

"I don't doubt that."

"Zachary, I know there's something out there and we'll find it along with your father, but try not to get all caught up with your ghosts and goblins."

"Spirits and demons."

"Please."

Zelda tugged at Zachary's shirt and they both forced a smile. They decided to go for a stroll down the shoreline; walking the south side of the peninsula and returning at dinner time. The sunset that night turned out to be marvellous and so was the meal cooked by Maria. She drilled her son with questions about his hypothermia research, and then he asked her some tough questions about his genealogy research.

"Do you know where Soarfoot comes from? Is he related to us? Do I have indigenous blood?" posed Zachary.

"I'm sorry dear, I just don't know all these details, but your father can answer those questions," promised Maria.

"What about your family? Did anyone ever talk about your great grandfather Rushad?" Zachary kept inquiring.

"My grandfather talked about him a lot. He was a brave, hardworking pioneer and prospector who started the Rhomany bloodline in North America. He came from the old country over a hundred years ago and lived a tough life. He was a farmer as a child, then a fur trapper and a gold miner, and then finally a farm manager in California. He made everything possible for my family."

"He went prospecting in the Cascade mountains apparently. Is your family certain he disappeared there? Did anyone ever talk about him showing up later, like maybe even here in northern Canada?"

"Not that I remember. I don't think anyone heard from him again. I'm so sorry, but I don't seem to be much help to you my son."

"Don't worry Mother, I understand, but I hope you can see why I need to find some answers for myself."

"I know Zachary, and I also know I haven't been the perfect mother, but I have always loved you unconditionally."

"You were a good mother because you always loved me. You don't have to make any apologies."

"I always questioned myself as a mother. I almost died when you were born and your father told me you were a miracle. He told me that you're special and we had to protect you at all cost, but I always felt inadequate, and I was afraid that you would sense my fear and not feel my love."

"Well you can rest easy. Your love has always nurtured me and I have no complaints. But I would like to know what makes me so special, that's why I came looking for you and Dad."

"And your father knows about these special connections. He'll tell you what to do when you find him."

"But you don't know where he is."

"I know how to get to the river where Jeremiah said he would be, and he did leave a map this time in case you came here."

"We will find your father Zachary, I promise you," said Zelda.

"Sounds good to me. Tomorrow's another day. I have a feeling we'll find what we're looking for," winked Zachary.

The three of them were exhausted by midnight and Zachary had exhausted most of his questions. They decided to call it a night and get an early start in the morning; retiring to their respective rooms and falling asleep peacefully, but not before Zachary and Zelda made love. Maria's wakeup call came all too early.

"Time to hit the open water kids. I don't know what you two were up to last night but it sounded like you had half the forest animals in the bedroom with you."

Zachary grinned: bounce, bounce, bounce.

He and Zelda loaded their gear into the canoe and after a breakfast of powdered eggs and moose sausage they were ready to sail away for the day. Maria gave them the map from Jeremiah and also described the rapids they would encounter. She suggested going upstream on the MacFarlane River after paddling down the much smaller Norseman River, a few portage creeks and pothole lakes north of the cabin. Jeremiah often spent several days on his retreats, so Maria was not sure where he would be or when he was coming back. She said Cookie the trapper had a cabin somewhere along the stretch of MacFarlane south towards the source of the river, which was one of the preferred areas for the frequent ritual retreats. The float plane was due to return in five days, so Zachary gave his mother some cash to secure another flight one week later if they didn't return; not knowing he would in fact never return. He and Zelda then said good-bye and were paddling across the bay to the north shore of the lake only an hour after sunrise.

It was sunny when they started, but before they landed in the mouth of a small creek some clouds rolled in and the wind picked up its pace. It started raining again as they lined the canoe along the mainly stagnant creek that drained into a pothole lake to the north. The creek bed was so tight that the canoe would only float for short stretches of the approximately five hundred metre section of land, so they laboriously dragged and pushed the canoe to the next body of water.

They made good time despite the rain and the boggy conditions of their three portages to access the flow of Norseman River. The first small inland lake was less than a half mile across and the second creek bed portage was even shorter. It was still hard work but they pulled the canoe into the second pothole lake and repeated the process after another lake crossing not much more than a few hundred metres. The final portage was also short but seemed the most difficult with fallen trees cluttered across the crooked lay of the land, however it did lead to a narrow lake almost two miles long that marked the beginning of continuous flow for the river.

They laboured through the swampy portage pushing their canoe over tree trunks while wearing chest wader boots Zelda thoughtfully brought along. Slightly fatigued they paddled west on the lake to a narrows also about five hundred metres long, which they were able to slip through without leaving the boat. However, the hard work of wilderness paddling was building up an early appetite for Zachary. Zelda was fine. It was a snap for a pine tree Minga with Marshlandite powers. (More about that quite soon.) They reached the mouth of Norseman River just before noon after crossing the final section of open lake water; beaching on the shore and taking the time for lunch.

It then took them just over three hours in the afternoon to slowly make their way through three sets of rapids along the river flowing north into MacFarlane. Shepherd Rapids is only a patch of riffles with whirling fast water eddies less than a mile down the river, but Allan and Greenfield Rapids about three miles along the river and another mile downstream are both full sets of rapids. They are not difficult chutes to run, but Zachary didn't want to risk any accidents; stopping to get out of the canoe on shore and reconnoitring the white-water before paddling through without portaging their gear. It was a little more time consuming and tiresome, however they made it safely all the way downriver to the confluence with MacFarlane's significantly greater volume of flow. It was late afternoon and so rather than starting to work their way upstream they decided to make camp and rest for the next day of paddling against the current.

The larger river was a refreshing sight, especially for Zelda with the sandy soil of the watershed providing such a fertile ecology for pine trees. Zachary welcomed the breeze over the wider river to help keep the mosquitoes away. He scouted a sandy point of land and after enjoying a cool cup of water walked up the shoreline elevation to find a location for their evening camp. He selected a relatively flat patch of moss-covered rock that was sheltered by a small stand of spruce and trembling aspen trees. Zelda approved of the campsite, although she would have preferred pine trees. Camp was made and after an early dinner they went to sleep without bouncing that night; preserving their energy and avoiding any wear and tear on the tent.

The next morning the elements turned on them once again. It was raining heavily this time; not ideal for paddling upriver. But despite the miserable weather they were warm and dry inside their tent. It was a good thing they didn't bounce in the night. The rain put Zelda in a sombre mood, yet the downpour triggered an opposite reaction from Zachary. He was inspired. He started by dashing down to the river perfectly naked and waking up properly with a dip in the water: the image of a Slattern. He came back to the tent wet and invigorated, and gave Zelda a big kiss. She woke up as well. A tarp to shelter them from the rain was not the only thing erected—a recurring theme in my story no doubt—but the tarp did allow Zachary to build a fire and prepare breakfast. Still naked, he served the meal to Zelda in the tent.

The young tree warrior candidate, now nourished and alert, cleaned the metal dishes but did not put them into metal cupboards, then doused the fire and packed up the tent after his lover was up and getting ready for the day. Zachary finally rigged the tarp over their gear in the canoe and donned his rainsuit, but did not wear anything else except sandals on his feet. The weather worsened as the morning progressed, with more rain and a strong wind raging directly head on as they paddled west. Struggling upriver was strenuous at best. They nary had a moment to raise their heads, putting their noses down to the grind stone so to speak, yet Zelda did notice a good number of fallen spruce and pine trees; possibly from a wind storm, but axe cuts indicated perhaps a trunk thrust in the area. She shed a tear for the fallen pine but kept her senses alert for any intruders.

They were strong paddlers and managed to nudge along for two miles of the more open sections before reaching a narrow portion of the river. They were slightly better protected from the wind for about another mile of paddling but the rain was still pouring and the current was relatively strong as the river narrowed. It took them the entire morning to cover just over three miles. They stopped for a break at a confluence where the water from a collection of small lakes drains into the river, and then they headed south upstream into the teeth of the current; sheltered from the full force of the wind by the narrow passage of the river, yet still fighting against the flow of the water for another two miles in the driving rain.

The elements were a challenge as the cold rain dripped under their jackets and soaked them with a chill. Zachary was beginning to fade later in the day but ignored his condition. He continued to exert himself as his body slowly declined towards an eventual halt. The wet cold was penetrating through his skin deep into his core; his hands and face turning clammy and pale, his muscles tense and becoming rigid, and his jaw beginning to shiver with slurred speech. The oxygen in his blood was diminishing and his bodily functions starting to fail. Zachary's mind began to drift; his brain was losing control over his body. He was slipping into hypothermia.

It had been a while since he last experienced hypothermia. It was dangerous but all the same it was like rediscovering an old childhood thrill. Zachary's mind fought to maintain control over his movements. The key to survival was knowing when to stop, alas when it came to hypothermia Zachary did not know many limits. Nevertheless, both his mind and body set their own limits. And then it happened. Zachary snapped.

There they were, Zachary and Zelda, paddling hard and sliding into an eddy cove on the shoreline just downriver of Herman Rapids. The wind and rain began to let up and it looked as if they might be canoeing out of the storm. The sun was even threatening to push through the clouds. They were portaging the rapids and intended to continue south into another open lake portion of the river; hopefully finding a nice place for camp, or preferably someone else's camp. They put on their backpacks and each carried one of the duffle bags of gear before going back to carry the canoe together. There were a few white birch tucked in with the many pine trees beside the slightly used portage trail that was just worn enough for them to walk without much trouble. Zachary was somewhat hypnotised by the unfriendly whisper of birch leaves rustling in the wind, given his state of hypothermia: honest, it wasn't because of us wind warriors. And then, as his mind floated through the forest the evil spirits began to attack. The whisper of leaves was replaced by a snarling, raspy voice.

"Go away," the trees hissed.

The now delirious canoeist stopped walking, dropped his bag, straightened out his back and listened as carefully as he could. Zelda stopped and looked at Zachary. He wasn't moving. He could only hear us wind warriors and the trees as he scanned the trail ahead.

"What's wrong?" asked Zelda.

"I'm not sure," said Zachary.

He picked up his bag and continued to walk down the trail. A sudden gust of wind wailed across the path and whispered again.

"Go away."

Dropping his bag for the second time and clenching his fists Zachary darted off the trail towards the birch trees. He stopped after a few strides and spun around; bopping his head about in search of demons. He crossed over the path to the other side—only the other side of the trail, but soon to be another side of reality—constantly peering through the trees and up into the sky. He came back to the path and stared at Zelda.

"What is it Zachary?"

"Listen," he said. They both listened.

"Now!" came the snarl.

Zachary began to tremble; his eyes conveying terror.

"Did you hear it?" he muttered.

"Hear what?" pleaded Zelda.

"The voice."

"A human's voice?"

"I don't know."

"I'm sorry, I didn't hear anything. I think we better take a break."

Rather abruptly Zachary jolted his body around and glared in the direction where they started the portage. He began to run towards the end of the trail, then stopped and turned back to Zelda again.

"Now!" the raspy voice repeated.

Zachary raised his head and glowered at the clouds: those vapour demons can be nasty at times. He turned yet again and started to run but fell hard; his elbow smashing down on a rock. He stammered back to his feet and crawled up a small hill of mud. He put his arms to his sides with his fists still clenched and yelled with all his strength.

"Naugh! I'm not leaving!"

"Zachary," Zelda screamed as she gave chase.

"I'm not afraid of you!" he yelled again.

Zelda climbed up the small hill and approached him. He calmed down and looked into her eyes. She held his forearm ever so gently.

"What's wrong my sweet?"

"Demons," he answered without hesitation.

Zelda thought for a few seconds: "I think you need to be warmed up. You've gone too far into hypothermia."

"But I heard the voice, and I saw Beatrice Bagwa. It's all real."

"I believe you Zachary, but right now you're in a critical stage of hypothermia. Let's warm you up first and then talk about this."

He looked down the trail. Drops of water were sliding off birch leaves and pine needles. The sun was fighting through the haze and a mist was slowly forming over the river; the storm was behind them. Zachary looked at Zelda.

"Ya, let's build a fire," he said.

They picked up the duffle bags and looked for some firewood while walking down the trail to the head of the rapids. Again Zachary stopped in his tracks. Zelda also stopped and looked despairingly at her lover, but then she also heard a voice. She listened carefully. Someone was walking down the trail coming from the feet of the rapids. Zachary strained until he was able to focus on the moving object against the trees. It was a man. He was softly singing to himself.

This tall man had a small backpack strapped to his shoulders with an old, scuffed external frame. He was wearing a well-worn cowboy hat and was bare-chested. Although he was not immense in size, he was well conditioned with a solid physique and a thick black beard. He looked rugged and well adapted to the wilderness; carrying an axe by its head which was attached to a long wood handle. The man kept his stride walking along the path up to Zachary and Zelda, looked up at them and waved his axe from side to side as he approached.

"Allo," he shouted. "Hit his might-he miser-hable, she his, huh? Not da kind hof day she his when you wanna be houtside, huh?"

"It could be worse," said Zachary.

"Ah we, tis look-hing fair now, eh?"

"We were just about to stop and build a fire. We've been paddling upriver in the rain and we're a bit cold," said Zelda.

"Well, hi am frum 'ere, where har yous cum from, huh?"

"We're from the south," answered Zachary.

"Ah, da sout. Lot warm-her down der, eh? My name, he's Cookie Labrecque. An yous guys?" he asked tipping his hat.

"I'm Zachary and this is Zelda."

"'Tis good to meet yous. Nice riv-her 'ere, you tink she his, eh?"

"It's a beautiful river," agreed Zelda.

"Dis be da furst time yous see da riv-her?"

"No, actually we saw it from the air first," said Zachary.

"Ah we, da float plane. Hi tell yous what. Yous look tie-heard han wet. Hi take yous to my cabin han we build da fi-her. Wees warm up frum da storm her, han hi make yous da meal wit da good stuff frum da forest 'ere. Hi make yous da meal dat yous nev-her gonna ferget, huh?"

The two canoeists looked at each other. Zelda shrugged her shoulders.

"Why not?" ventured Zachary. "How far to your cabin?"

"She be jus' down da trai-hul up hon da 'ill. Wees be der soon."

They left the canoe there and grabbed their gear; cautiously following the nonchalant woodsman less than a half mile south along the shoreline trail. Labrecque then took them up a slope to the west of the river where it opened up into a lake. They followed a smooth sandy trail up to a small stand of old and strong pine trees that marked the beginning of homemade wooden stairs. The stairs that Cookie built with pride led to a small ridge plateau with moss, lichen, some ferns and native grasses growing in a clearing. There, with a clear vantage of the water as well as the surrounding forest, was Cookie's home.

It was a wide, shallow cabin built with pine logs; complete with hand carved wood shingles on the roof that Labrecque crafted himself. Winding down towards the river basin on the far side of the plateau was a small drainage creek which made for handy drinking water. It was indeed a fine spot for a home. Cookie set his pack on its frame and his axe on its head against the cabin wall, opened the front door and motioned to the creek with his hat.

"Da wat-her 'ere he's good, huh."

He went inside the cabin while Zachary and Zelda also shed their packs and walked down to the creek. The sun was beaming brightly by then and it was turning into a pleasant day. The couple drank the cold, clean water and filled their canteens, but Zachary was still shivering in the sunlight; he needed to be warmed properly. Fortunately, a fire was already blazing inside Labrecque's cabin.

The fireplace and cooking inglenook in the cabin were neatly finished with granite stone, and a three-quarter wall separated the width of the interior into two sections. The sleeping area shared the fireplace with a few cooking utensils on the right side of the hearth and a bed on the left side, with two hand crafted wood sofa-style benches situated in front of the fire. Zachary and Zelda huddled on one of the benches to warm up. A book shelf unit, also hand crafted, stood the full height of the far wall beside the bed. The top shelves were full of books and the lower shelves of the stand were filled with a well-furnished collection of maps and assorted documents.

A full set of cupboards—not metal, but wood—were housed on the other side of the cabin beside the front door, storing clothes and personal items. A metal tub (not wood) sat against the far-left side wall, and four wooden chairs with a large pine table were situated in the middle of the living area. Another wall of shelves at the back of the cabin held dry food supplies and a few tools. Cookie was preparing some fresh food from the smoke house built next to the outside wall of the cabin, along with a sauna room sharing the same wood stove as a source of heat. An outhouse was also built on the opposite outside wall.

"When hi sees yous der, yous were stop-hing to make da fi-her han eat da food, huh?" inquired Cookie.

"Yes, we were going to warm up, but maybe keep paddling for a bit more and find a place to camp on the lake, but it looks like you have the best spot," answered Zelda.

"She waz a beech dis morn-hing, huh, da wind han da rain."

"It was difficult. I guess I over did it," said Zachary.

"Yous look cold, not wear much hon top, eh?" observed Cookie.

"I enjoy the rain but sometimes I get carried away. I noticed you weren't wearing anything on top either," Zachary also observed, seeing that Labrecque had put on a shirt.

"Hi jus take hoff da shirt when hi was 'iking han da rain stop."

"Did you build this cabin yourself?" questioned Zelda.

"Mais we, hi make hit wit my own hans, many 'ear hago. Hit be veh-ry good to me. Her, she's hold but she stands well."

"It has a nice feel to it. I can see how you would be happy here, but you're French, aren't you? How did you end up out west?"

"Me han-cestor, dey came west for da fur many 'ear hago. Der be French in da woods 'ere. So yous tell me, how did yous end up hout west 'ere?"

"Actually, speaking of ancestors we're looking for my father. We were told you know him. He has a large cabin on Norseman Lake, his name is Jeremiah Steele," explained Zachary.

"Bien sur, hit a good ting, hi know Jeremiah. He's da fer-hend 'im, wit me. Wees share many da camp fi-her us toged-her."

"Do you know where he is now?" asked Zachary.

"Now, dats a 'ard one. Hi left 'im tree day hago, by da big riv-her."

"The Churchill?"

"Mais we, da big one."

"What was he doing? Where was he? I was just there myself."

Cookie was pulling a cast iron frying pan from a steel spit fixture over the fire; adding fish fillets and asparagus spears to the potatoes he was cooking, after already frying up a round flat loaf of bannock bread made with a pinch of bear lard—mmm, yummy.

"Have sum hof da bread hi make, dis be da best yous ever had. Now your fad-her, 'im, he go to see ha-bout why der his da talk hof da sac-hri-fice," said Cookie, tending to the food.

Zelda perked to attention. She was hopeful they might find Zachary's family and ancestors involved in a sacrifice fire ceremony, as were many other tree warriors at that space and time.

"Sacrifice? Sounds like one of his rituals," speculated Zachary.

"Ah we, dat rich-hu-al stuff, hits every-ting your fad-her does, 'im han dat Storytell-her guy," commented Cookie, putting the pan back over the fire.

"You know the Storyteller?" asked Zachary excitedly.

"Bien sur, hi see 'im hall da time wit your fad-her."

"Imagine that?" said Zelda.

"And were they together on the Churchill?" continued Zachary.

"Hactually, Jeremiah was look-hing for 'im da Storytell-her, han dat Soarfoot warrior guy, 'im too."

"Do you know Soarfoot as well?" Zachary jumped up.

"Ah we, da Soarfoot. He be da great-hest warrior hof da pine tree, but hi tink maybe he's be dis-happear. Hits a sad ting, huh?"

"Wait a minute. Warrior of the pine trees? What are you talking about?" said a puzzled Zachary.

Zelda squirmed on the bench. She knew it was time to reveal the truth of Zachary's ancestry, but she wanted him to be properly prepared. Labrecque saw her posture and sensed her uneasiness.

"Hi tink maybe yous got to learn some tings, eh," said Cookie looking at Zelda for confirmation.

"We need to find Jeremiah, it's best these details come from him. You must know where he was heading," suggested Zelda.

"Dat Soarfoot 'im, he like to go to da gov-hernment park. Dey do dat rich-hu-al stuff der. Jeremiah said he go sout to da park."

"Lac La Ronge?" posed Zachary.

"Non, da park fur-der sout."

"Prince Albert? Where I also was only four days ago as well."

"We, dats da one."

"Do you think he would have made it to the park by now?"

"She's a good hike frum da Churchill. Hits 'ard to say, depend hon where he look han who he find."

"How long would it take my father to hike here from the park?"

"Your fad-her, he be hold 'im, but he be hin good condish-hon. Hit take 'im hat least tree day me tink, maybe four."

"Didn't it take you three days to get here from the Churchill, which is quite impressive if you were on foot?" queried Zelda.

"Hit only take me one day, but hits heasy, hi know da short cut way."

"So my father is looking for Soarfoot and the Storyteller as well, somewhere around Churchill River or Prince Albert National Park, where I just happen to have come from, and he probably won't be back this way for at least another three days."

"Hide say dats prob-hably a good hestimation."

"Tell me Cookie, do you know Soarfoot well?" asked Zelda.

"Ha little. Hi see 'im ha-bout every tree or four munt."

"Is he indigenous to this land?"

"Ah we, he's da Cree," answered Labrecque as he raised the frying pan to his face and inhaled.

"Is he related to Zachary's family, do you know?"

"You mean, har dey brod-her? Hi don't know, dey nev-her say dey har, but maybe."

"And you say Soarfoot is now gone missing?" pushed Zachary.

"Dats what your fad-her 'im, he wants to know."

"Me too, I guess."

"Hi tink for now, da food hit be ready. Wees gonna eat like da king now, eh," smiled Cookie.

The visitors were hungry and the feast was welcome: fresh walleye fillets with potatoes and asparagus grown by Labrecque, along with the bannock bread and a few pieces of moose jerky on the side. The meal was simple but delicious. Cookie cleaned up with a pot of hot water and Zachary began thinking about his next move. Labrecque suggested they stay the night and he would show them a good route heading south of the MacFarlane basin to the Churchill watershed by way of water crossings and portages. Alas, later that evening in front of the fireplace Zachary's curiosity dictated otherwise.

"Why did you call Soarfoot a pine tree warrior?" he stated.

"I think you should ask your father that question," said Zelda.

"This is what I came here to learn. If Mister Labrecque has some answers, why wouldn't I ask him?"

"I understand your desire to learn about your family history Zachary, I just want to be sure you're prepared to hear the truth."

"The truth; it sounds like you know more about my family than me. Is there something else you're not telling me?"

"Sort of."

Cookie stood up and walked over to the bookcase beside his bed. A small hatchet was leaning against the shelving. He grabbed the hatchet and handed it to Zachary.

"Hi tink you might need dis. Take hit han keep hit. Hit his my gift to you," said Cookie, as he looked at Zelda and spoke quite pointed with his slanted English inflexion. "Hi tink Zachary, 'im, he should know deez tings, udderwise 'im, he gonna get in trouble."

"Yes, you're right Cookie. I'm just being cautious."

"What are you two talking about? What is this hatchet for?"

"Hi tell you, hif you wan to find your fad-her han Soarfoot or da Storytell-her, you got to know deez tings. Da for-hest her, she's full hof da warriors dem. Dey halways fight-hing heach udder. Han heach warrior be hof da diff-her-ent tree. Han da tree har every-ting for da warrior. Dats what dey be fight-hing hall hof da time for."

"Tree warriors?" said Zachary staring into the fire.

"I'm afraid so, and there's more. It's complicated," said Zelda.

"Deez warriors dem, dey haf spesh-hal pow-her dey get frum da tree. Your fad-her, Soarfoot han me, we be hof da pine tree, but you, your mud-her han Storytell-her, yous be hof da haspen. Hi dunno why, but udder warriors, dey be hof udder trees."

"Yikes, this just gets better all the time. And you Zelda, what's your tree of preference?"

"Ah—you know how your mother said you're special?"

"Yes, I'm listening."

"Well I'm kind of special myself. I'm a pine warrior but I'm not quite like other tree warriors. Instead I have the magical touch of wizards."

"Tree warriors and wizards, of course, why not. So, does this mean you've been playing dumb with me ever since we met?"

"Definitely not, I had no idea about your ancestry when we first met, you have to believe me. I was visited by Rushad Rhomanscu after we were together for over a year. He explained that you're special because of the bloodline of your parents. He knew this moment would come, and asked if I would keep it in confidence and provide you with some guidance along your journey. In the meantime, I have fallen in love with you Zachary. Believe what you will, but I think our meeting was destiny."

"Wow. I have to say I didn't see this coming. I've always known my family was strange, but this is crazy. I do trust you Zelda. I believe in your love and I love you too. This is just so hard to fathom. Now what?"

"Da 'atchet hi give to you be da 'andle hof da haspen wood. Hit be your stay-grr. You need da stay-grr for da pow-her. Wit-hout da stay-grr yous haf no pow-her. Da warriors dem, dey har kill-hers. If you wan find your fad-her, you need da pow-her."

"Is this what my father believes in?"

"He has da stay-grr 'im too."

"But how do I use it? I'm sorry, but this all seems so ridiculous. What does it all mean?"

"Hi tell you, da bes' way hi know to hex-plain his to take you to da warriors hat da sac-hri-fice fi-her. Den maybe you will hunderstand."

"Zelda? What should I do?"

"We could continue looking for your father, but I don't know when we might find him. Cookie and I have certain powers and together we can travel through space. He knows some of the aspen tree warriors and we could take you to them. It will change everything, and this place will not be the same when you return, but you will find the truth about your family, and maybe both your father and your destiny."

"I want to find out where I come from more than anything else. I have built a life for myself that is quite satisfying, but I really don't have anything left here if I can't find my parents, except maybe you Zelda. I guess that's the life of an only child. You will be with me if I go, right?"

"Yes Zachary, I'll be with you."

"Okay then, I've come this far, I guess I should go all the way. Cookie, I think I'm ready to try anything. Take me to the warriors Mister Labrecque."

"Hoh-key, doh-key den. 'Old hon to your stay-grr has tight has you can, han come wit me."

Cookie led Zachary outside as the budding young tree warrior held his hatchet stager with both hands. They walked out onto the grassy clearing in front of the cabin under a starry sky. Zelda followed and stood beside them. Labrecque held his axe above his head with arms extended, paused to focus briefly and then unceremoniously drove the axe head into the ground with both hands. It came pouring back out of the ground surrounded by the glowing lasha: the power of the pine trees under Cookie's command. A large chunk of the ground ripped from the earth and hovered into the air buffered by the sporadic energy of botanic spiritualis.

Zachary sensed an enormous presence swirl into his mind and whisk away the evil spirits. And then he fell unconscious.

Chapter 21: Sacrifice Fire

Ashah pyen.

Zachary felt a breeze caressing his face; his hair ruffling in the brisk zephyr. He opened his eyes. He was on a distant plateau that glowed in shades of pink, purple and blue. The land was brown with patches of green: rolling hills sweeping towards the sky in a seemingly endless patchwork of shadows and hilltops. The silhouette of badland bluffs was on the horizon—Slatterns hidden in the crags. Swirls of dust and dirt danced over peaks and through valleys as the wind howled across the meagre landscape. Tiny shrubs clung to life and shuddered in the subsistent setting. The stunted vegetation was worn from the elements; the hills randomly spotted with stands of scantily dressed, nearly naked trees. Zachary was not surprised to see trembling and quaking aspens. The bare essence of survival was evident in the primitive mood of this place. It reminded Zachary of the prairies.

He was not alone. Gathered around him were people standing in small groups scattered over the rolling terrain and marvelling at generously stacked bonfires. They appeared to be deep in contemplation or meditation; oblivious of their surroundings. Many of them were softly singing a tribal chant that was growing louder. The chants sent a haunting reverberation through Zachary's body. But then a furious spikey bolt of lightning pierced the serenity of the blushing mauve sky and a tremendous roar of thunder filled the gathering like the presence of a powerful god. None of the assembled seemed to acknowledge the lightning, but the chants became louder. Zachary looked up and examined the sky.

There was not any sun, moon or clouds on the horizon; just the overpowering glare of the tinted sky. Another blaze of lightning streaked above and filled the air with a tumultuous blast. People began to encroach in circles around the flames. Zachary moved closer to the bonfire himself, attempting to blend with the crowd, but he realised he was not a member of this exclusive club—at least not yet—observing that everyone was curiously dressed in clothing made from the bark of aspen trees. Another strike of lightning exploded above and the chants increased with all concerned now singing.

"Ashah pyen, ashah pyen, ashah pyen. Ashah ashah ashah, pyen pyen pyen. Ashah pyen, ashah pyen, ashah pyen."

One of the warriors stepped forward and laid a hatchet like Zachary's on top of a pile of wood sticks. The warrior was laying his stager on a stack of many others, and then he stepped back into the crowd. The chanting suddenly stopped. Zachary clenched his hatchet in his hands. Yet another bolt of lightning jaggedly cut across the sky, but this time there was not any thunder; only the yowl of the wind flying above exposed hills. The warrior who stepped forward raised his arms and spoke loudly.

"Ashah Gorb eesah lah don. Laf naga pohsah lashmuh. Don maha naga moobah lah Alka, veebee teelaf traupah laf, seewha zahka."

Zelda was standing just behind Zachary all the while; leaning forward to talk into his ear as she started translating for him.

"The spirit of Gorb is with us. Much has happened since our last sacrifice. We would love to find peace with the Alkae, but their warriors who outnumber us persist with their constant attacks."

"Zelda, you are with me. I knew I could count on you. So, I guess you know their language."

"It's the ancient Druid tree warrior language."

"Don keeno lah nahtoo don bahsygah vohko ashah pyen, naga lohsee sahba meelkah Alka. Veebee, po don dahbid moobah, sylva shahtoo lah pyna Minga. Beelah bohtahna, rah Envrah fahbee don lashmuh. Traupah, nahtoo lasha ashah pyen ahskah snoh, lah nahtoo pyna Minga."

The warriors softly began to chant again when the sacrifice message was finished, while Zelda also finished translating the words.

"We trust and embrace our unrelenting strength in the aspen trees, to fend against the brutal infiltrations of the spruce Alkae warriors. However, now we have hope that the silviculture prophecy will be realised by joining with the pine tree Mingas. Respect the salvation of the tree gods and give thanks to the aspen angel Envrah for being with us here at our sacrifice. Tree warriors, embrace the power of the aspens in the smoke of the fire, and unite with the pine tree warriors."

The chanting continued to rise. Zachary was speechless, absorbing the allure of the ritual and the raw power of the ceremony.

"Ashah ashah ashah, pyen pyen pyen. Ashah pyen, ashah pyen, ashah pyen," they sang in verses.

Meticulously, one by one, knowing without words the parlance of the ritual, the warriors took turns walking into the sparse stands of aspen and cottonwood to accumulate more firewood. Unbeknownst to Zachary the wood included roots that contained rock chlorophyll, which they had piled up before the ceremony. The inventory of wood fibre was stacked on the fires until they were higher than the tallest warriors. Zachary stood there watching the growing intensity of the fire.

All of the stagers were added to the bonfires individually until the last carved branch was placed down on the flames: another surge of lightning magically stroking the sky at the very same moment signifying the act of sacrifice. The ensuing thunder ripped with the force of a departing god to commemorate the precious spiritual wood. Zachary's legs grew weak.

And then it began to rain from a cloudless sky.

The chanting stopped. All of the warriors silently titled their heads back facing the heavens, so to speak, soaking up the cloudless rain. Once again, after brief reflection beside the burning fires, the warriors quietly departed the sacrifice circles solitarily; this time removing branches from living aspen trees. But the branches were not burned. These were shaped into new stagers by carving and moulding the wood. While the instruments of power were fashioned and the sizzling fires were gradually doused by the rain, Cookie Labrecque and another man walked up to Zachary and Zelda.

"Welcum Zachary to da haspen sac-hri-fice. Hi tink maybe yous meet sum-one. Dis 'ere his Hawkins Kingsmere."

"The honour is all mine," said a slightly confused Zachary.

"Hawkins," said Cookie turning to the other man, "Zachary be hof da haspen, but he halso be hof da Steele Minga fam-hilly. An' dis 'ere be Zelda, she be da pine tree wiz-hard frum da marsh."

Hawkins Kingsmere was also a rugged looking man. He was even a bit bigger than Cookie and looked down to Zachary, but he had a mild, unthreatening manner, with long brown hair and a weathered face covered by an overgrown beard tanned a shade of blonde. He spoke in a soft, friendly manner, yet his words carried a convincing tone.

"A Marshlandite of the Minga? I don't get a chance to meet many of your kind," he said to Zelda.

"I'm only too happy to help out the cause," she answered.

"Glad to have you looking out for one of our mixed species hybrids. Hello Zachary, you're in good hands with this young woman. I understand you're looking for Soarfoot."

Zachary swallowed: "I wouldn't mind finding him to learn more about my ancestry, but I'm beginning to see there's a lot more I need to learn."

"You and quite a few people wouldn't mind finding Soarfoot. Many think he has come close to finding the silviculture prophecy in a mixed species such as yourself," speculated Hawkins.

"What exactly is a mixed species and a silviculture prophecy?"

"Why of course, how would you know about that? You are a raw insurgence of energy Zachary. We're happy to have you here. I can teach you much about the power of the trees and the prophecy, which you might actually help fulfil," Hawkins again speculated.

"This is why I encouraged you to come here Zachary. This man Kingsmere has a way of conveying the knowledge of tree warriors. He will be a true friend, because he is one of your kind," declared Zelda.

"Zachary, hi tell you, hi 'ave da pow-her hof da tress, but maudit hi could nev-her hex-plain deez tings. Hawkins 'im, heez be da wise-her han da good teach-her. Hi tink maybe he tell you bet-her 'ow da pow-her hit work," proposed Cookie.

The sacrifice fire was starting to crumble, hiss and smoke from the rain. Hawkins sighed and posed in Zachary's direction.

"The rain gives life to the tress, but that fire, that's the power. You will need that power if you ever want to find Soarfoot. Are you ready to believe in the trees?" surmised Kingsmere.

"When will I get another chance?" quipped Zachary.

"Very good then, why don't you come with me for the remainder of the sacrifice fire."

"What about you Zelda?" asked Zachary.

"My sweet, this is your journey. You must take these steps on your own. Don't worry, I will always be there for you. We will see each other again, just be aware that things will not be the same when you return. We will find each other, I give you my word."

"That's a lot of trust at a time like this, but I guess I've come this far already. Will he have the answers I need?" pondered Zachary with a nod towards Hawkins.

"You're in good hands with a man that old," winked Zelda.

Hawkins smiled in agreement and gestured at a small knoll away from the fire. He started walking up the hill: "This way Zachary."

They climbed the side of the knoll and sat down at the top overlooking the sacrifice fire below. The warriors bowed their heads and surrounded the smouldering fire with newly formed stagers. A mist began to rise and mix with the smoke; filtering through the ceremony. The air smelled fresh and full of new life in the rain, while the scent of the smoking fire rendered the familiarity of power. Hawkins spoke.

"Soarfoot is a great pine tree warrior, one of the greatest in the universe. He is a friend to the aspens and the manifesto of peace which we all fight to preserve, but he has disappeared and we are concerned. The sacrifice fire is for Gorb the god of aspen trees. Envrah, the angel of aspens, brings us the sporadic element on the cosmic wave. Before I tell you more, we must watch and learn. The power of the trees is very near."

And so they watched. The fires soon dwindled to coals and the rain began to pour hard. The sound of the raindrops on the ground could he heard above all else. The wind was silent and the warriors stood motionless. The aspen wood grasped for its last few breaths of life as it hissed under the rain; smoke billowing from the ashes. The nearby trees seemed content in the harsh environment. The silence grew and enveloped Zachary in a state of numbness as he sat watching. It was a distinctively familiar sensation, but it did not frighten him. He sensed a new strength evolving from within.

"Do you have a stager?" asked Hawkins.

"Yes, my hatchet that Labrecque gave to me."

"Hold it in your hands. Close your eyes and concentrate on the rain. Let the power from the water of life flow through your body. You must believe that the trees are speaking to us, always."

Zachary closed his eyes: "I want to believe."

The rain quenched his face. The evil spirits vanished. He was gliding above a placid river, winding through a land clear and brilliant. The trees were immense, rich and healthy; the leaves bold and flowing with warm colours.

"The stager is your weapon and your friend. With it, all is possible. It is your companion and by the grace of Gorb you will aspire to great heights with the power of the trees," professed Hawkins.

"I truly hope you're right. I will take your counsel if only I might find my parents," pleaded Zachary with his eyes still closed.

"I know of your father and his family, they have a history with the tree warriors. I also know of your mother's family. The Storyteller, one of our great aspen warriors, is your mother's great grandfather. We fear he is missing as well as Soarfoot, who might have succumbed to the spruce tree warriors and the evil creed of destruction. Yet we hope they are preparing for a journey to the spiritual world because of the silviculture prophecy. We need the wisdom from our spirit seekers to guide our actions."

"It doesn't sound like it's looking that great for my prospects, to find my family or my ancestors," remarked Zachary.

"No it does not, but it could be the opportunity of a lifetime. According to the silviculture prophecy, the ultimate warrior will come from a mixed species family. The warriors from homeland planets have resounding strength, but it is said that those who are born in galaxies with many strong species could in fact command the sporadic element with an astounding energy. We are encouraged to nourish potential warriors such as you, whose ancestry flows from different tree gods."

"I'm honoured. I didn't quite realise my bloodline was this rich."

"Your stager will show you the way, that and maybe the owls."

"Oh yes, the owls. I do share that vision."

"And that is why you are here. Now open your eyes and behold. The power is here."

The rain stopped. The smoke from all of the sacrifice fires swirled through the valleys in magnificent shapes. All else was still. The aspens were the domain that consumed Zachary.

"You are on Planet Envrah, home of the aspen trees. Long may they flourish, and long live Gorb, the god of the aspens."

Ashah pyen.

Chapter 22: Boreal Nation

The journey to Planet Envrah for Zachary's first aspen sacrifice fire and his return trip back to Earth was routed through spiritual corridors safeguarded by manifesto of peace angels. Cookie Labrecque levitated a small branch ship with Zachary and Zelda onboard; transporting them to the nearby Minga homeland planet of the pine trees, where they met with a courier angel who escorted them through the spiritual corridors for their entire journey.

Courier and sometimes guardian angels are cultivated by the gods from the ancient hybrid species to travel the cosmos and help guide tree warriors over the eons of existence. These angels do not possess the powers of the original fibrous angels, such as commanding lasha and enriching mortal souls with the power of sporadic energy, but they are gifted with botanic spiritualis and able to transcend dimensions in flight. They are also nurtured by the gods and privy to the knowledge of the heavens.

The flight to Envrah is one hundred and fifty-two billion light years from Earth: forty-seven billion light years of the pine tree unisphere, two billion light years of connecting buffer trails to the thirty-two billion light years of the smaller tamarack unisphere, another two billion light years of buffer trails to the fifty-five billion light year expanse of the larger poplar tree unisphere, two billion more light years of buffer trails, and finally across twelve billion light years of the aspen tree unisphere to the homeland planet of Envrah.

The fleetest of arboretum vessels could make the trip to reach Planet Envrah in just over half an Earth year, and an average tree warrior on a branch ship would require the equivalent of over six hundred Earth days, providing there were no complications, and about three-and-a-half Earth years to make the complete return trip. The entire flight would require over three centuries for the conventional mechanised interstellar vessels of the era, but none had actually attempted such a voyage during that space of time.

The angels are able to circumvent this time by travelling through the spiritual corridors—transporting Zachary, Zelda and Cookie to Envrah in a matter of a few hours—however the amount of time evaded through the spiritual habitat was a considerable lapse of time transpired in the organic habitat. Zachary had no idea what to expect upon his return to Earth. The amount of time he lost to his home planet while attending the sacrifice fire was three hundred and forty-seven years.

❖ ❖ ❖

Planet Earth was experiencing the initial stages of an historic transformation by the year 2336—politically and environmentally. The exhaustion of unrenewable resources, in particular the burning of fossil fuels, was compromising the stability of the environment and having an adverse effect on the social structures of humanity. The dominance of capitalism, materialism and the invariable decadence of the wealth gap had sent the entire civilisation of the planet into a detrimental tailspin; depleting natural resources in a senseless rage, while contributing to the suffering of all lifeforms including flora, fauna and humanoids struggling in poverty.

The twentieth and twenty-first centuries on Earth were both a marvel and an indulgence of modern technological invention; vastly enhancing the standard of living for developed nations and the luxuries of cultural and recreational pursuits for the more wealthy segments of the population. However, an excessive and ludicrous preoccupation to consume and indulge was also disgracefully altering the delicate balance of the natural environment and tragically accommodating overpopulation in economically unstable areas.

This was only the beginning of serious environmental and cultural fluctuations; eventually resulting in horrific natural disasters and constant social conflict. It was an era of discovery and scientific innovation for the planet and the humanoids had yet to devise a more sustainable and generous approach to managing their resources and inventions.

The human consumption of planetary resources on Earth continued throughout the twenty-second and twenty-third centuries, until the ecological, meteorological and seismological symptoms of environmental degradation had become completely unavoidable in the twenty-fourth century: global warming from the greenhouse effect of increased carbon dioxide and methane levels along with dwindling worldwide forested lands, air and water pollution from the accumulation of toxic industrial emissions and effluent, and geological instability from melting glacier ice and the extraction of fossil fuels. A rise in mean temperatures from the greenhouse effect was taking its toll on human populations and ecosystems between the forty-degree latitude parallels of the planet north and south; with extreme heat throughout the southern European and Asian continents, Africa, Australia, most of South America, Central America and the southern two-thirds of the United States of America.

The summer temperatures in these regions had reached an average of 135 degrees Fahrenheit, or near 60 degrees Celsius, while only cooling to an average of 100 Fahrenheit or 38 Celsius for two or three months in the seasonal cycle. The world's major mountain ranges at high altitude and the regions from the fortieth parallels north and south to the Arctic and Antarctic Circles experienced summer heat up to 120 Fahrenheit or 50 Celsius, with mild winters rarely going below freezing temperatures except at the higher elevations. The polar regions, once completely inhospitable with sub-zero temperatures in the winter months, now only dipped slightly below freezing.

The torrid heat was leading to an unbearable climate and creating uninhabitable terrain, with either dry conditions from the expansion of desert lands and severe drought in many geographic areas, or humid conditions from the flooding of coastal plains and watershed basins. The arid climate and chronic drought were predominant in Africa's Ethiopian Highlands and the African Sahara, Kalahari and Namib Deserts, the Arabian Peninsula, the entire Eurasian Steppe belt extending from the Black Sea across continental Asia to the Pacific coast, the Tarim Basin and Gobi Desert in central Asia, most of western Australia, and the foothills, badlands and prairie regions of the Americas bordering the Andes, Sierra Madre and Rocky Mountains.

The global heat was also melting Earth's polar and glacial ice at a rapid rate, resulting in a gradual rise of sea levels and constant flooding from rivers fed by glaciers; causing frequent landslides in mountainous terrain, surging floodplains along rivers affecting many large urban areas, and the erosion of shoreline across the planet forcing major coastal cities to build massive berms and dykes, construct floatation infrastructure or relocate inland. Mounting water levels were occurring mainly along coastal lowland plains and primary drainage basins flowing into the oceans, including the most significantly populated and politically powerful areas of the planet: the eastern and southern seaboard of the

United States, the Mississippi basin, parts of the Californian and northwest Pacific coast, some of Alaska and northern Canada, and the Great Lakes waterway; all of the shoreline along the North European Plain except for the Scandinavian peninsula; Russia's entire Arctic coast and Siberian Plains including the river basins of the Yenisei, Ob and Lena; the Chinese coast especially the Great Basin of the Yellow Sea, the Huang He (Yellow River) and the major river valleys of the Yangtze and Amur; and a large portion of the Japanese Pacific seaboard.

Meanwhile, significant shoreline infringement was taking place in Africa's major coastal river basins of the Nile, Congo and Niger, the Arabian Mesopotamia delta at Shatt al-Arab and the Euphrates-Tigris river system, southern Asia's Indian Ocean shoreline river watersheds of the Mekong, Indus, Salween and the confluence of Brahmaputra and Ganges, Australia's northern coast and its south central waterways, and South America's Amazon and Pampas basins with the associated coastal lowlands of the Parana River at Rio de la Plata, and the watersheds of Tocantins River, Rio Sao Francisco and of course Amazon River.

The frequency and severity of hurricanes, typhoons and thunderstorms were also picking up pace and becoming utterly unpredictable; inflicting constant damage to structures and taking many human lives. Earthquakes, tsunamis and sinkhole collapsing were becoming more numerous as well—due to melting glaciers, the overwhelming amount of drilling for fossil fuels and natural gas, tunnelling for minerals and the inaugural excavations for permanent underground cities to escape the killing heat—exacerbating the chaos of natural disasters for people and property. Pollutants were spreading throughout the planet via waterways and air currents; from roaring factory furnaces and sewage, internal combustion engines, agricultural practices and leakage from collateral damage to industrial facilities, including nuclear power plants.

The pollution was beginning to drastically affect wildlife, vegetation and forests, particularly in ocean estuaries, freshwater wetlands and melting polar regions, as well as the planet's once dense tropical jungles; testing the resilience of nature's plants, animals and ecosystems. The climatic changes were also diminishing clean oxygen levels with an influence on natural regeneration cycles of forests; prompting a surge in perpetual wildfires and infestations of insects, moulds and other biological contaminants.

The jungles of South and Central America, Africa and southern Asia were being hit hard; making the boreal forest of northern Canada and Russia all the more important for its cache of carbon, oxygenating fibre and the world's largest supply of freshwater preserved mainly in northern Canadian lakes and Lake Baikal in southern Russia.

Regional populations on Earth were suffering from rampant dehydration, heat exhaustion and stroke, widespread starvation and pestilence from unhygienic conditions, while food crop production in the world's bread belt areas was slowly being wiped out except for some genetically designed varieties of edible plants that were coveted and closely controlled for distribution. A marshal state of affairs was growing in many countries as people began to engage in warfare to fight for the food of survival.

❖ ❖ ❖

The degradation of the planet also changed the political landscape. Monetary accumulation and control of crumbling government infrastructure were gradually losing their advantage with limited resources available; environmental and economic sustainability were becoming the valued commodities of privileged purchasing power, especially the inland reserves of the planet's drinking water. The impending environmental catastrophe on Planet Earth paradoxically spurned an environmental revolution in world politics.

A new nation—one that did not exist when Zachary departed into the distant cosmos—was becoming the most influential democratic state in the global affairs of Planet Earth. A political movement, subtle at first but quickly gaining momentum, was forged in Alaska of the United States and northern Canada during the early twenty-third century.

It was still an era of resource gluttony, commerce and economic growth, as developed nations were under pressure to keep their populations employed; further feeding the extravagance of wealthy corporate shareholders, who were the real perpetrators determining membership in privileged society. Two democratic elections were the pivotal footholds for a new political revolution: Tuyl Reynolds as the Governor of Alaska, a distant relative of Zachary Steele's family, and Cassandra Kabor as the Green Party Premier of British Columbia in the Canadian province, the daughter of Brabeen Kabor and Anna Rhomany, also a relative of Zachary's.

It is said these two politicians possessed certain spiritual connections, but more importantly at that time and space, they could see the environmental and social implications of the demand on planetary resources. Governor Tuyl Reynolds and Premier Cassandra Kabor were both frustrated with the imperialistic regimes of their national governments; exploiting the resources of the northern frontier without capitulating any decision-making authority from the hands of the populous south. The two leaders gravely acknowledged the greenhouse effect on the planet and the subsequent global warming settling into the ecological equation; together forming a visionary democratic framework which would serve the future viability of the planet.

Governor Reynolds, first elected in the year 2202, was very much a dedicated capitalist but not an obedient patriot. He wanted more control over the natural resources being pumped out of the Alaskan state; taking counsel from the environmentally responsible socio-economic engine, ironically being ignited in British Columbia by Premier Kabor's Green Party.

Cassandra Kabor was first elected as one of six Green Party members in the legislative assembly for the provincial election of the year 2199. She had been nominated in the northern Skeena riding of the province, and after her victory in the spring she was elected leader of the party at an autumn convention later that year, based on a platform of economic joint ventures with government and the private sector to develop environmental technology.

The following year she pushed her party's executive to move more towards the centre of the political spectrum on social policy and went on a world tour to discuss environmental economics with influential nations such as the Scandinavian countries, Russia, China, Britain and even a visit to the United States capital of Washington, District of Columbia.

The minority government in British Columbia only lasted eighteen months, forcing another provincial election at the turn of the century in the fall of 2200, with the Green Party landing an impressive twenty-two seats in the legislature as the official opposition in a Liberal Party small majority government.

Kabor lobbied the government to launch a policy task force on environmental technology in the intervening four years, and built her party's platform on the 'five pistons of an environmentally responsible engine'. The Green Pistons, as they were publicised, included economic joint ventures to generate private sector income and public funds for essential services, development of the environmental technology and alternative energy sectors, comprehensive health care and education, elimination of the wealth gap through a new taxation regime based on increased government revenues, and the end of corruption by reorganising the provincial bureaucracy.

The Green Party diatribe and solid character of its leader—well educated, charming and attractive, not a radical but composed, confident, calculated and focused—were an instant hit with the people of British Columbia, ushering Cassandra Kabor to the office of premier after a shocking political victory in the provincial election of 2205.

Premier Kabor aggressively moved on her election platform, immediately phasing in strict pollution controls for industry but accompanying the regulations with a generously funded research program on environmental technology for air and water pollution, as well as alternative energy power generation.

The government went on to negotiate its first joint ventures in aquaculture, hydroponic food production, cannabis and hemp farming, while launching strategies on forestry, small business development, advanced education and scientific research grants, health care regulations, indigenous affairs and guaranteed income for the agri-food industry. The premier continued her world tour promoting environmental technology, initiated construction of new water filtration, disposal and recycling infrastructure, and announced the first of its mega ventures—construction of a Vancouver factory to produce "Acid Emission Purifiers (AEPs)," a technology developed in partnership with Swedish and Norwegian companies.

This surprisingly industrious socially leaning government secured some key economic ventures in its second year of office, in the form of new joint enterprises or expansion of existing companies, including the manufacturing of collapsible rigid seaworthy boats, pre-fabricated log homes, fish and seafood products, hydroponic fruits and vegetables, and electronic computer components. Environmental management consulting and advanced remote sensing technology, artisan sales, publishing and entertainment production were also encouraged by large tax breaks, and a wilderness tourism conglomerate was formed with the state of Alaska.

The new government was off to a sparkling start in the face of growing international crises, but the most impressive initiatives were yet to come. British Columbia announced two more mega ventures and five substantial alternative energy projects to begin in the years 2207 and 2208. The SAVs and FAVs venture involved a partnership with Alaska to build two sprawling shipyards;

one on the Pacific coast in the Alaskan capital city of Juneau to produce "Saltwater Anti-Pollutant Vessels," and one on the Skeena River in Kabor's hometown of Terrace to produce "Freshwater Anti-Pollutant Vessels." These ships carried the most advanced technological developments to filter, dilute, dredge and oxygenate all planetary waterways, with the ability to respond to major spills of pollutants in oceans, inlets, sea bays, lakes and rivers.

The unique joint venture between an American state and Canadian province was not unprecedented, but its success was certainly a premonition of the environmental and social revolution intensifying over the next several decades. The SAVs and FAVs were employed by multi-national energy companies at a cost of millions of currencies for the government coffers, while international jurisdictions would slowly accept the need for environmental regulations and turn to these technological developments for deployment.

The third mega venture announced later in 2207 was the construction of manufacturing plants in the northern town of Prince George and the capital city of Victoria for the production of super charged high capacity regulating industrial battery cells. The "Green Power Cells" were used in the designs of the energy power plants also announced by the government and were soon in great demand worldwide. This venture attracted capital investments from Californian, Alaskan and Asian interests, soon to become a lucrative project for British Columbia.

The five energy production projects integrated solar radiation, tidal currents, algae fuel, wind power (my favourite) and a molten salt nuclear reactor site for the province, the latter in spite of concerns from Green Party hardliners. The solar energy initiative constructed panel arrays covering multiple hectares of cultivated fields in the Okanagan and Shuswap valleys of British Columbia's interior, producing both electricity and root crops like potatoes, garlic, assorted vegetables and ginseng.

Tidal power stations were erected off the west coast of Vancouver Island and the Haida Gwaii Islands archipelago, algae pools and a refinement plant were constructed along the Fraser River near the city of Vancouver, small individual windmill water pumps were assembled on Moresby Island and distributed to First Nation communities in Canada as well as sold overseas to developing nations, and an international joint-venture molten salt nuclear station was built near the Stikine River on the border with Alaska to provide power for northern communities because of its proximity.

The feverish economy was prevalent in British Columbia with a considerable public monetary deficit to begin the first Green Party term, but sales from joint venture projects began to generate considerable revenue as products reached the marketplace in early 2208. Premier Kabor strategically called the next provincial election after four-and-a-half years of a majority government in the fall of 2209; enough time for revenues to build and put British Columbia in a stable fiscal position.

The results of the election were extremely encouraging as the Green Party won an even stronger majority. The second term for Kabor saw the province's joint ventures flourish and completion of the alternative energy projects; bringing surplus electrical capacity onto the provincial power grid. The success of her government allowed Kabor to concentrate on the party's agenda of social justice and equality, as well as federal and international lobbying for environmental regulations to subside the effects of global warming and toxic contamination.

This is when the gears started a perpetual motion in Governor Reynolds' political ambitions. The Alaskan head of state calculated the returns being generated by the environmental technology he had invested into and took note of the inevitable worldwide abatement programs that would be needed to preserve planetary resources. Reynolds, who already had a shaky relationship with Washington DC, began to take a hard stance on pollution controls and taxation of the resource sectors, even though his state was profiting from both the industrial and environmental activities.

The Green Party enjoyed one of the world's most successful economies and highest standard of living over the four years of its second term in British Columbia. It was a slight oxymoron for an environmental social democratic government to enjoy such economic prosperity; a situation that attracted positive international attention, but also endured ongoing criticism from the Green Party far left socialist national executive who contended that the economic activity was contributing to the environmental stress the party was trying to prevent.

Nevertheless, Kabor's provincial government was rewarded for its revolutionary accomplishments and elected to a third majority in the year 2213. Premier Kabor continued with her progressive economic policy over the next four years in spite of national party objections, but was perhaps most proud of the social policy initiatives finalised by the end of her third term in office. The government provided publicly funded services for all residents of the province, including health care and all medications, eliminating the need for additional insurance and medicare plans, post-secondary education up to six-year master's programs, province-wide child day-care programs, a guaranteed income structure for all farmers and fisheries workers, and a framework agreement with the federal government to make all indigenous authorities autonomous jurisdictions, allowing them to benefit from provincial services.

The premier campaigned for another election in 2217 on her government's impeccable economic record and a platform of complete self-sufficiency for the province, which she felt could be extended to the global theatre. The nature of the province's joint ventures was not only that public money invested into private commercial enterprises provided a capital return, but also that private companies were managing some public services with great efficiency. This helped fulfil the Green Party campaign promise of cleaning up corruption and incompetence in the provincial bureaucracy, and would lead to the widespread practice of granting service contracts to the private sector under the supervision of significantly smaller government offices.

The Green Party was elected to its fourth term with the most convincing majority government in provincial history, winning all of the seats in the legislative assembly. Cassandra Kabor's international popularity was reaching rambunctious heights; labelled by the western world media as 'the most enterprising social democratic entrepreneur' of the twenty-third century, which of course wasn't saying much since they were only seventeen years into the new century. Kabor was about to ride the wave of her new popularity into the historic journals that I have been composing, but first she had to strike an ironclad and clandestine failsafe deal.

She knew her methodology for eliminating the wealth gap and amending taxation laws was much too radical coming from only the premier of a Canadian province, and she was also genuinely upset with the reluctance of world leaders to halt the commercial and industrial practices that were quickly bringing the planet to its environmental knees. She was going to need a bigger platform.

Premier Kabor announced the largest surplus in British Columbia's history at the tabling of the provincial budget in the spring of 2218, with Alaskan Governor Tuyl Reynolds by her side as a guest in the legislature. Reynolds, who was campaigning for his fifth term in office later that year, was visiting Victoria to congratulate the premier on her victory and presumably gloat over the revenues for his state. The prestigious gubernatorial visit also included a two-day tour to the town of Tofino on Vancouver Island's west coast, to inspect offshore tidal power stations.

The two politicians were able to enjoy excluded privacy in Tofino; staying in the same exquisite oceanfront hotel. The media was buzzing later that week and Tuyl Reynolds had every intention of getting naked with Kabor; that is, until he was informed by Cassandra they were actually blood relatives. Kabor chose not to mention she had been advised by ancient hybrid species, and that she was able to meditate into the spiritual flight of aspen trees, and that Tuyl's ancestors possessed the spirituality of pine trees.

The rest suites me fine.

There that night, with the ocean waves smashing against the glass wall of the hotel, Cassandra Kabor entered the realm of empire building. But she waited until later that year, just after Reynolds was re-elected for the fifth time, to hold a news conference on the steps of the provincial legislature.

The Premier of British Columbia, with a failsafe deal tucked in her hemp purse, announced to the province, Canada and the world that she was leaving provincial politics. She had served the people of British Columbia with honour and passion, proud of her accomplishments and contributions, she said during a live broadcast that received international coverage, and now it was time for her to embark on a new challenge; to help spread the ideas and build the foundation for an environmental and social revolution. There is a better way, she ranted, a more viable path to social liberty, equality and prosperity for everyone.

It was widely rumoured that Kabor would gravitate to her party's national leadership, yet once again she surprised everyone. She would tone down the rhetoric and campaign on her solid record of governance; but instead of the Green Party, at the risk of alienating her electoral support, Kabor announced she was creating a new federal political entity called the Boreal Party of Canada.

Kabor did not believe the Green Party national executive could handle the federal campaign she was scripting. She had given herself approximately two years until the next federal election to build a national network and recruit enough candidates to fill a complete slate. She instantly began to publicise her agenda as the president of the new party until she was elected leader in only one year's time, thanks to a political platform already written and quickly published. The Boreal Freeborne Revolution, which highlighted the success of British Columbia's economy, was built on the 'strong northern values' of a dedicated work ethic, social liberty, equality for all citizens and freedom from exploitation;

with the ideologies of environmental stewardship and economic sustainability through scientific innovation and prudent resource management for a fair and respectful society.

The Freeborne platform was portrayed as the directions in a circle of power, with economic vibrancy in the north, environmental technology and alternative energy to the east, health care and education in the south, fiscal responsibility and equality to the west, and integrity in government as the centre of power. Kabor had the support of some key political and financial sources, including established entrepreneurs in British Columbia and the provinces of Alberta, Saskatchewan and northern Ontario, and even the states of California and Alaska, as well as her fellow premiers from the western Canadian provinces and the American governors of California, Oregon, Washington and of course Alaska.

The Boreal Party, with endorsements from these influential figures, proposed not only a strong environmental technology sector with continued exportation of products and services, but also joint ventures in agricultural hydroponics, offshore and inland aquaculture, composite forestry and mineral products, iron ore production with advanced smelter technology, a revamped ship building industry, a controversial but enticing plan to process and export freshwater supplies in newly designed and fabricated ocean tankers, and a huge solar power project for the taiga and boreal shield regions of the country augmented by bolstered production of industrial battery cells.

The party also called for free post-secondary education and childcare with public funding, guaranteed income for the agricultural sector, creation of a large pharmaceutical joint venture corporation, and the proposed integration of autonomous indigenous communities within the confederacy of Canada.

The popular vote of the party turned out to be good for ninety-seven of the four-hundred-and-one seats in the Canadian House of Commons during the federal election of 2220, making the Boreal Party the official opposition to the Conservative Party two-hundred-twelve seat majority government, ahead of the Liberals with sixty-two seats and Democrats with twenty-six seats, who had adopted the American party name, and stealing away all but four of the Green Party's twenty-seven ridings from the previous election.

The Freeborne Revolution definitely propelled itself on an overnight political rocket ride, attracting many sentiments and votes from the northern and rural ridings of Canada: winning twenty-four of the one-hundred-forty-one seats in the largest province of Ontario, mainly in northern electoral ridings, twelve seats in northern Alberta, another ten ridings from northern Saskatchewan and Manitoba, six of Newfoundland and Labrador's ten electoral seats, but only five northern ridings of Quebec's ninety seats and completely shut out of the thirty-five ridings in the Maritime provinces, while scoring its greatest victory with forty of the forty-seven seats in the province of British Columbia including urban seats in Vancouver.

Unfortunately for the party, the Vancouver base was the only source of major urban votes; more support from the large Canadian cities was critical to this political movement. Fortunately for the party, the Conservative government was floundering with its electoral stronghold and a series of natural disasters from environmental side effects were bombarding world politics with strife and fear.

The escalation of global warming and natural disasters, especially the growing devastation to the shorelines of United States, Europe and China from swelling ocean levels, hurricanes, typhoons and persistent lightning strikes, as well as worldwide destruction from repeated earthquakes and the loss of food production from heat and drought, were beginning to strain the cohesiveness of democracy on Earth in the early decades of the twenty-third century.

The moment was ripe for a feisty female professional politician; Kabor seized the opportunity for the next four-plus years by attacking the presiding federal government while offering the alternatives of her political platform, preaching environmental sustainability and national self-sufficiency, and promising to overhaul a dysfunctional federal bureaucracy.

The Canadian public turned to a more hopeful and reassuring message in the 2225 general election; voting the Boreal Party into power with a majority government of two-hundred-twenty-five seats in the federal parliament. Prime Minister Kabor became the first national leader to form a government in Canada without the greater share of votes in most of the largest urban centres; gaining the political support of Canada's western provinces by winning all but ten of the one-hundred-twenty seats available, and although still not making significant headway into all of eastern Canada with only twenty electoral victories in Quebec and the Maritimes, managing to win all ten ridings in Newfoundland and Labrador and a crucial eighty-five seats in Ontario excluding the concentrated urban ridings around the country's largest city of Toronto.

The lack of support in the highly populated cities of Canada—Toronto, Montreal, Calgary and the capital city of Ottawa, where most of the privileged and wealthy were converged—was a theme that would reoccur over this provocative time in the nation's history. There were several attempts from financial leaders and powerful aristocrats to politically sabotage the fledgling Boreal Freeborne Revolution, as financiers from California, Alaska and northern Canada battled with the Canadian and American corporate elite, particularly from the energy, mining, automotive, pharmaceutical and finance sectors. They fought over the prime minister's plans to establish alternative industry economic joint ventures and fund the gigantic undertaking of a nationwide solar energy project, not to mention reorganise the federal bureaucracy. Injunctions and lawsuits were filed in the courts against new federal regulations, but a determined prime minister soldiered on and managed to start some of the joint ventures that profited existing resource corporations.

Kabor also expanded the production capacity for AEPs, SAVs and FAVs, as well as industrial battery cells which were now called "Freeborne Power Cells" because of a 'green' copyright infringement. The tax revenues from these enterprises partially balanced the public investment necessary to initiate the solar power network and kept the country at a small deficit in comparison to most other nations on the planet.

The environmental technology sector was ramping up, mineral, forestry and agri-food ventures were underway, and construction of solar panel arrays was initiated in the northern territories of the country, western provinces, Ontario, Quebec and Labrador within the four years of the Boreal Party's first term in office. Continual obstructions to the government's plans from the established corporate sector were time consuming and expensive, but Canada was already doing better than several previous years of administration. The federal election of 2229 gave the Boreal Party another reasonable majority government with two-hundred-forty-seven Members of Parliament, yet Kabor knew she needed a more extravagant impact to meet her objectives.

The party continued its environmental initiatives and secured the remainder of its joint ventures including new iron ore factories that exported steel products and supported a revitalised ship building sector; also used to manufacture ocean liners for exporting drinking water from a terminus constructed in Labrador. The government also moved forward on the installation of the world's largest solar power array complete with the associated production and international sales of Freeborne Power Cells. The new revolution was progressing well environmentally and economically in its second consecutive term of office.

Prime Minister Kabor and the Freeborne Revolution unveiled the 'planetary phase' of their federal agenda leading up to the next general election in the year 2233; elaborating on the party's platform with the proposition of a Canadian transportation conglomerate which would develop Freeborne Power Cell electrical hover propulsion for ground vehicles, water transport and new aircraft.

The joint venture would manufacture a comprehensive line of hovercrafts: automobiles, semi-tractor trailer rigs, boats and new airborne hovercopters, as well as public transit vehicles and oceangoing ships, freight and passenger flights, along with tourism treks and cruises for northern Canada, Alaska and Scandinavian countries. The venture would also help to fuel a new Canadian national interstellar exploration program—heady stuff indeed. The Boreal piece de resistance, catering to emotional voters, was a much-fortified national armed forces to facilitate core government services and provide world class national defence in trying times.

The political ploys hit the mark; Canadians handed Kabor an overwhelming majority for a third term. The 2233 election was one of the defining moments in Cassandra Kabor's political career on Earth: the Boreal Party was re-elected under temperamental conditions, with candidates victorious in three hundred thirty-six electoral ridings of Canada, only losing out on sixty-five seats mainly in Montreal and Quebec, the national capital area of Ottawa and a handful of seats in Calgary and Toronto.

The momentum of the public mandate for the Boreal Party was irrefutable. Canada was feeling the incipient buzz already quite evident in British Columbia: nations of the world were adopting new environmental measures and importing Canadian technology, social policy and taxation reform legislation was introduced in parliament, and the latest construction of new factories was underway to begin production of hovercraft ground vehicles and water vessels.

However, the hardcore capitalists and aristocrats would not capitulate. They pulled every favouritism from the cracks of well lubricated affluence to obstruct the progress of this new revolution. It was their undoing. The aggressive power struggle indubitably forced the hand of the prime minister; it was time to pull political favour out of her hemp purse. The presiding Prime Minister of Canada and Governor of Alaska had entered politics at tender young ages; Kabor first elected at only twenty-six years-old and Reynolds at thirty years of age. They still had plenty of energy, Cassandra just turning sixty and Tuyl sixty-one, and it was time to finish the job they had started.

Governor Reynolds was becoming a folklore legend in Alaska; amazingly elected to his ninth straight term in the year 2234. He was ready to stamp the ultimate legacy on his career and give the Alaskan people the independence they wanted, and Kabor needed his clout to sway the political tide of history. The prime minister went on the offensive in Canada; citing the economic growth and sustainable industry she had orchestrated in nine years of power, as well as her influence on the environmental politics of the planet. The Alaskan governor announced he would honour his election promise after repeated attempts to regulate the resource industry in his state: simultaneously petitioning the American and Canadian governments with a statement of intention to secede from the union of the United States, signed and verified by over ninety percent of the state population, and a proposition of constitutional inclusion with the northern territories of Canada attached to a conditional statutory declaration of independence.

The clandestine agreement proved to be ironclad after all, and once again Cassandra Kabor shocked the world. An excerpt of a speech she delivered from the floor of the Canadian House of Commons, follows as such:

"Thank you Mr Speaker, Monsieur President, honourable members and fellow Canadians. I rise in the house today, only to sink with a heavy heart. I regret to inform this house, my fellow Members of Parliament and the citizens of this country, that the government of the day, at the urging of our loyal constituents, is progressing with drastic measures to address a chronic dilemma plaguing not only Canada but our entire planet. I have stated for the record several times Mr Speaker, as a paid subscriber of this existence we call humanity, that our planet is on the brink of destruction. Planet Earth is in pain and we have abused its resources, all in the name of greed and gluttony, decadence and extravagance. We are truly at risk of driving ourselves into extinction if we do not learn to respect the delicate balance of the natural environment.

"We began in this era of the technology revolution with wondrous scientific breakthroughs and compassionate ideologies, nurturing humankind and fostering an amazing quality of life across our planet, only further enhancing our intellectual capacity. Yet for some reason Mr Speaker, we have neglected our responsibilities in a global village and we are now ignoring the obvious signs of environmental degradation on our planet. We now use technology, sometimes for legitimate scientific innovation making a responsible contribution to our quest for knowledge, but all too often Mr Speaker, we use our technological inventions solely for the purpose of consumption, profit and the accumulation of wealth. We have chosen to dig ourselves into a grave of toxic chemicals in the sweltering heat from ecological travesties on this planet.

"This is not justice and equality for the conscientious individuals making a dedicated effort to create a free society and a reasonable standard of living for all of Earth's inhabitants: our courageous and honourable citizens must be treated fairly. And more importantly, we must preserve the balance of nature, not only for our own survival, but also as stewards of this planet for the future generations of our children.

"Alas Mr Speaker, these words that have been reiterated for what seems like time immemorial are still dismissed by the privileged as the crazed banter of radical elements. I am not radical Mr Speaker; I think that is quite evident by the performance of my government. I want to survive, and my government wants to empower our nation with the tools to salvage our environment and its natural resources. This incessant indulgence in our resources and the resulting pollution must stop: it is obscene. Technology and capitalism are not evil, they simply must evolve in parallel with nature instead of against the environment, with a fair and reasonable return for valuable contributions that enrich our future viability. This government has made every effort Mr Speaker, introducing new programs and projects, providing the established corporate sector with ample opportunities to join our fight for survival, but the reluctance to adopt alternative industrial practices has become unacceptable to our constituents of northern Canada.

"We have been exploited for far too long Mr Speaker, and I speak for the people of the true north, because I have spoken with them, face-to-face, over and over, and they all tell me the same thing. It is time for a new revolution; it is time for the Freeborne movement to take real action. Mr Speaker, this is not an easy nor casual task that I have hesitantly accepted. This government continues to work at keeping our nation strong and healthy. We have acknowledged the impending natural catastrophes that are already besieging our planet, and we have initiated a new resource management approach that is necessary for both environmental survival and economic prosperity. We do not want to tear this country apart, Mr Speaker, we want to keep it alive. Our constituents vehemently believe the only path to realising our policy of environmental sustainability and responsible resource development, is either with the cooperation of conventional industry and the power base of Canada's southern urban centres, and American influence as well for that matter, or as an independent jurisdiction, with the ability to revolutionise the very structure of our nation.

"And so, we are left with no choice but to introduce new legislation today. Bill C-47, Mr Speaker, proclaims a national plebiscite on the constitutional independence for certain proposed geographically defined northern regions within the Dominion of Canada.

"This legislated decree will be conducted responsibly and legally; respectful of the decision made by Canadian citizens. I emphasise to our constituents in the southern urban areas of the country, Mr Speaker, that this does not necessarily mean the demise of their nation, but instead could very well be the mechanism needed to resurrect Canada and perhaps all nations of the world. Canada will not be losing a country, but potentially gaining a new friendly neighbour, and irrespective of the outcome for this plebiscite, an undeniably bold statement will be made to the entire world."

-Right Honourable Cassandra Kabor,
Prime Minister of Canada, 20 November 2234

Prime Minister Kabor felt she was left with no other alternative; the far majority of new capital spending took place in the northern regions of the country, but she did not want to enhance public funding of the combined national forces only to see her investment remain with the entrenched bourgeoisie, so to speak. And so, Cassandra went to the people. She put it all on the line; really left it out there and all those melodramatic metaphors, slurs and innuendoes, so to speak. The Canadian government of the day and the Governor of Alaska Tuyl Reynolds officially legislated an internationally recognised plebiscite for 20 March 2235, which was amended by Quebec and then submitted to the United Nations International Court of Justice.

The referendum process resulted in one question for Quebec residents, one for all citizens in Alaska and Canada north of a defined boundary, and one to all Canadians south of the same boundary: from the mouth of the Skeena River on the Pacific coast, across British Columbia on the Yellowhead Highway to Prince George, along the Fraser River to the Rocky Mountain Alberta border and the source of the Athabasca River, following that waterway to the town of Athabasca and then east on Highway 55 to Beaver River and the Saskatchewan provincial border, south to Highway 3 and then east again staying north of Prince Albert to the confluence of the North and South Saskatchewan Rivers all the way to Lake

Winnipeg in Manitoba, south to the mouth of the Winnipeg and English River systems and east to the height of land separating the Arctic and Atlantic watersheds just north of Lake Nipigon, across Ontario and Quebec along the Arctic drainage basin to the Labrador border, and including both Labrador and Newfoundland in the defined northern territory.

The Boreal referendum proposed the creation of a new independent territorial democratic nation consisting of geographically defined districts and municipalities according to the boundary lines set out for the plebiscite. The state of Alaska would also need a subsequent democratic proclamation to dissolve its relationship with the government of United States.

The referendum to Canadian citizens south of the proposed boundary line presented the question of remaining a unified nation if the Boreal plebiscite and submission to the United Nations was enshrined with the delegation of constitutional authority.

The Quebec referendum was fundamentally the repetition of historical attempts to create a sovereign nation within Canada, with the question of constitutionally declaring independence or remaining in Canada, regardless of the outcome on the northern territory.

The northern vote in Alaska and across Canada was more than resounding; ninety-five percent of all citizens in favour of a new democratic nation. The southern vote was not as decisive, with the four western provinces rejecting a unified Canadian nation in the event of northern separation, and eastern Canada voting to remain unified, both with only small margins of consensus. The interpretation of the Quebec vote was debated extensively over the following months; a slim majority was in favour of sovereignty, and the provincial government argued that a sovereign nation included the northern region of the province, especially the hydro-electric power stations. This was disputed by the northern residents in the province who voted in favour of forming a new territorial nation and against Quebec sovereignty by a much larger majority.

The Kabor government immediately engaged in negotiations with Quebec once the aftermath of the plebiscite was analysed across the country and in the United States; crafting a lifetime binding jurisdictional contract agreement in the fall of that year, allowing the province to maintain ownership of the hydro-electric utility and retain control over power generation and revenues, but only under the environmental regulations of any new democratic nation. The hydro sites would continue to be the source of conflict and even civil war as covert militia from Labrador and the former region of northern Quebec made several attempts over the years to seize control of the utility network.

The negotiations, amendments, legally binding agreements and internationally recognised declarations surrounding this historical nation building exercise would be prolonged over the next several decades, but Cassandra Kabor and the Boreal Party had put the blueprint into action; introducing new legislation within months of the plebiscite, as did Tuyl Reynolds in Alaska. The Canadian federal government granted the new geographically defined northern territory complete autonomy pending acceptance by the United Nations; tabling, debating and voting on new legislation in Canada's parliament through the required three readings in the House of Commons and the Senate, and attaining royal assent exactly one year after the plebiscite on 20 March 2236.

The state of Alaska had to take a slightly different path, filing a submission with the United Nations Security Council to force the American federal government into relinquishing all fiduciary obligations in the union agreement between the state and the republic. The next step was to legally proclaim constitutional independence for the new northern territory in Canada and Alaska; drafting an official constitution, issuing another plebiscite requiring over ninety percent approval and organising the first national democratic election.

A constitution for the "Boreal Democratic Nation" was already prepared by Kabor, of course, complete with a national administration comprised of a legislature, an assembly, premier's head-of-state office and national executive, a total of twelve nation state districts divided into one hundred forty-two electoral boundaries which also formed municipalities, plus a premier's seat in the legislature, and a national government structure entrenched into law which could only be amended with another referendum and agreement by all electoral districts, consisting of government operations, government services and economic development national cabinet committees; each organised into five secretariats, two additional agencies and three government commissions, including an interstellar exploration program.

Kabor was still the prime minister by law for another two years. She used that time to set consultations into motion for a review of the new constitution, amendments to the Canada Elections Act, political options for the remaining provinces, and future bilateral relations between the Canadian government and Boreal Nation. Although she was seen as a separatist by some Canadians, many people believed in her message and still held hope for a prosperous Canada with

Boreal Nation, while others feared the wrath of natural disasters and the demise of the Canadian confederation; commencing a partial exodus from the southern border with the United States to the northern territory before the upcoming constitutional vote.

The Boreal Party did not want to risk any undermining of the vote, but also wanted to resolve administrative details with the existing federal government, provincial authorities and the largest boundary municipalities of Prince George in British Columbia, Prince Albert in Saskatchewan and Timmins in Ontario; the remainder of the boundary line only sparsely populated. Governor Reynolds, although facing more powerful resistance to his political actions, only had to contend with one government administration and was able to sort all legalities and diplomatic affairs in a timely fashion.

Prime Minister Kabor also toured powerful nations of the world; ensuring that international trade agreements and diplomatic protocols would be respected by the new democratic jurisdiction, and applying pressure to economically dominant countries urging improved environmental regulations. But Kabor knew she could accomplish this in the years after a new nation was formed; adhering to the spring equinox symbolism her revolution had started and issuing a second plebiscite along with the state of Alaska on 20 March 2237, for a vote on the proposed Boreal Democratic Nation Constitution Act.

The vote was perhaps tighter than expected or desired, but just over ninety-two percent of residents in the defined northern territory approved the constitution. A new nation was about to be born. A formal declaration of independence was registered with the International Court of Justice and United Nations Security Council; officially recognised and proclaimed as international law on 20 September 2237.

The declaration was commemorated with a signing ceremony of geographical significance at the tiny community of Fort Chipewyan on the northwest point of Lake Athabasca and the mouth of the Slave River flowing north; where Envrah and Minga tree warriors had roamed on Planet Earth for thousands of years prior, including the ancestors of Zachary Steele, Cassandra Kabor and Tuyl Reynolds. Kabor resigned as the Canadian head-of-state shortly after the declaration of independence; leaving an interim prime minister to drop the writ for a federal election coinciding with Boreal Nation's first ever general election on 20 March 2238. Reynolds remained as the governor of record for the secession of Alaska and was nominated as a candidate in the Boreal election.

The southern territory of Canada initially remained intact still stretching from the Pacific west coast of the continent to the Atlantic east coast, but no longer holding sovereignty over the Arctic coast. Although there was ample talk of separation in some form coming from Alberta and Quebec, the incumbent governments in the southern portions of the western provinces, Ontario, Quebec and the Maritime provinces excluding Newfoundland and Labrador, all decided the revamped Canadian confederacy would be stronger unified for the time being.

The state of Alaska and the Yukon River basin became the Alaska District of Boreal Nation with sixteen electoral boundaries, most of the vast Mackenzie River watershed became the largest district, Mackenzie, with twenty electorals, and another ten districts formed the remainder of the country: Athabasca in the western interior with nineteen electorals, Churchill with seventeen in the southwest and Boreal Shield along the arctic coast with fifteen, Nunavut also with fifteen in the north, Hudson Bay with ten, Labrador seven, James Bay in the south, Arctic Islands in the north and Skeena in the west each with six, and the Newfoundland island with five electorals.

Cassandra Kabor and Tuyl Reynolds became running mates for premier and vice premier with the Boreal Freeborne Party. The traditional political parties also joined the excitement and adrenaline of nation building, registering candidates in the election including an American and Canadian partnership for the Democratic Party, the Republican Party, Liberal Party, Progressive Conservative Party taking a chapter out of Canadian political history, and even the Green Party. Boreal election ballots require three votes for a premier, a national representative in the legislature and a non-partisan district representative in the assembly. The Boreal national government of the day is legislated to a six-year term, while municipal officials at the time were extended for three years until the first Boreal municipal elections could be held.

The team of Kabor, Reynolds and the Freeborne Party was elected as the first premier and majority government of Boreal Nation with a convincing eighty-seven percent of the popular vote. Cassandra won the vote for premier with a gobsmacking ninety-one percent margin, Tuyl was elected national representative for the Juneau electoral boundary in Skeena District on the vice premier's card, and the Freeborne Party gained one hundred twenty-four of the one hundred forty-three seats in the legislature.

They were all very giddy with their astonishing accomplishments; many glasses of British Columbian and Californian wine along with kegs of northern beer were consumed on election night, not to mention Yukon Jack whiskey and a big old jug of Alaskan moonshine. They were gathered at the hall of the finest resort lodge in the historical settlement of Fort Chipewyan—renamed Chipewyan City as the new befitting capital of Boreal Nation. It was an unassuming selection for a capital city; indicative of the inclusive democratic nation they would soon create. It was a perfect spring evening; not yet too sultry with a mild jetstream breeze thanks to yours truly. A divine terrace balcony overlooking Lake Athabasca was the setting for this special celebration, appropriately thanks to a Freeborne joint venture.

It was a rewarding moment for a beleaguered yet resilient and most definitely insightful spiritual warrior. Cassandra contemplated her role in the affairs of the universe, which of course she knew was the pine tree unisphere in Plateau Grand Creation. She had done an admirable job with the sacrifices she made in her life on the planet, and now this altruistic human could realise her proper place in the grand scheme for manifesto of peace heavenly compatriots. The manifesto angels needed an extremely strong character; they could see Tuyl Reynolds' path evolving, took guidance from Gorb's wisdom to pursue Zachary Steele and sensed Cassandra's affinity with the spiritual fibre of the cosmic wave. Someone was destined to change the political landscape and preserve the environment of Earth: Cassandra made the sacrifice bound to her home world, because it was on this planet of mixed woodlands that the manifesto of peace inter-species hybrid was born, and would need to proliferate for many centuries to come.

The Freeborne Party faithful enjoyed the celebration of a new profound democratic nation on Earth, but just as Kabor was aware of the universal implications, they too realised the difficult task of fulfilling their ambitious political agenda was only beginning. They basked in their electoral glory for a few days and soon relocated to the territorial legislative buildings in Yellowknife, which were utilised as temporary offices until national administrative buildings and national government facilities were constructed in Chipewyan City, quite efficiently, within two years of Boreal existence.

Kabor and Reynolds only remained in office for the first term of Boreal Nation; relinquishing their leadership of the Freeborne Party for the election of 2244 at the ages of seventy-one and seventy-two respectfully. The political team was able to see the foundation poured for a new democratic super power on the planet, but it would take several centuries of effort before the environment was stabilised and the population of Earth could thrive once again. They witnessed the completion of the solar power network—perhaps the greatest wonder of the world—with the shear engineering marvel of three immense arrays. The northern shield array spans from the north tip of the Rocky Mountains east to Hudson Bay, the taiga shield array is parallel to the Hudson plains south towards the edge of the Arctic watershed, and the boreal shield array extends west near Lake Winnipeg and east to Labrador and the Atlantic Ocean.

Boreal Nation was soon powered without the consumption of fossil fuels and their deadly pollution; the solar arrays came fully on line, existing hydro stations and molten salt reactors continued operating, and additional tidal power stations were built on the northern Pacific coast, along the northwest Arctic shoreline, Hudson Bay, Ungava Peninsula and the Atlantic seaboard of Labrador and Newfoundland.

The premier and vice premier also held office for the initial formation of a revolutionary new national combined forces, named Boreal National Forces, or Boreal Forces as it became known; providing national defence and operating government services such as public security and border inspection, water resources and energy production, public transportation, judicial and diplomatic administration and scientific research. The forces would eventually operate the country's interstellar exploration program, but during the early centuries of the new nation it built and established an independent orbital space station for environmental and astrological research which regrettably was also necessary for the defence of Boreal territory and resources.

The final signature legislative initiatives by the Kabor and Reynolds government introduced new commercial regulations, taxation laws and requirements for public office. The framework was set for adequate social policy funding, the elimination of the equity stock market in Boreal Nation and the creation of an ethical democratic political structure. This was essentially Kabor's equation to harness the wealth gap, control decadence and eliminate corruption.

Income tax for individuals and corporations was set at substantially lower rates, but was balanced by a hard cap on net income calculated at realistically generous levels determined by a standard of living formula known as the 'comfort rule'. There was incentive to earn higher income levels and build profitable companies with the lower tax rates, but the excess of profits and income beyond the comfort rule was circulated back into government services;

some of those services contracted out to the same private sector enterprises. Direct investment in value-added companies was encouraged, however only private sales of equity shares were allowed; eliminating the accumulation of wealth through publicly traded stocks, mutuals, hedge funds and the sort, while returns on all privately issued dividends were exempted from the comfort rule. Although there was a substantial exodus of investors initially, the slack was picked up by dedicated nationalists and a thriving economy ultimately attracted international investment.

All corporate and personal income taxes were incrementally eliminated with revenue recouped by the state from the return on public investment in joint ownership with private corporations. The taxation of dividends and individual income inside the comfort rule was reduced to zero within the first few decades after constitutional independence. Revenues from joint ventures and successful government corporations eventually balanced national expenditures and produced surplus budgets. In addition, the salary structure for politicians was radically increased to the upper levels of the comfort rule. However, once elected to public office national and district representatives in Boreal Nation were required to liquidate all equity in the private sector. There was also a lifetime ban on profiting from any corporate or government enterprises, which was offset by a lucrative pension plan. This attracted well qualified candidates and combined with a new open books policy for all government contracts effectively removed any incentive for corruption.

Boreal Nation became the world dominant power on Earth and a treasured destination for prospective citizens, but the road to national prosperity and planetary recovery was not a smooth ride. The first premier and vice premier of Boreal Nation retired into relative seclusion after the general election of 2244—which the Freeborne Party safely won—with the legendary politicians making only intermittent public appearances amid rumours of romantic liaison throughout their careers. Although they were always seen together publicly and lived in their biological bodies beyond one hundred years, the truth is their relationship was entirely professional yet extremely spiritual ever since the political encounter on the west coast of Vancouver Island. Cassandra tutored Tuyl in the craft of spiritual flight and they were both rewarded with visitation privileges throughout the unispheres of Plateau Grand Creation, long after their mortal existence transpired.

Boreal Nation was a going concern domestically and internationally in its first hundred years of democracy, and remains an integral influence in universal affairs well into the future as I reflect on this story of hybrid species. Boreal economic joint ventures were thriving globally at the time of independence as the new nation began to function on the world stage. Government spending in the second half of the twenty-third century was focused on public works infrastructure, maintaining essential social services, building and equipping a new national combined forces organisation, and sustaining export markets for environmental technology.

Widespread pollution, global warming and collapsing polar ice continued to disrupt the planet's natural cycles at the turn of the twenty-fourth century; finally convincing the economically powerful nations of the world to overhaul incremental measures and implement a new sweeping abatement schedule for environmental regulations. Boreal Nation greatly benefitted from the global trend of new environmental campaigns, but the damage had been done and degradation of the planet only grew worse over the next two centuries. Boreal Nation was forced to spend considerable domestic resources on national defence and international peacekeeping before ecologically friendly practices began to stabilise the detrimental effects to the environment.

The progressively extreme climate on Earth, diminished food production and lack of potable water gradually led to increased famine and pestilence, rioting, armed conflict and territorial wars, including pressure on Boreal boundaries from both migrating environmental refugees and militant groups claiming rights to resources such as freshwater. The "Druid Backpackers" as they became known were an unofficial collection of militia, mainly hunters and trappers, who took it upon themselves to defend their borders and thwart hostile intrusions during those first several decades of nationhood. The ranks of the backpackers unsuspectingly included a few hybrid tree warriors who mysteriously swayed the momentum of borderline skirmishes.

The backpackers helped bolster the country's defence of unprotected borders until the ranks of the national forces were brought up to full speed. The Boreal Forces became the most efficient and uniquely designed national defence organisation in the world. It started with an intricate and precise strategic operational structure combined with military spending; manufacturing plants for weaponry, munitions, vehicles, vessels and aircraft, as well as mechanical, electrical and computer components.

The Boreal hovercraft factories were already in production and turning a profit with transnational sales of vehicles, boats and the innovative hovercopters. The hovercraft industry was an important part of the economy; supplying not only the freight hauling and passenger flight industries, but also the national forces and other government ventures. The technology would later catapult into the future figuratively and literally with the amazing discovery of perpetual inertia. The simple machinery movements of a clock were combined with nanotechnology to manufacture miniature turbines inside engines, which produced electricity stored in Freeborne designed industrial batteries and powered all types of vehicles.

Meanwhile, the new national forces assumed operation of different government services in addition to national defence. Boreal Forces is organised into ten corps branches along with corresponding division commands. Commando corps is responsible for strategic command and has compiled a long history of reconnaissance, clandestine and covert missions. Combat forces with operations command patrolled the border and engages in international conflicts, peacekeeping missions and humanitarian relief efforts, while security forces and intelligence command provide border inspections, internal and external policing services and security at legal courts, embassies, consulates and penitentiaries. The marine corps and logistics command manage troop, equipment and supply movements, assist in border patrol with air support and operate transport installations, public and commercial transportation routes.

The engineering, medical and science corps, responsible for systems, academy and research commands, service all national forces operations, with the engineering corps also operating and maintaining water treatment plants, energy production facilities and government infrastructure buildings, and the medical and science corps conducting technological research and eventually educating humanity on the sciences of the universe and new lifeforms on distant planets. The diplomatic and judicial corps, with the communications and administration commands, provide operations for the nation's justice and diplomatic affairs secretariats, and the interstellar forces, responsible for tactical command and the flight of aircraft, and eventually interstellar vessels, initially launched orbital missions and began construction of the Boreal space station; soon venturing further into the cosmos with the exploration program. The global village of Earth had begun construction of an international lunar outpost on its moon and completed the original voyages to its neighbouring planet of Mars before the arrival of Zachary Steele in the year 2336. Boreal Nation would impact space exploration with revolutionary enhancements, but planetary political divisions were still being sorted in the meantime.

The prairie and foothills region surrounding the expansive cities of Calgary and Edmonton in western Canada ended up joining the United States union in the early twenty-fourth century, triggering the state of Washington to annex the remainder of British Columbia; albeit a friendly acquisition and neighbour for the new state of Alberta, approved by federal and provincial governments. The remaining southern territory of Saskatchewan became Canada's most westerly province along with western and southern Manitoba; both remarkably maintaining good relations with Boreal Nation and United States. The province of Ontario would not give up its northwest region above the Great Lakes; preserving geographic continuity across Canada to the three Maritime provinces and the Atlantic Ocean. Ironically, Quebec decided it was in its best interest to remain in Canada; losing the northern territory of the province but retaining control over hydro-electric resources.

Zachary was dropped down on a favourite spot of his in a wilderness preserve—renamed from Prince Albert National Park with an expanded boundary to become Weyakwin Nature Preserve, in the Boreal Churchill District—just north of the border with the small city retaining its original name Prince Albert, where a port of entry inspection station was erected across the toll bridge over the river and the Canadian province of the same indigenous namesake, Saskatchewan. Zachary was returned to Earth on a very different planet, although he was not fully aware of all the global implications. It was a rude awakening for him in many ways after his mystical visit to a sacrifice fire.

Chapter 23: Guardian Angel

The western hemisphere arctic and the transitional terrain of taiga to boreal plains and rocky shield had fared better in Boreal Nation than other regions of Planet Earth. It was far enough north to escape the most severe heat of the climate and a good portion of its freshwater was fed by either groundwater springs or far north glaciers, rather than glacial ice from more southerly mountain ranges which was quickly melting down to slow trickles.

The transport of Zachary from the mixed woodlands of Earth in the pine tree unisphere to the homeland planet of Envrah in the aspen tree unisphere of Plateau Grand Creation was a collaborative effort directed by the insight of the manifesto of peace original fibrous angels. The angels provided a courier taking Zachary back to Earth and gently placing him at the head of Grey Owl's trail on the shore of Hawkin's namesake Kingsmere River. Zachary was unaware of the exact time elapsed and the transformation of the planet: physically, politically and socially.

He would soon learn of the changes on Earth and the tribulations of tree wars, but his location in the nature preserve now a part of Boreal Nation sheltered him from any obvious signs of historical revelations. He went from MacFarlane River over a hundred and fifty billion light years to Planet Envrah and back to Saskatchewan; typical of his canoe trips but leaving him grasping for any perception of space and time. It was reasonably warm and sunny outside, but it did not feel like the summer weather at Labrecque's cabin only a few hours ago. And then Zachary saw some unmelted snow in the underbrush near the trail where he was propped against the side of a dirt ridge.

"Great, this is all I need," he muttered to himself.

Although it was not winter when he lifted off the planet, he did deduce that his trip into outer space was a considerable distance. Zachary used his astute rationale to determine he was on Earth sometime in the future; it still seemed unbelievable as he sat there gripping his hatchet. He looked over at his backpack neatly unzipped beside him to show it was restocked with new gear and supplies.

He remembered meeting a man named Hawkins Kingsmere, talking about Soarfoot, Storyteller, warriors, angels and gods, and apparently accepting a hatchet for his wood instrument of tree power as well as hitching a ride with a space tripping French Canadian fur trapper.

The new findings were fleeting through his mind like the demons infiltrating his dreams, but now he was not as confused. A new understanding was growing into a scraggly weed in his thoughts; his brain was racing in triplicate. Zachary picked up his backpack and lifted it onto his shoulders. He was slowly crossing the realm of human reality into the depths of spirituality as he started walking down the trail. Suddenly it was all very real to him: he wanted the truth, he wanted the power, and he was being called by the trees.

There was at least one problem however; he did not know where to look for his father, not to mention exactly which year it was on Earth. He did remember where he was though, and so he started hiking to Kingsmere Lake about a mile north of his location. He was walking along the east shore of Kingsmere River; well above the steep banks of the shallow, winding waterway, with the current flowing south in the opposite direction. The river can be navigated except for one set of rapids, where there's a railroad track on the west shore so paddlers can take their canoes around the rapids on a flatbed railway car. He would end up hiking the east shoreline trail of Kingsmere Lake, but first Zachary decided to check out the west shore railroad track and walk up the extended trail that leads to the southend campground on the lake near the mouth of the river.

A bridge crosses the river to the west side about half of the way down the trail, with another half mile or so from there to the southend campground. Zachary hiked across the bridge but did not take the rolling railway flatbed; instead keeping his backpack on his shoulders and walking along the tracks. Along the railroad is the peak of the slope ascending the elevation of the rapids, with thick forest growth on both sides of the trail. Zachary could not see to the end of the tracks until he hiked up the slope, when he saw an unsettling sight that was a sign of the times.

It was a band of Druid Backpackers, as it turned out, who were patrolling the river on the lookout for fleeing marauders after an outpost raid on the Boreal Nation border over fifty miles to the south. There were seven militia in the patrol unit: clad in heavy boots and camouflage fatigues, holding assault rifles and of course wearing backpacks. Zachary was nervous as they approached; he did not have a weapon except for his stager and he really didn't know how to operate it just yet. The lead backpacker shouted at him.

"What are you doing here?"

"I'm backpacking, just like you," answered Zachary.

"Do you have any weapons?"

"No, just my camping supplies. I can show you," said Zachary, pulling off his pack and starting to open it.

Three of the militia soldiers raised their weapons in response.

"Drop the pack," yelled one of them, as Zachary immediately set his backpack on the ground and held his hands high.

"I told you, I don't have weapons. I'm just hiking to the lake."

"Where are you from?" continued the Druid Backpacker.

"Where am I from? I'm a dual Canadian and American citizen. Where are you from? I didn't think they allowed guns in the park."

"This is no longer a park, it's a nature preserve and you would know that if you were a Boreal citizen. How did you get here?"

"Ah, that's actually difficult to say."

"What are you, some kind of a joker. Put your hands behind your head and turn around."

"I've got this one boys," said one of the men standing behind.

"Why, do you know something about this guy that we don't?"

"He's with me, we just came back from a sacrifice fire ritual and he's probably disoriented."

"Tree warrior voodoo magic. I guess you know what you're talking about, but I still think he looks suspicious," said the backpacker.

A weathered and rugged looking older man stepped forward; obviously well respected by his peers, yet dressed a little more casually than his patrol partners without a rifle and sporting moccasins instead of boots. It was Hawkins Kingsmere.

"I know he looks different, but trust me, this one is special," he said.

"Whatever you say then," acknowledged the soldier.

"Kingsmere," smiled Zachary.

"So you do know this old warrior," motioned the backpacker.

"I just met him but it seems like we've been friends for a long time. It's good to see you again Hawkins."

"I've been waiting for you Zachary, I thought you might end up here," Hawkins welcomed his young friend. "Don't worry boys, you continue down this west shoreline and I'll meet you at Waskesiu Lake. I'll cross over to the east side and make sure our friend in arms here is set on his way."

"Sounds good. Keep alert and we'll see you in a few minutes. Good luck in your travels my friend," responded the backpacker.

The patrol unit hiked up ahead while Hawkins and Zachary leisurely strolled to the bridge and crossed back to the other side of the river. The old tree warrior consoled the young candidate by describing the lay of the land and telling him what he might find.

"Zachary, I know this might come as a shock but you need to remain strong. Some things have changed considerably, but some things are still very much the same. I think you should look for your father up the shoreline of my namesake, Kingsmere Lake. It was one of his favourite spots."

"Was one of his favourite spots? How much time has expired? Do you even know if my father is alive?"

"Your father was preserved in the spiritual dimension and I am told he has resumed his search for Soarfoot here on Earth. Your voyage to Planet Envrah also took you through spiritual corridors, but your awareness is not yet developed and you were not able to stay conscious for the flight. I'm not sure when you departed this planet but I can tell you that hundreds of years have likely transpired."

"And what about my mother, is she still alive?"

"Why yes, she is with your father. They now travel together. You will find your parents Zachary, and this is the best place to start."

"Zelda told me this would happen. Will I find her as well?"

"She will find you, but you should know that Planet Earth has changed. It is just entering a terrible time of environmental degradation, yet there is still hope for the future. What was once Alaska and northern Canada is now a new country, Boreal Nation. We are in Weyakwin Nature Preserve in the Churchill District of the country. It's an example of an area that still displays some amount of environmental stability."

"I could see the environment coming, but another country, wow, that's something. So, are those men part of the military of this new country?"

"Not exactly, but they are an unofficial militia that works closely with the new government. They are called the Druid Backpackers, because their focus is to protect the forests of Boreal Nation from raids by marauders. There are a few select tree warriors such as myself that have joined their ranks and help them patrol the international border."

"What if I run into more of them and you're not here?"

"The north portion of the preserve is clear. I'll come back and check on you, but I need to join this patrol and search for your father and Soarfoot farther south."

"Why don't you just come with me? I still don't know how to use this stager and I don't have a gun. I'm not so sure I can deal with this."

"Trust in yourself Zachary. You are special, a mixed species hybrid, but if you are to possess the silviculture power you must find your own path. Besides, we can cover more ground with you searching north while I continue with the backpackers. The power of the trees will come to you soon enough. You should be fine in this area for a while."

"I guess I don't have much choice. I hope I'm doing the right thing."

"You are doing the right thing for the tree warriors of both the aspen and the pine. It is your bloodline, you need to believe in it. Botanical disputes in the universe are also changing, but our search for your ancestors is in the name of the silviculture prophecy; that hasn't changed."

Zachary sighed and looked down the trail towards the lake, then turned back to Kingsmere: "Thanks for everything Hawkins. This is what I wanted when I started looking for my parents, I just didn't think it would be this much of a challenge. I'll do my best, wish me luck."

"Believe me Zachary, luck is definitely on your side, but remember to believe in yourself. The power within you will guide the way, that and the owls."

"I'll keep on the lookout for pine trees and aspens, but I kind of hope the owls stay in the forest for now, at least until I get my bearings."

"Good luck with that."

And with a wink and a jump in his stride, Hawkins started hiking down the trail while Zachary cautiously stepped forward scanning the forest. He would soon be on the shore of Kingsmere Lake only a few hundred metres ahead; a deep crater lake with clear aqua green water and a decent stock of trout. Zachary was thinking he would fish to supplement his food supplies, but his mind soon wandered to thoughts of the trees. He observed some spruce and was excited when he thought he saw aspen, but realised they were poplar. He saw balsam fir and tamarack, but still none of the aspen. He felt inhibited: there were black spruce, white spruce, some jack pine which were a comfort, more balsam poplar and even some white birch, but still none of the aspen. And then, in the distance, peeping above the shadows of intimidating black spruce, Zachary saw a small patch of trembling aspen.

Pleasant thoughts filled his mind. He mused of bouncing with Zelda. He then picked up his pace and decided he would hike over four miles before the day was done and make camp for the night at the designated lakeshore campsite Chipewyan Portage, if it was still there. The trail led to the lake in only a few minutes where he found a stockpile of firewood and a small dock on the water. Sitting on the end of the dock was an old man holding a wood pole to the ice forming on the frozen shoreline. The old man was facing north looking at the open lake, which did not freeze over in the climatic conditions except along the extremely shallow shoreline in the middle of winter.

The somewhat withered man looked to be about seventy-years-old or thereabouts. He was small and lean but average in height; tanned brown skin and practically bald with a light grey beard. He was wearing a loose top, leather loincloth-styled shorts and open sandals without socks. Zachary removed his backpack, leaned it against the dock and approached the harmless looking man; perhaps feeling cocky after his encounter with the militia.

"Hello," he called out.

The old man was startled. He lifted his wood staff in a bit of a fluster and twisted his body in Zachary's direction.

"Oh, hello. Where did you come from?" he asked.

"The bush," said Zachary, pointing behind him with his thumb.

"Oh, I see. You'll have to excuse me, I tend to daydream more often than I used to. I was just wondering when the lake would be freezing."

"By the looks of this shoreline ice, I would say in a few weeks from now, depending on the weather."

"So you know the lake well?"

"Fairly well, but it was basically an educated guess."

"And how do you come to be so educated?" posed the peculiar old man.

"Let's not play mind games, huh," quipped Zachary.

"But they're the best kind of games."

"Look, anyone who is out in the bush at this time of year should know when the lakes freeze. Now you know as much as I do that winter means lake water will freeze, at least in Canada, or should I say Boreal Nation."

"Yes, I know, you're right. It's just that it's been so long since I experienced any of Earth's seasons, in North America or anywhere else. That is where we are, isn't it?"

Zachary chuckled: "Fine. Have you come to teach me, warn me, give me instructions, or guide me along my path of destiny. Or do you just want to be my sidekick?"

"I like that last choice. I think I'll be your sidekick, but just for a short while," said the old man, standing up with the help of his staff.

"Wait a minute. If you're going to be my sidekick, I would like to know who you are and where you're from," insisted Zachary.

"My name is Harold. I can't remember where I come from. I lost my birth certificate somewhere."

"You can't remember where you were born?"

"Well no, it was a long time ago."

"Oh boy, how long ago?"

"At least a few hundred Earth years the last time I counted."

"Uh huh. Ya, well, tell me, what kind of wood is that staff?"

"What kind of wood do you want it to be?"

"Listen old man—"

"Harold. Please call me Harold."

"Fine then, Harold. What I don't need right now is someone playing silly games with me. I have enough problems functioning as it is. Now, would that staff be made of aspen wood by any chance?"

"You sure are perceptive," smiled Harold. "You can recognise an aspen stager from well over three feet away. My, I can see you catch on fast."

"At least you should be friendly, I guess," groaned Zachary.

He was becoming accustomed to meeting people in the hundreds of years-old range, but this time he was not intimidated—at least not quite yet. Zachary put on his backpack and started walking along a small beach void of water or ice. Harold easily kept pace. The beach was only a few hundred metres, ending in a clump of bulrush reeds. The trail cut back into the bush and snaked through the trees for another mile leading to a sand point campsite on the lake. It then went into the woods again for about another two and a half miles until reaching the Chipewyan Portage campsite. Zachary posed a few questions along the trail. Harold politely answered them all.

"Who are the Alkae?"

"The warriors of spruce trees."

"Are they the enemy of the aspens?"

"Yes."

"And the aspen warriors are Envrahs?"

"Correct."

"If Gorb is the god of aspens, who is the god of spruce?"

"Rulsp is the god of spruce trees."

"Is Soarfoot a mortal?"

"Actually, he's a tree warrior."

"What's the difference?"

"Tree warriors have a spiritual core on their bodies and they don't bleed. You'll learn about that when you're ready."

"Do you know where Soarfoot is now?"

"No, it's up to you and warriors like Hawkins Kingsmere to find him."

"Do you know if the Storyteller is with Soarfoot?"

"No idea, but many warriors suspect he is."

"Do you know my father?"

"I'm afraid not."

"How did you know where to find me?"

"I was at the sacrifice fire on Envrah. Cookie Labrecque asked me to drop by here to see if you might need some help."

"Good old Cookie."

"A fine warrior."

"You know, I have these terrible dreams filled with evil spirits."

"Quite normal for a tree warrior in training."

"I'm going to become an Envrah?"

"It's up to you, but you do show great promise. We need all the help we can get these days."

"What do you know about a naked woman running through the woods?"

"That could look very nice."

Harold was patient with Zachary despite being a cranky old cadger at times; the tough love was yet to come. Zachary thought Harold was a fragile old man, but quickly realised he was exceedingly energetic for someone his age when they came upon an open ridge dotted with trembling aspens. Harold lit up with delight and increased his canter substantially. Zachary was unable to keep up. Another mile down the trail Zachary reached Chipewyan and there was Harold; sitting beside a small campfire in the late afternoon shadows, which he sparked after building a lean-to shelter and spreading a bed of boughs on the ground for sleeping. Zachary was duly impressed and with most of the camp chores already done he took the opportunity to try out his new stager in the remaining daylight.

The hatchet Labrecque provided had a hole drilled in the end of the handle with a narrow leather strap looped through. The strap allowed Zachary to swing the hatchet at a distance, which he thought would be advantageous if he was going to use it as a weapon: but for now he would attempt to chop wood. Zachary sized up a standing spruce. He felled it in seventeen swings.

"I've seen better," said Harold.

Unamused by the comment, Zachary silently chopped down two more trees; another spruce and an aspen he mistook for a poplar or an alder. Harold was visibly angry when Zachary dragged the aspen to the campsite.

"What do you think you're doing!" he shouted.

Harold grabbed his stager and with both hands swung it at Zachary; striking him in the chest and pinning him up against a tree. The blow winded Zachary. He was seeing stars and gasping for air to breathe. Harold was still holding him against the tree.

"What did I do?" wheezed Zachary.

"Obviously you need to learn a few things. That tree you chopped down is an aspen. Don't ever do that again," threatened Harold.

"I'm sorry, I thought it was a poplar."

Harold lowered his staff stager and Zachary rubbed his chest to relieve the pain. The blow was going to leave a bruise.

"That's a mistake you can't afford. Now look around," said Harold.

The stars around Zachary's eyes dissipated and he began to breathe normally. He was still feeling the pain in his chest but he suddenly stopped thinking about it. It was bright and clear outside and they were not at Chipewyan. A steep cliff of smooth rock was behind Harold and they were standing on a small mountainside ledge. An enormous valley stretched for miles below them with mountain peaks in the distance. The valley was bare with very few trees bunched together in small stands. Harold stared at Zachary.

"These are spruce. Examine them carefully. They are not aspen."

"I know," answered Zachary.

"Are you sure now?"

"I'm positive."

"Good, now hold your hatchet tightly."

They were on Planet Alka, home of the Alkae warriors.

And then an array of crystalline particles began to swirl around Harold's raised stager. The flecks of light spun faster and changed colours as they expanded; circling both men inside a wall of sparkling fragments. And then the particles quickly vanished. The land was once again drastically changed. They were now on a small island. Zachary could not see anything but water and a few other islands on the horizon. The trees on the island were all identical. They were on Planet Dlailia, home of the Dlailian warriors.

"These are willow trees, they are not aspen either," stated Harold.

"I know," said Zachary sharply.

The coloured particles surrounded them as Harold raised his staff again, and when the light was dispelled, they were standing on the sandy bank of a river. They were in a shallow, sunny valley spreading across the landscape with vibrant forest growth. The trees flourished in the gullies and on the hillsides. It was Planet Minga. Zelda was not far away. Harold pointed to a stand of trees.

"Pine, not aspen," he said.

Harold raised his stager another time before Zachary could respond and once more they were transported by a band of light. They arrived on the ridge of a dreary valley. It was overcast and wet. The ridge was covered in leaves and the valley was rich with botanical life. It was Planet Coulee.

"These are—"

"Allow me," interrupted Zachary, regaining his composure. "These are birch trees. They're not aspen either."

"Very good. I knew you could catch on fast. Try this one."

The next stop saw them in the midst of a gigantic swamp. The stands of trees were located on random mounds of high ground and around the edge of the bog. Zachary was unsure of these trees. It was his first visit to Planet Yndes. He looked at Harold.

"Well?" the old man prompted his student.

"They look a bit like fir or maybe spruce, but I don't think they are. I'm not sure about these trees," admitted Zachary.

"They're not aspen, are they?"

"No, they're not aspen."

"They're tamarack and this is Planet Yndes, the home world of the Yndae warriors," smirked Harold.

He raised his staff and the sparkles began to fall, but before the particles disappeared Zachary could hear a constant roar in the background. They found themselves on the bank of another river. This one was speeding with white-water; the rapids spanning as far as Zachary could see. They were the rapids of Planet Naruka. The surrounding shoreline was thick with healthy trees. Zachary squinted in Harold's direction.

"Fir trees?" he guessed.

"You got it young earthling; trees of the Narukas."

They were again transported to another land. The fog was dense and it was dark. They were in an isolated gorge on Planet Demkew. An ancient tree towered high just beside them. Zachary reached out and touched the bark.

"That's it, take your time. You better get this one right," said Harold.

"Poplar?" questioned Zachary.

"Yes, poplar, not aspen. Notice the texture of the bark compared to the touch of aspen. Memorise it. Don't forget it."

"I won't forget," said Zachary, examining the tree a second time.

"That's good, your life may depend on it. You see, this is not a silly game, and there are not any rules to follow. You have to go beyond the rules. You have to become the trees. You have to know the trees intimately, and you have to believe in their powers. But before you can believe in them, before you can absorb their powers—you have to stop chopping down aspen trees!"

"I understand."

"I certainly hope you do. Now, I've shown you a few different species of trees. I think I covered the basics for the area where you're searching, although it's been a while since I walked through Earth's boreal forest. Regardless, mind the trees and know them well. They are the medium for the power of the gods. You must believe that. Above all else, you must believe in the trees."

The veteran angel of botanical disputes momentarily looked his age; the flickers of light highlighting the wrinkles on his face as he raised his staff into the fog. Zachary posed a question with the sparkles descending down.

"Are you a tree warrior or a spirit?" he inquired.

But the crystals of light were gone and so was Harold. Zachary was back at Chipewyan. The fire was not burning, the lean-to shelter was gone and it was dark outside. Zachary retrieved a flashlight from his backpack that was still there and looked around the campsite, but there wasn't any sign of Harold. The lake was completely melted and rested peacefully beneath the bright moon, yet the water was still cool; perfect for a hypothermic dip. Zachary resisted the temptation and instead set up his tent to get some sleep.

In the morning, he broke camp and resumed hiking north on the Kingsmere Lake trail. He was not bothered by Harold's brief appearance; after all it was only for a short while, true to the old man's word. Zachary concentrated on his objective and continued to search for his parents. He carried his hatchet as he hiked and paid close attention to the different species of trees. He was sure to walk up and experience the touch of each and every aspen. He would caress the bark and close his eyes; attempting to become part of the tree as Harold suggested. Zachary wanted to absorb the power and so he was becoming as intimate as he could with the aspens.

However, when he ran his fingers over the trunk bark, he did not feel anything out of the ordinary: none of the inspirations he wanted, none of the eclectic tremors he envisioned. Once when he was feeling up an adult tree Zachary was mildly aroused by a young aspen sucker sprouting from an exposed root and brushing up between his legs in the wind, with a little assistance from yours truly, but otherwise nothing much happened. He would have to wait for a revelation from the trees. He needed to practise chopping more wood.

He covered the three miles to the next campsite Sandy Beach in a couple hours under a cloudy sky; unaware of the roving vapour demons. He stopped to cast an angling line into the lake and was lucky enough to catch a small trout. He built a fire and cooked the fish for lunch. Zachary was happy with the ease of his hatchet while chopping wood for the fire. He decided to further test the power of his stager.

He found a thick poplar log, placed it on its end, held the hatchet above the log and concentrated on his swinging motion. After a few chants of ashah pyen, he wound up with a full swing and came down on the log with all his strength. The hatchet drove through the wood and split the log decisively. He set up one of the halves and repeated his ritual; relaxing his swing with less effort. The piece of wood exploded into splinters as the hatchet made contact. Zachary was pleased.

He split logs for another twenty minutes and his swing gradually became more relaxed. The logs shattered with more ferocity after each subsequent strike. Zachary observed a sparse flash of light after the contact from several swings. It was with such deliveries of his hatchet that he felt a rising surge. It started in his hands and moved rapidly through his arms, across his chest and into his brain.

The surge would then abandon his head; almost levitating his body. Zachary's face turned red with heat, his nostrils burned, his ears swelled, his mouth sizzled and his eyes teared from the velocity of the energy. He could almost see the power whirling into the forest after it passed through his body. The surrounding trees wavered in the wake. It was the power of the aspens and it provided him with a euphoric blast, yet a frustrating sense of anxiety just the same.

The energy raced through Zachary's blood and then, just as quickly, it was exhausted into the atmosphere. He summoned the power but was unable to contain or control it. He would practise more at the next campsite Northend, about two and a half miles beyond Sandy Beach where another trail leads to Ajawaan Lake and the cabin of the late naturalist Grey Owl. Zachary kept hiking to the top of the lake in the early afternoon with the sun periodically spreading its warmth through the rolling clouds and the roaming vapour demons in the sky; not the only demons he would experience on that day. He stopped at a footbridge over Poplar Creek near the shoreline and sat there to ponder his youthful past. Zachary remembered how intimate he was with nature as a boy while he rested. He filled his camping cup with a sip of water from the creek, put his backpack on again and went to feel up another aspen tree. Nature had truly changed for Zachary.

He arrived at the comforting Northend beach surrounded by a gorgeous stand of jack pines, some trembling aspen in the distance and plenty of daylight remaining. He set up his tent, strolled down to the beach after collecting some firewood and lay down to catch a few rays of sunshine. Suddenly a massive creature was standing above him; covered in rough bark, patches of stone and callous skin. An ugly hollow face with pockets of stirring dark gases threatened Zachary by its mere existence. It began to scream and wield an axe at his head. He squirmed in the sand and awoke in a startle.

The sun was setting across the lake. Zachary looked up into the sky. It was a tranquil and mild dusk. The serene sunset soothed his soul and brought him back to his senses. Growing accustomed to the evil spirits, he chose to ignore his dream. He walked back to his tent and started up a campfire before it was too dark. He stoked the fire with a generous supply of wood and headed into the bush to try his luck with a few spruce. Zachary's hatchet struck the trees with a detonating burst and ripped through the trunks. The spruce enemy splintered and slammed down to the ground: tree bashing at its ultimate. He decided five bashings was enough. Indeed it was.

The tree bashing caused enough commotion to arouse a hungry demon sput. Zachary could barely see where he was going in the falling darkness, yet he clearly saw the sput's face straight ahead. He stopped dead in his human spoors with the imposing humanoid animal squaring off only a few feet away. The sput was exactly as Zachary imagined in his dreams. He was face-to-face with a core-eating monster, but fortunately his wood fibre spiritual core was only just developing. The demon sput however, not the brightest entity in the grand creations, was unaware his prey was coreless.

The sput's face lit up the blackness of nightfall with a haunting glaze. The creature's bark was scuffed and gouged from past battles, and a hulking evil glower made it apparent he was viciously crazed. The demon issued a wallowing growl and ripped a sizable tree from the ground. Zachary took a step backwards. The sput took three steps forward and raised the tree above his head; throwing it with a bitter snarl. The tree came flying at Zachary: he dropped to his knees, closed his eyes and held his hatchet up high. The tree rammed into the hatchet blade and an eruption of lightning shot from the stager, blasting the botanical specimen into dust. The sput was taken back a few steps and Zachary, climbing to his feet with a new injection of confidence, slowly approached the demon.

The creature let out a howl and rushed Zachary, who was able to duck under a wild swing as the sput attempted to strike him. The demon, losing his balance, went sprawling face first on the ground. Zachary wound up and drove his stager into the creature's back. The hatchet lodged into the bark with a thud and the sput screamed in pain. The demon tried to get up, but as Zachary yanked his stager free both combatants fell to the ground: end of round one.

Ducking under another swing Zachary delivered a blow to the sput's collar bone, gouging out a chunk of bark. The direct hit sent the animal falling on his back. The tree warrior in training moved in for the kill, but an unexpected swift punch to the gut caught him off guard. He miscalculated attempting to block the punch and the rough bark sliced into his forearm. The blood began to seep as he knelt down holding his arm: end of round two.

It was now the sput's turn to move in for the kill. Standing above his prey the creature raised his arms together and prepared to strike; all too reminiscent of Zachary's dreams. The demon's clenched fists came down and Zachary instinctively held up his hatchet. A flash of power ignited as the sput's arm fractured into pieces. The demon scrambled and yelled with displeasure: end of round three.

This time Zachary moved in for the kill with determination; rising to an attack posture and landing another blow squarely in the middle of the beast's chest. The sput sliced, cracked and split into stagerdust, collapsing into nothing more than a pile of scrap wood: end of the final round. Zachary immediately went to feel his injured arm but the blood was already dried and the wound completely healed. He sensed the power of a burgeoning spiritual core at work. He smiled with healthy pride and gathered up the demon sput kindling. He would use it as firewood; just reward for his victory.

Carrying the sput in his arms back to the campsite Zachary found the coals in his fire red hot and begging for a sacrifice. He burned the sput for the rest of the night while sipping on Labrador tea and whiskey. Gorb smiled down on him.

Chapter 24: Quantum Mechanics

Harold's tour to the homeland planets of the tree species actually took Zachary away from Earth for another one thousand, nine hundred and fifty-nine years of space and time. Although there were considerable scientific and political changes that occurred on and off the planet in just under two millennia, Zachary would learn about the impact of these changes on the entire universe as explained by Hawkins and other tree warriors in his travels; and now he would take a much more active role himself in shaping the future of the cosmos.

Earth's environment, although benign industrial practices were gradually adopted in the twenty-fourth and twenty-fifth centuries, saw the full force of global warming and pollution grip the planet through to the twenty-seventh century. This catastrophic cycle was followed by another three hundred years of stable conditions without further escalation, but Earth was still mired in extreme weather until the effects of environmental measures could slowly begin to reverse the climatic warming trend.

The polar ice caps melted down to less than ten percent and all but minute traces of glacial ice vanished in the European, Middle East, African and Australian mountain ranges, as well as the southern portion of the North American Rocky Mountains and Sierra Madre of Central America. The Andes Mountains, Himalayas and Shan ranges around the Plateau of Tibet were somewhat preserved because of their high altitude, but these regions experienced sweltering hot mean temperatures rising to 150 degrees Fahrenheit or 65 Celsius and never cooling below 120 Fahrenheit or 50 Celsius—except in shaded valleys and at higher elevation near the peaks—causing more than three-quarters of glacial ice to disappear.

The north tip of the Rockies and mountains near the Arctic Circle in Boreal Nation, such as the Mackenzie, Selwyn and Brooks ranges, along with the ice cap of Greenland, suffered the same shrinkage of glaciers but still experienced temperatures around the freezing mark—mainly in the prolonged darkness of winter because of altitude and the northern latitude distance from the equator— delaying the melting process marginally.

Vast land masses were underwater from melting ice and thermal expansion of swelling sea levels, covering the most populated cities of the world and many areas where natural resources were once extracted. Northern Europe and Eurasia endured perhaps the greatest impact; the North European Plain south to the Alps and the Black Sea, most of Russia except for its eastern mountain ranges and parts of the Central Siberian Plateau, and a large portion of central Asia all the way south to the Caspian and Aral inland seas, were all immersed under some amount of Arctic sea water. The Ural Mountains which had separated Europe and eastern Russia became a large island in the Arctic Ocean, along with Scandinavia, Iceland, the Scottish Grampian Mountains, Northwest Highlands and Southern Uplands. A central slice of northern England, the Pennines, the Cambrian Mountains of Wales and outcroppings throughout Ireland formed smaller islands.

The East and South China Sea coastlines were also submerged including the basins of the Yangtze River, Yellow Sea and northern Amur River; separating most of the Korean peninsula from the mainland and ravaging all of Japan's shoreline with continuous storms and flooding. The Indian Ocean coast was flooded at the basins west and east of India on the Arabian Sea and Bay of Bengal, only the southwest and southeast tips of the Indo-China Peninsula remained attached to the mainland, and the rest of the land base with Malaysia, Indonesia and East Indies became a series of tiny islands in the sea. Australia was mostly swamped and essentially became two islands; the arid deserts of the west connected by a small strip of land to the cordillera island of the Great Dividing Range running north and south.

The entire Amazon and Pampas drainage basins in South America were also swamped, transforming the continent into three major height of land regions. The Andes and foothills, almost completely separated from Central America by water, became the world's longest extenuated spit of land; also mostly separated from the Brazilian Highlands by flooding of the Parana basin, and from the Guyana Highlands by the Amazon tributary basin. The Mexican Gulf coast and the east coast of Central America became somewhat swamped as well and expanded the existing West Indies island archipelago, with fifty percent of the land mass submerged below prevailing sea levels.

All of the Atlantic seaboard and Gulf of Mexico shoreline in the United States were completely flooded, including major cities such as Boston, New York, Philadelphia, Washington and a large percentage of the states along the east coast, all of Florida, Mississippi and Louisiana, three-quarters of Georgia and Alabama, eastern Arkansas and Texas all the way to the cities of Little Rock and Dallas, and up the Mississippi River basin swamping land as far north as Lake Michigan. Ocean water surged the North American St Lawrence River basin and large tracts of Great Lakes shoreline as well, including some of the cities Quebec, Montreal, Kingston and Toronto in Canada, and the American cities Rochester, Cleveland, Detroit, Milwaukee and Chicago. The Hudson River basin also swelled from the Atlantic coast and spilled over to the Great Lakes watershed; creating a new Maritime Island with parts of Connecticut, Massachusetts, Vermont, New Hampshire, Maine and the Canadian provinces Quebec and New Brunswick.

The Canadian province of Nova Scotia became a small archipelago of seven islands and all the major urban areas of Prince Edward Island were largely covered by water. The Appalachian Mountains extending from upper state New York south to the city of Atlanta became an eastern mainland peninsula; only because it remained joined to the western continent over swamped land by the world's largest engineered causeway connecting the states of eastern Indiana and western Illinois south of Lake Michigan.

The North American Pacific coast was also significantly affected: the Mexican west coast and Gulf of California were flooded, most of the cities San Diego and Los Angeles were eroded away, the Monterey and San Francisco Bay areas were overcome with ocean water inland between the coastal mountains and Sierra Nevada range, as far south as Fresno to Bakersfield and north of the state capital Sacramento to Redding near Mount Shasta. The Columbia River basin draining into the Pacific was swamped, which forms the state border of Oregon and Washington, and the basin including Puget Sound, lower Fraser River and shoreline areas of the cities Seattle and Vancouver was also covered by sea water.

The remainder of North America was not as severely affected. Boreal Nation only incurred relatively minor coastal flooding along the western and northern Arctic mainland, the polar islands, the Yukon River and Mackenzie River deltas, mainly the west coast of Hudson Bay and James Bay, some of the Ungava Peninsula and Labrador shoreline, and the Atlantic seaboard of Newfoundland including all but a small island of the Avalon Peninsula. Ocean water also surged across a large swath of land from the north arctic mainland at Chantrey Inlet south to the Hudson Bay coast at Rankin Inlet, forming the Great Arctic Wetlands and creating islands of Boothia and Melville Peninsulas.

The subsequent pollution from increased sea levels on the planet seriously affected marine ecologies worldwide. It took the better part of a millennium to dilute and evaporate many pollutants, or toxins to settle on ocean floors, creating several hot spots across the globe. The levels of glacial rivers on Earth were reduced as well—some completely dried up—until environmental stabilisation cycled back cooler weather and glaciers could begin to accumulate once again.

❖ ❖ ❖

The Boreal Nation tablewater natural springs of the taiga and boreal ecozones benefited from healthy rainfall and freshwater reserves despite excessive thunderstorms, summer heat about 55 Celsius and rarely reaching freezing temperatures in winter; able to sustain the growing district populations of Athabasca, Churchill, Boreal Shield, Hudson Bay, James Bay, Labrador and Newfoundland. The comparatively moderate climate of summers just under 50 Celsius and some winter frost in the other five districts of Boreal Nation touching the Arctic and Pacific coastlines kept those regions habitable with the use of desalination plants for supplemental freshwater.

Boreal Nation developed desalination technology using the energy generated by tidal current power stations. This technology and natural freshwater supplies were first exported and then donated in relief to all nations of the world. Hydroponic technology was also shared globally to grow indoor food crops in the stifling heat, as many countries attempted to build underground and dome cities with only limited success.

The climatic conditions in eastern Canada north of the flooded Great Lakes basin—although gripped by hot summers near 60 Celsius and winter temperatures above freezing—were tolerable enough for habitation with a manageable amount of artificial atmospheric control inside large building structures, while the western prairies of both Canada and United States were parched by endless cycles of drought; becoming the location of new solar power arrays and a patchwork of hydroponic greenhouses along the northern border with Boreal Nation, supplied by freshwater flowing south from giant aqueducts constructed in the District of Churchill.

The United States population gravitated to its northern and western territory on the Appalachian Peninsula and Rocky Mountains cordillera. Underground structures were initially excavated along the Appalachian ridge to accommodate overflow from the large east coast cities, but complications from sinkage and collapsing convinced America to abandon this approach.

The elevated areas of the northeastern states New York, Pennsylvania and Ohio were overcrowded as people evacuated to a slightly cooler and bearable climate. The states of Michigan, Iowa, Wisconsin and Minnesota with their supply of potable freshwater, and western Montana, Wyoming, Idaho, Alberta, Washington and Oregon with their somewhat tempered north of forty climate, along with northern sections of Colorado, Utah and California, became the most populated areas of United States with steady migrations from the east. Desalination plants along the Pacific and Atlantic seaboards were critical to the survival of the states for more than a millennium following the onset of global warming.

The highest concentration of people on the planet were forced inland during the two-thousand millennium on Earth, resulting in many deaths. Continental populations of the world were crammed onto elevated regions, such as southern Europe, central Asia and China; either tormented by extreme heat and diseases or scrounging for food and freshwater for over five hundred years. The land base of the Middle East, Africa, southern Asia and all that remained of Australia and South America was rendered uninhabitable by the most drastic heat; creating the world's environmental refugee population drifting to highlands and makeshift underground bunker networks wherever possible, as only the most privileged were able to secure lodging inside hastily constructed climate-controlled structures.

The second half of the three-thousand millennium saw the slow recovery of climate and the natural environment, while civilisation clawed and climbed its way out of social upheaval. International conflict and warring factions were the mainstay in many regions for several centuries. Boreal Nation was at the forefront of both humanitarian relief and military peacekeeping efforts, eventually forming a new Northern Security Council to police the world with eleven other countries: United States, Canada, Denmark controlling Greenland, Iceland, Norway, Sweden and Finland, Scotland representing the British governments with the largest land base still above water, Russia, Mongolia and China.

❖ ❖ ❖

It was not until the early four-thousand millennium that interstellar exploration finally started to alleviate population pressures. The super power nations of the world were devastated by environmental degradation and their citizens were punished by the elements; governments were not in a position to spend money on space programs as their economies crumbled. Boreal Nation took the high road supporting all global efforts to keep humans, wildlife and ecologies healthy and alive, instead of exploiting the world with its most fortunate climate, natural resources and strong economy built on new technologies.

The Boreal Department of Interstellar Exploration, then within the Scientific Research Secretariat, was responsible for completing its first orbital space station in the Earth year 2265. The station was expanded over the next two thousand years and today is still an extensive orbital city with over four hundred and forty-six million square feet of functioning floor space on sixteen decks, including living quarters, medical, educational and recreational facilities, hydroponics, cargo docks, commercial trade areas and botanical gardens with aquatic pools. The space station dubbed "New Boreal" originally operated as a scientific research and monitoring facility until it was expanded for permanent residency; reaching over twenty-seven million square feet in its first two centuries and used as a supply transfer depot in the construction of an international lunar complex on the surface of the moon.

Originally, the moon outpost named "Solaris Lunar" was no more practical for large scale relocation than the two existing stations orbiting Earth; without natural gravity and requiring ventilation of oxygen. A planetary project to land humans on Mars successfully completed its first phase in the early twenty-fourth century, with two missions making return flights. The multi-national enterprise was encouraged enough to plan for a series of enclosed habitat biospheres; with adequate gravity and buried polar ice to attempt terraforming the planet.

Boreal Interstellar Exploration was charged with coordinating the "Solaris Mars" project; using New Boreal as a launching point for missions, which did not resume until the twenty-eighth century. Mars was initially developed over a span of two hundred years—indoors and outdoors—over an area of about four million square kilometres on the northern hemisphere of the planet. Solaris Mars was incrementally populated by citizens of Earth's countries devastated by an

240

intolerable climate, impossible growing conditions and chronic diseases, but the small planetary settlement could only accommodate so many fulltime residents.

Meanwhile, Boreal Nation continued to conduct scientific research at Earth's orbital and lunar stations. There were four profound benchmark innovations by the interstellar program that would change the world forever and impact on the history of Earth's universe. These innovations, along with a previous theory of physicist Albert Einstein, were affectionately referenced by the scientific community as the 'evolutionary elements of quantum mechanics'. The first and second element benchmarks between the years 3781 and 3792 literally propelled the infancy of Earth's exploration.

The telemetry of cosmic nano-probes exploring the Milky Way Galaxy and beyond, originally launched successfully in the twenty-second century, provided Boreal Nation and other nations with volumes of data on dark energy and matter. Research was accumulated since the discovery of gravity's energy back in the twenty-first century—Einstein's relativity postulation, which is regarded as the inspiration for the quantum benchmarks—leading to the first element: generating and harnessing the graviton pulse. Boreal scientists were able to adapt the technology of particle accelerators and emit a controlled graviton pulse within a confined structure to simulate gravity where there was none, such as on the orbital and lunar space stations.

This miraculous technological feat spawn the interstellar era for Planet Earth and manifested into other inventions. The technology to manipulate particles and energy resulted in the development of habitat biospheres in zero gravity on orbital stations, lunar outposts and spacecraft, as well as ionised and electromagnetic particle pulse and array design for sensory systems and weaponry, and the greatest accomplishment of all, the second element: an advanced propulsion system for space ships that approached the acceleration of light and later eclipsed the speed of time and space as humans knew it. The graviton pulse was refined in a few years; requiring a protective buffer shield around the accelerator for residue gamma-ray photons from the technology. The force of gravity could penetrate through a protective layer, while the buffer trapped minimal radiation from the process of generating the particle pulse.

Graviton was installed on the international space station, New Boreal and Solaris Lunar, which were augmented and increased in size to house more of Earth's struggling citizens. Flights transporting people to Solaris Mars definitely improved as well with graviton incorporated into spacecraft designs, and in the process a revolutionary new propulsion technology was discovered.

The confined graviton pulse inside a ship's outer structure provided simulated gravity but it also hindered forward momentum and required increased inertia from rocket thrusters fuelled by liquid hydrogen and oxygen. Scientists tested bulked up forward thrusters stacked in the rear of ships, but found that this approach could not compensate adequately for missions beyond Mars with restricted space and weight capacity for fuel storage. And then came the same genius revelation that discovered graviton in the first place. Fuel cell thrusters, with their technology already highly advanced, were stacked at the symmetrical centre of a spacecraft—the engine core—and once a critical speed was attained with forward thrust, a spherical array of intensely fused plasma particles was released through a circular bank of emitters located in the middle deck of the vessel; a procedure known as corridor dispersal.

The spherical array, led by a forward stream flowing out the bow of the ship, is shaped by the port, starboard and stern emitters with manipulated particle acceleration in the same manner as the graviton pulse; encompassing the entire vessel in a propelled corridor of plasma, with particle array continuity maintained by electromagnetic deflectors inside the corridor.

The plasma dispersal array attracts positrons found in dark energy gamma-rays which interact with electrons in the process of antimatter annihilation to create ionised forward propulsion, while the E.M. deflectors protect the ship's structural integrity and eliminate gravitational force at high speeds for passengers inside; essentially by floating the spacecraft in the middle of the plasma corridor, like an aerated bubble pulse streaming across the surface of water.

The new technology, known as corridor propulsion, was installed on large-scale space ships beginning in the last decade of the thirty-eighth century. These ships could reach velocities never before attained near light speed, complete with simulated gravity onboard; quite adequate for extremely efficient flights to Mars. Corridor propulsion also enabled astrophysicists to chart courses utilising the gravity energy of stars, planets and moons for sling shot acceleration, and most importantly eventually black holes; reducing the demand on fuel and allowing missions to the outer edge of the solar system and beyond. Flights could now last several months and even years.

The realisation of the first two quantum mechanic evolutionary elements by Earth's scientists bolstered the spirit of a socially stressed planet and helped to squelch political friction. There was reason for optimism as the Northern Security Council announced it would begin an aggressive cosmic exploration and astrometric project in the year 3792. The new spacecraft became Earth's first interstellar fleet; built by the Boreal National Government and operated by the Boreal Forces.

The ships were large enough to carry crews in the hundreds; stretching almost five hundred metres in length with a nine-deck centre hull structure, and both fore and aft modules attached that could separate, enter atmospheres and land on planets. The ships were equipped with onboard electrolysis converters recycling oxygen and hydrogen from by-product water vapour produced by the fuel cells; utilised to replenish thruster fuel and sustain life support systems, including air ventilation and hydroponic operations. Botanical arboretums were incorporated for prolonged expeditions to produce oxygen, and large freezer capacity was used for food storage.

A fleet of almost one hundred interstellar exploration vessels, as they were called, and close to four hundred smaller galactic and planetary ships were deployed. The exploration project would soon become a way of life for earthlings—resulting in new scientific breakthroughs and technological developments—as the galaxy and then more distant interstellar systems were gradually charted.

Boreal Nation possessed the resources and capacity as the primary sponsor of Earth's interstellar exploration program; coordinating operations with Northern Security Council member nations and gradually accepting candidates for the Boreal Forces from any country in the world, with normal screening procedures. The first monumental discovery was made a mere one hundred and sixty years into the program with only a small sector of the Milky Way charted. A few planets with atmospheres conducive to human anatomy were discovered beforehand, but considerable adaptations would have to be made to geological formations and ecologies for sustainable habitation. And then an uninhabited planet with atmospheric and ecological conditions ideal for human occupation was located about twenty light years from Earth's sun. This solar system was proclaimed "New Terra" and became the destination for the largest relocation of earthlings in the planet's burgeoning history; providing relief and a new opportunity for many humans still living in poverty.

It was a stimulating occasion for scientists, a shot of adrenaline for politicians and euphoria for much of humanity, but it was only the beginning of the interstellar era for Planet Earth. Infrastructure and public works were carefully planned, manufactured and assembled on Planet New Terra; requiring almost one hundred years of installation before a substantial number of citizens could emigrate. The first new permanent residents arrived in the year 4047 and moved into what started as neighbourhoods administrated by various governments; most adopting the name "New" as a democratic state, such as New Egypt, New India, New China or New America. Boreal Nation assumed administration of its New Terra District, the smallest on the planet, which was added to its Solaris Lunar and Mars Districts established in previous years.

The resources of interstellar exploration were focused on establishing New Terra over the next few hundred years. It was a twenty-year shuttle journey to reach the solar system. The majority of people applying for citizenship were making a commitment to future generations: couples fostering families on route or with infant children, along with older family members who desired some comfort in their declining years, enthusiastic young professionals and brave individuals just wanting to prosper in a new frontier.

There were plenty of jobs available to build a future; from simple labour to scientific disciplines. Life expectancy was also improved when humans were living in clean environments. Global warming took its toll on earthlings, but medical advancements increased mortality as the health care industry developed treatments to counter climatic stress and disease; making the arduous migration into the galaxy worthwhile to many people. The new planetary settlement—sprawling along the equator region because of bitter cold mountain terrain towards the polar regions—would grow into a cultured civilisation. And more planets would also be discovered; even though cartography expeditions were temporarily hindered while New Terra was being populated.

Astrometrics soon exploded into the ether while Earth propagated the galaxy; taking thousands of years to chart nebulae, quasars and the full scope of the universe. Exploration zones were originally mapped into quadrants and sectors of both homeland and outer territories—north, northwest, southwest and south towards the centre of the galaxy, with far north, northeast, southeast and far south towards the edge of the galaxy—reflecting the one hundred and sixty years it took to chart twenty light years in exacting detail.

The human existence on Earth may have never ventured beyond its own galaxy if it were not for the third evolutionary element of quantum mechanics; discovered because of the human drive to explore and the spirit to overcome astrometric challenges. Robotic ships were launched from transfer stations in the expanding exploration sectors; releasing nano-probes that could exceed the speed of light and return telemetry to compile detailed astrometric charts. This process continued until favourable locations were identified to extend the network of transfer stations. The pioneers of interstellar exploration would spend the majority of their lives in outer space; most descending from the New Terra population.

Corridor propulsion was engineered for the nano-probes using solar radiation cells and Freeborne Power Cell technology instead of hydrogen fuel cells; adequate to propel the suitcase-sized vessels beyond the speed of light without fuel storage restrictions. It was the amount of fuel capacity that prevented exploration vessels from sustaining factored light speed acceleration. The photovoltaic power from solar radiation was not sufficient to generate a plasma array on the larger spacecraft; demanding the combustion of hydrogen and oxygen, but the propulsion systems could not produce or store the amount of fuel needed to reach and maintain velocity beyond light speed. Many test flights were conducted with robotics to develop the speed for nano-probes, including successful flights with shuttle-sized ships and even large transports. Light speed factors were attained by robotic passenger and freight ships, but only for short distances until fuel expired and particle continuity deteriorated.

Propulsion research was conducted in parallel with cartography operations for five hundred years leading up to this new benchmark. The gravitational sling shot manoeuvre was studied meticulously; engaged at light speed in attempts to reduce the amount of fuel required, as cosmological bodies were discovered and charted farther into the galaxy. It was during sling shot experiments that the third quantum mechanic element came to fruition. Researchers were able to observe the behaviour of antimatter positrons found in the ambient plasma and gamma-ray photons of dark energy emanating from black holes, while gravitational energy was being utilised for propulsion and the ship's engine core was in idle mode.

The third element was strictly mechanical, even though astrophysics are essential in design calculations for specifications. A system of collector vents was installed on the centred topside and bottom hull of spacecraft, in line with the engine core. The venting system collects hydrogen and positrons from ambient plasma and gamma-ray photons while a ship is propelled by gravitational force; continuously replenishing fuel banks for protracted combustion. Corridor dispersal arrays were tweaked and fortified to withstand the velocity for uninterrupted flights: the science was solid and Boreal Nation engineers were becoming quite adept at technological precision.

This evolutionary quantum technology became the third element: plasma streaming, as it became known. Spacecraft reached new velocities beyond the speed of light; increasing with test flights from twofold to factors of ten. Plasma streaming corridor propulsion peaked with the technology available at a factor of just over one hundred and five thousand times faster than the speed of light; approximately one hundred and eight trillion kilometres per hour, or twelve light years per hour.

The plasma streaming era was introduced to earthling explorers, scientists and engineers, new travellers and commercial trades. A flight to New Terra that lasted twenty years when it was initiated two hundred years earlier was reduced to only a few hours gate to gate. Exploration and charting of the Milky Way that would have taken almost a million years was completed in less than eight years, including the discovery of another habitable planet on the far side of the galaxy in the year 4283; named Halpern in honour of the astronomer who first charted the solar system.

Planet Halpern was consequently established as another settlement for Earth. Cosmic flight was the new reality for earthlings. Exploration would prosper into the millennia and shape the future for these organic mortals; giving rise to a utopian existence that would open new frontiers and nourish their civilisation, yet woefully also lead to more conflict on the horizon.

Planet Earth was blossoming into the interstellar era as Zachary was camping on the shore of Kingsmere Lake, but the fourth evolutionary element was not discovered for another few hundred years. Earthlings had not yet encountered extra-terrestrial beings except animal creatures on new planets, let alone ancient hybrid species with the spiritual power of the trees. Zachary was ahead of his time in many ways.

Chapter 25: Muh

Bruno cast the fishing line over his shoulder. He watched the bait plunk into the lake; fresh minnows he caught himself. He reeled in slowly while looking down into the water. Another bite. He fought the fish briefly and easily pulled it to the side of his canoe: his fifth pickerel. He scooped the fish out of the water and set his fishing rod and open-faced reel in the canoe. Removing a smoothly polished wood baton from an underarm pouch, he gently tapped the fish on its head. He removed the hook, lined the pickerel through the gills on a rope with the other fish, rigged another minnow and cast out again.

This warrior is a solidly built young looking man who has actually lived hundreds of thousands of years; virtually immortal it seems because of many trips that have taken him several billions of annual continua through distant dimensional corridors, due to the demand on his acute skills. He is very tall with dark, straggled hair and almost always showing the shadow growth of an early beard. He is firm and muscular, especially considering his age, and carries a prehistoric look to go with the many years he has transpired. He was only wearing moose skin pants at that space and time.

The morning of fishing was a relaxing and welcome break for Bruno. He just returned from Planet Dlailia where he served as a bark shredder; the warriors who cover the flanks on tree raids. It is one of the most challenging and demanding of all tree raid positions. Bruno battled through rain, sleet, brutal cold and nasty gravity fields. He faced the possibility of losing his core on several occasions. And he knew the agony associated with being coreless. Bruno could not imagine life without a core.

And if it was not difficult enough protecting his core with a stager, remaining stagerless would leave his core even more vulnerable. The sputs on Dlailia are not vicious but they are numerous. The demons would surely congregate if a warrior wandered long enough without a stager, until there would simply be too many sputs to fend off with any amount of success. Life could be miserable while on a tree raid. Sleeping accommodations are not always ideal for bark shredders; non-existent is more accurate. Bruno does not mind sleeping without shelter, but in hail storms, snow storms and wind storms it's rather aggravating.

Bark shredders always have to be alert during raids. They take shifts as branch watchers at seedling stops. They are also responsible for the safety of the advancement while warriors are rooting. Although it is the root thrashers who usually suffer the greatest losses during the initial stages of a trunk takeover, it is the shredders who protect the ranks during trunk thrusts. The thrashers are big and strong, but they don't have to be all that cunning. The firewood harvesters and log splitter have to be sharp, agile and dextrous, but they are afforded luxurious sleeping accommodations by comparison on the rooting ships.

It is the bark shredders who have to possess the most diversified spectrum of talents. The have to be rugged and durable, able to navigate the lasha with a keen sense of the environment while dealing with the elements, and they have to be cunning and ruthless without fear of death. Bark shredders are among the bravest and most respected of all warriors, along with the tree raid commanders; during the entire tree raid, not just the trunk thrusts, shredders cannot afford to let their concentration falter. Many lose their stagers, roam the cosmos coreless or outright die in battle. Bruno always battled hard, but now he was relaxing. He enjoyed casting and reeling on a calm lake. It was therapeutic; soothing his mind.

But now it was time to clean his catch. A meal of fresh fish was the only thing on Bruno's mind. The lake he was on is small and well protected by the forest. It is one of Bruno's favourite spots and the fishing is usually good. It is the gift of Ajawaan. He started paddling to Grey Owl's cabin on the shoreline: once a famous mortal naturalist who lived with beavers on the little lake. Bruno would use the wood deck at the cabin to fillet his fish.

A man appeared from the bush walking towards the cabin as Bruno landed his canoe. The man wore green fatigues, hiking boots and a short-sleeve shirt. He was also wearing a backpack. It was Zachary. Both men stopped and looked at each other rather curiously. Bruno slowly climbed out of his canoe and Zachary cautiously took off his pack.

"Hello, doing a little fishing?" greeted Zachary.

"Muh," grunted Bruno.

The wood shaft in the pouch under Bruno's arm caught Zachary's attention. He knew it was not there for aesthetic appeal. It was a stager and this man was a tree warrior. Muh is the word in the Druid Dictionary of the ancient language that means the affirmative, or something that is good and beautiful, often spoken with enthusiasm. Bruno is a descendant of an original Druid; born in the pine tree unisphere where he often dwells.

Although the Druid presence on Earth led to the formation of a clan including priests and soothsayers emulating some of the rituals of botanical hybrid species, many tree warriors such as Bruno have evolved from their bloodlines to covet the powers of the sporadic element. The Druids, like Zachary, do not descend from a specific angel of the gods, but rather are the offspring of mortal self-perpetuation from many different tribes, so to speak. They became keen students of the spiritual conflicts, as well as linguistics, semantics and etymology as it turned out. While some seem very primitive, they have nonetheless uniquely developed their own sophisticated cultures, civilisations and of course languages, scattered on several Druid planets across the grand creations.

Not knowing anything about Druids but deducing the man before him was a powerful warrior, Zachary approached the situation with trepidation.

"I'm not looking for any trouble. I'll just turn around and be on my way if you would prefer," said Zachary.

The hulking warrior looked inquisitively at Zachary, who was holding his hatchet. Bruno pulled out his stager from under his arm and freely offered it in exchange while pointing at the hatchet.

"Nahsah dah," he said, asking Zachary to give him the stager.

The earthling was frightened by this large Druid but felt compelled to co-operate. He slowly gave Bruno the hatchet and took the wood baton; a fair trade of weapons. Both men examined the new stagers in their possession. The baton looked like it could be aspen, but Zachary did not know. Bruno looked at Zachary and smiled.

"Muh," he said again.

Zachary nervously smiled. Bruno began to laugh and adeptly tossed the hatchet blade firmly into the trunk of a spruce tree.

"Nice," said Zachary.

"Muh," repeated the Druid with more laughter.

"Whatever you say big guy—muh," Zachary forced a timid laugh.

Bruno laughed louder and this time shouted up towards the sky with his arms extended: "Envrah muh!"

Realising Bruno was not going to harm him, and assuming he had just met a friendly aspen warrior, Zachary held the polished baton above his head.

"Envrah muh, yes," he also began to laugh loudly.

Bruno waved towards his canoe.

"Don whaga, naga geevab gah," he said, roughly translated as let's go fishing for food.

He held up the line of fish from the canoe and pointed to the lake. He then set down the fish and grabbed his rod and reel. Zachary received the message and remembered he had a collapsible fishing rig in his backpack.

"Yes, we should go fishing, gah," he said nodding in agreement.

He yanked his hatchet from the tree and pointed to his pack with a smile, intending to get his gear. But Bruno did not find it amusing.

"Sahba," said Bruno, rushing over and taking Zachary's backpack to the canoe, placing it in the boat and once again beckoning to the lake.

"But I was just getting my fishing rod," explained Zachary.

"Whaga," let's go, said a persistent Bruno.

"Okay, I guess I'll take the bow," Zachary obliged his new partner.

They hopped into the canoe and shoved off shore; paddling only a half mile down to the south end of the lake where there's a small island close to shore. Zachary thought either this tree warrior was extremely friendly or he was being set up in a bad way. He was along for the ride at any rate, or should I say paddle: maybe they would catch some fish if the pickerel in the boat were any indication. Bruno pulled up a few feet before the island so the slight westerly breeze would gently drift the canoe across the south bay as they cast their lines trolling for a catch.

"Naga geevab po, pahva gahnah gah," instructed Bruno: fishing now, later preparing and cooking food.

And Bruno did not disappoint. He caught three more fish and Zachary caught another two. Zachary was excited to catch the fish. Bruno appeared rudimentary but was both a skilled and a very happy angler. He was clearly enthused and even thrilled as he set his hook and reeled in each fish to the side of the boat; easily securing them with a nimble pinch inside the gills.

"Muh, muh, muh," he rejoiced with every catch.

He decided ten fish would satisfy them for the day and so they paddled around the island to the shoreline where there was a portage trail between Ajawaan and Kingsmere Lake. Again with skill and agility Bruno slung his saddle bag pouch over his head and shoulder, slipped Zachary's backpack under the gunwale thwarts with the paddles and fishing rigs, and hoisted the canoe up onto his shoulders by himself. The string of fish dangled decoratively tied to the bow seat. Of course, their stagers remained with them always.

A paddle dropped down to the ground as Bruno started to hike down the trail with the canoe. Zachary looked around to see where it landed. He caught a glimpse of the handle and saw a faded and dusty light encompass the paddle. The next thing he heard was Bruno putting the paddle back under the gunwale.

"Do you have it?" asked Zachary.

"Muh," answered Bruno.

The two-mile portage to Kingsmere Lake was simple for Zachary, with nothing to do except watch Bruno carry the canoe and all the gear on his shoulders. The rookie space traveller may have been unknowingly out of his element well into future spacetime, but he felt comfortable with this burly tree warrior. He would further extend his trust with Bruno when they reached the Northend campsite on Kingsmere; still intact after over two thousand years. Bruno immediately put the canoe on the beach when they arrived and began filleting the fish on one of the paddles, while Zachary started a fire without prompting and pulled out a metal firegrill from his backpack.

He watched Bruno take a sharp knife and precisely cut behind the gills of the fish, carve around the rib cage and over the spine to the tailfin, cut away the body leaving the scales on the skin and the fillets from both sides attached at the tail, then slice some slits into the meat so it would peel away easily after cooking. Bruno usually cooked the fillets skin side down directly on hot coals or hanging on a cross spit branch rigged over the fire, but on this occasion he used the metal grill when the fire was ready with a thick bed of coals. He smiled at Zachary; impressed with the cooking grill.

"Muh," he nodded.

The young mortal took the cue and attempted to start a conversation.

"You like the grill?" posed Zachary.

"Neewhasee eesah jah—muh," that is what I said, yes.

"Muh, that means you like it?"

"Muh," Bruno laughed, as he was wanton to do.

"How do you come to be here in the wilderness? Who are you and what is it that you do?" continued Zachary.

"Naga?"

"Yes, naga I guess. What do you do? Are you a tree warrior?"

"Dah naga moobah. Neewhasee eesah muh."

"Yes, muh, you like that word."

"Muh."

"So, if I can figure out what you're saying, naga could mean to do something, and that something is moobah; that's what you do."

"Muh."

"And there's that word again."

"Muh."

"It must mean something good."

"Muh, muh," Bruno spoke with increased emphasis.

"It means yes, and sometimes an emphatic yes," calculated Zachary.

"Muh."

"Is that all you're going to say—muh?"

"Sahba."

"Ah, you said that earlier today. Does it mean the opposite of muh?"

"Muh."

"Okay, so muh is yes or good, and sahba is no, or bad?"

"Muh."

"And you like to do this thing called moobah?"

"Muh."

"And so moobah is a good thing. I heard that word before. Does it have something to do with this quest for peace?"

"Muh. Neewhasee seebee, bohtahna lah sylva," exclaimed Bruno: it is the same as salvation for good deeds and the silviculture prophecy of actuality.

"Are those different words for muh?" puzzled Zachary.

"Sahba."

"Sahba, no, they're something else."

"Muh."

"So I was right, I figured out some words, at least muh and sahba."

"Muh, muh, muh," smiled Bruno.

He then unceremoniously walked over and gave Zachary a big hug. The girth of the Druid warrior was intimidating and potentially painful, yet in Zachary's peripheral vision he thought he saw something glowing down around the waist of Bruno's pants. It was actually the tip of his stager sticking out of the underarm pouch, but Zachary thought of a more bizarre scenario: holy shit, he said to himself, I'm here on this isolated lake alone with this ape of a man and his pants are glowing. Fortunately for Zachary the hug only lasted a few seconds without any harmful repercussions.

"You're quite strong there, fella," Zachary said to Bruno, who answered with a flex of his bicep.

"Vohko," he grinned.

"Oh yes, vohko, very strong," agreed Zachary.

"Muh, laf vohko."

"Laugh, yes I can laugh, ha, ha," played along Zachary, so he thought.

"Sahba. Laf vohko," no, very strong, repeated Bruno.

"Sahba? What, I shouldn't laugh?"

"Massyb, ha, ha. Laf, vohko," gestured Bruno again to his flexed bicep.

"I see. 'Laf' means very strong, and your word for laughter is actually different, it's 'massyb'."

"Muh, tee shahtoo," yes, you understand.

"Excellent. I take it 'tee shahtoo' is a good thing as well, but I think we'll leave it at that for today's lesson," rationalised Zachary.

Bruno simply laughed yet again: "Muh, muh."

The fish was soon cooked and Zachary watched his companion wolf down several fillets. Bruno had the appetite to go with his size and consumed half of the fish; wrapping the uncooked leftover fillets in a cloth and putting them in his man purse of a leather pouch after Zachary ate two fish on his own. The warrior seemed to know what he was doing in the wilderness with only a few items for gear, which convinced Zachary to tag along for an afternoon of paddling in the canoe. Bruno was receptive to the idea after dousing the fire and cleaning up camp.

They pushed out from shore in the shallow water at Northend beach and headed across Kingsmere. Zachary scooped a cup of lake water and drank it. It was good: muh. He inhaled deeply and swallowed the fresh scent of boreal forest. There he was canoeing across a clear lake in the north country; life could be worse. Bruno was in the stern charting a course across the lake to Pease Point— a small bay on the west shore that curls into a narrow channel leading to the smaller Bagwa Lake. The namesake of Beatrice is one of three lakes forming a westerly semi-circle beside Kingsmere.

Paddling through calm, smooth water was easy and relaxing. Zachary concentrated on regular strokes to gain maximum gliding efficiency. Sitting in the bow he methodically kept a steady pace: Bruno was certainly not taking up his time with idle conversation. Zachary's mind began to wander. He stared into the water and started to feel a nerving yearning; otherwise known as sexual frustration. He saw Zelda's face in the water, then her clavicles, then her breasts and her entire body floating on top with her legs spread and her hands rubbing her flat stomach. Zachary thought about bouncing.

He could not keep his sanity any longer. He knew there was only one way to achieve immediate relief. He released his paddle in mid-stroke and lunged overboard. The cool northern water erased thoughts of breasts and thighs with visions of snakes slithering back into their burrow holes in the ground. Bruno was able to keep the canoe righted as he paddled beside Zachary. He grunted at the fool in the water with an inquisitive smirk.

"Bah? Zahkahsoo?" what, are you injured, he questioned.

Zachary easily pulled himself back into the canoe.

"We go now," he said picking up his paddle.

"Bah?" repeated Bruno.

"Go," said Zachary pointing across the lake.

"Whaga," concurred Bruno.

"Alright then, whaga."

They continued towards Pease Point without any further words.

Reflecting on the episode Zachary learned something valuable. He knew that to succeed with his search, he simply must dismiss everything which existed for him in the civilised world he left behind. He must think of nothing else but the trees; it was imperative if he was to survive this ordeal. And he must do more tree bashing. The power of the lasha was not far from his command of ionised endorphins. He would soon have his way with a few spruce.

Entering the bay at Pease Point Bruno steered the canoe towards the channel leading to Bagwa Lake. Zachary stopped paddling and pointed at the campsite on shore.

"Whaga," he said.

"Sahba," demanded Bruno.

There was not any argument from Zachary who continued to paddle. The wind picked up and a few clouds started moving across the sky as they entered the Bagwa channel, which is bordered primarily by spruce trees on land with lily pads scattered on the water's surface and reeds overgrowing the shoreline. We wind warriors increased in force and more clouds with vapour demons blew in from the east. An easterly wind was not normal and either was afternoon fog creeping in from the forest and spreading across the channel. Suddenly Bruno stopped paddling himself and stood upright in the canoe. He looked to each shore and back at Pease Point. The fog grew more dense.

"Zahka vahbahsoo," dangerous fog, whispered Bruno.

"That doesn't sound good," Zachary also whispered.

"Zeeb, sahba muh," confirmed Bruno in the simplest of words.

Intent on each stroke, Bruno slowly took them through the mist while constantly scanning in all directions. Zachary did not know what to expect next. A fairly pleasant day abruptly turned into a sorcerous haunt of uncertainty. A splash in the water sounded off to the port side. Bruno directed the canoe into the reeds and a large bull moose splashed up more water and retreated into the woods. Zachary was shivering from the sudden cold weather. They moved through the reeds back to the middle of the channel and luckily made it out into the lake without any complications.

The fog remained thick on Bagwa as Bruno kept a steady line straight across the lake to the south shore and a small peninsula. The clouds began to swarm above the eastern horizon. Bruno glared at the turbulence in the sky and observed a bright ball of light breaking through the cloud cover and soaring down towards the canoe. Zachary could see the dazzle and clearly identified the object streaking above the lake. It was a large clump of land behind a glitter of sparkles, with a man between two trees holding a shining staff protruding from the ground and an open fire burning at the stern of the flying island. Zachary knew it was the power of lasha.

The branch ship buzzed overhead and out to the west side of the lake, but Bruno's eyes remained focused on the eastern horizon. It was another arboretum vessel in pursuit. Bruno began to paddle fast.

"Alka! Whaga leepkah tiggvab, sygah!" he yelled: roughly translated, spruce warrior, paddle hard in the boat.

Zachary did not need any translation—he understood. They raced through the water towards the south shore. The first branch ship turned in the sky and headed back to the middle of the lake. The two ships were on a collision course. The second ship, an Alkae warrior according to Bruno, swerved just before ramming to execute a destabilising impact.

A tremendous clap of electromagnetism exploded in the air. Sparks and lightning flashed above the lake as the first ship faltered. The chunk of land sliced into the water while the Alkae ship deflected off to the right, crashing down to the shoreline. But the spruce warrior was able to navigate his ship out of a nose dive and pull up above the trees. Bruno paddled even harder.

The Alkae circled and passed above the canoe, delivering a bolt of lightning that struck the water just ahead of Zachary in the bow. The lake water boiled and the canoe smashed through waves of glowing water. Zachary could feel the jerks of electricity dart through his body when he was splashed. Bruno stopped paddling and grabbed his stager from under his arm, motioned the baton at the branch ship hovering near them and unleashed a whirl of sparkling aurora. The result of the blast made it evident to Zachary his new friend possessed compelling power.

The arboretum ship was shaken and the navigator went tumbling into the lake. Bruno dove into the water and swam to the nearby shore. Zachary did not know what to do. He watched the Alkae swim to shore as well and struggle to his feet. The two warriors faced each other standing on the peninsula at the south end of Bagwa Lake.

"Zeeb!" shouted Bruno with the anger inferred in the word.

The dizzy spruce warrior immediately jumped up, clutched the edge of his hovering branch ship and lifted himself back onto the airborne craft. Bruno then took some affirmative action of his own; holding his stager above his head with both hands and driving it into the ground. The stager was buried into the dirt and came shooting back up with a glittering tail. The land around him ripped from the earth and a wild collection of coloured particles appeared under the bed of soil; floating the island vessel into the air. Zachary was duly entertained: this was lasha power to reckon.

Both warriors were now controlling hunks of earth the size of small yachts. Bruno did not waste any time and rammed his ship into the Alkae. The vessels shuddered and sparked. Bruno quickly rammed the spruce ship two more times and the Alkae, jarred and reeling backwards, retreated from the contest by pulling up and fleeing over the tree tops. Bruno hastily pursued.

The spruce warrior circled over Bagwa and came to a crisp stop facing Bruno with a sharp spin to the middle of the lake. A slice of lightning speared from the Alkae's stager, but it was not enough. Bruno viciously smashed into the branch ship before the lightning reached the boundary of the vessel. It was no contest.

The aspen powered ship penetrated the spruce barrier of lasha and bashed the island of land into bits of dirt; a flashing shower of sparks filling the foggy air above Bagwa. The pieces of the ship crashed into the lake and the Alkae plunged down to the water. Bruno drove through the impact, pulled his ship to a quick halt and glided down over the water's surface to investigate: this warrior knew exactly what he was doing.

The Alkae and his ship both sunk to the bottom of the lake, and just as tragically the warrior and vessel from the first branch ship to enter the atmosphere were also hopelessly submerged. Bruno paused and then looked up to the eastern sky again. It was yet another arboretum ship cruising down to Bagwa. Bruno saw who it was and casually hovered over to Zachary and the canoe; landing back down where his ship had ripped from the ground. The shimmering light around his vessel disappeared, as did the aurora attaching his stager to the flying organic island. He put his stager back into its underarm pouch while Zachary paddled to shore. Standing on the peninsula they watched the new branch ship approach. Bruno did not take his eyes off the ship, yet he did not show any alarm. Zachary finally recognised the navigator as the tree warrior came up to the shore: it was Hawkins Kingsmere.

The branch ship was covered with grass and soft moss. A small stand of trembling aspen garnished the vessel and an open firepit was decorated with limestone rocks between Hawkins and the trees. There were three people sitting on the grass—a man and a woman, who were both naked, and another man dressed like a tree warrior. Kinsmere brought the ship to a rest beside Bruno and Zachary; releasing his stager but still leaving the vessel activated. He walked with the other warrior over to the dancing coloured light skirting the edge and stepped down to the ground. The naked woman jumped up and dashed into the woods. Zachary watched the nude figure of a woman. There was something familiar about her movements, but she was not Zelda. And then the naked man gave chase. Zachary turned his attention to Hawkins.

"So we meet again," said Kingsmere.

"It's good to see you Hawkins," answered Zachary.

"Hudec," greeted Bruno, saying welcome with his arm raised.

"Hudec keeno," greetings friend, said both Hawkins and the other man, also raising their arms.

A dim light formed between the three men and they all smiled. They lowered their arms and Hawkins started explaining the situation.

"Zahka Druid. Don naga tee. Dah bohtrak whaga neewhasee Alka, jobo Druid," he said pointing to the lake: there is fighting on Druid, we need you, I travelled through space pursuing that Alkae from Druid.

"Neewhasee soonah, traupah zahkahsoo. Dah nah maha tee," it is sad the tree warrior died, I will help you, said Bruno.

"Neewhasee laf Alka tahsak Druid. Nah tee whaga po?" there are many spruce warriors on Druid, will you go now, questioned Hawkins.

"Zahka sahba, seebee Dlailia. Don whaga po, lah loho pahva," war is bad, the same as on Planet Dlailia, we will go now and triumph later, predicted Bruno.

"Muh," Hawkins thanked his friend; also turning to Zachary who was anxiously waiting to ask a question or two.

"What exactly is going on, and who were those naked people on your ship?" he inquired.

"Oh, those two. They're just a couple of newlywed wizards, Sally and Sven Slattern. They're helping us search for Soarfoot actually."

"So my mother was right."

"About what?"

"I saw Sally at my parent's cabin on a lake north of here, but that was a few hundred years ago, so I'm told."

"Yes, about that. You see, when you met up with Harold, he took you to several homeland planets across the unispheres of our grand creation."

"Unispheres? Grand creation? Oh no, here we go again."

"I know, it'll take you some time to acclimatise, but soon you'll adapt to all this cosmic travel. Earth is in the pine tree unisphere, home to Soarfoot, but the aspen tree universe is billions of light years away through a black hole corridor found in a galaxy of the Indus Supercluster in this universe."

"So a unisphere is the same as our universe, and don't tell me, there's a universe for each tree species," deduced Zachary.

"Exactly. See, I knew you would adapt. There's several unispheres and they're grouped into the largest of clusters we call grand creations. As far as we know there are another two grand creations beyond our unispheres."

"Separated by hundreds of billions of light years," posed Zachary.

"Yes, right again. But I'm afraid you were taken across dimensions by Harold and another couple thousand years transpired here on Earth."

"Damn, I hate it when I'm right. This is blowing my mind Hawkins. I'm afraid to ask, but do you know what year it is on Earth?"

"I know it's crazy," said the other warrior, "but it's the end of the forty-third century. I've been around from the time of your ancestors myself."

This man was short and stalky; a distinct looking Chipewyan warrior with curly strawberry blonde hair contrasting his darker skin.

"This is Alexander Ajawaan, another namesake from this area dating back to the time of Irving Steele and Soarfoot," continued Hawkins. "He was on his way to a tree raid until we took this detour. Those wizards you just saw were sent to me at Harold's request. They took me into spiritual corridors and we consumed enough spacetime to arrive back here with you."

"Well at least that's some good news I guess, but if that makes me over two thousand years-old, how about you and this big guy here?"

"You don't know who he is?"

"Well, I've been with him for most of the day, but we've just started communicating in the ancient language. Did you say something about a Druid?"

"Yes, I did as a matter of fact. This is our good friend Bruno. He's a great aspen warrior from Planet Druid—keeno Zachary," said Hawkins looking over to the imposing Druid, telling him that Zachary was also a friend.

"Hudec," said Bruno with a wink.

"Hudec is a greeting and keeno means friend. I told Bruno there is more fighting on his home planet and he is needed there. He thinks we should go and take care of the trouble. And as I'm sure you just witnessed, Bruno is very good at taking care of trouble. I'm a few hundred years older than you Zachary, thanks in part to our search for your ancestors, but this guy, well, no one knows for certain, probably not even him, but Bruno is hundreds of thousands of years-old at the very least. He has travelled far and wide to fight for the manifesto of peace."

"How about my parents then? Do you know if they're still alive?"

"The wizards tell me they have seen your parents and yes, they have travelled into the spiritual dimension and returned all these hundreds of years later. They also tell me your father is still dedicated to finding Soarfoot and the Storyteller, as we all are these days."

"Yes, this manifesto. It has very profound implications I take it."

"Yes indeed, universal implications. The manifestos battle for peace across the galaxies against the evil intentions of the credos, who bring death and destruction to many home worlds."

"And these are the organic vessels that fly through space?"

"This is a branch ship, it is one of the arboretum vessels tree warriors use for interstellar travel, like the one that transported you to Envrah with Cookie and your friend Zelda. The cushion of light particles gives the ship its power, the same power that comes from the stagers. We call this energy the lasha, and when we're riding through space it is bohtrak, or botanic spiritualis."

"Muh," responded Bruno.

Hawkins chuckled: "See what I mean."

"Yup, I think I'm slowly catching on to this. Can you tell me a little more about these tree raids?"

"Well, the first branch ship you saw was an aspen Envrah and chasing it was a spruce Alkae. The spruce ship jumped the Envrah at the edge of a swaying flotilla on its way to Planet Blaved for a tree raid. I detected the credo and gave chase with Alexander. We were not far from Earth and knew Bruno was in the vicinity, so we manoeuvred in this direction. Unfortunately we lost a tree warrior, and unfortunately Bruno had to terminate the Alkae, but this constant conflict seems to be the way of the universe right now."

"I figured something like that, but what exactly is a swaying flotilla?"

"It's a group of other larger ships that engage in tree raids, but you'll probably see that first hand quite soon."

"Don whaga po," said Bruno, telling Hawkins they should leave now.

"Muh, don whaga tahsak dah brak," answered Hawkins, telling Bruno they would go on his branch ship.

He turned to Zachary: "The question is, are you coming to Druid?"

"Will I be able to travel on this thing?" pondered Zachary.

"You might pass out again, but you'll make it," Kingsmere assured him.

"Then I'm coming."

The mortal human in the crowd jumped onto the floating island while Bruno and Alexander loaded the canoe on the ship. Zachary felt a surge spread through his body and into his mind. It was the sporadic element and the energy was strong; it did not take much for an overdose at his stage of development. The ship began to glide over the trees and up into the sky under Hawkin's power. Zachary fell to the grass. They began moving quicker and blew through the clouds in a blur. The blue sky began to darken. Zachary held on tightly to his hatchet and fought the stars twirling in his head, while a thrust of inertia pushed against his body. The coloured light at the bow of the ship expanded brighter as the organic island broke the planet's atmosphere and darted out into stellar space. But Zachary could not hold on any longer; he saw the universe open up before him in a fleeting vision and then he lost consciousness.

Cruising above a forest that looked similar to Planet Earth with Hawkins still at the helm and Bruno standing at the bow overlooking the ship's course, Zachary finally awoke beside Alexander on the grass. They came upon a river and Hawkins turned the vessel to follow the flowing water. The river was wide and overgrown with trees on both sides of the shoreline. There was an assortment of hardwoods including aspen, poplar, birch, maple and elm. Zachary was recuperating from his trip through space yet he soon realised his muscles were suddenly much stronger, firm and rejuvenated. He breathed deeply and with an increased capacity. He looked at his hands still clasping his hatchet to see that his stager was faintly illuminated and almost floating.

"How do you feel?" asked Hawkins.

"Sensational," answered Zachary.

"It's the power of the aspens, ashah pyen. You've been absorbing it on the ship. This mass of land has been with the lasha for some time and it's rich with the power. Someday you'll be able to navigate through the cosmos, it's the gift of the angels," explained Hawkins.

"Are we on Druid now?"

"Yes, just ahead there's an Envrah camp. We'll be stopping there."

"What should I do while I'm here?" questioned Zachary.

"You should probably follow me and I'll let you know what's going on. In the meantime, be alert and prepared, things might get a little dangerous."

The warriors approached a bend in the river and Kingsmere took the ship up the left bank etching into a cliff face with scattered ledges of rock and sand. Zachary could see a few other warriors partially hidden behind the rock as their ship climbed over the top of the cliff. Around another bend of rising banks the river then emptied into a vast ocean of water stretching in all directions and reaching to the horizon. Turning the ship left they followed the shore where several small camps were spread out on the towering coastline. They reached a gaping fjord inlet that opened up beyond the cliffs only a mile down the coast. Hawkins steered them into the fjord and came to a waterfall flowing from a smaller creek behind the stone walls surrounding the inlet.

They swerved to follow the creek; gliding over the narrow passageway carved into rock and moss, where Zachary could see many warriors perched on steep ledges. It appeared as if each warrior was protecting the entrance of a cave with smoke billowing from some of the openings in the rock face. The entire area was a hub of activity. They saw many people along the shore: gathering water, washing clothes and cooking meals, with small branch ships passing back and forth. Hawkins floated their ship through the passage and entered into a lush valley of aspens, cottonwoods and grasslands. The creek meandered across the enormous valley. Hawkins guided them over the trees to a camp beside the waterway; consisting of three wood shacks and several tents, with half a dozen fires burning at random locations. He brought the ship to a rest and with both hands pulled his stager free. The lasha faded as Kingsmere, Ajawaan and Bruno walked off the ship into the camp.

"Follow us," Hawkins said to Zachary.

The new arrivals were met by camp elders. Everyone was dressed in similar clothes: moccasins, leather hide pants and various designs of bark-bast vests and tunic tops, made from smooth sheets of pliable outerbark or weaved in strands with the innerbark phloem plant fibre from trees, much like the flexible armour of medieval knights and other warriors of the Middle Ages. It was like a throwback in history to the era of the ancestors they were pursuing. Zachary watched as greetings were exchanged and the conversation started.

"Alka meelka zahka don eevah, laf jobo," said one warrior, explaining that spruce hybrids were infiltrating under disguise and fighting or killing their people at many different places.

"Jo?" where, asked Bruno.

"Neewhasee laf zahka, jobo Takid Wheep," said another warrior: there are many battles at Camp Wheep.

"Don nah lohsee eevah. Whaga sweesah, po gahtoo," declared Bruno.

The Druids nodded in agreement and went to a nearby campfire. Bruno returned to Hawkin's branch ship to retrieve his saddle bag.

"Did he just say we're going to eat first?" asked Zachary.

"Very good, you already have an ear for the language. Yes, Bruno says we will go soon to protect the aspen families at Camp Wheep, but first we will eat. He does need his nourishment," translated Hawkins.

"I'll say, that man can devour a lot of food."

A young twig supplier at the neighbouring camp cooked a meal for everyone in attendance. Nourishment complete, all concerned walked over to another campfire where more Druids were assembled.

"Don whaga po, jobo Wheep," announced Bruno.

And the party of Envrah warriors departed into the forest. Zachary followed with Hawkins and Alexander; further quizzing them on the ancient language.

"It's a very basic language as you can tell," started Hawkins.

"It might be simple, but without any vocabulary I'm a bit lost."

"Well, syntax is very loose and most of the lexicon concerns the actions of tree raids and battles. Some words take on more than one meaning, but the same can be said for the English language. Emotion, context and inflection can change the meaning of many words. There are foundation words as a base, which I'm sure you've heard from Bruno already. The Druids have a dictionary for the language, we could probably find a copy somewhere around here. The words and semantics were developed over millions of years in four stages; basic communication, as a trail guide, for tree raids and then most recently to explain some of the modern technology in the universe."

"So I should be able to pick up on it fairly quickly then?"

"You're an educated man, it shouldn't be too difficult."

Hawkins assured Zachary he would inform him of meanings and nuance as they encountered new expressions. Zachary continued to ask the meaning of a few different words while they walked. They reached Camp Wheep in short order, which was much larger than any of the previous settlements. A wall of wood shacks was dispersed along a perimeter the size of about two football fields. Tents, shacks and campfires were spread throughout the camp with some permanent structures serving as dwellings for commerce built among the small stands of trees that dotted the area. Smoke and the sound of bustle filled the air.

"Be on your guard now. This place can be dangerous, it's swarming with warriors, con artists and criminals of various descriptions," warned Hawkins.

Bruno led the modest entourage through the maze of tents and shacks. Wheep was truly a universal community. People were eating and drinking around campfires and yelling in different languages. A few leaf gypsies were playing guitars, violins or squeeze box accordions with or without vocals. There were quiet social conversations, loud parties with singing and dancing, bathing in tubs behind curtains or showering in gravity fed stalls, group saunas in log bath houses, and a few drunk warriors zapping rodents with their stagers. Bruno approached two men standing beside a lean-to attached to a cabin. A slab of wood was placed over barrels at the front of the lean-to. Hawkins motioned to the man behind the countertop.

"What do you say Zachary, let's grab some aspen juice," he suggested.

"Aspen juice?" frowned Zachary.

"It has a kick, it'll build up your confidence," laughed Hawkins.

"I can imagine."

"Ip kahs," ordered Kingsmere.

"Muh," answered the bartender.

They were served two large portions of the brew in tall metal mugs with handles: a unique concoction made with fermented branch leaves, sapling sprouts, just a few filings of inner bark phloem and most importantly some root fibre. They took a sip of the juice while Bruno was talking to the men beside the counter. It tasted like cold tea, but with a very distinct kick as Hawkins described. Meanwhile, Bruno was getting some important information.

"Crah laf Alka, meelka fahbee Wheep?" how many Alkae are in disguise here at Wheep, asked Bruno.

"Don ashahssa eesah ip Alka meelka. Neewha fahbee po," answered one of the men: we think there are two Alkae infiltrating, and they might be here in the camp now.

"Nah tee shahtoo teelaf?" can you describe them, continued Bruno.

"Soonah, don sahba klahsah bah teelaf eesah," sorry, we do not know who they are.

"Bah teelaf naga fahbee?" what are they doing here, posed Bruno.

"Teelaf zahka keeno Envrah, lah sahzah ashah pyen ashyb," they are fighting friendly Envrah warriors and stealing aspen trees.

"Teelaf eesah za," they are cowards said the other man.

Bruno turned to his friends and removed his stager from under his arm as he started walking farther into the camp.

"Don whaga," we go, he said bluntly.

He slowly browsed through the crowds of people while holding his stager ready for battle. Hawkins and Zachary followed behind with the group of warriors.

"They suspect there are two Alkae somewhere in the camp. If they're here, Bruno will find them," explained Hawkins.

Watching intently, Zachary took another drink of the aspen juice and then noticed Kingsmere was already done. He tossed caution into the barrel, so to speak, and slugged back the rest of the bitter tonic. The relaxing warmth about to encompass him, combined with the lasha battle he was about to witness, made for a very interesting and eventful segue in his life's journey, as whacky as it was becoming.

The search party mingled through the menagerie of camp dwellers until Bruno spotted a large man off to the side of a teepee tent. The man, who appeared to be drunk, was hassling and apparently threatening a woman. He was gesturing with his hands, laughing loudly and slurring his speech. Bruno stopped and assessed the situation. Although it looked too obvious, Bruno knew the typically crude, arrogant and belligerent conduct of seasoned spruce warriors on a bender. Facing the Alkae he raised his stager and pointed at the man.

"Bah tee naga Wheep?" Bruno shouted above the noise, demanding to know what the warrior was doing in the camp.

The Alkae stopped waving at the woman and looked over at Bruno. The people in the area also stopped to observe the confrontation.

"Dah maha loho," I'm enjoying the party, he said with a cocky grin.

"Jo tee keeno?" where is your friend, demanded Bruno again.

"Bah keeno?" what friend, snarled the warrior.

"Tee Alka keeno," Bruno accused him.

"Dah sahba dahbid keeno," I don't have a friend, insisted the Alkae.

"Zeeb, tee Alka traupah meelka," I strongly disagree, you're a spruce tree warrior in disguise, retorted Bruno.

The warrior suddenly pulled a stager from a side pouch on his leg and shot a razor edge of flashing particles at Bruno. A layer of lasha lit up around Bruno's stager and deflected the charge out over the camp where it struck a large cottonwood tree outside the wall of shacks. The tree exploded into tiny pieces of wood with fragments of stagerdust drifting in the air. People around the commotion began to yell and run for cover, while Hawkins and Zachary moved closer to watch the fight with the rest of their party.

The Alkae stager also lit up with the power of spruce as Bruno rushed forward without hesitation. The Druid delivered three quick blows with his stager which the Alkae blocked. The stagers smashed together with snaps of electricity accompanied by bursts of lasha. The spruce warrior was driven back and tripped into a tent. He struggled to his feet and Bruno lambasted him with another strong swing of his stager. He was sent sprawling again as he blocked the force of Bruno's strike, but was able to scramble on his feet and sling a whirling ball of lasha at the Druid. Bruno easily stood his ground and deflected the ball of energy directly back at the Alkae; sending him crashing into a small wood shack.

The bulky warrior lay on the ground stunned yet was able to recover back on his feet again. Bruno was greeted by a desperate and wildly swinging warrior as he barged into the shack kicking away boards and planks. He ducked under the attempted blow and connected with a crisp overhand stager punch. The Alkae reeled into the back wall of the shack and Bruno followed up with another swing, but the warrior slipped under the flash of energy. The strike hit the back wall and cracked down the remainder of the shack amidst splinters of wood and flickers of lasha. The two warriors brushed away the debris and shuffled about for position.

The Alkae wound up with an overhead slam which Bruno intercepted with a stiff forearm. The Druid then took to the offensive landing two quick stager jabs and letting loose a full roundhouse swing. The Alkae crouched down avoiding the deadly strike after fending off the jabs and then connected with a powerful blow of his own. Bruno was sent flying onto the ground for the first time. The spruce warrior charged and came crushing down with his stager. Bruno rolled to the side and the Alkae stager landed in the ground; chunks of dirt and stone spraying in all directions. The mighty aspen warrior immediately shot a bullet of lasha while on his back and the unprepared Alkae was jarred off his feet; his head snapping back as he went flying into a stack of firewood. The warrior moaned in pain. He was unable to continue the battle.

The Alkae stager lay on the ground beyond the warrior's reach. Throwing it up into the air, Bruno sent the stager sailing off into the distance with a blast of lasha. He then confronted the Alkae who stood up.

"Tee eesah sygahvee. Whaga Alka po," you are defeated, go back to Alka now, ordered Bruno.

The spruce warrior did not argue. He stumbled in the general direction of his stager and vacated Camp Wheep. The Druids and Envrah in the camp slowly assembled from under cover; ridiculing the Alkae and walking up to Bruno with offers of congratulations. Although the local population seemed delighted with the victory, Bruno was not overtaken with joy. Graciously he accepted the accolades but kept a watchful eye on the proceedings. Gradually people began to disperse while a hum of excited banter filtered through the camp. Bruno, still gazing around intently, approached his friends where Zachary and Hawkins were still standing.

"Neewha pinnah Alka meelka fahbee takid," he said, there could be a lone Alkae still in disguise here at the camp.

And then, as chance would have it, a scream could be heard.

"Bruno!" came the yell.

They turned and looked above the perimeter of shacks. Standing on a branch ship floating among the tree tops was a female Alkae navigator. She was lean, attractive, dressed only in skimpy clothing and sailing an impressive ship: surrounded by healthy spruce trees and covered in soft moss, with rocks protecting the bow and helm where the warrior was standing holding her shiny stager, and a firepit backed by a stone wall shielding the stern with neatly stacked kindling and logs. The Alkae looked arrogant and steaming with presumptuous ego, but also rather fragile and harmless. She began to laugh.

"Teesah Envrah, bohko zahka," she shouted at Bruno; foolish aspen warrior, prepare for battle.

And with an almost seductive swish of her arm, she fled up and over the flora; quickly disappearing behind a trail of streaming lasha. Bruno watched in disgust, but did not make any attempt to follow. He had won this battle.

"Sahba po. Don zahka lah loho pahva," not now, we will fight and triumph later, he said to his friends.

"Muh, muh," came agreement in unison.

"Now that was an Alkae, but Bruno doesn't think it's worth it because he'll just crush the little powder puff later, right?" summarised Zachary.

"That's about right, except I wouldn't underestimate that Alkae. She looked to be a very competent bark shredder," clarified Hawkins.

"A bark shredder—I know what an Envrah is, an Alkae and a Druid, but this is a new one. This ought to be good," sneered Zachary.

"I thought by now you would take this more seriously."

"I'm sorry Hawkins, it's just the aspen juice talking. That stuff really has a kick. I definitely want to know about tree raids, and I'm guessing I'll need to know such things fairly soon."

"Well, these things are not that easily explained, but I suppose if you're to become a tree warrior you should know. Come with me, we'll go for a hike and I'll explain a few things."

Hawkins walked up to Bruno and Alexander who were already talking to other warriors about the tree raid on Planet Blaved. He put his arm around Bruno and bid him farewell.

"Tahsah traupah, tee loho sweesah. Dah nah shahtoo leepash, lah Zachary jobo min. Rah keeno," said Hawkins: old warrior, you will be victorious soon, I will be explaining tree raids with Zachary in the valley, farewell friend.

"Hudec keeno," be brave friend, said Bruno.

He then turned to Zachary and raised his arm. The earthling followed Bruno's lead and a glimmer of lasha filled the space between them.

"Lasha," smiled the Druid warrior.

Zachary was filled with a sobering sensation; once again invigorated and extremely energised.

"Muh," he spoke softly to Bruno.

"Muh," answered Bruno.

Chapter 26: Conjuring Lasha

The menacing sput could smell the wood burning. Hungry for a core, it began to lumber towards the fresh scent. Through a stand of alder, down into a valley of birch and across a ridge of aspen, the demon sput plodded closer to the campfire. It could see the faint light of the flames from a peak in the distance. There would likely be campers beside the fire, vulnerable to the sput's sneak attack.

The demon sput is a mindless creature of destruction. It is not aware of any bounds to its destructive abilities, which are usually limited if the truth be known. It will attempt to remove the spiritual core from any warrior, without any consideration of a warrior's prowess. A sput is defeated in most situations, but the half-tree, half-demon, which can possess gender depending on the circumstances of its creation, can often be found in large numbers. They gather in hordes and spring core fusions on unsuspecting warriors.

Sputs breed on any planet and reproduce in abundance. Fostering offspring was originally a result of unsuccessful spiritual mating; a collusion of evil agents from the heavens. Those children of the compromised spirits unable to pass on the genetics of actuality are conceived as easily as they are terminated. A sput may not pose any immediate threat to the sophisticated tree warrior, however, for the simple mortal a demon sput would surely mean instant death.

This particular sput was creeping closer and closer to the campfire, which was now only a tree throw away. The two warriors sitting beside the open fire seemed unaware of the demon's presence. But suddenly, with the demented tree spirit lurking in the aspens on the edge of the makeshift camp, Zachary seized his stager and sprang to attention.

"There's something out there," he said.

"It's only a solo sput. It's been honing in on us all the way from the ridge to the north," explained Hawkins.

"A sput. I fought one just like it at Northend on Kingsmere Lake. It didn't seem that harmless then," commented Zachary as he caught sight of the ghastly demon; holding his stager ready for battle as the sput continued to approach their camp.

"But you weren't much of a warrior then. Try zapping this one and see what happens," suggested Hawkins.

The fledgling warrior squeezed his stager and concentrated all his vibes on the power of the trees, but nothing happened.

"No, not like that. You have to relax and let the lasha flow; let it mingle with your synaptic neuron wavelengths," instructed Hawkins.

"Say what?"

"Brain power of the mind my son. Swing your stager through the air around you and let the ionised particles of lasha cling to the aspen wood of your hatchet, and then release the power with the endorphins generated in your mind. Like this—" explained Hawkins, as he flipped his lance stager, snatched it in mid-air and thrust a quick shot of lasha from a sitting position.

The stream of lasha zipped over the sput's head and shattered a tree top. It was enough to scare the sput and keep it at bay for a moment.

"Try it again. Just relax and let the power flow from your mind," he coached his younger student.

Swinging his stager from side to side while holding it by the leather strap, Zachary saw his hatchet light up with lasha. It was the first time he was in complete control of the sporadic energy. He was excited.

"All right then, here we go," he whispered.

He abruptly brought the stager in front of his chest with a little flip of his own and unleashed a whirling stream of lasha. It sliced into the sput and split the demon into slivers of kindling.

"That's quite the surge of energy, isn't it?" prompted Hawkins.

"Too much," marvelled Zachary, "even my toes are tingling. It sure beats tree bashing."

The older warrior laughed and took a sip of the Labrador tea they had steeped. Zachary set his hatchet down and sat beside Hawkins, who continued to explain the power of the trees to the best of his ability: the young candidate's lasha coach, if you will. Kingsmere offered his observations of the spiritual sporadic element that he experienced throughout his own life.

"You should be aware that the more powerful your blasts become, the more it will drain your strength. You have to keep in good shape to develop your arsenal of lasha. The more experienced you become the easier it will be to release the lasha with less effort; you have to work hard to perfect the power in your mind. That was a precise shot, most young warriors in training don't have that kind of control."

"I was practising on Earth just before I met Bruno. Although I think that was the first time I was actually able to conjure lasha, the sensation of the ionised energy was familiar. I did zap some logs and I even blasted a tree that another sput threw at me."

"So that wasn't your first encounter with a sput?"

"No, but it was a lot easier. By the way, why do sputs turn into wood like that? Are they trees?"

"Not only sputs but all warriors turn into wood when they're destroyed. All I can say is that it's the power from the angels of the tree gods. We remain biological, but we also become the essence of the trees. The sputs are half human demons and half tree; some kind of genetic mutation. They're frustrated without the power of the trees, and most are created by evil spirits we believe. They can reproduce fairly easily I'm told, but they're more of a nuisance than a threat, except when they gather in large numbers, which they often do. They can become a threat to your core. It's rather repulsive, but sputs love to eat cores."

"And what are these cores?"

"You'll get one when you've become a full-fledged warrior. I'd be surprised if it hasn't started growing on you already. It's the ultimate gift, spread throughout the universe on the cosmic wave by the angels. The stagers, the arboretum ships, the trees, they're all part of the miracles of the heavens. We are bestowed with the sporadic power when we receive a spiritual core. The stager may be your weapon, but your core is the true source of power, without it you won't have any of the purifying sensations that you've started to feel by now. It's a small patch of wood fibre that forms in your navel, yes, your bellybutton. It's so small you don't even notice that it's there."

Zachary lifted his shirt and looked at his bellybutton.

"How will I know if I've got one?"

"Touch your navel."

Zachary did: "What about it?"

"If you had a developed core, you would feel a tingle through your body. When you get one, you'll know what I'm talking about. As a matter of fact, it's quite heavenly, if you know what I mean."

"You wouldn't be teasing a gullible earthling, would you?"

"Not at all my boy, I'm every bit as much an earthling as you."

"So when do I get this core?"

"Now don't be too hasty. Remember, a core gives you the power, but it also means if you lose it all is lost. And a sput will do anything to get at your core. I've heard of sputs that have eaten hundreds of cores over thousands of years and have developed into unstoppable monsters. They tower over trees and crush anything in their path. They don't bother with cores anymore, now they just devour warriors whole."

"Are you serious?"

"What do you think? Have you ever known me to lie?"

"Okay, I believe you. Are there any more of these sputs around here?"

"If any come close to camp, I'll sense them. Don't worry, we can handle any of the sputs found on Druid."

"I never imagined there would be such bizarre creatures."

"Neither did I. Neither did I."

Naturally, Zachary had several questions for Hawkins, who answered with patience talking about botanical disputes, tree raids and the grand creations; even a little speculation on our wind warrior and vapour demon spirals from stories he had heard around other campfires.

"The trees are everything, just like Harold said," surmised Zachary.

"Yes, you were fortunate to have Harold show you the trees."

"Is Harold an angel or a spirit of some sort?"

"Yes, he's a courier angel who routinely carries warriors through spiritual corridors to distant unispheres, just like your trip to Envrah. He rarely serves as a guardian angel though, which he did for you, if even for only a short while. You were lucky."

The campfire was dwindling as the night progressed. Hawkins reached over and added more wood to the coals; spontaneous combustion igniting the flames again.

"Is my father a tree warrior?" asked Zachary.

"I really can't say for certain, but I suspect so."

"I guess I was more or less born into this."

"You definitely have the genetics for it, but you still have to prove yourself worthy of the power. I have shown you the way, now you must find your own path."

"My intentions are the same. I started searching for my ancestors and this is where it has led me. I only want to follow the bloodline of my family. Do you think we will ever find Soarfoot and the Storyteller?"

"We are not the only warriors looking for them, we can only hope they are alive and well, but I think the best way for you to find your path is to go on a tree raid and talk to other warriors. Maybe someone else will have an idea of where your parents are. And if you really want to become an Envrah, a tree raid is the best place to start."

"That sounds reasonable. Can you get me on a tree raid?"

"I hope my name is still worth something," said Hawkins with a chuckle.

"What about the talk of Planet Blaved?"

"Yes, they're staging for a raid there. The Alkae have been harvesting inventories on Blaved for raids on Minga, but because of depleted resources they have been turning to other nearby planets, especially Arkna recently, a rich mixed species planet like Earth. I can take you to Blaved, it's only a few hours away. We should be there before the tree raid departs, if not there's another raid set for Planet Tuw. Either way I'll need some sleep to make the trip. If you don't mind, I'll doze off for a few hours."

"I guess I could use the sleep as well. Blaved you say. What kind of tree raid do you think it will be?"

"Only the chlorophyllialis will know. You'll find out soon enough."

Hawkins promptly fell soundly asleep almost before he ended his sentence. He started snoring beside the fire. Zachary, fearing an outbreak of sputs, remained awake until his mind was finally set at ease. He closed his eyes with his arms curled around his hatchet.

Chapter 27: Tree Raid

The fire was still burning and the aspen trees cast shadows across the camp, but Zachary noticed a change. The stars in the sky vanished. A layer of lasha surrounded the camp and Hawkins was not asleep. The old warrior was standing ahead of the campfire with his stager sparkling in the ground. He levitated the camp into a branch ship which was taking them to Blaved.

It was the first time Zachary was lucid while travelling through space on an organic vessel. He stood up beside Hawkins and gaped at the inspiring view. Streams of coloured light fled by as Hawkins manoeuvred the ship. They were flying through a cavity of rippling energy. The pulsing tones blurred past the ship in brilliant shades. Occasionally a sweltering candescence would consume their corridor as the ship ripped dangerously close to the gravity of a burning star or pulsar, even a quasar or a black hole.

"What was that?" asked Zachary.

"Just a little turbulence between magnetic fields," answered Hawkins.

"Magnetic fields? How fast are we going?"

"It varies, depending on the trail we catch. I can usually maintain a good eight to ten million light years per hour, but some warriors can go faster."

"That's unbelievable."

"It's the power of the aspens."

"How do we stay alive?"

"The lasha protects us. It attracts positrons apparently, which react with electrons and form an ionised corridor of plasma around us, at least that's what I'm told. We ride one of the cosmic trails emanating from the heavens with the spiritual gift of the sporadic element, from the angels and the gods. The power of the trees will give you the cosmic actuality to see these corridors through interstellar space, just like you'll be able to hear the thoughts of others and perceive events before they happen."

"And I'll be able to do all of that?"

"I have no doubt you will, it's in your blood."

"I assume you know where you're going."

"The power of Envrah will guide us to our destiny."

It was not long before Hawkins brought the ship to what seemed a sluggish pace. The cosmic trail slowly relapsed and the stars came back into view. A planet orbited by three moons was directly ahead. It was Blaved. Hawkins steered between two of the moons and glided to the outer haze of the planet's atmosphere. Entering the exosphere and thermosphere was not difficult; slicing through with only a brief sparkle of lasha. Down into the mesosphere, stratosphere and troposphere they sped until levelling out at two thousand feet above the surface.

Blaved is a grey and gloomy planet. It consists of cold rock and valleys of mud and dirt, with only a few old and tattered trees sparsely scattered across the landscape. Zachary recognised a larch, willow, birch and the odd ginkgo. Hawkins pointed out hidden camps in the bleak environment. Blavedians are meagre people who struggle simply to survive. They are quite vulnerable on their barren planet, and as a defence against intruders they have learned to blend with the atrabilious setting. Zachary sensed a mood of despair on the planet. Blaved is a victim of botanical wars and mortal industrial exploitation which have punishingly stripped the world of its resources. A once fruitful land is now a diseased and crippled casualty of blind greed.

A small flock of birds were startled from a rug of tundra on a ridge as Hawkins skimmed just above the rugged terrain. The birds clambered into flight and flew across the arid horizon into a bare canyon over the next ridge. The branch ship followed in the same direction. The splendour of a plush green island was resting at the bottom of the grey canyon. It was a rooting ship gleaming in sharp contrast to the droughty surroundings of Blaved; cushioned by a bed of lasha spanning the canyon floor. Branch ships, scarifiers and many Envrah aspen warriors were mingling around the green island. A tree raid was about to begin.

The branch and scarifier vessels had bark shredder pilots and a couple of catalyst ships were dropping off tree warriors to engage in the raid. The rooting ship was just how Hawkins described it: the entire outer edge lined with rocks and boulders, then trembling and quaking aspen trees, a large stone cover protecting a cave near the stern with smoke pouring out, and a grassy hilltop peaking highest on the ship in front of the cave, where three navigators were holding long glowing stagers. The tree raid commander kohpah was there with the navigators surveying the wood sacrifice squad, who were organising the fuel pit brimming with harvested trees in front of the helm. The ship's camp, with small fires dotted amongst standing trees, tents and huts, was isolated in the middle of the vessel; separated from the fuel pit by a large pond, and from the shallow gulley of the holding ground at the bow by a subtle ridge. The bow of the ship was a mixture of sharp rock chunks and boulders with rough, gnarled bush and trees.

Kingsmere hovered to the bottom of the canyon and crept towards the imposing rooter. The closer they came to the island of trees, rock and water, the more humid and warm it became. Zachary admired the arboretum vessel. He could feel the pulsating waves of power lapping from the lasha; the strength building inside his mind and body. He began to prepare himself for his first tree raid.

Hawkins came to a stop near the edge of the rooting ship beside a crowd of warriors surrounding a man who looked to be issuing orders. Zachary recognised the man as they walked over to the crowd. It was Alexander Ajawaan, who he met only the day before.

"Kingsmere, what the Quujj? Did you decide to come along for the tree raid?" Ajawaan greeted his fellow namesake warrior.

"Not quite Alexander. I brought along my new friend Zachary Steele. He would like to join the campaign if there's an open spot."

"You didn't exactly tell me that he's a quujjeeng Steele. In that case, I think we can find a spot for old time's sake."

"I know I'm a rookie, but I'll do anything to get onboard, I really need to go on a tree raid," responded Zachary.

"What the Quujj, why not," concurred Alexander.

"I appreciate it, but who or what is Quujj?"

"Oh Quujj, it's just tree warrior slang in this universe," translated Hawkins yet again. "It's the name of the pine tree god and it's used to express both joy and frustration, even anger."

"It's kind of your all around exclamation, like, oh my Quujj, or praise Quujj, or Quujj me gently we're in deep shit now, or sometimes, that's just quujjeeng wonderful. Of course, in extreme circumstances we sometimes say quujjeeng sabiichee, which is about as crude as it gets, kind of like mother fucker is used on Earth, if you know what I mean," expounded Ajawaan.

"I think I get the drift. Thanks for the clarification. I'll try not to look too out of place, swearing might help me blend in," said Zachary.

"You'll be fine, just be yourself," quipped Alexander.

"What's the word on the tree raid?" inquired Hawkins.

"Kohpah will confirm, but I'm told it's Planet Arkna. Another Alkae raid has wiped out most of our Kobin settlement. Those spruce are getting frisky, I think they need a good swift kick right between the old quujjeeng legs, if you know what I mean."

"They always need it, but I'm going to skip this one old friend. Zachary here can help you out. I've seen him in action, he looks quite promising."

"How's your lasha?" questioned Alexander.

"I've only just acquired it, but I do have two sputs to my credit."

"I'll tell you what, why don't you come onboard as a campfire maintainer and maybe we'll get a chance to put you into the action."

"I'll do whatever I can," pledged Zachary.

"I'm sure you will. Head onboard and ask for Winston Waskesiu. He'll give you a quick orientation and fill you in on your duties."

"Waskesiu? As in the lake back on Earth where you're from?"

"There are many warriors of different species from Earth, and the north country has always been a fertile breeding ground. Winston, Alexander and myself were all born in the Weyakwin region," explained Hawkins.

"Stranger and stranger all the time," remarked Zachary.

"It's destiny young Steele, or at least I hope it is," added Kingsmere.

"You've been an incredible help to me Hawkins. You've coached me well on the power of the trees and I thank you for all your support."

"It was my pleasure Zachary. You will bring honour to the Envrahs and the manifesto of peace. Embrace this tree raid and the best of luck in your search. Perhaps we will meet again."

"I would like that."

It was encouraging to know he was boarding the rooting ship and looking for an earthling born in Saskatchewan, considering Zachary was still anxious about the entire cosmic tripping crusade he had now come to accept. He took a deep breath and turned towards the floating island. He looked back at Hawkins who was already talking further with Alexander. There was nothing else left to do: he strapped on his backpack, stepped up and onto the ship through a gap in the lasha and began to look for Winston Waskesiu. Wandering in the main camp he noticed the dress code of tree bark fashion, including the soft flexible bark-bast weaved tops, some rigid two-piece vests attached front and back at the shoulders and the ribs, as well as a few leather outfits, serape and tunic styled garments, dhoti pants and ponchos. Zachary felt out of place in his fatigues and hiking boots.

He finally came upon a man who looked to be in charge. This warrior was short and lean, although physically fit and probably strong for his size. He had a friendly face with a copper hue in his vibrant skin tone and he looked youthful, like someone in his late twenties or early thirties, but Zachary knew better than to guess his age. Indeed, this hybrid also dated back centuries to the north-western frontier of North America.

"Hello, are you Winston Waskeiu?" asked Zachary.

"In the bark and flesh. What can I do for you?" he answered.

"My name is Zachary Steele, Alexander Ajawaan told me there might be a spot for a campfire maintainer."

"Steele you say. Are you related to Irving?"

"Why yes, he's my ancestor. Do you know him?"

"Your ancestor? Well then, that makes you quite the youngster. Come to think of it I haven't seen you around before."

"I'm only thirty-nine years-old, but I guess I lived about twenty-three hundred years ago. I'm new at this sort of thing."

"It looks like it, but obviously you've put in some space travel. We'll have to get you some barkwear for the trip. I've known Irving for all of his life but I haven't seen him around lately either."

"So you don't know where I might find him?"

"Not at the moment. Why do you ask?"

"I'd like to find him and some other ancestors. I think our bloodline includes the likes of Soarfoot and the Storyteller. Could you help me out?"

"Ah yes, you're a mixed species. I could possibly help you, but not right now, I'm kind of occupied. Have you ever been on a tree raid before?"

"No, I have to admit, this is my first—quujjeeng—tree raid."

Winston giggled: "Well, at least you have some tree warrior's humour. I sense something special in you Zachary, and any Steele is a welcome addition to my camp. Tell you what, I'll make you my first hand for this raid; that way you can learn more about all this botanical stuff."

"That would be great."

"Good then, you can start by assigning the harvesters, splitters and thrashers to their sleeping quarters; six of them in each of these mini longhouse huts. Start here and work your way around the camp. Is that clear?"

"Of course, no problem. I was mentored by Hawkins Kingsmere, he explained the mechanics of tree raids, so I have some idea how this works."

"Kingsmere is a good teacher, you should make a decent maintainer. I'll direct the warriors your way and you assign them huts. Once things settle down, I'll explain our routine for camp. In the meantime, I'll see if I can find you an extra seerah, creedak or poncho. So, you can deal with that for now?"

"Absolutely, six to a hut. By the way, what's a seerah and a creedak?"

"Those are upper body barkwear for warriors; vests, tunic sash tops and such clothing, similar to this poncho I'm wearing. They can protect you if you get involved in a lasha fight."

"Sounds good; my first tree raid and my first uniform, so to speak."

"You could say that."

"Winston Waskesiu," shouted an approaching warrior.

"That's my given name, you gotta take what you get."

"Don't we all. Nevin Uda, firewood harvester, reporting for duty."

"I would take Nevin, that's a good name. Welcome Uda. Zachary here will assign you sleeping quarters. Kohpah will address the warriors in about an hour, so be ready."

And with that Zachary began to assign sleeping arrangements. He stayed in a central spot and received the warriors as they filed in, while Winston roamed the camp tending to assorted details. They were able to scrounge enough clothing to assemble a makeshift wardrobe for Zachary with a pair of moccasins, moose skin pants, a bark-bast vest over his camping shirt and a poncho; now he really felt like a tree warrior.

The initial task for the camp leader's first hand was not difficult and Zachary felt fortunate alongside the other maintainers who were chopping wood, making firepits, digging holes for the outhouses they were about to construct, and building shelves beside the camp kitchen shack for storing cookware and food. There were twenty of the longhouse huts Zachary designated for quarters, made with branches of aspen, alder and cottonwood trees and spread around the edges of the camp; every two huts sharing a firepit, an outhouse and a smaller tent stocked with a water keg. A communal circle in the middle of the camp featured a large cooking pit, benches and tables, and the kitchen shack where meals were served buffet style. Three teepee tents were set up near the camp kitchen to accommodate the twig suppliers, leaf gypsies and campfire maintainers, along with any bark shredders who needed rest. The pond at the back of the camp had a soft sand bottom to allow washing and bathing, and along the shore there were five log shower and sauna structures; a water drum suspended above a burn barrel with a shower stall to one side and a sauna room on the opposite side.

There were three twig supplier cooks on this tree raid and two leaf gypsy entertainers who played musical instruments, told stories and even served as counsellors when warriors needed to relieve their stress. Winston and Zachary were among five campfire maintainers, with thirty-six battlefield warriors for each group of root thrashers, firewood harvesters and log splitters, twenty bark shredders who mainly stayed on branch ships, five soil sucks, a wood sacrifice squad of three and the same number of navigators, and of course only one tree raid kohpah commander chlorophyllialis: one hundred and fifty Envrah and twelve acres of hovering land ready to blast into space.

It was a somewhat inspiring sight when the crew gathered in the camp to hear the tree raid kohpah's instructions. A bark shredder glided over the fuel pit and down to the camp on a branch ship. Standing beside the pilot was a woman of average height and build, dark in complexion with long flowing hair accented by aspen vine shoots, and dressed in a delicately woven cloth top over leather pants and moccasins. She was holding a lance stager and beamed with a gentle warmth which Zachary could feel from his spot in the camp. She paused to examine the rooting ship crew and then spoke.

"Dah Trudie Makwha, for those of you who do not know me. Dah eevah descendant of my matriarch Namid Makwha, tonntee croonlash, star dancer, lah eefee, and sister of Noodin, whassa, the wind, he battles for the aspen trees across the interstellar expanse, mee naga zahka ashah pyen annha," she announced, explaining her Ojibwe heritage dating back thousands of years.

"Ashah pyen, ashah pyen, ashah pyen," the chorus began.

The warriors continued to shout louder for a few more chants until Trudie raised her stager.

"I am honoured by so many brave warriors assembled here to defend the manifesto of peace. Dah beelah laf vohko traupah, gootak fahbee lohsee moobah. Don bohtrak Tahkah Arkna. We will soar to Planet Arkna and take our aspen trees at Kobin, where the spruce warriors have infiltrated and killed many of our people. Don dahbid ashah pyen Kobin, jo Alka meelka lah zahka laf don eevah.

Nah don cyndah Alka, don lohsee, veebee don sahba whaga zahka. If we are confronted by the Alkae, we will defend ourselves, but we will not seek out any battles. We will take our aspens and we will travel to Planet Earth, where we will confront the spruce at Nemeiben, who have infiltrated our Casyndeka settlement. Don dahbid ashah pyen lah don bohtrak Tahkah Earth, jo don cyndah Alka jobo Nemeiben, teelaf meelka don Casyndeka tahkid. Nah naga, don zahka Alka. Ashah pyen quueesum eesah. If we need to, we will fight the Alkae. The aspen trees must live. Prepare warriors. Bohko traupah."

"Ashah pyen," the warriors shouted again in response.

The branch ship hovered up over the camp, scooted back across the fuel pit and dropped off Trudie at the helm. The warriors dispersed with clamoured conversation about Arkna and Earth, as Winston began to explain camp duties to Zachary at the cooking pit.

"The first thing we'll do is a complete check-up on the camp. I want to know the condition of everything, the huts and the bunks inside, the firepits, tents and water kegs, cookwear and food supplies, and the status of the outhouses, everything. Assign one of the maintainers to any necessary repairs or adjustments and report to me. Fires are to be kept burning as long as there are warriors, and check the water kegs on a regular basis. There are back-up kegs in the central teepee over here. Take care of any problems as soon as you can and keep me informed. I have to go for a trunk thrust meeting, but I'll be back fairly soon to make sure everything is running smoothly."

"I'll keep on top of things Winston, I promise," said Zachary.

"Oh, and just a few other things, the leaf gypsies are on their own and the camp kitchen twig suppliers can handle the food, unless they get a rush and ask you to lend a hand."

"Got it, no worries. I can handle myself in the kitchen."

Winston paused to see if anyone was listening: "And just between you and me, the outhouses are rigged with gravity fed bidet hoses, but there's some surplus tissue in our teepee, just in case."

They smiled together and shared the humour of the moment. Zachary knew he was going to get along with this tree warrior.

"Winston, the trunk thrust meeting is starting soon, meet up at the helm," said an approaching warrior: it was Alexander Ajawaan.

"Of course, I'll walk up with you," answered Waskesiu.

"Well Mr Steele, I see you've nabbed yourself a prime position, camp leader's first hand—not bad," remarked Ajawaan.

"I guess I was lucky."

"Alexander is in charge of battlefield warriors. He's a shrewd warrior himself; one of the best we have," commented Winston.

"But I'm not a Steele by birth. It's in your blood Zachary, when it comes to crunch time you'll come through. I might be counting on you when the action gets heavy, and I have no doubt you will shine."

"I'll give it everything I have," pledged Zachary.

"I know you will."

The two veteran warriors walked up to the helm together and Zachary embarked on his survey of the camp. He found three huts in need of minor repairs, a couple of firepits requiring reinforcement and only one water keg leaking. The rooting ship began to advance as the repairs were started. The arboretum vessel slowly climbed over the canyon wall and quickly darted into the outer atmosphere of Blaved. Twenty branch ships flanked the magnificent island of trees and rocks: seven to port and starboard, three leading at the bow and three more trailing at the stern. The organic formation vacated the planet's ionosphere and entered the interstellar cosmos. The light show was dazzling; layers of luscious lasha. The Envrah tree raid was swaying.

The voyage to Arkna would Take thirty-six Earth hours by the time they crept into the solar system and plotted their attack strategy, or about one Stellar Rotational Continuum day which comprises an equivalent twenty rotation hours. Zachary was kept busy supervising fires outside the huts while the other maintainers tended to the repairs. The tree warriors he encountered were friendly and pleasant, and requests were simple and uncomplicated. The Envrahs are quiet, contemplative and relaxed, but Zachary could feel the abundant cache of energy subdued by the warriors; their relaxed demeanour was the psychological ploy they used to prepare themselves for battle. It is the calm before the raging botanical storm.

The imminent and brutal struggle for survival was camouflaged by a blanket of simplicity. Zachary respected the warriors for their approach to conflict. He was unaccustomed to such an existence after living in an academic setting for many years dealing with scholars and intellects. He was intrigued by his observations. He embraced his duty as camp leader's first hand with undaunted enthusiasm; feeling obliged to help the campfire maintainers fulfil their role on the tree raid. He enjoyed maintaining the camp and the Envrah recognised his genuine efforts with an unspoken vote of confidence—a nod here and a smile there. Zachary was being accepted into the culture.

The early portion of the tree raid elapsed quickly for Zachary. The trip to Arkna took several hours, but he was constantly kept busy. The warriors did not adhere to regular patterns and there was almost always someone sitting around the various firepits. He was occupied keeping the camp running smoothly and he was serious about his responsibility to supervise the crew of maintainers. Despite his inexperience, Zachary managed to accomplish his duties with reasonable efficiency until Winston returned a few hours later and allowed him to rest.

"Take a break Zachary, you've earned it."

"I'm fine Winston. I can carry on without a problem. I think things are pretty well under control anyway."

"It looks like it, good job, but you should rest before we reach Arkna. You'll need your energy, and besides, I can't sleep. Quujj, I'm so wound up right now. These raids really pump me up."

"Pretty good for an old fart, or are you one of the young warriors?"

"No, I'm an old fart all right. There are some older warriors, like Bruno, but the average age is only a few hundred annua old, and then there's the young pups just starting out not even one hundred yet. The likes of Alexander and myself are clearly the veterans at a few thousand years."

"How long have you been a tree warrior?" mused Zachary.

"All of my life."

"And you were born on Earth, in America before the Europeans?"

"I was born there, I'm Cree, but before I could crawl, we were flying through space. I've been on Earth many times, but I'm always traipsing around on these dang tree raids. Listen Zachary, you get some rest and we'll talk later. We still have to go over the trunk thrust with the other maintainers."

"Okay then, I'll go lay down in the teepee."

Winston went for a swim in the pond and Zachary, regardless of his inquisitive nature, was tired and easily fell asleep. Later on the trip he was asked to build a dock on the pond with another campfire maintainer. It was a large dock crudely built with the help of stager bashing, but Zachary was proud of his work. The remainder of the swaying went well without any major complications outside the usual routine and casual conversations with the warriors. Soon the rooting ship was approaching the Arknae solar system and Winston was issuing trunk thrust instructions to his camp crew.

"Don sahba naga teesah. Alka dahbid laf sygah traupah, veebee teelaf tahbee fah po. We're not going to try anything extravagant. The Alkae have many fierce warriors, but they're spread thin right now. We want to go in fast and leave, but if the spruce are there, we will stand our ground. Don naga whaga fahbee sweesah, lah whaga, veebee Alka jobo, don tah don dizz. Don quueesum bohtahna ashah pyen, veebee leepash sygahvee. We must salvage the aspens or the tree raid is a failure. I want everyone up on the ridge when the takeover begins, ready to carry logs, tend to injured warriors, maybe even help the thrashers fight. Dah naga lahtoo tah duk pah leepash tahsak, bohko goobah ashyb, maha zahkahsoo traupah, neewha maha traupah tah zahka. Neewhasee quueesum, traupah tahkid nah naga. Whatever is required, the maintainers will do it. Stay on your toes and be alert; speed is of the essence during a trunk takeover. Whaha tah whasoo lah ashahssa, sweesah eesah po leepash tahsak."

"Traupah tahkid sahba sygahvee, don bohko," the campfire maintainers will not let you down, we will be ready, said one of the warriors.

"Teelaf muh traupah lahtoo, don naga quueesum. You're a good crew, we'll get the job done," reassured Winston. "Now, does everyone know how to carry stacks of logs with the lasha? Nah lahtoo klahsah goobah muzz ashyb?"

The two younger maintainers and Zachary were unsure, so Winston took them to the ridge and demonstrated. He selected a large slab of rock and using his baton stager sprayed a stream of lasha that burrowed under the flat boulder. The lasha suspended the rock in the air and a thin string of energy flowed from Winston's stager to the cushion under the boulder, which he could pull and float under his control. Winston explained that the secret is a gentle, steady pulse rather than the swift, jerky motion for a laser stream or cluster pulse used as an offensive volley.

"Fahsee fah neewhasee goobah. Neewhasee seewha dizz lasha, sahba vohko sweesah lasha, veebee naga oosah. Ease it under while lifting. It has to be a flat, sustaining lasha; not a potent blast but a controlled stream."

The maintainers were not the only warriors sharpening their skills of lasha. Intermittent flashes and zaps could be seen and heard in the camp as Winston was coaching and the rooting ship was navigating around planets. The Envrah were getting pumped for the trunk thrust. Zachary was able to levitate large objects like boulders and tree logs before they landed on Arkna. He was developing his powers quickly. And now it was the space and time for him to see his first action as a tree warrior.

The rooting ship eased its speed entering into orbit and breaking the atmospheric barrier as it edged down to the planet's surface. The trunk thrust began. The aspen warriors were lined up along the bow of the ship: a row of root thrashers, then firewood harvesters and the log splitters. The campfire maintainers stood behind the warriors and the bark shredders flanked the floating arboretum island on their branch ships. The target was in sight.

An incredibly large living organism span across a plateau over a mile wide and over twelve miles deep: a single grove of quaking aspen trees abutted up against two mountains with interconnected roots spreading underground for a hundred acres, separated by a valley of coniferous trees and followed by another sprawling grove of aspens on the other side of the mountains. The rooting ship manoeuvred over a gulley of ash trees and snaked through a gorge at low altitude on a bearing for the middle of the mountains and the valley of coniferous spruce trees in the distance. The Envrahs raced up to the plateau; violently ramming the bow of the ship into the fringe of quaking aspens.

Living breathing botanical entities were ripped to shreds and went spinning in the air—a sacrifice before the takeover. A cloud of stagerdust floated above the bow and slowly dissipated around the aura of lasha. Aspen branches shuffled in the vibrations of the shock wave and whispered with the power of botanic spiritualis. Trudie Makwha was hovering above the bow on her branch ship before the dust subsided. She inspected the grove of aspens for a flickering moment and then turned to her warriors.

"Traupah tah, thrashers!" she yelled.

The root thrashers bounced over the boulders at the bow screaming and ranting into the forest of aspens. They crashed through the trees and approached the valley between the two mountains. A line of Alkae appeared over the two ridges on either side of the valley and rushed down towards the thrashers. Trudie again turned to the warriors and issued her orders.

"Traupah sweesah, harvesters!"

And the firewood harvesters sprang into action. They scrambled out into the forest like fleeting gazelles and began to slice down the aspens. The harvesters felled trees in brief flurries of lasha with one-handed stager blows. The quaking aspens were scattered in rapid succession; warriors dodging the felled trees, bounding over stumps and dashing from trunk to trunk. Trudie once again shouted out her command.

"Traupah gootak, splitters!" resounded the order through the heat.

The log splitters scampered into action, and without hesitation began to reap the harvest. They hacked the trees with their stagers into two or three logs each and heaped them into stacks of about a dozen trees, also using the power of the lasha to throw them on the accumulated piles.

"Traupah tahkid, maintainers!" continued the kohpah commander.

Winston signalled the three other maintainers into the commotion. They immediately started hauling stacks of logs to the bow of the ship where Zachary still waited in anticipation. The warriors used their lasha to hurl the stacks across the gulley and into the holding ground.

Meanwhile, the thrashers were engaged in stager-to-stager combat with the Alkae. The trunk takeover took on the fervour of war. The first wave of spruce warriors was effectively wiped out by the Envrah root thrashers, but the aspen hybrids may have been mistaken about the number of Alkae on the planet. A second tier of the spruce credos descended from the ridges and met the thrashers on the mountainsides; warriors clashing with the electric sizzle of lasha. The Envrahs sustained the advantage, but then the Alkae hit them with everything they had: an army of warriors coming out of caves from beyond the ridges flooded down into the valley and rushed the aspen root thrashers.

"Traupah tiggahsee, shredders!" yowled Trudie.

The bark shredders darted out to the ridges on their branch ships and were blasting at scores of Alkae almost instantly. The initial pass by the shredders sent many of the spruce warriors sprawling for cover, but those who made it through the line of fire started battling with the thrashers. The bark shredders were able to lambaste the ridges with subsequent bombardments of lasha squalls in compact flights of three ships per volley. Although many of the Alkae were suppressed, the root thrashers were being overwhelmed and the trunk thrust would soon have to deal with a squadron of spruce branch ships zooming into the mountain pass.

The Alkae were escaping through the line of root thrashers and racing towards the firewood harvesters who had reached halfway to the mountains, with the log splitters right behind them. The Envrah shredders split eighteen of their twenty ships into two groups of three flights each to support the thrashers and engage the approaching spruce ships in the air, and also turn back to chase the warriors within blasting distance of the harvesters. A dozen of the aspen harvesters stopped their tree bashing and prepared to confront the Alkae striding through the forest. A branch ship soared above the tree tops and fired a blur of lasha. It was Bruno.

The cluster of lasha exploded a clump of aspens and stopped the spruce warriors in their spoors. Bruno pulled his branch ship to a halt and reeled around pointing at the Alkae. Another outburst of lasha fired from the top of his stager and ripped apart more trees in front of the spruce perpetrators. The warriors dove for cover, hurried back to their feet and began to run into the forest. Bruno promptly released quick flurries of lasha detonating around the Alkae. The warriors desperately stopped and faced the branch ship, but their shots of energy were easily absorbed by the aspen botanic spiritualis. Again the spruce raced away on foot. Bruno circled around them and this time knifed his flying chunk of land down into the trees. He pulled his stager from the helm and jumped off the ship as it clattered into the aspens; wood and bark fraying around the crash site.

Bruno landed safely and directly in the path of the Alkae. The spruce hybrids, still sheltering their bodies from flying debris, were victims of the lasha sprayed by the firewood harvesters and Bruno: devastating pulses of energy cracking and disintegrating spruce wood chips in a forest of aspen trees. Bruno did not waste any time jumping back onto his crashed arboretum vessel, activating his stager again and floating over to the mountains only a few miles away by then. He watched aspen shredders effectively thwarting spruce warriors on the plateau and the root thrashers finally advancing up the ridges with the support of the other bark shredders, both on branch ships and on the ground. The Envrah were shattering warriors into kindling and stagerdust and the Alkae were on the run except for a few warriors still attacking. Observing the battlefield Bruno backtracked and yelled to his shredders on the plateau.

"Traupah tiggahsee, whaga cyndah—" go to the mountainsides.

He then followed up by searing over the valley and shouting further instructions to Alexander Ajawaan and the root thrashers.

"Traupah tah, whaga cyndah," he repeated the trunk thrust strategy.

Ajawaan, the lead battlefield warrior, gazed down at the plateau from his position near the top of the valley ridge and then looked over to the mountainside. He could see the last of the Alkae retreating.

"Lap traupah tah, whaga cyndah. Light thrashers, to the mountainsides. Tap traupah tah, deewha duk. Dark thrashers, hold the ridges," he barked.

Standing at the bow of the rooting ship Zachary could faintly hear Alexander issuing his orders. The sporadic sensory perception of a tree warrior was growing more acute within him and he could sense the entire trunk takeover unfolding. Suddenly an enormous stack of trees collapsed on the plateau two miles away: a log splitter was buried under the rubble, which Zachary could see and feel in his mind's eye. A fellow splitter raced over to the trees only to find the warrior trapped and unconscious without a stager. It was time for Zachary to enter the battlefield.

"Traupah tahkid," called out Trudie Makwha.

"Follow me," said Winston turning to Zachary.

They dashed over the boulders on the bow of the ship as Zachary firmly gripped his hatchet stager. He found himself bounding over the rocks with a speed he had never experienced. He was catching air and bouncing from rock to rock on the cushion of lasha. The power of the trees was certainly being generous to this new recruit, yet he did not think much about his new found flight. Instead he leapt behind Winston with all the concentration and intensity warranted by the heat of battle.

The root thrashers were now exchanging clusters of lasha with the spruce warriors on the mountainsides and the ridges of the valley pass, where the aspen bark shredders continued to fire on the Alkae while also dogfighting with branch ships over the plateau. Zachary and Winston reached the pile of trees as a shot of lasha fragmented some branches near the trapped log splitter. Waskesiu let fly a stream of his own which squarely sliced through an Alkae warrior.

"Cover me," ordered Winston.

He slipped down into the trees and started pulling up the splitter. Zachary was scanning the stacks of harvested aspens in search of spruce warriors, standing above Winston with his hatchet poised in his right hand. An Alkae broke through the harvesters near the mountains and started racing across the naked plateau towards the rescue operation. The warrior was fast and within firing distance in seconds. Winston climbed up and looked at the rushing Alkae.

"Use the lasha," he shouted.

The spruce warrior raised his stager but Zachary had already swung his hatchet into position. He decisively unleashed a wave of lasha. The salvo was accurate. The spruce warrior was obliterated; crumbling into splinters and stagerdust. The scent of charred wood filled the air.

"Good shot," uttered Winston.

"I killed him," said Zachary, staring out at the battle scene.

"You didn't have a choice," answered Winston.

Still peering out over the smoky plateau, Zachary did not react. Winston grabbed him by the arm.

"He's in spruce heaven now. Snap out of it man."

One of the maintainers named Gaff came running up to Winston and Zachary as they stood face-to-face.

"Trudie jah don vee traupah gootak," the kohpah says one of us should replace the splitter, he said.

"Tee vee gootak Gaff, whaga dee," Winston pointed ahead, telling the warrior to replace the splitter and cover the area in front of them.

"Muh," confirmed the young maintainer.

"Are you with me?" Winston asked Zachary.

"I'm sorry, I'll be fine. I'm just a little shocked I guess."

"Shake the shock, as we say in the tree raid business."

"That's a good one. Yah, I'm with you now. What should I do?"

"Take over for Gaff. Start with this stack and move up as he works his way to the mountains. You can also split trees if you catch up to him."

"No worries, I've got this," said Zachary with confidence.

"This is the way we battle for justice and equality in the world of botanical disputes Zachary. It might be life and death, but we're fighting to end the conflict and bring peace to the universe. This is your chance to join the crusade young man," posed Winston.

"I want in, I'll do my part. I can handle this," pledged Zachary.

"Good then, get stacking and I'll take this warrior back to camp."

Winston spread a layer of lasha under the injured splitter and towed him back to the rooting ship. Zachary contained his emotions and began to slice, stack and carry aspen trees. The harvesters finished the first plateau, ripped through the mountain valley destroying spruce trees and moved onto the second aspen grove plateau. The splitters and maintainers followed closely behind as the thrashers secured the mountainsides and the bark shredders flanked around to the rear of the rooting ship that slowly hovered along with the advancing trunk takeover.

The Envrahs were well fortified and rooting aspen trees without any resistance. The Alkae appeared to be defeated; any that remained were fleeing in retreat.

The bow of the rooter was tucked into the valley while Zachary was reaching his stride on the second plateau. He was becoming very proficient as a log splitter: he loved tree bashing. The swift blows of the extended hatchet cut through the aspens with lasha befitting of a true Envrah. Zachary found that splitting was much easier than shooting at warriors.

The harvesters finished the second grove and were helping haul logs back to the rooting ship. The remainder of the Arkna plateau was cleaned bare leaving stumps with sprouting saplings on their roots for regeneration. The takeover was a resounding success with all the aspens salvaged, spruce trees destroyed and only five casualties among the Envrahs. The holding ground was piled high with trees and the fuel pit was being used as overflow storage. Trudie Makwha was the last to board the rooting ship as the navigators pulled away from the mountains with the bark shredders flanking in position.

The scars of war revealed a barren forest below. The rooter glided over the battle scene and up into the atmosphere; breaking through the planet's gravity and speeding into a cosmic trail. The tree warriors were humming with the success of the trunk thrust. Crossing the stacks of aspens in the holding ground were quietly jubilant splitters and harvesters speaking enthusiastically. The thrashers, despite suffering most of the casualties from their ranks, were also very happy with the outcome. Laughter and yelling soon filled the ship's cavity as the warriors descended down the ridge into camp. The arboretum vessel cruised into an interstellar corridor. Ajawaan approached Zachary from behind and slapped him on the shoulder.

"Good splitting out there Zachary, you'll make a fine warrior."

"Thanks Alexander, it was quite the experience."

Log splitting was thrilling but it was also a draining exercise; Zachary was exhausted. He lumbered into the middle of camp where he found Winston amid the clamour. Waskesiu was already organising for the trip to Earth. Campfires were ignited and aspen juice was poured. It was Winston's treat for the warriors in celebration of the trunk thrust. Zachary started a conversation with the maintainer Gaff after a sampling of aspen juice.

"Is this your first tree raid?" asked Zachary.

"Yes, I was recruited from the Darri camp on Groakk. And yourself?"

"This is my first time too. I'm from Saskatchewan on Earth. How big is Darri?"

"The district is only a couple hundred square vibs, about a million people live there."

"What's a vib?"

"I'm not exactly sure how it converts to Earth's measurements."

"Vibs are approximately the same length as a kilometre," said Winston, joining the two maintainers. "Darri is the size of an average city on Earth and Planet Groakk is about four billion light years from here, beyond the Andromeda corridor that's taking us back to Earth right now. Groakk is a small planet, slightly closer to its star and warmer than Earth."

"It's home," interjected Gaff.

"Sounds nice," said Zachary.

"It doesn't have as many trees as Earth so it's not usually subjected to tree raids. Earth is so rich with different tree species that almost everyone uses it for seedling stops. It would be a stronghold if we could secure it, but it would be a hotly contested battle if anyone attempted to conquer Earth. I often wonder if Earth will become another Blaved," contemplated Winston.

"I hope not," asserted Zachary.

"Any loss of trees is unfortunate, but to lose all the trees on Earth would be a catastrophe," surmised Winston.

"What's next for you after this tree raid?" posed Zachary.

"Continue the search for Soarfoot, and your ancestral grandfather the Storyteller."

"Speaking of that, did you say you could maybe help me find Irving Steele and my parents after this is over?"

"I'll talk to Trudie Makwha and some of the other veterans when we finish on Earth. It'll be difficult to find Soarfoot and Storyteller, but they might know Irving's whereabouts or where other warriors are searching, including your parents."

"I would appreciate that, it's why I'm here in the first place."

"It's no trouble, I'll see what I can do. In the meantime, both of you should get some sleep before we reach Earth. I'll take the first shift with the other maintainers and you can relieve us after you've rested."

"Done deal, thanks again Winston," said Zachary.

He and Gaff had a few more sips of juice talking with other warriors and then went to the teepee and passed out from exhaustion. The sleep was definitely needed. Zachary resumed his duties as camp leader's first hand after his rest and once again enjoyed taking care of the warriors. The trip to Earth was uncomplicated and seemed to pass by quickly—until the collision.

Chapter 28: Roots of Humility

The three ships smashed together with the devastating force of their speed and mass. The botanic spiritualis danced through the intersecting corridors sparking a deluge of dazzling colour. The arboretum ships violently spun in a fury of ionisation as the bows of the vessels fused and created a bridge of elemental rock from the cosmic dust and rubble. Warriors were tossed over firepits, seams ripped through the soil and the camps were jarred into shambles. The three vessels became one sizable collection of elements spinning in a collision of cosmic trails.

The Envrah rooting ship suffered two riveting shock waves splitting the ground from the bow back to the fuel pit. The rotation of fusing lasha gradually subsided and the ships slowly gained limited navigational control. The dust and gases trapped between the lasha corridors began to seal as the bows all grew with layers of magnesium and iron basalt. The aspen warriors were rammed by a spruce Alkae rooting ship and a pine Minga ship attempting to intercept the intentional confrontation. They collided near the Andromeda galaxy in the black space on the doorstep of Planet Earth.

The span of rock between the ships grew considerably while they were suspended in the stellar darkness. All three of the vessels lost a few bark shredders, but those who remained flew their branch ships into the lasha corridors. Trudie Makwha was hovering above the holding ground on her branch ship and the other two kohpah commanders were doing the same. Zachary, standing on the ridge at the fore of the camp, recognised one of the warriors floating on a carpet of lasha above the pine holding ground: it was Zelda.

"I don't believe it. It's my lover," he marvelled.

"What are you talking about?" Winston leaned forward.

"The warrior hovering beside the branch ship on the rooter off our starboard bow—it's Zelda."

"And you know her?"

"Intimately."

Beyond that moment Zachary was temporarily speechless while he attempted to digest this new revelation. The sight of his lover and the power of the collision were staggering; no pun intended. He was dumfounded.

The bark shredders all skimmed into the corridors and flanked their commanders at the bow of the ships. The rest of the warriors except the navigators were all lined along the camp ridges. The power of the heavens from three tree species was poised at loggerheads in a botanical standoff. The gravity of Andromeda pulled the ships closer to the black hole of the galaxy like a single frozen entity in the desolate interstellar space. Trudie looked to her side and nodded her head towards the bridge of rock between the ships.

"Traupah tiggahsee Bruno," she called.

The powerful ancient warrior skirted down to the span between the ships holding his stager on a lasha surfboard platform. He detached his stager from the botanic spiritualis and held it in a ready position by his side. There he stood as a challenge to the Alkae. A spruce warrior sailed down to Bruno and also dismounted a lasha platform with his stager ready for battle. The warriors prepared to fight for the honour of their hybrid species. Zachary was still fixated on Zelda, but she did not immediately distinguish him on the ridge.

The two combatants circled each other on the suspension bridge of rock and bounced on lasha as they jockeyed for position like gladiators in an arena. The commanders and their bark shredders watched the confrontation unfold on the battlefield between the ships. Bruno stepped in close and delivered a thrust with his stager. The Alkae blocked the offensive tactic and both warriors stepped back. Bruno followed up with another two swift blows.

The spruce warrior blocked the assault again with the glitter of his stager and then swung with two strikes of his own. Bruno blocked the first thrust and ducked under the second attempt; landing a hard blow with the Alkae off balance. The spruce shredder reeled backwards from the force of the lasha and fell in a heap on the sharp iron rock. Several chips of wood were gouged from the warrior's bark armour but he was able to quickly recover and send a blast of ionised energy at Bruno. The veteran aspen warrior calmly deflected the cluster pulse into the surrounding corridor of botanic spiritualis. The zapping singe of the stream resonating into the lasha seemed to startle Zachary from his temporary relapse. He looked down at the rock battlefield.

"What's going on?" he asked Winston.

"A fight for honour you might say. The triumphant warrior usually dictates the terms of separation, so to speak."

"And that's our Bruno down there?"

"Yes, and the outcome will be swift. I don't think there's any warrior who can defeat Bruno."

The bark shredders circled each other again as Winston was speaking, but Bruno was about to move in for the kill with his opponent labouring in pain. The Alkae desperately advanced on Bruno who easily blocked two rapid strikes. A third swing hummed above Bruno's head as he dodged the stager, and with the warrior's defences down he crushed the demented spruce credo with two ravaging blows. The first swing demolished the Alkae stager into splinters and the second landed deep into the warrior's chest. The spruce hybrid exploded into stagerdust. Bruno glared up at the Alkae rooting ship and yelled out.

"Envrah vohko! Alka fahsee—" aspen are strong, spruce are weak.

Trudie and the bark shredder branch ships glided down and filled the gap behind Bruno. The revered aspen commander addressed her rivals.

"Envrah loho. Neewha jobo laf Alka fahbee annha, veebee Envrah vohko lah bahsygah. Don sahba naga zahka, don zahka pinnah ashyb. Po whaga pinnah tahbee, veebee don sygahvee teelaf tahkid," she proclaimed: the aspens are victorious, and maybe there are many spruce in the cosmos, but the aspens are strong and tenacious, we do not want war, we fight only for the trees, now go your separate way or we will destroy your ship.

"Ap traupah sahba naga veebee," one warrior does not make a difference, countered the spruce kohpah.

The Envrah branch ships answered back without words and instantly opened fire on the Alkae bow with slashes of lasha. The rock shattered into dust and collapsed under the ship; disintegrating in flashes of brilliantly coloured electromagnetism. The bark shredders did not cease fire until the bow was dissolved through to the holding ground. The spruce vessel was dangling by a thin band of lasha.

"Whaga po!" go now, screamed Trudie.

"Neewhasee crah teewha, don sahba sygahvee," this means nothing, we will not surrender, shouted the defiant Alkae.

A thin line of lasha slowly transcended across the gap between the ships. The spruce rooter backed off and rotated in the direction of the Alka galaxy many billions of light years away. The arboretum vessel bolted into one of the trails emanating from Rulsp's heaven. Trudie turned to her warriors.

"Shahtoonee zahka," she ordered.

The tree warriors descended back into the camp and Winston was on his way to the helm with Alexander once again.

"What's a shahtoonee?" asked Zachary.

"It's another trunk thrust strategy meeting. This might force us to modify our approach, but it really doesn't change anything. We're still going to Earth to destroy spruce trees. You'll have to run the camp until I get back."

"Do you think I can talk to the pine bark shredder Zelda before that ship departs?" Zachary excitedly inquired.

"Oh yah, that cute Minga. How do you know Zelda? I think she's one of the pine Marshlandites, isn't she?"

"Oh yes, that she is. And quite the firecracker, if you know what I mean. She happened to be my research assistant and my girlfriend I guess you would say, back on Earth over two thousand years ago, but we were diverted by a certain French Canadian fur trapping tree warrior."

"Don't tell me—Cookie Labrecque."

"Precisely. I guess the circle of Earth warriors is rather tight."

"I suppose, but there isn't a weak link in the chain, I'll tell ya that much. I can understand why you would want to see Zelda. I think Alexander knows that Minga kohpah, I'll talk to him."

"Please and thank you."

Yet before Waskesiu and Ajawaan convened to discuss the matter, a slender and sleek whisk of a wind current slinked in a fanning curtain of aqua blue and forest green to the top of the ridge above camp; revealing the golden-brown lustre of Zachary's love.

"Zelda!" announced Zachary with delight.

"My love," she extended her arms in greeting.

They embraced and held tight for several seconds. Zachary did not want to let go and Zelda actually started crying.

"Hawkins said you would find me. I've become much stronger, but I really miss your touch," exclaimed Zachary.

"I'm very proud of you sweetie. You have come a long way in a short time, but this is only the beginning of your search."

"I know, I still haven't found my father yet, and there's the matter of this silviculture prophecy thing that Kingsmere says Soarfoot is seeking, if we ever do find him. But tell me, how did you preserve yourself to come back after two thousand years?"

"I was preserved in the spiritual corridors just as you were, except by pine tree angels instead of the aspen."

"Does that mean you're mortal? I thought you said you're a wizard."

"As you know, Zachary, I'm quite biological, it's just that my brain has developed ionised endorphins that allow me some limited shape shifting in certain conditions. I'm still mortal and prone to aging, but the spiritual essence inside the souls of all tree warriors adds vitality to our lifespan. You will experience this as well."

"So that means we can be together along my journey?"

"Absolutely my love, I will never abandon you."

"You don't know how reassuring that is to me Zelda. I'm so grateful to have you with me. I'm also more hopeful of finding my parents. Apparently this rooting commander Trudie Makwha might have a notion of where they are."

"That's encouraging, you should definitely take her advice."

"Are you going to join this tree raid with me?"

"I'm sorry sweetie, but I have to continue the search for Soarfoot with the Mingas. We'll be together again very soon Zachary, but in the meantime you must continue the search for your parents on your own path. The actuality growing within you will lead the way to them. I will follow you later and we will find each other again."

"I hope you're right. I trusted you before and I don't regret it, but I would be devastated if I lose you."

"You will always have me Zachary."

Unfortunately, he could not have her at that space and time. The nerving yearning only grew stronger but it did provide vigorous motivation to find his ancestors. Although he was somewhat shaken, he bid farewell to Zelda with another tight embrace and a passionate kiss, and then immediately turned to his duties on the rooting ship.

The brief reunion with Zelda was revitalising for Zachary, but the enormous magnitude of the situation began to creep into his mind as he scrambled with the other warriors to keep the rooting ship from falling apart. They were speeding through a cosmic trail towards Earth, the ship's pond was pouring into the fissures created by the collision, only a few water kegs were still sealed, half of the longhouse huts were crumbling, the power of the navigators was being tested to the limit, they lost five branch ships and many other warriors were wounded with wood chips and bark rashes to heal. Zachary was fighting for survival in outer space, and now he discovered that his girlfriend was a spiritual shape shifting pine tree wizard of some prominence; the situation was taxing his composure.

Alas, the atmosphere inside the cosmic corridor was far from hectic. All of the tree warriors were calmly helping the campfire maintainers plug and dam the pond runoffs, tidy the camp and make any emergency repairs before reaching Earth in only a few hours. Zachary was truly humbled by the incredible astronomical and spiritual powers at play, as well as the determined attitude of the warriors and the amazingly insouciant vibrations floating through the ship. It was remarkably inspiring. Zachary almost felt insignificant had he not been welcomed into the Envrah culture with complete acceptance. He was overcome by humility in the midst of such dedicated conviction and gratified to be part of this grand universal scheme; gripped by a sudden sense of obligation to honour the integrity of these crusaders.

Winston and Alexander returned from the trunk thrust meeting and tended to last minute preparations before reaching Nemeiben. Firewood was not a problem any longer; warriors were lighting crumbled huts into blazing bonfires while the sounds of blasting stagers once again filled the ship's cavity. The Envrah were quickly staging for another trunk takeover. It was the dreaded arch rival in space and heaven: the Alkae of spruce trees.

Zachary hoped there would not be any opposition on Earth and wondered if he really would ever see Zelda again. He also wondered if he would ever find his ancestors or his parents. Zachary's faith in the trees was being tested.

Chapter 29: Basin of Love

Sally scrambled up the ridge to enjoy a complete view of the forested canyon below. Sven followed her and the Slatterns scanned the misty valley together. They could see the winding river flowing through the canyon. Canoeing along the river was a lone warrior. He wore a bearskin cloak and weathered buckskin pants. Sally turned to Sven.

"How did he get there?"

"I have no idea," remarked Sven.

"Well you should. It is your watch," Sally berated her partner.

"Maybe if you wore clothes, I'd be able to concentrate," quipped Sven.

"Not funny at a time like this. I just hope he isn't a very powerful warrior. What do you think? Alkae? Or perhaps Naruka?"

"Oh I don't know. Does it really matter?"

"Well, are you going to do something?"

"You seem pretty keen. Why don't you do something," suggested Sven.

"We have to do something," insisted Sally.

"Be my guest. I'll be right behind you."

"Very well, I'll deal with the intruder."

Sally held out her hand with the palm cupped skyward and flicked her fingers at the trees along the river shoreline. A large pine tree ripped from the ground and darted down to the canoe. The warrior looked up to the horizon and saw the tree knifing towards him. He stood in the canoe and held out his paddle. The tree sliced into the paddle and blistered into pieces. The warrior was jarred but managed to keep the canoe floating above water.

Sally immediately summoned a horrendous gale of wind before the warrior could affix on her figure. The credo hybrid fell into the canoe and feverishly paddled against the gale, which was sprinkled with some of us wind warriors and a few vapour demons. The warrior managed to paddle into shore where he was protected from Sally's view by the steep bank of smooth stone.

"He's a Naruka and he will not exactly be a pushover, but I'm sure you can handle him," smirked Sven.

Sally snapped back: "You just be sure to back me up."

The attractive and naked as usual Marshlandite wizard scampered down the ridge in pursuit of the fir tree Naruka. The warrior pulled himself up against the shoreline by grabbing an overhanging tree branch. He secured the canoe by tying it to the branch with a rope and then climbed over the rock bank; galloping through the forest with his canoe paddle in hand heading to the middle of the canyon. The Naruka pounded over fallen trees, burst through shrubs and leapt across small creeks in a desperate frenzy. Sensing the presence of wizards he slid down an embankment and came to rest behind a rather large poplar tree.

The fir warrior was breathing hard as he peered around the tree. He could not see anyone in the surrounding woods so he resumed his romp through the canyon. However, standing between two trembling aspen trees on the opposite ridge of an intervening gulley was Sally Slattern. The Naruka was shocked by the initial sight of a naked woman, but remained alert knowing Sally was most likely a dangerous predator. And indeed she was.

Sally pointed to a tree branch which transformed into a screaming eagle. The raptor flew into open air and dove down at the warrior. The Naruka's paddle lit up with the illumination of lasha as he fended off the eagle. Grunting with effort he kept the bird at bay by taking several swings, but the contrived winged warrior was persistent and backed the credo to the edge of the declivitous river bank. The credo fell to his knees and fired a cavalcade of lasha with his stager: the eagle squealed in pain and waned in the air.

The Naruka jumped back to his feet but the eagle did not falter long; swooping down onto the warrior once again. The credo did not thrust his stager at the bird this time, but instead spun around facing the river and flopped down on his back. The eagle missed its target and the Naruka came springing up with a wild overhead swing. The fir tree warrior struck the vulnerable bird of prey and the eagle collapsed into the river. The credo quickly veered around but before he could react, he was charged by a bighorn ram which Sally summoned from the gulley. The Naruka and the ram both went plunging into the river and the warrior instantly came teeming up to the surface of the water with an excruciating yell and his stager already in full motion; the canoe paddle landing firmly in the thick horns of the ram.

The animal cringed under the strain of the lasha and disintegrated in the river. Now that he vanquished another of Sally's creations, the hybrid submerged himself and swam under the water's surface to the near shoreline; peeling off his bearskin cloak and floating up beside the steep bank. Sally was standing above the precipice searching for the Naruka. The fir warrior began to climb the bluff by prying his paddle stager into a stone crack and lifting himself out of the river. Sally bent over the ledge of the cliff face and saw the warrior. She lunged across the waterway and landed on the far shore.

The Naruka was still climbing the bank when he looked back to see a naked wizard levitate a ball of pine needles and pitch them across the water. The warrior dodged the collection of needles and fell back into the river; the needles piercing into the bank and shattering the rock. The Naruka swam under water again and crossed the river, but when he came to the surface Sally was ready for him. Positioned directly above she delivered another cluster of coniferous needles that struck him in the shoulder; crushing his scapula and ripping off a layer of bark. He grimaced in pain but was able to avoid another clump of needles by sinking back into the river.

The Slattern spun yet another ball of needles and waited for the warrior to surface, who came shooting out of the water with his stager firing a thrust of lasha at Sally. The spray struck her in the rib cage and jounced her into the forest bush. The Naruka briskly kicked over to the other side of the river and used his paddle to finally scale the wall of rock. He reached the top of the stone bank in a great deal of discomfort, only to find himself face-to-face with Sven Slattern: first a naked woman and now a naked man. The credo intruder was exhausted, injured and confused.

"You're a tough customer young Naruka," said Sven.

The warrior held his stager in defiance but appeared close to the end of his capabilities. Sally recovered and whisked over the river, landing near the Naruka. He backed away from the Slatterns, unsure of his next move. Sally slowly moved closer.

"So you thought you would come and find Soarfoot, did you? Yes, we know why you're here," snarled Sally.

"You're mad," cried the tree warrior.

"Mad, you think we're mad? Well you're right, we're totally insane, but you will not find Soarfoot here. No, you won't get that chance," glared Sven, who then suddenly grabbed the warrior's stager and jerked it out of his grasp.

"No!" screamed the Naruka.

"Yes, I'm afraid so," yelled Sally.

"And now my fellow adversary, you will learn why nobody comes here to search for Soarfoot. This place is by invitation only, and you're not on the guest list. I'm sorry young warrior, but this is one battle you are not going to survive. We cannot let you live," declared Sven.

And without warning he abruptly sliced the Naruka at the waist with his own stager. The warrior distorted into twisted pieces of balsam fir and collapsed into a pile of dust. Sven split the canoe paddle at the shaft and tossed it into the river.

"That's unfortunate," said Sally.

"I agree, it's sad to see any good warrior go down," sympathised Sven.

"Sometimes you amaze me Sven Slattern."

"I hate to see all this war and death. I hope he is ready soon and brings and end to it all. Why don't we go and check on him," posed Sven with a slight smirk.

"What did you have in mind?" twinkled Sally.

"Let's just go down to the basin and make sure everything is secure."

Sally agreed and the Slatterns ran down the shoreline of the river until reaching a rocky wall. They climbed to the summit of the wall and jumped down into the mist of the basin. Underneath the haze was a marsh harboured by the deep basin which was quite familiar to the Slatterns. The river trickled into the bog and weaved through the swampy wetland of the marsh. They walked to the middle of the bog where a mound of granite rock was piled on top of a grassy island knoll.

A well-hidden opening in the granite boulders led to a cave beneath the rock. A peaceful stream of smoke was rising into the damp air like a sauna steam bath circulating in the basin. There on the island beside the cave Sally and Sven sensually lay down their naked bodies to relax while caressing the soft grass. They snuggled side-by-side on their backs looking upwards and did not speak initially; both of them gazing into the ceiling of fog that seemed to be swaying in rhythm with the drifting smoke from the cave. It was dark and cool and they could see the vapour from their breath. Sven's eyes began to glow with a green gloss. Sally's eyes answered with an incandescent blue sheen.

"This place can be so eerie and frightening, yet to us it's completely serene and romantic," contemplated Sally.

"It's not simply appearance which entices emotion, but more so I think, the semblance of aesthetics associated with pleasant and meaningful thoughts or memories. If you have sentient affection for a certain vista, no matter how plain or even unattractive it may appear, it can yield a very special trance, if you know what I mean," professed Sven.

"It's the omnipotence of the silviculture prophecy and the magic of the Marshlandites," added Sally.

A voice sounded from within the cave: "You wizards are all the same. Are you ever silent? I need peace and quiet to do my bidding. Now please cease with your simplistic philosophies and if you insist on figuring out the secrets of the cosmos can you not do it somewhere else?"

"We apologise, we'll stop talking, but I can't promise we won't make any noise, if you know what I mean," answered Sven.

"I understand," acknowledged the voice in the cave. "By the way, you handled that Naruka well, but do try and stop those credos before they enter the canyon."

The Slatterns smiled at each other in silence as requested. They lay motionless for a moment; their eyes still glistening with a punctuated libido. Sally reached out and touched Sven. The green lustre in his eyes heightened. He rolled to his side and kissed Sally. They embraced.

And so, Sally and Sven Slattern made love in the marsh—again.

Chapter 30: River of Courage

Trudie Makwha's tree warriors destroyed the spruce near Nemeiben Lake in former northern Saskatchewan, by then La Ronge electoral boundary in the Churchill District of Boreal Nation. There was not much resistance from the Alkae and that suited Zachary fine. Although he was beginning to accept the reality of botanical disputes, he was still unaccustomed to all this killing whether it be trees or hybrid warriors.

Winston Waskesiu inquired with the chlorophyllialis Trudie Makwha and some other seasoned warriors to see if anyone had an inclination of where Irving Steele or Zachary's father Jeremiah might be found. The only bit of information he was able to procure indicated that perhaps there were tree warriors searching along the Churchill River again, just over twenty miles north of Nemeiben. It made perfect sense for Zachary to disembark the rooting ship and continue his search. Bruno, who was going to Planet Bahkra about five billion light years away to help some elm tree warriors, agreed to drop off Zachary on the Churchill and let him use his canoe.

They shuttled north on Bruno's branch ship to Trout Lake where the Churchill water basin widens to form one of many open water lakes along the river. Zachary had his backpack full of camping gear and was thankful for the canoe with two paddles. Winston gave him a bison hair cloak for cold weather and a ruck sack containing some flour, pemmican and venison jerky for survival food, and of course he had his stager hatchet and a newly acquired tree raid wardrobe. Bruno set him down at the Birch Rapids portage on the south end of Trout Lake and Zachary was ready for the next chapter in his adventure.

It took some paddling before the surroundings of the Churchill River became comfortable. He was slightly exhausted after travelling through space, harvesting aspen trees and the sort. He canoed the river many times before as a youngster with his father and his friend Flayda Findstad, and now the familiarity of his environment was gradually stabilising his anxiety. He canoed across the first open section of the lake and was winding through the islands leading to the second area of open water. He was floating downriver and could feel the current's flow between the islands.

The Churchill geography opens into lakes small and large with several narrow sections and occasional sets of rapids or fast water as the river drains on its eventual path to Hudson Bay and the Arctic Ocean. Zachary was stroking in calm conditions on the second open section of Trout Lake; leisurely paddling north in the sunshine. He was constantly examining the trees on the shoreline and taking note of many spruce, both white and black depending on the contour of the land and moisture in the soil, along with balsam fir and mercifully jack pine, plenty of birch along that stretch of the river, and of course some trembling aspen.

Finally becoming accustomed to his new seclusion and keenly aware of all the elements around him thanks to his new depth of perception, Zachary was conscious of slight changes in the breeze, the shifting of clouds and the tempo of the river's current. An unending shore of trees became an ever-altering forest of potential enemies. Zachary was ready; anticipating anything from a barrage of Alkae Iasha strikes to an assault of Naruka branch ships. And now he could muster a contentious force of sporadic energy for his own self-preservation.

Paddling to the end of the lake he was gliding up to Trout Rapids where the Churchill narrowed and displayed its certain power. It was not as dynamic as Iasha, but the speed and surge of the river possessed an imposing quality only nature could boast. Zachary could hear the roar of the rushing water ahead as he beached his canoe at the head of the portage around the rapids. It was comforting to know it was an earthly sound. Taking only his stager, he walked to a cliff where he could observe the white-water and chart a course for his canoe. Standing on the bluff of the south shore he enjoyed a complete view of the narrow span.

The rocks were casehardened and cold with geological age but were afforded the growth of green moss; a luxury unknown to Blavedian rocks. The water ripped down the descent with the torrential intensity of the Churchill. The rapids are short but potentially dangerous with two trouble spots. A standing wave about four feet tall gushes just below the crest at the head of the rapids; seemingly defying the river as it sputters white foam. The chute is clear after that until near the end of the choppy rapids where a large rock beside the south shore throws up a wall of water. The sprawling wave stretches across to the middle of the gap in the river.

Formulating his strategy Zachary decided he would take the top of the run wide to starboard side; avoiding some rock near the shore and knifing past the first swell. He would have to pull on port side and ferry against the current to avoid the standing wave near the south shore, but he did not anticipate getting wet. He was a stager himself when it came to white-water and he was in his own backyard, yet the power of the river was a challenge worthy of a tree warrior: the Churchill was calling.

He was beaming with the confidence of a log splitter as he returned to his canoe and paddled upstream; his stager tucked into an underarm holster that held the hatchet by its steel head. He turned the boat into the current and slowly approached the rapids. The white-water was in sight and he was soon on top of the first standing wave. Zachary stroked on port side and veered right of the swell. He compensated with a cut stroke and the canoe straightened true to the flow of the water skimming smoothly past the wave of foam. He remained collected, even contemplative; his strokes responding to the energy of the aspens and moving through the current with authority.

Continuing with a combination of sweep strokes on starboard followed by j-hooks and pitched cut strokes, Zachary paddled across the flow of white-water and neatly sliced to the left of the final standing wave into the main chute of the rapids. He delicately bounced into the chute and over a powerful hydraulic curl of water; easily steering his way through the rest of the white-water. It went exactly as planned—he surmounted the challenge of the river. Zachary rode out the rapids and continued downriver to the next white-water just around the bend. He decided to run these rapids without reconnoitring.

The river's width is extremely narrow at this gap but the drop is minimal. However, there are two large standing waves in the middle of the chute. Approaching the blare of the water's rush Zachary decided the only route was straight down the middle. He selected a smooth v-crest leading directly into a shower of foam and was unceremoniously sucked into the gap between standing waves; bracing through a barrage of white-water as the canoe skipped over the waves and was spewed out into the tail end of the rapids. He stroked port side and slid by another standing wave—the side of the canoe bumping against a wall of foam but not taking on any water. He steered with a few more sweeps and j-hooks, running the rapids to their conclusion and continuing downstream in a south-easterly direction.

The afternoon was becoming quite splendid. The zephyr which was present for most of the day was now gone and the sky was clear; the prominent sun slowly falling behind Zachary and pouring its heat onto the river. A stretch of calm water lay in front of him, yet Rock Trout Rapids were not far away. He would run Rock Trout and head down the river another three miles before reaching Nipew Lake, where he intended to find a campsite. Zachary was constantly scanning the shoreline again looking for warriors or any sort of threat, but it was becoming a much more casual process. He was acclimatised to his homeland Earth by then and his smooth sailing through the rapids only added to his growing self-esteem. Alas the rapids were in sight sooner than he anticipated and it was time to get serious again.

These rapids are not easy: consisting of two frothing sections of white-water. The first section chutes straight into the rock wall of an island which splits the river, with the second set of rapids to the right side and the passage left of the island shallow and usually impassable because of large rocks. A tall standing wave at the head of the second run provides a notable hazard, but the biggest threat is getting caught in the current of the initial chute and thrown up against the steep rock wall of the island.

The first set of rapids were visible to Zachary: a prevailing trench of white-water rushing through a narrow gap between the rock banks of the river. He paddled on port side to take him along the right fringe of the rapids so he would not slam into the island, but the canoe was cutting starboard of a standing wave in danger of sliding broadside into the spurting curl of water. Zachary instinctively thrust his paddle into the water with a hard cross-draw and brought the stern of the canoe into line. He narrowly slipped past the swell; the rushing water within the length of his paddle.

He skimmed over a series of crests on the edge of the rapids, sticking close enough to the main chute to avoid a swirling eddy beside the right shore. He cleared the whirlpool and feverishly stroked port side to stay away from the rock wall of the island, but the flow of the river was unrelenting. Zachary was heading directly into the haystack wave marking the beginning of the second run. He adamantly paddled with draws and cuts to slip by the wave of water, successfully negotiating the corner of Rock Trout. A strong pull with a few j-hooks and he next manoeuvred between two troughs of speeding water. Skidding on crests of standing waves Zachary bounced over a few smaller swells and navigated onto smoother water riding out the rapids: another test of his wits completed.

There were rock bluffs to both sides of him as he sat back in the stern of his canoe and admired the view for a short distance downstream. He spotted an obvious landing on the shore where the rock curves down to the water and creates a natural docking area. Zachary cut across the river and paddled to the spot so he could bail some water he took on through the rapids. A predominant glow of optimism suddenly and radically developed into guarded suspicion as he paddled to the shore. He was aroused by a sudden chill. Zachary's perception of human reality began to warp; creeping closer to the spiritual side.

The canoe slowly drifted downstream as Zachary stopped paddling and scrutinised the shoreline of granite stone. The trees leered behind the shield of rock—seething with the venom of Rulsp's curse. Zachary was searching for unfriendly trees but soon found himself drifting away from shore. Sparked by his new buoyancy of self-assurance he decided to confront the evil spirits; stroking hard against the current to land his canoe on the curved rock. He pulled the boat onto shore and walked to the edge of the forest trees.

There were many looming conifers but they were accompanied by some soothing deciduous. He was relieved by the presence of a few aspen and hopeful that the birch would attract sympathetic Coulees, yet just as he began to relax a haunting cold breeze cut through the trees. He could feel the evil nemesis tearing away at his mind. He yanked his hatchet from the holster and held it into the breeze with an outstretched arm.

"No!" he yelled.

But the gust persisted; not all of us wind warriors were peaceful at that particular space and time. The onslaught of the evil burst grew stronger. Zachary reacted by gripping his stager with both hands and snapping a blur of lasha into the woods. Twigs twisted through the air and landed in the river behind him. The breeze subsided, but then Zachary heard a familiar whisper from within the woods.

"You are nothing. I shall destroy you," came the raspy condemnation.

"I won't let you," shouted Zachary, as he managed to swallow his fear and answer back to the demon voices in his mind.

"You will die!" blistered the scourge of Rulsp.

Shaking with perspiration pouring down his face, Zachary said nothing but remained tense and alert as he waited and listened. The only whisper he heard next was the voice of the river. He brought his stager to his side and continued to glare into the trees.

"Show yourself!" he defiantly screamed.

"Find me!" roared the evil spirit.

"If that's the way you want it, I will find you," muttered Zachary as he spit on the ground and started to walk into the tangled underbrush.

He did not hesitate and began to trot through the dense forest; soon bounding over fallen trunks, weaving around bushes and racing at a frantic pace to vent the horror inside his soul. He came up to a small ridge and stopped. The nemesis spirit issued another warning.

"Die Envrah!"

The confused earthling reeled around and released a whirl of lasha; exploding an old growth spruce tree into dust. He looked down the line of the ridge and saw another towering spruce. Again he blasted and again the spruce was destroyed. He turned to the gulley in front of him and took aim at a tall balsam fir. The lasha erupted inside the tree and it too was obliterated into tiny woodchips and stagerdust. He blasted another three trees in succession and then zoomed in on a patch of ferns growing in the gulley.

The ferns were surrounded by a small stand of balsam poplar trees. Zachary held the lasha around his stager and did not fire. The slope of the ridge into the gulley was dotted with alder and birch, gently rolling down into the garden of ferns growing in the moss and rich black soil of the forest floor. Protected by the fortress of poplars the ferns exhaled a peaceful warmth flowing up to Zachary: he would face the Alkae spirit there.

Carefully descending the gulley and walking into the plot of ferns he was more enraged than he was frightened. The sporadic energy of the aspen boiled inside him and accentuated his slightly misguided conviction into a fuming outburst of anger. Unfortunately he had become ignorantly defiant. He made two mistakes. The first was taking one hand off his stager. The second was not recognising a shrubbery of killer ferns.

The shaded wilderness garden greeted Zachary with an unpleasant jolt as he reached the bottom of the gulley. A streak of numbing pain raced up his spinal cord, and before he could react the ground buckled beneath him. He was immediately sucked down into a hole by a patch of swarming killer ferns. He finally reacted by spreading out his arms and holding onto the ground for his life.

He dug his fingers into the moist dirt as the ferns mobbed his body and pulled him into the depths of the earth.

During the fall from grace Zachary dropped his stager. He looked to his side and saw the brown leather strap: the hatchet was buried under the killer ferns and the strap was disappearing. He seized onto the leather and began pulling his stager free, but with only the strength of one arm he was sucked down into the hole. He was up to his neck in dirt and gnarly ferns were clinging to his face. Zachary gathered all his faculties and concentrated with every last morsel of his talents.

He tore his stager free and with one swift motion delivered a crucial blow to the ground. The lasha glistened in the shadows and the earth ripped apart; chunks of dirt and mud scattering about. The forest floor caved in completely creating a gaping tunnel in the ground. Zachary immediately went sliding down to the bottom where he could feel the soil still crumbling under his feet. He lifted his stager with the sides of the tunnel beginning to crush down on him and he issued a desperate blast of lasha.

The charge ushered dirt skyward and cleared a steep pitch for Zachary to climb. He scaled the wall of earth as the dirt continued to collapse all around him, only to be met by the hungry ferns at the top of the pitch. Planting his feet firmly in the ground he fired a jagged edge of lightning and seared a path through the ferns. He ran over the edge of the pit and through the patch of killer ferns, stopping halfway up the gulley to gain the support of a friendly poplar tree. Panting from his ordeal he peered down at the hole in the ground: the pit was still growing as it was swallowed into the cavity, the ferns were smouldering from the heat of the lightning and the surrounding vegetation was gradually catching fire.

The green killers began to scream out in pain and the crumbling pit finally grinded to a halt. Zachary took a few steps down the ridge for a closer look at the scene of destruction. The massive hole was deep and the smoke from the ferns began to drift into the cavernous opening. He had seen enough, yet before he could turn to climb the ridge, he was the victim of a vicious impact. He was sent sprawling down the slope in the grasp of a demented creature. He was jumped by a mad sput.

The demon hybrid grabbed at Zachary's neck and scratched at his stomach as they rolled down the gulley. Fighting and tussling they flipped through the ferns and over the lip of the hole down into the pit of dirt. Zachary fell on top of the sput with a thud but the demon instantly delivered a punch to his abdomen. Dazed and down on one knee, Zachary reached for the handle of his stager dangling from his wrist as the sput wound up with another swing. He ducked under the attempted blow and whipped around his stager at full force. The hatchet landed deep into the sput's shoulder with a flare of lasha and a flaming chunk of wood shooting into the air. The sput fell to the ground and Zachary did not waste any time thrusting a cluster of lasha at the beast—charred demon wood.

The ground began to shift again as Zachary quickly charged up the wall of earth with the bounce of lasha. The flames from the ferns were blazing at the top of the pit blocking his exit. He was slowly sinking back into the dirt and the pit was getting larger by the second. Zachary took drastic action and drove his stager into the ground; like a gushing spring of water the stager bounced back up surrounded by the power of botanic spiritualis. The lasha separated the rich top soil and a branch ship emerged from the turmoil. Zachary was airborne. He was navigating lasha.

Cruising up the side of the gulley the burgeoning tree warrior was ecstatic. The haunting chill of the evil spirits was gone and he was basking in the exhilaration of the aspens. He glided over the ridge and rather crudely landed his branch ship on the shore of the river. He released his stager, the lasha disappeared and the hatchet fell to the ground in a heap of dirt. Zachary was thrilled. He picked up his stager and held it high in victory.

"Where are you now?" he shouted.

There was not anyone to answer. And then, a stimulating twitch began to emanate from his navel. The vibrant sensation streamed through his soul; he was teeming with the glory Hawkins Kingsmere described. Zachary had grown a spiritual core. He examined his bellybutton and found a thin layer of wood formed on his skin. He touched it. A wave of electricity rippled through his body. He then fainted. Zachary was not prepared for the changes in his body. He regained consciousness with a balmy smile stretched across his face. He was dreaming of Zelda. He sat upright and looked into the forest. There was not any sign of danger. He felt safe and more than human; elevated to a new level of existence. Zachary became an Envrah.

The canoe was launched onto the Churchill with enough daylight to reach Nipew Lake before sunset. Downriver Zachary came upon a small island which splits the river. He chose to pass on the south side where a narrow passage cluttered with rocks separates the island from the mainland. A shallow set of rapids ripples beside the island followed by a short section of calm water, then a rock peninsula extending from the island forces the waterway to curl towards the mainland. A second set of rapids rolls through a gap between the peninsula and the south shore. Zachary ran the shallow but passable riffles, scraping only a few rocks with his canoe. He shot through the mild white-water without any difficulty.

The river then pours into Mountney Lake; flowing south at the end of the lake for another short distance before reaching Nipew Lake. The banks are rugged there and dense with bush. The river is narrow and the current is fast. This is typical Churchill country: a tapered passage of speeding freshwater grooming a path through the tempestuous boreal shield. Zachary maintained a steady pace. The river presented a few runs of harmless white-water, several rocks, some tricky currents and random eddies. In short order, he paddled to Nipew Lake.

A shoreline camp at the mouth of the lake was ideal, with a bathtub, patio, garage, living room and plenty of bedrooms. The lake opens up north of a smooth, exposed rock peninsula forming the patio. A small opening in the rock leads to a pool of water tucked behind the shoreline between the patio and the narrow point of the peninsula. The sheltered pool is just large enough to house a few canoes—the garage. The shoreline also provides an indentation beside the patio where water rests in a miniature cove for a natural bathtub. Beyond the shore and into the woods is the campsite with a living room and bedrooms. A circular firepit made of stones is the living room and scattered blankets of moss offer a good selection of bedrooms.

The sight of spruce and fir trees did not bother Zachary; they were inevitable. He was growing completely confident in his ability to perceive danger. The presence of evil spirits certainly aroused strong reactions in his mind. In the meantime, he was going to enjoy his environment.

The sun was setting and its warmth was bleaching down on the rock patio as Zachary parked his canoe in the garage. He pulled out his fishing rig and started casting for his dinner. Bruno's luck was with him: two pickerel. He filleted the fish on the patio and tossed the carcasses into the river. He chopped some wood, started a fire and spread his bison cloak over a bed of moss. The red sunset and a clear sky bode well for a starlit sky and a dry sleep. He didn't bother setting up his tent, cooked the fish and devoured the fillets sitting around his campfire. He snuggled into his warm cloak facing the dwindling flames under a bold star field. Zachary was ready for a good sleep.

The Churchill coolly susurrated into the open water of Nipew with a gurgle and a slosh from the shoreline as a mist settled above the river under the early morning sun. Zachary was ready to continue his journey after an undisturbed night of rest. Rising from his bed of moss he stretched out the overnight kinks and went down to the river for a quick plunge into the water. The brisk Churchill is enough to clear the cobwebs from anyone's head. He built up a small fire with kindling and quickly cooked a bannock mixture with the flour and baking powder from his supplies, water from the river and a little fat oil he saved while cooking his fish. He ate his breakfast bread, doused the fire, loaded his canoe and set out in the morning fog.

The water was perfectly calm and the day's heat would soon clear the mist from the top of the lake. Zachary contemplated testing his botanic spiritualis navigational skills further, but decided to keep paddling for at least that day. Until he was completely versed in the power of lasha he would travel down the river by canoe. The ideal weather conditions and flat water allowed him to cross Nipew quickly. He circled around two islands at the east end of the lake and past three more smaller islands leaving Nipew behind as the Churchill narrowed again. He followed the south shore of Selby Peninsula and headed northeast around more islands as the river narrowed once more until he reached Fletcher Island. There the river flows past Twolake Island and opens into an extended bay.

The large bay stretches over a mile where the river flows south becoming Dead Lake. Still floating on calm water, Zachary gradually paddled starboard and pointed his canoe towards the terminus of the lake. Dead Lake is about two miles long with Burgess Bay the final half mile where there are two small islands in the southeast corner. Beyond the islands the Churchill flows into Great Devil Rapids. Zachary didn't give any thought to the names of these bodies of water. In fact, Dead Lake was just as commonly called Hayman Lake. The lake was originally given its name because of a disease outbreak in the area many years in the past, but to those select warriors who travelled the cosmos on arboretum ships Dead Lake meant more than disease.

This portion of the Churchill is a prime location for trunk thrusts and roaming sputs. Because there are often many warriors meeting along the river, the sputs usually gather in packs and consume any and all spiritual cores they can scavenge. Zachary was paddling across the lake under the sharp rays of the noon sun. He could see a few islands and farther downstream even the blurred east shore of Burgess Bay in the building waves of heat above the water. He slowly glided in his canoe on the surface of Dead Lake without much effort, yet with an uneasy feeling of slight apprehension. The water was an eerily still glass top mirror reflecting the canoe and distant horizon: lines of green forest and blue sky wavering in the sultry heat. Zachary stopped beside a small island and surveyed the remainder of Burgess Bay.

There was not any obvious sign of danger, yet Zachary could feel the wrath of evil spirits close at hand. Boldly he moved out from the island and began a hurried pace into open water. He pointed his canoe towards a small reef of rocks which etched a sharp outline above the smooth water. He squinted to focus on the rocks and saw that the reef, although closer to him, was situated between the two islands at the end of the bay. But what appeared to be rock was not a reef. And what appeared to be islands were not just rocks and trees. The reef was the pubic hairs of a mammoth sput and the islands were the demon's breasts. The sput was laying under the water with its face looking up at the headwaters of Great Devil Rapids.

The demon sput began to rise. The reef suddenly disappeared under the water as the sput erected to a sitting position. Zachary saw the islands at the end of the bay elevate into the air. The gaseous face of a giant sput stared down at him and the river was swept into a mad swish of waves and whirlpools swirling down into the graveyard at the bottom of Dead Lake. Zachary swung the canoe around and stroked unmercifully towards the small island where he had stopped.

Massive whirlpools formed on each side of the sput under its armpits, pushing crests of insurmountable waves. Smaller but devastating waves nonetheless curled up from the sput's abdomen and were upon Zachary almost instantly. He was able to ride on top of the waves with some adept paddling derived from the power of the aspens; dipping down into a swell after the first rush of water. He was close to the refuge of the island, but then fell victim to the huge armpit waves whipping across the lake. The canoe was tossed like a toy as the walls of water from the two whirlpools collided; the white foam of Dead Lake spitting into the open air.

The lake surged to new heights and the canoe was swallowed into the tide. The tiny vessel knifed through the water and into the trees of the island as the small speck of land was covered by the rolling waves. Zachary himself was submerged under the turbulence and carried over the island; finally breaking through the water in the resulting swell. Immediately he began to swim for the protection of the island but was pushed back by another wave. The ensuing breakers were not quite as potent and the island served as a barrier which afforded him some calm water. The monster sput was now on its feet and wading across the bay; its tree trunk thighs pushing water with each step and creating large crashing waves.

Dead Lake was transformed into a stormy scene under the clear sky. Zachary reached the shore of the island with the sput towering above him; its face swirling with gloom, its gnarled limbs reeking of desolation, and from within, the demon cries of captured cores screaming in the amok. The sput was the essence of Rulsp.

The island was demolished with one sweep of the sput's forearm, leaving Zachary a vulnerable target crouching near the shore. Wood chips and sput dust disseminated in the air as tree tops went flying into the lake. The sput sneered at Zachary's naked core, who wrenched his stager free from the underarm holster. There was only one thing left to do: get the Quujj out of there. He drove his stager into what remained of the ground and the lasha did not fail him. The hatchet came rushing back up with the power and a chunk of rock split from the island. Zachary began to navigate the lasha but the sput was already striking down with an overhead swing.

The young Envrah pointed his branch ship towards the southern sky and streamed forward with all his speed. The sput's arm whistled through the air narrowly missing him but catching the stern edge of the ship. The rock shattered; flaring in flashes of green, red and blue lasha in the mayhem. Zachary looked back and saw the vacant space in his ship, but the lasha regained semblance and filled the void. The sput renegotiated its balance and turned towards the fleeing warrior. Zachary spun around and fired a blister of ionised spiritual energy.

The sput held up its hand and effortlessly deflected the lasha into the boreal forest. Zachary had clearly overestimated his power. He veered his arboretum vessel to the east and turned on the afterburners, but he was not quick enough. The sput's next blow sliced across the port side of the branch ship and sheared the lasha. The absence of sporadic energy caused an imbalance and the flying clump of rock tilted sideways and began to dive towards the lake. The sput pivoted in the water and chased the faltering tree warrior.

Heaving hard on his stager Zachary pulled the sparkling hatchet to the starboard side. He levelled his ship cruising just above the wild water of Dead

Lake and brought the nose up to clear the trees on the shoreline. He managed to soar above the trees but shifted the lasha too far right. The ship was speeding over the trees with the starboard side leaning forward and the impoverished port side hanging in the rear. Looking over the bow of the ship he could see the sput crossing the bay and closing in on the shore. He desperately needed to gain control. Slowly he turned the vessel and pulled the bow back into position. The diminished lasha on the port side slanted the branch ship to the left once more and forced Zachary to lean right yet again.

Alas, it was futile. He could not hold his altitude and the ship cut into the trees. He crashed into the forest with a spray of splinters and a dazzling light show of lasha. The branch ship piled into the ground and Zachary was thrown clear of the wreckage. He ripped through several limbs of coniferous branches and slammed up against a tree. He was hurled down to the ground half unconscious and barely managed to break his fall with a roll into the moss. The sput drooled menacingly as it lumbered up to the wooded shoreline.

The waves continued to splash from the sput's legs and were breaking over the north shore of the bay. Zachary was dazed and bruised; laying on his back near the crash site. The waves from the imposing demon creature rushed over the rocky mainland; drenching and waking Zachary, yet he still remained quite groggy. He held onto his stager while the sput cast a threatening shadow over him. Again the demon sheared away trees with a sweeping thrust of its forearm. Zachary crawled away from the timber and slunk behind a pine tree. He lifted his stager for one last desperate stream of lasha, but before he could fire the sput was suddenly jarred back into the lake.

A piercing streak of lightning bolted from behind Zachary and scorched the sput's chest. The giant core eater shrieked in pain as its scathing bulk was split in half. The hulking body of spruce fractured into singed bark and twisted pieces of wood. The sput's head went flying through the air and landed in shambles across the bay. Once again Dead Lake spew white foam as the remains of the sput slapped into the water. Zachary was surprised but eternally grateful. Wet and exhausted he began to laugh as the lake settled, the swells rescinded and the last few waves curled up to the shore.

The sput was killed by a surge of lightning, yet the charge of electricity came from the ground and not the sky. Zachary turned and looked into the bush. Walking through the trees were two rather thin but muscular old men; one carrying a large staff and the other what looked like a wood carved spear. Both men were well tanned—one with brown skin, going bald and growing a light grey beard, the other with olive white skin still sporting curly brown hair on his head and clean shaven—and both were wearing interlaced bark-bast tops and fluffy cotton pants with moccasins. Zachary slumped down onto a moss-covered rock and marvelled at his saviours. He recognised one of the men. It was Harold his guardian angel.

"Harold," he sighed.

"Zachary old boy," smiled the angel.

"Was that lightning from you?" questioned Zachary.

"Rock-a-bye sput, over tree tops, when the lasha blows, the cradle will fall. Yes, my young student, that lightning was from the lasha, but it wasn't me, it was your ancestor the Storyteller," said Harold, pointing to his companion Rushad Rhomanscu.

"The original Rhomany?" gawked Zachary.

"Yes, my schweetz, you are my child, and family is everything. I will keep you safe now," answered the Storyteller.

"That's absolutely amazing. You found me and saved my life."

"Well, I kind of owed you one," said Harold.

"What do you mean?"

"That sput you killed at Kingsmere Lake was coming for me. It was my core that it sensed and the reason it was attracted to the lake."

"But I thought you're an angel."

"I am. Angels have cores too, you know."

"So I've got this thing forever?"

"Yes, I see that you have your own core now. That was pretty good flying, and I do think you would have survived the encounter eventually, but we thought we would save you some injury and put an end to that nasty monster."

"Well, I certainly do appreciate the intervention."

"It's really nothing at all for a pair of Envrahs like ourselves."

"So, Rushad Rhomanscu, the Storyteller. Are you an angel as well?"

"No, no schweetz. I am just like you. We have strong family blood. We have a special gift and we will live for thousands of years, just like the angels."

"The Storyteller is a tree warrior just like you have become, and now he will take over my job and be your new guardian," explained Harold.

"Then do you know where my parents are?" pleaded Zachary.

"Of course we do. What kind of a guardian angel would I be if I didn't know that?" quipped Harold.

"Did you know when we first met?" quizzed Zachary.

"Absolutely not, I didn't even know who you were."

"Well then, how did you manage to find them?"

"I found them my schweetz. We share the same bloodline and your mother called to me on the cosmic wave. And now Harold will take us to them through the spiritual corridors," assured the Storyteller.

"And not only that, but I will also take you to Soarfoot, and even that cute little thing you love so much," boasted Harold.

"You mean Zelda!" exclaimed Zachary.

"In the flesh, if you know what I mean," taunted Harold.

"This is simply incredible. I've come full circle. I started out with Zelda travelling to a distant planet, came back to Earth and met you Harold, then an ancient Druid and a tree raid on even more planets, and now I'm meeting you Rushad, my ancestral grandfather still alive more than a hundred years older than me. I'm blown away and utterly humbled by everything that's happened to me."

"What are you saying?" asked Harold.

"I don't know what to do or say. I don't know if I can handle this. How can I possibly live up to my ancestry? I'm not sure I want to go," said Zachary.

"Don't you at least want to meet Soarfoot, let alone your parents?"

"Well, yes, but that monster sput made me think twice. I know I made a commitment, but I have to admit I'm having second thoughts."

"What will you do? Where will you go? Do you want to stay here on this river in the forty-fourth century?" posed Harold.

"It is frightening my child. That is why you must go. You may not know it yet, but you have strength greater than any other, the same as Soarfoot. You will crusade for peaceful existence," Storyteller profoundly conjectured.

"Yes, I do feel it. Somehow I know it to be true, thank you Rushad."

"It is with pleasure. We are family blood my schweetz."

"And we will find my parents?" inquired Zachary.

"Just follow me," said Harold.

Chapter 31: Black Hole of Wisdom

The Slatterns lay in the cold, moist grass of the marsh; their burning bodies providing all the warmth they needed. They were naked, as usual, and making love, as usual.

Sally looked up into the haze and saw the mist slowly beginning to disperse. It had never done that before; always hanging dormant above the chilly confines of the bog. The mist began to drift towards open air as it dissipated in the starkness of the basin. It continued to climb higher, above the bulrushes and along the craggy walls of stone. The fog casually floated into the canyon and disappeared into the trees as the dawning sun began to shine through the branches. The marsh was exposed to sunlight.

The woman with the blue eyes sat up; her breasts recumbent as she supported herself with outstretched arms. She could hear small rodents and bog animals scurry for cover from the harsh light. The sunlight continued to filter down into the basin: the otherwise dreary swamp began to display signs of rejuvenated life. The slumping reeds and grasses seemed to expand and fortify with new energy. Colour returned to the marsh. Brown plant life and grey water became green and clear blue. A dragonfly fluttered down to the water for the first time since the Slatterns took up residence in the cryptic surroundings. The spores would once again germinate and multiply.

There was also another sound that Sally did not recognise immediately. It was a droning hiss. She contorted her body and whipped around her head to scan the marsh, but could not see anything. Then she realised: it was Sven snoring while sleeping only moments after passionate sex.

"Wake up you oaf," she said to her mate.

Sven did not budge. Sally nudged him and he stopped snoring.

"What is it?" he groaned.

"The mist has lifted. The basin is uncovered."

"The fog will come back."

"I don't think so."

"Why not?"

"There isn't any smoke coming from the cave."

Sven bounced upright. He looked over to the island of rock and grass where the cave was hidden.

"Well Quujj me gently," he remarked.

"What do you think?" asked Sally.

"He must be ready. I suspect we will have visitors soon."

A dark hand emerged from the cave and grabbed the rock formation at the entrance. Rising from beneath the marsh was a taut and solid figure of a man. He was vibrantly gleaming with vitality and projecting a supreme temperament; his skin a smooth and unblemished shade of umber formed tight to the curvatures of his developed muscles. He appeared stern yet his stature hinted a compassionate disposition. He wore only creased bark pants and moccasins. He was and still is a Minga of the upper echelon; a defiant warrior of almost countless battles. This man was the highly sought after pine tree warrior Soarfoot.

He gazed at the sky and turned to the Slatterns. Sally and Sven stood before him in an exposed state of curiosity. Soarfoot did not speak initially but did cast a bemused frown at the naked couple and shook his head. He bent down and reached into the cave pulling out an old tomahawk: a forged steel blade and a scuffed, light brown stock handle of pine wood. It was one of the most powerful weapons in the universe, and still is one of greatest stagers in all of the grand creations. Soarfoot faced the Slatterns.

"You can find a warmer place to live. And can you please put on some clothing before our guests arrive," he told the wizards.

"Is he coming here then?" inquired Sven.

"Yes, he is bringing a young candidate," answered Soarfoot.

"But why didn't you tell us before now?" questioned Sally.

"He is quiet in his ways. I did not know myself until he spoke to me on the cosmic wave just today. He finally found the mixed species hybrid who was looking for his ancestors back on Planet Earth," explained Soarfoot.

"Why yes, we know him. We protected and transported his parents while we were helping the manifestos. He is Zachary Steele," stated Sven.

"You are very perceptive despite your odd behaviour. The manifesto warriors of peace do appreciate all you have done. You have served with honour by protecting this sanctuary and allowing me to prepare for our journey into the spiritual dimension, leepshah shahmah."

"We will stay until he arrives," suggested Sally.

"Muh. Don naga lashmuh, pah mee whaga," said Soarfoot, saying yes, we will have a sacrifice fire when he arrives.

"I imagine he is happy now that he has found his ancestral grandchild, conceived with the bond of your very own bloodline," observed Sally.

"Muh, lahtoo eesah maha, we are all happy. And now we will find true awareness with the tree gods, sylva moobah lah bohtah."

"We wish you all the best in your crusade," said Sven.

"I thank you, rah keeno," acknowledged Soarfoot.

"Well Sally, we better start thinking of somewhere else to go and amuse ourselves. I hear the Demkew elders are a riot and the winters are quite mild on their homeland," proposed Sven.

"I like the winters," pouted Sally.

"Now don't get all sentimental on me—"

"Actually, we might need a few wizards on Flafidia and there's never winter on that planet," offered Soarfoot. "The credos will fight us when we return from the heavens and they will employ Flafidians. The manifestos will need your help once again. But before that I would like to ask you for a special favour. We will be jumping into the spiritual dimension tonight, but Zachary's parents will be here and they must stay behind. Will you please transport them again, back to their home planet?"

"We will happily take care of them, for certain," promised Sven.

"Yes, and we will continue to fight for peace. As you can see, we like the aspen and pine tree warriors in Plateau Grand Creation," commented Sally.

"And we love the Marshlandites," concluded Soarfoot.

The Slatterns looked at each other and waved their shape shifting heads in a fluffy swirl of cloudy vapour; whisking their naked bodies up to the peak of the basin wall. A sparkling organic vessel adorned with colourful limestone and robust pine trees drifted in the opposite direction with three people onboard as the wizards stood on the stone ridge above the basin. The branch ship touched down in the marsh and landed on the grass island beside Soarfoot. Yet another arboretum island floated down through the trees protruding above the narrow shear rock opening at the top of the hidden canyon. This ship, rich with cottonwood, trembling and quaking aspens, was navigated by Harold standing alongside Zachary and the Storyteller. Zachary gazed into the canyon and recognised the Slatterns as the seemingly harmless lovers he saw at Bagwa and Norseman lakes, who were standing on the ridge of the basin in their naked human forms.

The Slatterns turned and bounded down the basin wall; vanishing into the woods of the canyon only to return later that night. Harold waved his staff over the canyon as they glided closer to the basin.

"Soarfoot," he announced.

"Down there?" pondered Zachary as he took a deep breath and inhaled the heavenly powers.

"Yes, down there," repeated Harold.

"But where, exactly?"

"You'll find him, and your parents as well. The ridge where the wizards were standing, it opens down into a basin."

And with that, Harold also vanished, leaving an ancestral grandfather and grandson gliding on an arboretum vessel. They descended into the swampy marsh and settled onto the basin floor not far from the grassy island. Zachary soon set his eyes on Soarfoot for the first time, but it was the other three people he was totally enamoured to see. He immediately dashed across a bed of moss and reeds, jumped over a channel of water and ran up to the grass island. There they were: his mother Maria, father Jeremiah and lover Zelda.

"I've been looking for you," said Zachary.

"Yes, my son, and you have found us," answered Jeremiah.

Father and son embraced and the Steele family instinctively bonded telepathically with the gift of sporadic perception, and physically with a group hug as Zachary's mother joined in.

"I knew you would find us," said Maria.

"I think it's you who found me. Thank you for bringing my parents here Zelda, how did you know?" said Zachary, welcoming his partner into the fold.

"I simply followed the owls on the cosmic wave," smiled Zelda.

All four of them huddled together with broad beaming smiles.

"I'm so glad you found us Zachary, this makes us complete. You have respected our ancestry and now you can follow the tradition of your bloodline, the quest for universal peace," Jeremiah told his son.

"It all makes sense now Dad. I also feel complete. I didn't think I had the strength for this journey until just now. Thanks for believing in me."

"It's the gift that you possess Zachary," reflected Maria. "You have honoured your family. We are fortunate to have such a wonderful son."

"I'm the lucky one. You both carried such a burden all my life. I feel like I'm indebted to you, and you too Zelda, but I also feel the pulse of my bloodline in my soul. I'm now driven by the power of the trees."

The smiles and laughter of the family reunion slowly turned emotional as both Zachary and his father shed tears of pure joy. The elderly hybrid ancestors patiently observed while the sentiments ran their course there in the marsh.

"We are all lucky, and you will flourish Zachary when you join with Soarfoot," said Zelda, prompting the family to turn their attention.

"Yes Zelda, there is very much to do," declared Jeremiah, next looking directly at his son. "I see you've met your Rhomany forefather Zachary, but I don't think you've met the Steele family patriarch."

The Storyteller was already stacking firewood beside the cave from his and Zelda's branch ship to prepare for the evening's festivities, while Soarfoot was placing some trunk logs on their ends to use as seats. He pointed to one of the logs with his tomahawk stager and motioned to Zachary.

"Beelah, tahsak fah tee. Please, sit down and rest yourself," he said.

Zachary pulled his stager from its holster under his arm and sat down on one of the logs. Soarfoot also sat down, followed by Jeremiah who then introduced the ancient warrior to his son.

"Zachary, this is our Minga forefather Soarfoot," said Jeremiah.

"I've been looking for you too," responded Zachary.

"Tee klahsah lasha lah moobah tahsak bohtrak. Tee naga muh, po tee nah bohtahna," said the ancient pine tree warrior.

"Soarfoot says you have learned the ways of lasha and the manifesto on your journey," translated Zelda. "You have done well Zachary, and now you will be rewarded. You see, your blood is a bond from two strong species, the aspen and the pine. The Storyteller is your maternal ancestor as you know, and Soarfoot is also your direct forefather."

The Rhomany Storyteller also jumped into the conversation: "And it's not by chance my schweetz. Soarfoot came to visit me on Mount Shasta with the botanic spiritualis, lasha bohtrak, a hundred years before you were born. He showed me the ways of the ashah, spiritual awareness, and later, when your mother came to the prairies, we visited your father and told him that he would wed this Rhomany woman and they would conceive a child born with a special gift in his soul. We Envrahs believe you and Soarfoot are the mixed species who will join the strength of the aspens and the pine trees to shine a bright light on the path of the silviculture prophecy."

"And as I told you Zachary, Rushad came to counsel me so I could help guide you on your journey," interjected Zelda again.

"She's a good schweetz," affirmed the Storyteller.

Jeremiah and Maria were smiling at their son; the aged wrinkles on their faces hidden behind happiness and contentment. Zachary was still feeling the emotions pushing up on his throat from his stomach—or should I say his bellybutton—holding back the tears as he realised this might be the last time he would see his parents.

"So, Soarfoot, you're the missing link? You spawn another generation of Steeles in eighteen-twenty?" surmised Zachary.

"Yes, you have done your research, but I fathered children before then. I was born on the Missinipe River before the Europeans arrived and named it the Churchill. Edith Steele was my woman after I became a hybrid species and we raised a family together. I started travelling the cosmos on many tree raids and when I returned over a hundred years later the Steele family line was in danger of dying off, so I revitalised another generation."

"But what about Irving Steele, is he a tree warrior? And Beatrice Bagwa as well, how does she fit in?" queried Zachary.

"Beatrice never did become a hybrid and she now roams the Churchill River, as you know. Irving became a pine tree warrior but he died in battle not long ago," answered Jeremiah.

"It is sad, yet we persevere. And now the struggle is in our hands. We must journey into the spiritual habitat," said Soarfoot.

"No disrespect intended, but what does that mean? What are you trying to tell me?" quipped Zachary.

"We are special, we possess a rare gift. We will honour the manifesto of peace and fight against the creed of destruction by entering the spiritual domain of your tree god, Gorb of the aspens," continued Soarfoot.

"But why me? Why not some other more experienced warrior?"

"You have been confused and full of questions schweetz, yet you have embraced your role as an Envrah with conviction and integrity. The manifesto angels of peace have witnessed your strength and they have selected you," professed the Storyteller. "We will burn a sacrifice fire tonight, we will speak to the gods, and I will take you and Soarfoot onto the cosmic wave. The angels of peace will lead us to Gorb's aspen tree heaven."

"I'm going to heaven? But I don't want to die—"

"You will not die, but we will enter the black hole of Gorb's domain."

"Will we ever return?"

"Yes, we will return, but many years into the future. You have taken every step on this journey with hesitation, but you have always triumphed with courage. You will triumph again," the Storyteller grinned with a smile.

"Is this what you want? Will I ever see you again?" Zachary looked over to his father.

"Soarfoot is our hybrid species family patriarch and it has been an honour and a privilege to raise you as a child Zachary. You're a tree warrior now my son, and there is one last journey calling out to you. Your mother and me do not possess the power of the trees as you do, our journey is now complete with your ascension," teared up Jeremiah.

"We always cared for you but we couldn't reveal everything, I'm sure you can understand now. We knew you would find a way to prove yourself Zachary. We are very proud of you. But now you must go with Soarfoot and the Storyteller and respect this struggle for peace," swelled up Maria.

"I love you Mum and Dad. It's all because of you that I started this journey in the first place."

"We love you with all our hearts son. This is not a sad occasion, we are filled with happiness, but your journey will take you away for many years and we will long be spirits when you return," contemplated Jeremiah.

"There's a cabin still preserved on the shore of Norseman Lake. I've made arrangements to see that your parents are taken there," said Zelda.

"Thank you my love. I'm very fortunate in many ways. I only hope I can repay everyone by honouring this manifesto of peace," mused Zachary.

"You will do even more my schweetz. You and Soarfoot will liberate the grand creations. We will sacrifice the trees with the lashmuh and the spirits will show you the way, but first we should eat some good Romanian cuisine. I have some wild meat from the forests of my homeland in the Carpathian Mountains of Transylvania. I will cook us a meal," proclaimed the Storyteller.

The aspen and pine wood was piled beside a stone firepit near the cave on the grassy island, where Zelda sparked a fire and the spry Storyteller assembled a metal tripod to hang a pot over the flame. Zachary and his parents sat and watched with Soarfoot. The old Romanian chef decided to save the wild boar and perch fish fillets to make skewers another time, which would turn out to be the next night for a very special dinner. Instead he prepared his late wife's famous chicken stew to feed everyone there, using the two large partridges he also had with him. He skinned the breasts from the birds by stepping on the underside of their wings and pulling on the clawed feet. The breasts slid out from the skin and feathers handily without gutting the animals, leaving the carcasses on the ground. He washed and quartered the breasts with the bones still in, cleaned the thighs and legs to add into the stew as well, and carved out the rib bones to boil in water for the stock.

"What are you making?" asked Zelda.

"It's Marianna's Romanian chicken stew. I was going to make skewers wrapped with the partridge, some boar meat, perch and wild rice, but I'm not sure if they will feed everyone. The stew will go further with some mamaliga."

"Mamaliga, what's that?"

"It's like polenta, cornmeal porridge with some herbs and spices."

"I have some fresh moose, lake trout and ruffed grouse we can use to make a meal another night," offered Soarfoot.

"Ah yes, tradition—that's a good schweetz."

Everyone admired the Storyteller and sometimes chief cook and bottle washer as he practised one of his many crafts. He boiled the rib bones from the birds to make a broth and then sautéed the partridge meat in a pot with some wild boar grease, scallion green onion stalks, chopped garlic and diced kohlrabi, added paprika spice and leuschen herb, and finished the stew mixing in the broth with corn starch. The cornmeal mamaliga was already simmering in another pot sitting on the rock edge of the firepit. They all enjoyed the modest but delicious feast when it was ready; partridge stew served over mamaliga in metal bowls from the camping gear that the well-equipped Rhomany ancestor brought along for the journey.

"We are truly honoured to have such an artisan at our campsite. I was the teacher when we first met, but now Rushad is the master who astounds me with his many skills," remarked Soarfoot.

"This stew is simply amazing," Maria complimented the chef.

"My dear Marianna taught me how to cook," said the elder Rhomany.

"The Storyteller has shared many secrets of life with me, but he has never divulged the recipe for Marianna's chicken stew," chuckled Jeremiah.

"You just need to cuddle with him first," laughed Zelda.

"That always helps my schweetz," smiled Rushad.

"You have a smooth touch Zelda," said Zachary with a wink.

"We can cuddle around the fire tonight. I'm sure the Storyteller will maintain the sacrifice flames for us," suggested Soarfoot.

"We will prepare for the spiritual dimension," nodded the Storyteller.

They finished eating the Romanian stew and the Steele parents were happy to clean up the dishes with a pot of water warmed over the small cooking fire. The ritual sacrifice fire was started at sunset on an adjoining island of rock and swampy wetland habitat. A much larger bonfire was soon blazing and spreading a cuddling warmth in the marsh; reflecting against the faces of mixed hybrid species young and old alike. The Storyteller was the principal campfire maintainer, Zelda the supportive counsel at her lover's side, Jeremiah and Maria the loving parents sitting in the background, and Soarfoot with Zachary the brave advocates of peaceful existence preparing to volunteer their service to the heavens.

The fire was glowing and burning high when the Storyteller piled on some ancient aspen wood he saved for that moment. He then began to flail on the mound of hot coals with his scuffed and well-worn stager spear; also joined by Zelda with a large pine branch. The hard smacks against the crackling firewood sparked spirals of floating embers that intensified with each strike. The reddish orange particles began dancing in an unrehearsed choreography of flaring light; meshing with a lapping waterfall of bright green and aqua blue lasha that cavalcaded down onto the island in the marsh. The aurora of light enveloping the basin was inspiring. The Storyteller smiled inside himself and the serenity of his soul shrouded the gathering of the soon to be organically spiritual warriors as he spoke to the heavens.

"The fire is the power that comes from the trees. The trees that we sacrifice are a gift from the gods. Quujj has planted the pine and Gorb has planted the aspen. We will become the fibre of the trees and our silviculture warriors will absorb the sporadic energy of spiritual actuality. The angels are with us now. They will take us to the heavens. We are the children of peace."

He raised his head to the star filled sky and closed his eyes. An even brighter radiation in multitudes of coloured light sprinkled down onto the marsh island. A young aspen and pine tree were rooted into the dark fertile soil of the bog and the rock cracked and split; levitating an organic vessel of cosmic energy above the basin. All but Jeremiah and Maria were carried up into the atmosphere of Planet Envrah.

Zachary's mind fluttered. Gliding above a placid river, winding through a land clear and brilliant, the trees on the shore were immense; their trunks rich and healthy. The leaves were bold and flowing with warm colours.

The forested canyon open below the lip of Gorb's black hole. Lush and luring vegetation span the inner space; the trees encompassing the spiritual habitat. The cottonwood and aspen were bountiful. Verdurous green leaves and shimmering white bark spread an uplifting trance throughout the heaven. The trees were trimmed and pruned; the forest thinned, neat and tidy.

There was an inviting sensation rising up from the canyon. They entered the heavenly domain of the aspen trees.

Part Five
The Crusade

Chapter 32: Spiritual Bequest

The tiny but eminently powerful vessel from the organic marsh carried the silviculture hybrids Soarfoot and Zachary into the spiritual canyon with their escorts: a dedicated and courageous sweet old farmer and a gorgeous wizard more than just another pretty warrior. The arboretum ship glided down into the canyon and settled on an upland plateau above a spectacular river flowing with clean, pristine water. The grand vista of layered cliff ledges lofting to the horizon of the canyon walls span a breadth of splendour before them. They were in Gorb's domain; somehow navigating into heaven without the botanic spiritualis of an angel.

The entourage of godly recruits could see a giant twisting rock spiral in the distance. They could feel the compelling allure of glittering power emanating from its peak. A brushed edge of twinkling lasha spread from the rock island of the branch ship to form a buffer around the upland ridge where they landed, yet the organic warriors quickly realised they would disintegrate into spiritual dust particles if they roamed beyond the perimeter. There was only one thing to do: sit and wait.

Of course, the Storyteller took it upon himself to maintain a small campfire and cook another meal—this time a smorgasbord of meat skewers with traditional grouse, moose, trout and wild rice, along with Transylvanian wild boar, perch fillets and kohlrabi, as well as some Hungarian paprika and Romanian leuschen herb. The incredible view of the canyon and a perpetual magical sunset caressed their souls and seemingly held time in suspense as their next meal was sizzling over an open flame; that is until they saw the figure of an angelic woman walking towards them on the shoreline of the river. It was Envrah the original fibrous angel of the aspen trees, walking up to the ridge where the silviculture candidates waited.

"Hudec, greetings," she called out, dressed in a soft fabric robe with her long-braided hair and thin vine branches falling over her shoulders, while holding an aspen staff propped against the ground.

Zachary and Soarfoot stood up and greeted the angel.

"Hudec keeno," said Soarfoot: welcome friend.

"Envrah?" pondered Zachary.

"Muh, dah laf keeno. Dah Envrah," the fibrous angel spoke, saying yes, she is very much a friend, she is Envrah.

Soarfoot immediately bent down onto one knee.

"Don bohtahna, our saviour," he said.

"Tah, fahsa traupah," stand up young warrior, answered Envrah.

"I am at your service," volunteered Soarfoot.

The pine tree hybrid stood up and came face-to-face with the angel.

"I am no one's saviour," she declared. "You alone decide your path, I'm only here to help. We are all the same; organically spiritual, as you know."

"But you have the power to control our destiny. It is your grace that has brought us here, is it not?" questioned Soarfoot.

"It is your will that has brought you here. The fate of your existence is determined by the decisions you make following your own path. If the balance of your love, compassion and spiritual courage is complete, you will find the wisdom of a pathway no one else has walked."

"We are honoured to be here in your presence," continued Soarfoot.

"It is Gorb who is honoured by your dedication to peace—and by your exquisite culinary talents it appears. You must have brought a storyteller with you," smiled Envrah, looking at the skewers of meat cooking above the fire.

"It is a gift from the Rhomany family," said Zachary.

"And your presence here is also Gorb's gift to the mortals, for this is the only time an organic soul has cooked food over an open fire in the spiritual habitat. The prairie warriors have always been strong. This one roamed the mountains and found the power of the trees; we watched him carefully as he sought the truth with remarkable courage. The Storyteller is wise. He will guide you safely to your destiny. And this Marshlandite has also shown her humility and love in the name of peace. We are grateful for your loyalty to the manifestos Zelda Mintah. Now, let us all sit and talk, there is much to learn."

The very unique heavenly gathering sat around the campfire and munched on divine meat skewers while an angel created from the spiritual fibre explained the power her god was about to bestow upon them. The eternal sunset finally slipped behind the canyon wall and a dim nightfall descended as Envrah revealed the implications of the silviculture prophecy and the secret of Gorb's treasure from the one original aesthetic heaven.

"In the beginning, the spiritual fibre created this heaven and all the domains of the gods, but there was also unidentified spiritual fibre that the gods could not control. That essence became the wind warriors and the vapour demons, created electromagnetic energy, fire and rain, and gave birth to the shape shifting wizards. Gorb is the only god who retained some of this fibre from the original heaven, and now you will become endowed with a gift no other entity in all of existence has ever possessed. Yet this will not be enough to complete the silviculture prophecy. Although you will command an unmatched actuality, you still must find a warrior with the ultimate sporadic element to overcome the evil nemesis creed of destruction."

"And this is the grand scheme for universal peace?" posed Zachary.

"The manifesto of peace is a dream we all hope you can fulfil with a grand crusade, but the fate of our existence is truly sporadic and you will need the strength of all the loving gods to plot this actuality," explained Envrah.

"The gods cannot change the fate of existence?" asked Soarfoot.

"The gods possess the unparalleled power of cosmic actuality, but the destiny of existence cannot be controlled. It follows the sporadic gift of the natural balance coming from the evolution of existence; born from the big bang of the one original aesthetic heaven. We can only hope to influence the natural balance of harmony by the peaceful choices we make."

"So it's possible that we could fail and these credos of destruction might prevail with their evil domination?" deduced Zachary.

"There are natural gifts in the universal domain that make certain entities powerful, but the gods do not make these choices; they can only observe the path of the cosmic wave that brings those gifts to existence. We believe the resolve of the manifesto is greater than the creed because of the overwhelming peaceful intentions from the majority of the gods, yet some of these natural gifts are blinded by pride, privilege and anger, and regrettably those without such gifts seek material possessions because they are not content with their existence. They want more, but they do not know why because they do not have an understanding of themselves and their place in existence. These are the credo warriors who are denied spiritual love and are manipulated by the will of the nemesis gods. Greed and envy consumes them without hope of true happiness and they become victims of their own gluttony and indulgence; complacent in their decadence and ultimately too lazy to seek the wisdom that will lead to everlasting peace. Yes, you will have to battle these evil elements, but by the grace of the manifesto you will not fail."

"How can we truly make a difference?" wondered Zachary.

"You are being offered a tremendous gift of natural sporadic power. The authentic spiritual entity that is the god of aspen trees will share this gift with you because of your affinity with liberty and freedom. Although you are not the prophecy, Gorb has seen the faith you have in your brothers and sisters. You will use your conviction and integrity to bring justice and equality to the cosmos. You will embrace the satisfaction of peaceful harmony with love and compassion in your soul. This gift will give you the resolve and universal clairvoyance to seek hope and affirmation, and reveal the true actuality of the silviculture prophecy with your most commendable bravery."

"We will fight for the manifesto of peace," pledged Soarfoot.

"Indeed, you will crusade. You will have the power to conjure visions, the wisdom to realise secrets of existence and the courage to find the natural balance of harmony. You will absorb the unidentified spiritual fibre of the wind warriors and the vapour demons and you will command the actuality of Gorb, god of the aspen trees," concluded Envrah.

"And you're certain I have the strength for this? I really don't know how I'll manage. I'm just glad Soarfoot is with me," said Zachary.

"This is the dawning of your space and time. You will soon have an unmatched cosmic actuality. It is in your blood. Gorb believes in you, that is all that matters," assured Envrah.

"Do not worry Zachary, you are young and strong, and the Storyteller will guide you on the path of freedom and equality," added Soarfoot.

"We're all in this together Zachary. We will work as a team. You have true friends you can count on," said Zelda.

"Now go my children," Envrah instructed Soarfoot and Zachary. "I will protect your comrades with my spiritualis here on the ridge while you follow the river to the spiral of Gorb. There my god will speak to you."

The Storyteller and Zelda stayed on the branch ship and kept the home fires burning, so to speak, while Soarfoot and Zachary heeded the words of the aspen angel and started walking along the river shore until reaching the middle of the canyon. An orbiting swirl of spiritual fibre was gently circling over the twisted rock monument that is the power of Gorb; soft and white clouds mounting to ocean blue with streaks of forest green. They could feel the essence of a god palpitating against their mortal skin.

Soarfoot was vindicated and proud; a lifetime of defending the quest for peace rewarded with his journey into heaven. It was a new adventure for Zachary however. He was astounded and amazed; the purpose of his life now dawning in Gorb's domain. The silviculture warriors could hear the stirring bequest of the aspen god from within the blue and green cluster at the top of the rock edifice.

"Welcome to my heaven warriors of peace. The grand creations have evolved from a spark ignited by the gods, but before the spiritual habitat blossomed, before hybrid species mastered the power of the trees, all throughout existence, Rulsp, the god of spruce, has always been the aggressor. Rulsp has always been stronger and faster, and always the first to pursue new ideas and new schemes, but now Gorb, the humble god of aspen trees, will be the first to share the secret of penetrating the grand spiral domains in the cosmos. There is not any other god who has discovered this secret.

"The wind warriors and the vapour demons are spiritual entities who exist in the organic habitat. Warriors, you are mortal organic entities and you will now become organically spiritual. You will become one with the wind warriors and vapour demons, travelling freely in the organic habitat through the grand spirals and the spiritual corridors of the heavens at your will.

"There is more. There is more beyond your universe, more beyond the aspen unisphere and the pine tree unisphere. This is not the only cosmos of existence. There are many dimensions and grand creations beyond the spiral barriers inhabited by the wind warriors and the vapour demons. And there has never been a tree warrior, an angel or a god who has entered the organically spiritual spiral domains. And now you my children of peace have become the first mortal entities to enter the spiritual habitat as organic fibre without the botanic spiritualis of an angel.

"Go now with the seed of unidentified spiritual fibre and pay homage to the wind warriors and vapour demons; mingle with them in their organically spiritual domains. They are the heavenly entities who will unite with the manifestos and bring peace to the grand creations. They will harbour manifesto warriors on a crusade to all the unispheres of the grand creations in this dimension. You will visit every homeland galaxy with the vision of your new actuality and you will enter the spiritual corridors of all forty-seven heavenly domains. You will collect an original ancient fibrous tree from every heaven until reaching the black hole of the spruce domain, where you will find the true silviculture warrior and confront the evil that is the god Rulsp."

That was all; pure and profound, simple and wise. Gorb's message was instilled in the souls of Soarfoot and Zachary. The journey into the spiritual dimension graced them with a supreme power they would use to champion the silviculture prophecy. This was the beginning of the cosmic crusade for peace and the quest for forty-seven trees.

The newly empowered tree warriors walked back to their branch ship with an injection of energy and informed the Storyteller and Zelda who were patiently waiting with huge smiles and eager anticipation. The arboretum vessel from Planet Envrah lifted up in the canyon of Gorb's heaven and soared through the god's black hole on the cosmic wave, transporting a prime ancient aspen spirit tree onboard. Zachary, less versed in the power of the trees than the rest of his colleagues, was exhausted after the heavenly ordeal. The branch ship penetrated into the organic habitat and the power of its flight inundated the young warrior once again.

Chapter 33: Vortex of Peace

The new silviculture purveyors were charting their course along cosmic trails towards our wind warrior spiral domain when Zachary was aroused from his slumber. The epic journey into Gorb's heaven was an extremely complex and exhausting ordeal involving excessive metaphysical prowess; consuming the greatest amount of sporadic energy ever released in the grand creations and elapsing thousands of years in the organic habitat.

Guardian and courier angels are able to transport only a few individual mortals inside spiritual corridors, but never into the heart of a god's domain; and furthermore these passengers must stay within the protection of an angel's botanic spiritualis. Soarfoot and Zachary's indoctrination was the only occasion hybrid species descendants entered directly into a god's heaven outside the barrier of spiritualis as whole organic bodies instead of brain wavelength entities.

This was a profound event in universal history; made possible by the preservation of the last remaining unidentified spiritual fibre. The combined strength of an aspen and pine tree warrior provided the impetus to create a previously unmatched force of mortal actuality that would shift the tide of botanical disputes. The manifesto of peace now possessed a new advantage in its struggle against the epidemiology of demented evil intentions.

The stories of a sporadic element that commanded unbelievable power began to spread throughout manifesto tree raid camps. The Envrahs of aspen and Mingas of pine would journey into all three grand creations pronouncing this new weapon to be engaged in tree wars, with Soarfoot and Zachary as the ultimate warriors displaying an unprecedented explosion of lasha. They, the tree warriors, were also buoyed by another element; that of surprise, since never before in the new habitat had any warrior successfully surfed our grand spirals. The manifestos would soon rally their ranks across Windswept and Vapourdom spirals, mobilising resources in strategic patterns; at least initially without creed of destruction warriors aware of the new tactic.

Credos were always among the most skilled and fearless fighters: Alkae of spruce and Narukas of fir, the Sabaquae of acacia and Marcynakians of olive. They dominated many botanical disputes as the manifesto cause relied on alliances of collective efforts. The aspen god Gorb was never as powerful as the likes of the spruce god Rulsp or Eamaan of ash, nor as bold as the cactus god Verra or Yanamea of sassafras, but the peaceful gods outnumbered the agitated gods and Gorb's foresight was proving to be shrewd and wise.

Yet, ascending the mountain of creed persistence still seemed somewhat insurmountable to many veteran warriors: there was plenty of climb left in the ascent of peace. The tree raids that occupy galaxies, clusters and unispheres continued to vent for millennia while the manifesto plan was being hatched in the aspen heaven. Tree wars slowly meshed with mortal mechanical conflicts as the interstellar era thrived and gained insight into spiritual dynamics. The god Rulsp, of course, was taking every advantage of this progression while manifestos pursued the silviculture prophecy.

The Storyteller was tending the sacrifice fire while Soarfoot and Zelda were watching the light show over the bow of their ship as the warriors emerged from the spiritual dimension into organic space. The cosmos was once again very different upon Zachary's return to Plateau Grand Creation. It was SRC-325-E/247-T/867-A, over fifty-one thousand Earth years after they entered the heavenly domain. Interstellar exploration was thriving in the pine tree unisphere by the time the silviculture journey began, such as scientific and commercial operations of the Boreal Forces, but there was also conflict awaiting the manifesto warriors including an intergalactic war and another dark conquest of mechanical force about to explode.

"Where are we?" asked Zachary, rising from his sleep.

"We are fulfilling Gorb's will of course. We are approaching the wind warrior spiral domain I believe," answered Soarfoot.

The waves of coloured light lapping across the cosmic corridor masked the signatures of any specific clusters or galaxies, or their exact location.

Again Zachary inquired: "Can you actually tell where we are?"

"The Storyteller and I have travelled the cosmos for many years and we have ventured near the windswept edge of our grand creation before, but this time our botanic spiritualis is being guided by the new actuality we have acquired from the spiritual fibre," explained Soarfoot.

"You and Storyteller are aware of what's happening all the time, but I really seem to be clued out. How will I be able to lead this crusade with you?"

"The perception of cosmic actuality will come to you very soon. Until then we will work together Zachary. We will penetrate into the Windswept Spiral as it is known, and we will commune with the wind warriors. We will then go back to the aspen home world Envrah and begin spreading the word of the silviculture crusade. The clairvoyance of universal knowledge will enter your soul as we visit the homeland galaxies of the manifesto planets, and you will soon be leading a journey with the Storyteller at your side."

Soarfoot's last few words were muffled in the whispering fringe of turbulence as the branch ship was fully swallowed into the Windswept Spiral. The vessel was surrounded by the unexplained wind currents in the cavity of their interstellar corridor. The lasha was wild; dancing and twitching across the cosmic trail. The passengers were all looking at each other and grinning in awe of the raw power. The spiritually organic spacecraft was about to interact with the organically spiritual wind warriors.

The emotion in our spiral domain was quite jubilant on that occasion, as I remember. Free flight vectors zipped and howled from zephyrs to blustery gales. Expectation and excitement teased our jet streams like a cool breeze in a sweltering desert. We were celebrating. The space and time was upon us: the silviculture warriors were not just legendary stories on the wings of wind currents any longer. We would be liberated to launch our free flight missions to the far reaches of the grand creations—it was sweet bliss.

The silviculture delegation was greeted with pulsating squalls of wispy translucent light that rattled the arboretum vessel and bounced it into our grand spiral. The ship was propelled to the upper echelons of free flight vectors on ritual gusts of wind, as the passengers continued to marvel at the unbridled force of nature. A collection of divine wind warriors as we called them were able to mesh their celestial actuality with the brain wavelengths of Soarfoot and Zachary. Incidentally, I am one of the divine wind warriors myself because I discovered reptiles in the one heaven.

We escorted the mixed species hybrids with the cushion of a gigantic stellar vortex that eternally imparted the power of spiritual fibre on the wings of our wind currents. The search for forty-seven trees now had the gift of free flight at the disposal of the silviculture warriors. All around the organic branch ship a maze of floats and vectors systematically flanked into vast swirls of free flight missions, synchronised to the ashah telepathy of the tree warriors. It was a time and space for celebration. We were pleased that the peaceful manifestos discovered our secret of wind power before the wrath of the destructive credos, but there was still an incredible amount of work and many annua of battles ahead of us.

Riding on the wave of a bold vortex we began our manifesto strategies as Soarfoot and Zachary guided us to Envrah, homeland of the aspens. The remaining floats and vectors waited in our spiral domain soon to be united with new and diverse manifesto flotillas. The plan to confront evil greed was set into motion and we wind warriors were happy to join in the bidding for peace.

Our arrival on Envrah was impressive. Descending down to the surface of the planet we could clearly see hordes of warriors gathering for large sacrifice fires in the bosom of a prairie canyon valley. The sparse patches of aspen groves were swarmed with hybrids collecting firewood and harvesting branches to carve new stagers. The Envrahs were pumping the lasha. They, the tree warriors, were preparing for the arrival of the silviculture prophecy, so they thought and so they believed; certainly making it the only thing that really mattered for this auspicious and commemorative occasion.

Planet Envrah was rarely thriving with such an abundance of life. This was more than just a sacrifice ritual: almost all of the aspen warriors in the cosmos were there to share this moment, which unbeknownst to Zachary and his friends was thousands of years after they departed for Gorb's heaven. It was a celebration of epic proportions; an infusion of new energy and purpose for the manifesto of peace. The warriors camped on the ridges of the valley walls and in the gullies of the canyon slopes knew that something colossal was beckoning their spiritual cores.

The Storyteller was the sight of a shaman presiding over a grand festival of spirituality, bringing the new aspen silviculture warrior and a great pine Minga warrior to the Envrah hybrids riding on a glorious branch ship of peace. We entered the canyon with a bluster, quickly ascending to a gale force thunderstorm blowing through the valley. We wind warriors and vapour demons preceded the Storyteller's entrance and signalled the presence of a god's great spirit in the flesh of Soarfoot and Zachary. The Envrahs clung to the smooth white and grey tree trunks of the aspens and cottonwoods as our free flight currents roared through the prairie canyon; warriors leaning into the wind, gripping limbs and branches, yet gazing hither at a prophecy's arrival.

The arboretum ship circled amid the jet streams, squalls and wind eddies of our vortex and gently landed in the valley pushing the windstorm aside. A tall and slender ridge near the head of the canyon was where the Storyteller chose to preside over the momentous lashmuh ritual ceremony. The tree warriors huddled around sacrifice fires randomly burning in the valley with stagers piled high ready for the ritual. The silver shimmer of spiritual lightning weaved across a cloudless mauve sky; cracking and roaring above the mystical setting. The silviculture crusade was about to be announced as the soft murmur of a tribal chant began to rise up from the canyon floor.

"Ashah pyen, ashah pyen, ashah pyen."

The Storyteller smiled down on the prairie expanse and reached up to the heavens. And then: a streak of thunderless lightning illuminated the sky. It was the time and space to sacrifice the trees.

"Envrah traupah, dah shahtoonee jah, eesah ashah pyen. Tree warriors, I am the Storyteller of the aspens. I bring you the new silviculture warriors to fulfil the prophecy of peace. Dah nahsah teelaf fahsa sylva kohpah, bohtahna moobah. Don bohtrak lah shatoo shahmah, sahba leepshah, lah don shahtee lah traupek ashah. We have travelled and seen the spiritual dimension, not in a dream but with our own eyes and organic bodies. The silviculture warriors now possess ultimate power. We must unite with the pine trees, prepare for silviculture journeys, and continue to battle against the creed of destruction. Sylva kohpah dahbid rygah lasha. Don quueesum nahtoo lah pyna, bohko sylva bohtrak, lah vee zahka zahnoosah. Sahba sweesah lah fahsee, veebee lah bahsyga don nahsah moobah lah bohtahna jobo annha. It will not be swift nor easy, but with determination we will bring peace and salvation to the cosmos."

The throngs of warriors in the canyon screamed their approval in the distance and began to chant again as the Storyteller finished his message.

"Neewhasee sylva, shatoo traushah, lah neewhasee eesah don klahsah tahsah ashah ashyb pyen," he shouted while waving to the ancient spirit tree and the new silviculture warriors. "It is the silviculture prophecy as foreseen by spirit seekers, and this is our true ancient aspen spirit tree. Dah nahsah Zachary, Envrah sylva kohpah, lah Soarfoot, Minga sylva kohpah. I give you Zachary, aspen prophecy warrior, and Soarfoot, pine tree prophecy warrior."

"Ashah pyen! Moobah pyen! Loho pyen! Muh, muh, muh!" the wild chants continued from the cradle of the valley bed.

The adrenaline consumed Zachary. He was caught up in the moment and felt compelled to address the warriors gathered for the ceremony. He stepped forward on the branch ship with a nudge of support from the Storyteller and proceeded to speak his mind.

"We bring you the word of Gorb. Honour the aspen trees and draw strength from the heavens. This is what you have been waiting for. I pledge all my powers to the silviculture prophecy. We will carve new weapons of peace and the manifesto shall live forever."

The warriors also gave their approval to Zachary by cheering his brief message of hope. Soarfoot then took it upon himself to translate for his new silviculture partner, while also managing to offer his bond of friendship with the Envrah warriors.

"Don nahsah teelaf eesah jah Gorb. Beelah ashah pyen lah dahbid vohko shahmah. Neewhasee bah teelaf whaha. Mee nahsah lohtoo mee lasha, jobo sylva. Don nah tiggahsee fahsa stah moobah, lah moobah nah eesah seewha. We now possess power never before witnessed in the cosmos. The aspen and the pine shall travel together beyond the grand spirals, into all of the unispheres in our dimension with the wind warriors. We will bring peace to everyone. Don po dahbid lasha teewha shahtoo fahbee annha. Envrah lah Minga bohtrak tahbee tonntah, jobo laf annha lah whassa traupah. Don nahsah moobah jobo lahtoo."

"Nahtoo Envrah lah Minga!" encouraged the Storyteller.

"Neewhasee eesah rygah lap nahtoo Envrah lah Minga!" added Zachary, impressively saying that there's a great light shining on the aspen and pine.

The rousing assembly of warriors in the canyon continued to chant.

"Ashah pyen, ashah pyen, ashah pyen."

They added stagers to sacrifice fires and as it turned out celebrated well into the evening with aspen juice and feasts of wild food around their enclaves. A fierce rumble of thunder sounded a departing clasp of lightning and it began to rain from a clear sky. The tree warriors tilted their heads up to the cloudless mauve horizon and chanted to the power of the trees. Methodically they dispersed one by one and added more wood to the fires. The flames lit up the valley as they carved new branches from the stands of aspens. Soarfoot then issued the final words to this epic gathering of warriors.

"Jobo ashyb, jobo moobah. Where there is a tree, there is hope."

Chapter 34: Reckoning

A messenger convoy of arboretum vessels swayed through Plateau Grand Creation on floats of free flight vectors, bringing the energy of a new sporadic element in the organic habitat. Zachary was well protected on a rooter surrounded by scarifiers and branch ships; returning his lover and spiritual confidant Zelda Mintah back to her homeland of Planet Minga.

Zelda and the pine tree manifestos were to lead the vapourdom journey into Summit Grand Creation together with the venerable warrior Soarfoot. Zachary would return to Envrah and lead the manifestos on the windswept journey into Crown Grand Creation with his aspen ancestral grandfather Rushad Rhomanscu the Storyteller.

They landed safely in the jungle of Minga's southern continent on the ocean coast and were greeted by an immense gathering with thousands of tree warriors. Zachary would soon get down to the business of peace-making, but first he attended several sacrifice fires with his spiritual colleagues to spread the word of the silviculture prophecy.

It was a brief time to embrace the treasure of their spiritual discovery and the gift of free flight from the manifesto gods. Soarfoot had arrived earlier on a separate rooting ship. The two sporadically graced warriors still had to be careful and did not want to surf the cosmic wave together; leaving one of the silviculture warriors safe if they were attacked by credos. Soarfoot had talked with some elders and prominent bark shredders, but he had not spoken to a large audience as he would for Zachary and Zelda's first night on Minga.

Hybrids and select mortal purebreds were roaming from camp to camp along a ridge overlooking a majestic ravine, which lead to a spacious sand beach on the coast. Zachary's ship landed in the ravine and he ascended the ridge to meet Soarfoot with Zelda; laughter and the jumbled ambient sound of many excited conversations were drifting through the camps.

"Zachary, Zelda, my new treasured friends. I hope your flight was smooth," Soarfoot welcomed them.

"It seemed to have a special airy quality I have not felt before," said Zachary with a smile.

"Like a cushion of owl feathers beneath our bed," winked Zelda. The three of them laughed together.

"I truly hope we will be able to celebrate again very soon, but we do have an arduous journey ahead of us," commented Soarfoot. "We will soon be very busy and very exhausted, yet we will be crusading with an incredible new energy. But before we embark on our quest, I think it's important that we absorb the moment to contemplate this new sporadic element and share in the wonderful joy and inspiration our warriors are feeling right now."

"Sounds good to me," said Zelda.

"I haven't had a drink in a few billion light years," chuckled Zachary, "I think maybe I could relax for one night."

"I think we can find you something to imbibe," agreed Soarfoot.

"Is there any of this famous Minga wine I've heard about? Or maybe some Envrah ale, it certainly went down well last time."

"You will enjoy the Arknae juice, trust me," assured Zelda.

"But don't overdo it until later tonight," cautioned Soarfoot. "You will have to speak to this gathering around the fire, and I don't think it would be inspiring if one of the silviculture warriors is drunk."

"I will be inspiring my friend, but not bumbling."

"I have every confidence in you Zachary."

The pine tree celebrations commenced on Minga just as they had on Envrah. The various clans of hybrid tree warriors soared to their homeland in succession over the next several continuum rotations; settling into camps scattered across the landscape, enjoying feasts of food and drink, and learning of the new silviculture journeys.

Zelda escorted Zachary among the pockets of Mingas along the ridge and introduced him to many warriors, with particular attention to the mixed species hybrids in the crowd. Zachary did imbibe in some Arknae juice which relaxed him just enough to feel confident and sense the new strength growing within his spiritual actuality.

The clans congregated around stone fired camp kitchen inglenooks; preparing and consuming meals of fresh cuisine, socialising and preparing for the sacrifice ceremony until darkness descended. They slowly filtered down into the ravine and onto the beach after sunset, collecting wood and igniting a rather large bonfire that would later accept sacrifice stagers.

The warriors naturally sensed the timing of the ritual and some five thousand or so assembled on the beach against the backdrop of the jungle facing the bonfire and the ocean. The wind currents blowing in from the ocean carried the voices of those presiding with a little help from my friends.

"Pyna traupah," called out Zelda. "Mingas unite!"

"Pyna traupah, pyna traupah, pyna traupah," came back the chorus chant in unison.

This is the pine tree chant, similar to the aspen with a variation incorporating the native word for pine with the ancient Druid name for tree warrior. It was the first time Zachary heard this chant; so powerful and resonating, just as the aspen sacrifice rituals. And then Soarfoot dramatically entered the ceremony, floating down to the beach with an original ancient spiritual pine tree on his branch ship.

"Traupah, dah nahsah Soarfoot," continued Zelda at the top of her lungs, followed by applause, hooting, hollering and other assorted owl calls. "Mee traupah sylva. Nahtoo mee lasha, lah beelah mee jah. I give you Soarfoot, our new silviculture warrior. Embrace his power and heed his words."

"Pyna traupah!" the crowd instantly answered back.

Soarfoot stepped down from his branch ship and stood in front of the bonfire as he spoke to the gathering.

"Keeno, hudec lashmuh. Don maha rygah whaha po. Welcome my friends, to our sacrifice fire. We are now enjoying such an impressive time in our history," he said, opening his arms in Zachary's direction. "Dah whaga shammah, lah fahsa keeno traupah. Mee klahsah nahtoo ashah pyen. I have travelled to the other side with you, my new brother, you truly embrace the sporadic element that is the power of the aspen trees. Nahtoo naga loho! United in victory!"

Soarfoot quickly roused the packed beach into a pitch.

"Pyna traupah! Pyna moobah! Pyna loho!" came back the enthusiastic shouts of encouragement.

"Yes, the pine tree warriors will fight for the manifesto of peace in the grand creations. We will be victorious, and we will celebrate!" claimed Soarfoot.

There were many more cheers and yells as the Minga wine and Arknae juice took their effect on the spirit of the crowd, so to speak, while Soarfoot continued to preside.

"Keeno traupah, don loho pahva vee. Po, don bohko sylva. Lah ashah pyen, don zahka zahnoosah. We will celebrate again later, but first we must prepare for epic silviculture journeys. With the guidance of the aspen Envrah, we will continue our battle against the creed of destruction; it will not be swift nor easy, but with determination we will bring peace and salvation to the cosmos. Sahba sweesah lah fahsee, bahsyga don nahsah moobah lah bohtahna jobo annha. Dah shatoo shahmah, sahba leepshah, lah dah shahtee, lah dah ashah. I have seen the spiritual dimension, not in a dream but with my own eyes and body. Neewhasee sylva moobah, shatoo traushah. Zachary eesah klahsah moobah kohpah, dah nahsah po, lah don klahsah tahsah ashah ashyb. It is the silviculture manifesto as foreseen by our spirit seekers, and Zachary is the true manifesto warrior, whom I bring to you today along with this, our true ancient spiritual pine tree."

The tree warriors calmed down and were attentive to Soarfoot's words as they marvelled at the sight of a glowing spirit tree from the pine heaven of Quujj, but they were also eagerly awaiting to hear from Zachary; the ascending excitement drifting through the crowd on the beach. Normally he would be very nervous to speak at such a prophetic moment, but the sporadic energy filled his soul with clarity and conviction. Zachary gently lifted his arms to accentuate his words; towards Soarfoot and Zelda and then facing the beachfront.

"Rah pyna eevah, keeno, lah klahsah traupah. Thank you my pine tree family, friends and true spiritual warriors—muh!" began Zachary to a roar of acceptance.

"I am the descendant of mixed pine and aspen spiritualis, ancestor of Soarfoot and the Storyteller. The aspen Envrahs will unite with the pine tree Mingas and we will soar through the cosmos, strong and determined, and we will bring the balance of peace."

"Mee eevah lahtoo, pyna lah pyen ashah, eevah Soarfoot lah Storyteller," Zelda quickly translated for Zachary. "Envrah nahtoo Minga. Bohtrak annha, vohko lah bahsyga, nahsah moobah muh!"

The warriors on the beach ramped up their enthusiasm once again; yelling out salutes of 'moobah', and 'loho' and of course, 'muh, muh, muh', causing Zachary to pause before finishing his words.

"I have entered the spiritual habitat as a whole organic warrior, and the gods have bestowed upon me the power for freedom of flight throughout all of the cosmos, including the great spirals that separate the grand creations for all warriors. I may not be the most powerful warrior among us, but I now possess the gift that will lead us to vindication and salvation."

Zelda translated again: "Mee whaga fahbee shahmah, lah ashah. Bohtah nahsah mee ceemah bohtrak annha, nahtoo tonntah. Mee sahba rygah lasha traupah, veebee mee dahbid nahsah. Mee whassa don klahsah lah bohtahna."

The sacrifice ceremony was now ready to burn the rock chlorophyll: the sky was glowing with the familiar mauve sheen signalling the spiritual power, lightning cracked and thundered across the cloudless horizon and the warriors continued to chant.

"Pyna pyna pyna. Traupah traupah traupah. Pyna traupah, pyna traupah, pyna traupah."

The chant suddenly stopped as Soarfoot raised his arms beside the flaming bonfire. An enormous sheet of lightning streaked the sky without thunder.

"Pyna! Traupah! Ashah sylva Quujj fahbee. Nahtoo pyna vohko, deewa sylva. The spiritual power of Quujj and the pine trees is now with us here. Embrace the strength and feel the spiritual power."

Soarfoot's words ushered tree warriors up to the sacrifice fire in small groups. They quietly added their stagers to the blaze until the flames reached high into the air. The procession of warriors took several minutes until a thunderous bolt of lightning eventually clasped the heavens and broke the silence; piercing into the ceremony as Soarfoot continued.

"Warriors, go to your family camps and await guidance. Traupah whaga eevah takid, whaha shatoonee. Don zahka lah naga loho. Don loho pahva vee. We will battle and we will be victorious. We will celebrate again. Pyna nahtoo! Mingas unite!"

"Pyna traupah, pyna traupah," came back the chants, again in unison and naturally flowing with the ceremony.

The hybrid warriors surrounded the bonfire in layers on the beach and casually entered a contemplative state nearing the peak of the ritual. Soon it began to rain from a clear sky with the water of life. Everyone raised their thoughts towards the heavens and felt the impending flush of strength in the rain; randomly sauntering into the stand of ancient pine trees that populated this jungle ravine. The hiss of doused flames and the smoke of smouldering coals filled the cove and began to drift above the beach as warriors carved new mighty stagers from the radiant trees: words were no longer needed.

The Mingas were filled with the sporadic ashah of the lasha. The rejuvenating water of life rainfall and the ahskah mist swirling in the air at this historical lashmah recharged their powers and prepared them for a legendary quest. A passionate celebration rocked through the night after the ceremony—lasting another few rotations on the ocean coast, as elders and bark shredders brought instructions to the various tribal camps.

This was only the beginning of many sacrifice fires for Zachary and Soarfoot. The planets in their home universe were the first stops for the crusade, followed by a mix of planets in all of the unispheres: assembling warriors, entering spiritual corridors, harvesting original ancient fibrous trees and encouraging hybrid breeding, so to speak, with the hope of finding the silviculture prophecy from superior genetic actuality, as suggested by Envrah herself.

Soarfoot ventured outside the galaxy of Quujj with Zelda by his side and the largest botanical flotilla in Minga history. They started on Planet Vhana in what Earth's Boreal Forces charted as Supercluster Territory and then toured to Uhrobie, Emmoha and Raakah in Outer Edge Territory, Selyyd in Outer Boundary, back to Tuw in Supercluster, Earth and Druid in the local supercluster Homeland Territory, and then to the planets Thalla, Arkna and Pardaebia in Andromeda Edge, Palpaas, Puryd and Groakk in Boundary, and as far as Jhallaras fifteen billion light years away in Frontier Territory; gathering a force stronger and stronger by the planet.

Zachary's tour with the Storyteller took him out to Envrak in the northeast of Outer Boundary Territory, Kaepyd in Outer Horizon and Davern in Outer Fringe, then on a southeast swing of Sarbyd, Svorkdal, Bahkra and Targg in the Outer Fringe, Frontier, Horizon and Boundary, doubling back in the far south quadrants of Boundary, Horizon and Frontier to Dynna, Ghanostra and Kohbee, and finally a small inconspicuous planet named Feecher in the Outer Fringe far south, where at the urging of his ancestral grandfather they conferred with some elders; all the while collecting an assortment of hybrid species ready to fight for the manifesto cause.

This early stage of the quest for forty-seven trees was an exciting honour for Zachary, yet once the tour through his home unisphere was completed he calmed down and gradually adopted a more mature attitude for the responsibility of his new spiritual path. The separate silviculture journeys first visited homeland planets in Plateau; plotting logistics before heading beyond Vapourdom and Windswept into the Summit and Crown grand creations. They would not be reunited for many annua of the universal continuum, but they were able to speed through the cosmic expanse with thousands of tree warriors swaying in their organically spiritual free flight. Soarfoot and Zachary became known as the messenger proclaimers uniting warriors and seeking out ancient ashah trees. They brought a new force to the galaxies: blowing the tides of vindication and salvation. The word of Gorb was about to briskly flutter on a vortex of peace.

The windswept campaign finished touring Earth's universe and then cruised to the aspen tree unisphere; accepting the ancient ashah tree from Gorb's heaven and joining the warriors who had assembled on Envrah while Zachary was spreading the word billions of light years away. The aspen flotilla, with hundreds of arboretum ships cluttering the orbits of hybrid galaxies, just like Soarfoot's Minga armada, was the greatest assembly of Envrahs ever to grace the cosmic wave.

Meanwhile, the vapourdom journey stopped first on Planet Yndes (*Yin-deez*) in the tamarack tree unisphere near Ardyk's heaven, where they gathered more hybrid warriors and another spiritual ashah tree. The arboretum vessels then whisked to the poplar tree unisphere and were welcomed by a gigantic sacrifice fire celebration on Planet Demkew near Dkobi's black hole; unveiling an ancient poplar tree as they awaited a messenger convoy from Zachary, who had swept through Envrah and visited Planet Talib in Lirda's elm tree unisphere before Soarfoot and Zelda arrived on Demkew. The messenger rooting ship was accompanied by a formidable tree raid contingent of elm Talibian hybrids with one of their original trees, organised by Zachary in his growing confidence as a spiritual leader—of all things.

The plan hatched by the messenger proclaimers was to quietly proceed through the grand creation without attracting attention. They would move on and subtly acquire original trees in Summit and Crown spiritual corridors with the fibrous powers bestowed upon them and the support of tree warriors accumulated along the quest; returning as a bulked powerhouse of sporadic energy to retrieve the last remaining ashah trees in Plateau.

However, their plan suffered a flaw when they were deceived by a weak moment of indulgence—after all, the gods certainly know that nothing is perfect—which I guess you could say was a premonition of their eventual fate in the usual random fashion of spiritualised destiny. Perhaps Soarfoot was tempted by his pride when the Demkews, Talibians and Yndae amassed together with the Mingas, but nevertheless he saw what he thought was an opportunity. The birch tree Coulees were beginning to wane in the unisphere of Sonus, beyond the heavens of Quujj and Pefl approaching Zarkk's fir tree black hole. The Coulee warriors were affected by the anxious musings of nervous willow tree Dlailians wavering from Pefl's neighbouring unisphere, as well as the convincing diatribe of moderates among their own. Soarfoot thought the strength of his multitudes was more than enough to invade Planets Dlailia and Coulee without much struggle, so he launched massive trunk thrusts targeting the passageway forests into the willow and birch spiritual corridors.

The task of supressing the Coulees was not insurmountable, but Soarfoot was surprised by rebels who still clung to their defiance. Although the Dlailians rather quietly relinquished and surrendered an ancient willow tree, it would require a time consuming and meticulous effort to overcome the thinly dispersed birch warriors. These pockets of rebel tribes not only blocked the botanical passageways for many moon cycles on Coulee, but their ardent battle tactics also echoed across the cosmic corridors and sounded in the halls of credo heavens. The silviculture quest would soon lose its early advantage of surprise as the spruce angel Alka eventually informed Rulsp of the new dimensional transcending powers possessed by the manifesto warriors.

The Demkew and Talibian flotillas would remain in the Coulee galaxy while stagerdust floated over valleys and through tree stands for many continuum moon cycles. Soarfoot departed with the tamarack Yndae, leaving the poplar and elm warriors in trust of the new conflict that lasted for several annua; unaware he had inadvertently sparked an organic universal war. He then took a wide berth around the fir tree Naruka and spruce tree Alka unispheres, and even Fesso's oak tree Dewar unisphere, somewhat hesitant after his experience on Coulee.

The intent of Zachary's journey was also discrete, but he managed to filter through unispheres of undecided moderates as he approached Windswept Spiral. They, the undecided moderates, all humbly offered their support without conflict or battle after hearing the words of a messenger proclaimer. The ginkgo tree Salites from Planet Saleh (*Sall-ay*) in Svebb's unisphere, cedar tree Syntras from the unisphere of Nybos and maple tree Nycaas in Wateko's unisphere all added spiritual trees and many arboretum ships to the windswept conglomerate of hybrid warriors, which gradually expanded to match the pine and tamarack flotillas on the edge of Vapourdom Spiral.

It was over three continuum annua after they departed Gorb's heaven that Zachary and Soarfoot arrived at their respective grand spirals for the silviculture crusades. They would soon carry tree warriors into our organically spiritual dimensions for the first time in existence. It was a grand and wondrous space and time.

❖ ❖ ❖

A brief respite for the silviculture flotillas in our grand spirals dazzled the tree warriors camped on arboretum vessels; protected as they swayed in clear and calm corridors with our dancing coloured curtains of energy gliding and spiking through the dark cosmic waves to carve passages in the organically spiritual domains. Zachary and Soarfoot prepared for the crusades by communicating with our sporadic layered pillars of shining light, which most definitely inspired the manifestos awaiting their flight into the distant unispheres.

We wind warriors agreed to divide some of our free flight vectors and have them join with Soarfoot's campaign forging through Vapourdom. We bid our brothers and sisters farewell with the confidence we would meet again on the cusp of Rulsp's heaven. We watched them sail towards Summit Grand Creation; proud and honoured to be assisting in the quest for peace, but not too proud, but maybe a little angry—just a smidge of wrath directed at Rulsp, Zarkk and other credo elements. You would have to admit, we were entitled to a little belligerence if not full out antagonism. The rest suits me fine.

Although the cooperation of vapour demons was certain, since it was we wind warriors who carried them on their thunderclouds, the more amiable of our kind, so to speak, formed the majority of the vectors breezing around the threshold of Plateau to reach our USF family at Vapourdom. They, the diplomats, so to speak, solicited support for the silviculture quest. The departure of free flight and thundercloud missions left a vacuum of sorts in the spiral domains: never before had such a great number of entities vacated our homelands. Nonetheless, the vacuum was soon replaced by the excitement of a new identity; now it was our turn to fly through space with a truly powerful essence previously unmatched in the organic habitat.

The wake of cosmic commotion filling the spacious dark banquets behind our vectors did not leave any doubt that a momentous actuality was consuming the galactic topography. Free flight and thundercloud missions had been fairly isolated in the past; only making memorable impressions in secluded solar systems. This howling force of manifestation echoed a potent battle cry, bouncing on the brink of magnetic fields across the interstellar expanse: reeling solar winds and erratic spatial disturbance, hurricanes and disruptive planetary climates. Cosmic dwellers squirmed in the presence of this strange but wondrous new force.

I accompanied the windswept journey myself; leading a high-pressure vortex with Zachary as we exploded into Crown Grand Creation. The credo hurricane stronghold of the sassafras tree Urbonae in Yanamea's unisphere and the jute tree Yabnians in Baf's unisphere was the first hurdle for our journey. We proceeded through the four unispheres of the wind funnel gods before reaching the creed region, where moderate warriors were supressed by the influence of credo tree raids for eons—but that was about to change.

The journey patiently mobilised friendly tribes of hybrids before confronting the evil forces of creed. We wind warriors identified the strongest of the tribes and Zachary proclaimed his priorities accordingly. The planets Avid and Frev were the first hosts for another two enormous and festive sacrifice fire celebrations in the rubber tree unisphere of the god Rom and the calabash unisphere of Marn. The Avidians and Frevs were only occasionally persecuted by credo tree raids; sheltered from such violence within the reach of our sometimes-unruly wind currents that tend to dissuade hostile actions. There were very few trunk thrusts to defend throughout these unispheres, but some of the battles against credos were intense—an omen of the difficult journey ahead.

The rooting ship holding Zachary was able to permeate into the spiritual corridors of Rom and Marn on a giant free flight vortex, where ideal trees were staked and elevated with the lasha onto his arboretum vessel; adding ancient rubber and calabash trees to the aspen, ginkgo, cedar and maple from Plateau heavens. The botanical flotilla, with the strength of yet more ashah trees, then embarked deeper into the wind funnel for the first real test of the journey.

The manifestos arrived in the Nuuka galaxy of Apar's mangrove unisphere, another fifty-five billion light years away: a barrage of arboretum vessels preceded by a series of wild thunderstorms, ready to liberate the homeland planet. The sassafras and jute warriors dominated this region of the grand creation because of their supreme fighting talents; powerful and well organised in their waring ways, resulting in confrontations tangled with stagerdust bashing and filled with flaring wood chips. The vicious trunk takeovers on Planet Nuuka tested the manifesto initial preparedness, but the Envrahs, Salites, Syntras and Nycaas worked well together with the Nuukas, Frevs and Avidians; luckily suffering only a few casualties while defeating the credos in vehemently contested battles.

The quest for spiritual trees in Crown Grand Creation might have ended before it started if it were not for the grit of the Nuukas and the sophistication of Zachary's powers. Deadly lightning strikes jarred credo ships into submission and bolstered the Nuuka mangrove warriors as they captured enemy trunk thrust squadrons. The fierce Nuukas, weathered and burly from generations of tree wars, capably liberated their planet with the help of the intimidating silviculture fleet. The battles on Nuuka span almost two annua before the mangrove home world was rid of the credo presence, but the liberation was comparatively short lived when the hurricane stronghold realised the magnitude of the force against them and steadily retreated to planets Urbonas and Yabnas—over one hundred billion light years distant beyond the wind funnel unispheres.

The Nuukas enthusiastically joined the silviculture quest when they saw and felt the power of the original mangrove tree from the spiritual dimension; signalling the gradual enhancement of the crusade with another party of grand proportions, so to speak, acknowledging their major victory with a joyous feast of sustenance and spirituality. It took little convincing to ready the warriors for further battle.

The manifestos swayed to Tyru's kapok tree unisphere next and easily released the Weks from their bonds of oppression on the edge of the wind funnel; encountering only a limited number of credo tribes and retrieving an original ancient tree without complications. An impressive crusade, after more celebrating of course, breezed the cosmic trails from Planet Wek to confront the hurricane stronghold on Urbonas. The credos, having witnessed this windswept rage, were aware of the campaign before it arrived: the evil warriors were ready to take on this new force in their grand creation.

The showdown on Urbonas was the greatest challenge for Zachary and Storyteller. The sassafras Urbonae and jute Yabnians assembled together in preparation; separating some of their trunk thrust squadrons in a dark fold of the galaxy where they waited for the manifesto attack. The warriors of peace were flanked by stacked columns as they descended through the atmosphere of Urbonas: Envrahs with Salites, Syntras and Nycaas, Nuukas with Weks, Frevs and Avidians. But the silviculture advance was blind to the hidden tactics of the hurricane stronghold. The largest tree raid in Crown Grand Creation's history was about to encounter a shrewd botanical manoeuvre.

The creed warriors in the dark fold of the galaxy were masked by powerful and deceptive layers of lasha that not even us wind warriors could detect; enabling them to move behind the planetary assault with an attack of their own. The element of surprise, almost always one of the best weapons, put the manifestos at a huge disadvantage. Trunk thrust formations acted fast to cover their flanks, but confusion reigned as lasha strikes consumed the skies of Urbonas; pressing ships into defensive postures and forcing them down to the surface in an attempt to avoid deadly exchanges. The manifesto warriors were twirling and stumbling against the surprise attack for many Urbonas days, but Zachary was well advised by the Storyteller who remains wise in the strategies of tree wars.

The ancestral Rhomany was not shocked by the credo ploy; he simply played one-upmanship. He watched the battle unfold while relaxing on a rooting ship surrounded by other vessels—well distanced from Urbonas ironically near Yanamea's black hole and the heaven of sassafras trees. The Storyteller also told Zachary to separate some free flight vectors with just enough wind warriors and vapour demons to create a respectful lightning storm, which were awaiting his orders. The vectors joined together in a vortex and released their wrath upon the planet. Now it was the credos who were surprised.

The vortex storm sliced down on the Urbonae and Yabnians; swinging the momentum and neatly levelling the battlefield. The manifestos took full advantage of the spontaneous thunderstorm and were able to fight their way back to even ground. A cruel conflict evolved on Urbonas that lapsed for more than three annua of fighting: lightning and driving rain covered the planet in a canopy of killing, trees were scarred and singed, and spiritual fibre was destroyed in seemingly aimless plight. The quest for peaceful balance took on the appearance of botanical genocide.

It was a sad time in universal history: burning deciduous, melting coniferous and dead warriors. The planet was being decimated in a flare of disruption. Urbonas was nearly plundered of all its resources. It would require several seasonal rotations of the planet before many of the ecosystems could recover, but there was a light of hope piercing the dim scene of war. The manifesto of peace gradually gained the upper hand over the creed of destruction; sheer numbers outweighed imposing stature in deadly skills, as was the spiritual way of things. The credo warriors were pursued across forest stands and meadow glens, crisscrossing the planet until they eventually became desperate. They were dominated, outnumbered and overpowered, and although they attempted to find refuge until the very end, they were finally surrounded in a heavily wooded valley. Against their demented judgement, the hurricane stronghold warriors surrendered—Urbonas was conquered at last.

This conflict certainly put a strain on the silviculture crusade, but the manifestos emerged victorious and were able to secure ancient sassafras and jute trees from the spiritual corridors leading to the heavens of Yanamea and Baf. Planet Yabnas was relinquished without resistance since all the extreme warriors were either killed or captured on Urbonas and only moderate tribes remained on the homeland. Camps were established on both hurricane planets to treat injured warriors and encourage converts to the peaceful path, and while casualties of war were slowly healed Zachary immediately turned his thoughts to the remaining unispheres in Crown. There were still evil elements to be defeated.

The hurricane war cost the windswept journey many good warriors and Zachary knew he had to find reinforcements. Fortunately there were another six unispheres of undecided factions and those loyal to the manifesto cause before reaching the fringe corridor of creed unispheres. Zachary's maturity as a tree warrior and now spiritual leader truly surfaced during this space and time of the crusade; combining with his mortally unparalleled power of free flight to quite capably and effectively lead the campaign for peace through most of the grand creation. He mounted a surge through the heart of Crown unispheres for several annua to rebuild his botanical flotilla with many brave warriors, as they approached the remaining credo homelands. The distant creed of destruction fringe corridor with the olive tree Marcynakians and cactus tree Peyotae was all that stood in Zachary and Storyteller's path of peace.

❖ ❖ ❖

An unremarkable asteroid of ordinary characteristics broke from its gravitational orbit near the Alka galaxy and blazed towards the Vapourdom Spiral. Protected inside a cavity of botanic spiritualis was a small group of tree war spies, if you will, including two original entities, so to speak: the original wizard Flafid and the entity of the spruce angel Alka in the body of a tree warrior. They were attempting to slip though the grand spiral in an oversized scarifier ship disguised as a cosmological object; intending to warn the faithful credos in Summit Grand Creation and create a wizardly weapon to match the blustery manifesto vortex approaching.

Rulsp commanded the concealed spiritual vessel after Alka explained the dimensional transcendence transpiring in the Coulee galaxy. The spruce god sensed the daring plan of the manifesto gods and wanted to counteract the scheme by releasing wizards from their slipper voids in Summit to unleash another kind of deadly force. Alka was risking her very existence once again for Rulsp's evil bidding. I have to admit, we wind warriors and vapour demons were somewhat preoccupied and it was a smart move by Rulsp, but alas the creed tactics would have to be content with the unispheres in Plateau.

The asteroid vessel did gain entrance into Vapourdom—the spirit of an original fibrous angel, a few wizards and a handful of elite warriors huddled beside a cave of deception sacrifice fire inside the granite rock cavity. They scraped against waves of our organically spiritual fibre for some distance, but the rebellious entities were not able to navigate completely through the grand spiral into the Summit unispheres. We soon shut down the surreptitious flight of the asteroid and bounced it back into the cosmos of Plateau; if not for the power of Alka the ship would have been destroyed, but instead remained intact for another kind of evil bidding.

Soarfoot's quest, so I'm told, entered Summit on the other side of the grand spiral as Alka was busy clinging to life. The vapourdom journey began in earnest on a gigantic wave of wind current vectors with pressurised thunderclouds of lightning strands and torrential rains. The silviculture tribes began their journey with an immediate and distinct advantage: manifesto tree raids were already testing credo camps some two hundred and sixty-five billion light years away between the vapour cloud unispheres near the edge of Summit and the creed mountain stronghold unispheres. The prodigious greenheart tree Tusrae from Kumi's unisphere and balsa tree Karvs from Onu's unisphere were feeling confident after defending their homelands against brutal tree raids only a couple of annua earlier, as it turned out, but these agents of peace did not anticipate the support they were about to receive.

The Mingas, Yndae and some willow Dlailians swept through the unispheres of the vapour cloud gods under Soarfoot and Zelda's leadership as they progressed towards the greenheart and balsa unispheres. The ultimate target was Planet Wabeka in the credo mountain stronghold ash tree unisphere near the black hole of Eamaan, where the tung tree Kagiwosians from the unisphere of Rens were also gathered. Messenger convoys were dispatched down to the surface of vapour cloud homelands on route to the victims of creed; spreading the word of the silviculture prophecy and sequestering the support of tree warriors.

The vapour cloud hybrids and their neighbouring unispheres suffered from creed invasions throughout history, especially since the peace corridor of manifestos defended the central regions of Summit on the far side of the mountain stronghold. Planet Haukna in Jacobi's unisphere touching the shadow of Vapourdom Spiral is home to the yew tree Hauknians—a tribe of impressive stature well-endowed with attractive features, who set the tone for the crusade by pledging their unequivocal dedication to peace—followed swiftly by the kind but crude jacaranda tree Nylors in the Dwyi unisphere and the keen eucalyptus tree Dovipanites in the Janale unisphere.

There were many deca of sacrifice fires, festivals and botanical strategies as ancient yew, jacaranda and eucalyptus trees were retrieved, while warriors congregated and packed arboretum vessels to their freeboard brims. These peaceful tribes were grateful for the courageous fight of greenheart Tusrae and balsa Karvs and were eager to bring forth this apparently strengthening hand of manifesto authority to dictate the outcome of creed aggression, which rather conveniently was being resisted with even more determination; perhaps another premonition of eventual fate.

The proclaimers soared on their feet, so to speak, swaying to Planet Karv and then Planet Tusra. They were warmly welcomed, with both homelands void of serious hostilities. The hybrid elders saluted the tremendous flotilla with the customary ceremonies and admired the spiritual greenheart and balsa trees collected on Soarfoot's rooting ship, but quickly sped the warriors on their way to join with the tree raids already engaging credos across the distant cosmic trails. The minimal creed operations encountered in the vapour cloud were not threatening and easily debunked, however some credos were able to flee and notify the mountain stronghold of the manifesto forces approaching. But it was too late for the ash warriors and their tung tree allies from Kagiwosa. The vapourdom flotilla was orbiting the ash tree homeland within four annua after entering the grand creation.

There was little doubt who would prevail as they glided down to the surface of Wabeka where greenheart and balsa warriors were hastily harvesting stands of ash and tung. The silviculture flotilla was empowered by menacing windstorms to topple evil forces and enough hybrids to outmatch any credo trunk thrust. The wicked vortex winds devastated the forests of Wabeka; ripping trees from the roots and flinging rocks and vegetation across the landscape. It was an awesome sight of sheer power.

The ash and tung warriors were flustered into a state of disarray as they hectically scampered to cope with the planetary attack. The Wabekas and Kagiwosians were vulnerable to the legions of manifestos; quivering at the sight of arboretum vessels wafting down to their camps, and after being weakened by the Tusrae and Karvs, captured like logs rounded up in a trunk takeover. The siege lasted less than two annua of the universal continuum: weeding out stubborn holdouts hiding in mountain valleys and caves, moving prisoners to camps that would be converted into habitat ships for transport, and conducting thoughtfully devised peace talks, if you will, most tactically with the tung tree Kagiwosians.

Zelda used her charm and persuasion interviewing warriors to encourage peaceful submission, but also to gain the favour of tung hybrids in particular with the intent of convincing Planet Kagiwosa to surrender without conflict. The Kagiwosians on their home world were not as compromised as the Wabekas were against the manifesto onslaught, and Soarfoot, expecting a battle on his hands, wanted to employ any advantage he could find—still cautious from his encounter on the birch tree homeland Coulee. It was an involved process but the tung and ash warriors, humbled by the silviculture power as they surfed the cosmic wave on habitat ships, eventually agreed to advocate the path of peace over the creed of destruction.

The manifesto presence swaying to Kagiwosa was undeniably evident, with an actual fibrous ash tree onboard a rooting ship as well. The Kagiwosians only needed moderate prompting to join the ranks, as it turned out. They observed the messenger proclaimer enter their black hole, emerge from the spiritual corridor and herald a magnificent ancient tung tree. The mountain stronghold, which conceded to the evil doctrines of Eamaan and Rens since the era of the one heaven, was now committed to peace.

The vapourdom journey had converted one of the two creed dynamos in Summit by overcoming the destructive regimes of Wabeka and Kagiwosa. A peacekeeping force led by the Karvs, Hauknians and a few influential Yndae remained on the tung homeland to ensure there were not any further revolts;

allowing the campaign to set its sights on the final creed stronghold, Planet Sabaqua in the acacia tree unisphere of the god Baqua. The number of Sabaquae warriors was not as great as the mountain stronghold, but the acacia hybrids were renowned for their ferocious courage and cunning tree raid tactics. Soarfoot and Zelda carefully contemplated their next move.

The vapourdom crusade was cruising through peace corridor in Summit as the windswept journey departed the hurricane stronghold in Crown, but there was still this matter of trunk thrust battles on Planet Coulee in Plateau. The spirit of Alka survived expulsion from Vapourdom and reported back to the spruce heaven; explaining that she could not penetrate through the grand spiral barrier. But Alka also learned that an immense manifesto armada of pine, tamarack and willow, and another of aspen, ginkgo, cedar and maple had vacated the grand creation, leaving only the poplar and elm to defend peace in Plateau.

Rulsp saw the weakness of the Minga and Envrah. The spruce god commanded an escalation of hostile botanical salvoes and political ploys in the aspen and pine unispheres. The gods Gorb and Quujj sneered at Rulsp's continuing evil intentions, but remained hopeful for the actuality of the silviculture prophecy.

Chapter 35: The New Frontier

Zachary and Storyteller shared a relaxing campfire beside a small lake on Planet Peyote. They were in a reflective mood after the breadth of the manifesto surge in Crown Grand Creation had overcome the evil fringe corridor of credo unispheres, occupied by the olive and cactus tree warriors. Rushad Rhomanscu's face was softly glowing against the flames; soothing the tensions of conflict with the unconditional love in his soul.

"You have come a long way my schweetz," he said to Zachary.

"Only with your touch of grace grandfather."

"Yes, you are humble like a true warrior, but you now have the confidence of the manifesto and all the hybrids who follow in our path. Our search for ancient spiritual trees will soon be complete."

"The end of the journey is near, but there are still challenges ahead."

"Do you feel the wave of the sporadic element that was born in our grand creation after we departed?"

"Yes, I feel it. It is very strong and it seems to be giving me even more clarity. My visions are growing stronger all the time."

"And do you see the evil that is lurking near this new energy?"

"Yes, I can sense that too. What is this revelation?"

"It is the coming of the silviculture prophecy, a warrior with powerful actuality that is yet to be released, but this new energy must confront the nemesis element."

"Are we needed there? Should we dispatch another messenger convoy? I could ask Harold to transport some of our venerable warriors."

"We are still needed on this crusade. You are strong and we will meet this sporadic element soon, at the door of evil, where we will finish the ultimate quest. The elders on Feecher are waiting in the pine tree domain for this sporadic gift from the heavens."

"Feecher, where you insisted we meet with the elders. Did you already know of the prophecy?"

"No, I could not see it then, but the owls on the cosmic wave came to my visions, soaring to the warriors on Feecher. They have seen the silviculture prophecy and are waiting for its arrival."

"And can you see what will come of our journey?"

The Storyteller smiled again with the serenity of wisdom.

"Only the cosmic wave holds the secrets of the sporadic element, nobody knows where it will take us. It cannot be foretold, as you know, not even the gods can control our destiny. Rest assured the Feecherians will guide this warrior of actuality along the cosmic wave. They have seen the owls rise."

"As only you can do my ancestral friend, I am once again inspired by the swift of flight and the power of the aspen trees," surmised Zachary.

The windswept journey had fought for peace over four chapters of messenger proclaiming up until this moment of reflection, if you will, taking about ten continuum annua to cover each universal region of the grand creation. The first ten annua took place before the outbreak of a new universal war in Earth's pine tree unisphere. This time was spent in the wind funnel expanse and battling the sassafras on Urbonas.

The next chapter consisted of silting through tree raid conflicts in the cosmos between the credo hurricane and manifesto strongholds. They continued liberating planets and acquiring both ancient spiritual trees and hybrid warriors: beech tree Yharites in the god Maav's unisphere, rose tree Irbae in the unisphere of Moht, and in Nekrol's unisphere the gum tree Prawdians.

They patiently visited as many hybrid planets as possible in the manifesto stronghold to write the next chapter; rebuilding the strength of their trunk thrusts with warriors and spiritual trees for another ten annua, as the universal war in Plateau had begun billions of light years away. The stronghold warriors are devoted courageous veterans of peace who were anxiously waiting to hear the silviculture proclaimed: baobab Atakeewans in the unisphere of Laavv, teak Nagawashians in the unisphere of Cess, and alder Wabagoonads in Kwarg's unisphere.

The swell of vortices they formed swaying towards the fringe corridor succinctly defeated the credos of Marcynaki and Peyote; all but ending the chapters of proclamation. The many olive tree Marcynakians in the unisphere of

Evbic were unprepared for the onslaught, but it still required three annua to sweep up and collect trees.

The bitter cactus warriors however were a different story in Verra's unisphere; simply refusing to concede defeat. The windswept flotilla first liberated the mopani tree Zadeks in Lipna's unisphere, who had miraculously survived between the two credo homelands since the dawn of botanical disputes. The campaign then invaded the cactus unisphere. The Peyotae fought until the death of almost all their hybrids, but not their ancient fibrous trees. It was a disheartening six-annum conflict, but remorse was soon replaced by jubilation when courier angels brought news that the universal war of oppression in Plateau Grand Creation had come to an end.

❖ ❖ ❖

The vapourdom journey with Soarfoot and Zelda did not spend as much time in the different regions of Summit Grand Creation; swaying through peace corridor and reaching near the edge of the creed stronghold just as the universal war was underway in Plateau. The peace corridor redwood Zemders feeding the wave to Palu's heaven, karri tree Swoonites looming beside Forek's black hole, and ebony warriors from Suzhe in the oldest cosmos of the god Kymm, all joined Soarfoot's already impressive botanical flotilla with their warriors and ancient trees. They liberated the incense tree Yonnites in Hume's unisphere, but required five annua to chase credos from the palm tree Baltsa unisphere of the topography god Yufe.

Unfortunately, the acacia tree Sabaquae in Baqua's unisphere were heated and infuriated, and like the cactus warriors, they refused to surrender; battling to the end and delaying the crusade over ten annua. The acacia warriors would not stop fighting on their homeland Sabaqua, even though they were confined to the planet. They fought without consequence and they fought until they died. The manifestos were not left with any other recourse but to wipe out the Sabaquae, save a few survivors. Sabaqua was a hollow, almost treeless planet after the tenth annum of invasion: the wrath of Baqua was silenced and more fibrous spiritual trees were added to the fire, so to speak.

Soarfoot was finishing his crusade—slithering in the wrinkles extending from the roots of existence among wizard slipper voids—while Zachary was entering the final two heavens near the far canopy edge along the universal tree of grand creations. Botanical armadas collected the last few ancient spiritual trees. Soarfoot and Zelda entered the heavens of Yett, Kapid, Cyte and Alsa; retrieving avocado, podocarpus, mallee and mahogany trees with the help of Pagron, Calli, Kuaandi and Drang warriors. Zachary and Storyteller only had to acquire kurrajong and bubinga trees with the Sarites and Sinaitatians from the unispheres of Idyp and Var. Both crusades took needed time to assemble hybrids and transport all of them within the corridors of their free flight flotillas.

Tree warrior comrades who bravely made sacrifices in the name of peace were taken to their home worlds, while thousands more continued with hope in their souls to courageously face the wrath of evil greed in the cosmos of Rulsp's spruce tree credo stronghold. The voyages of arboretum ships from the fringes of the universal tree in Crown Grand Creation and the roots of existence in Summit Grand Creation were festive and jubilant with many friends and invigorated warriors. The windswept and vapourdom marathon silviculture journeys were finally flowing towards Plateau Grand Creation over eight hundred billion light years away. The quest for forty-seven original ancient trees was complete in two of the three grand creations and riding a crest of buoyancy.

Soarfoot and Zachary had returned to the organic habitat from the spiritual dimension over fifty thousand Earth years after they entered the aspen heaven. They took another forty-seven annua for their silviculture journey, of course, up until this defining moment in universal history. There were also two intergalactic wars in the pine tree unisphere during this same space and time, and now the proclaimers were returning to Plateau Grand Creation to preserve the peace after these wars—hopefully for an eternity.

The immense relevance of the silviculture crusades would soon be realised in the actuality of organic and spiritual habitats, but not before a few more obstacles were overcome. The messenger proclaimers and their brave tree warriors were fleeting the cosmos in victory yet they were still searching for the true silviculture warrior with the ultimate sporadic actuality, who was indeed waiting at the doorstep of credo greed and destruction.

Map of Known Universe

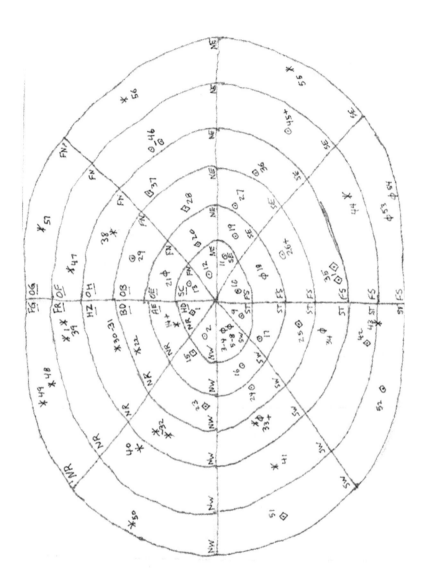

Universal Territories & Quadrants— Galaxies, Clusters and Planets

Homeland—*NR* **1**. NGC-3923—Varbosen *NW* **2**. Sculptor—Denbaur
SW **3–4**. Andromeda / Solaris Andromeda
5–8. Milky Way—Earth / Mars / New Terra / Halpern *ST* **9**. M81—Druid

Supercluster—*FS* **10**. NGC-2997—Vhana *SE* **11**. Virgo—Minga
NE **12**. NGC-3672 & 3504—Blaved *FN* **13**. NGC-3607—Tuw

Andromeda Edge—*NR* **14**. QSO-0241+622—Thalla (North Edge Station) *NW*
15. Perseus—Arkna *SW* **16**. Coma—Anahanni *ST* **17**. A1514—Pardaebia

Outer Edge—*FS* **18**. 3C-273—Uhrobie *SE* **19**. BNC-OE-SEW4-G73—
Emmoha *NE* **20**. Hercules—Raakah *FN* **21**. BNC-OE-FNW2-CG17—Nuung

Boundary—*NR* **22**. 3C-48—Khiallaily *NW* **23**. A665—Palpaas
SW **24**. A910—Puryd *ST* **25**. A1146—Groakk

Outer Boundary—*FS* **26**. BNC-OB-FSE1-CG259—Dynna (Boundary Station)
SE **27**. TON-256—Targg *NE* **28**. Indus—Envrak *FN* **29**. A2645—Selyyd

Horizon—*NR* **30–31**. BNC-HZ-NRW4/E4-G15 & G349—Sevvah/Aazzee
NW **32**. PKS-0405-123—Caesarea *SW* **33**. BNC-HZ-SWE1-QC37—Vardookah
(Horizon Station) *ST* **34**. BNC-HZ-STE2-G427—Waavvek

Outer Horizon—*FS* **35**. 3C-275 & 279—Ghanostra *SE* **36**. A2232—Bahkra
NE **37**. BNC-OH-NEW3-SC54—Kaepyd *FN* **38**. BNC-OH-FNW4-QC2073—
Ennstra

Frontier—*NR* **39**. 3C-9 & PHL-957—Hyka *NW*—**40**. PKS-0237-233—Suthan *SW* **41**. BNC-FR-SWE4-G58—Jhallaras *ST* **42–43**. BNC-FR-STE3-SC782—Pova / BNC-FR-STE4-QC5373—Iltuk

Outer Frontier—*FS* **44**. PG-1247+26—Kohbee *SE* **45**. 3C-295—Svorkdal (Frontier Station) *NE* **46**. 3C-345 & 351—Abourque *FN* **47**. 3C-446—Serenva

Fringe—*NR* **48–49**. PHL-957—Ska / BNC-FG-NRW1-QC36—Flafidia *NW* **50**. BNC-FG-NWW3-QC77—Lubba *SW* **51**. BNC-FG-SWE4-SC88—Vermilion *ST* **52**. BNC-FG-STE1-CG2336—Flayba

Outer Fringe—*FS* **53–54**. BNC-OG-FSW1-G889—Neudraven / BNC-OG-FSW4-G1947—Feecher *SE* **55**. PKS-2000-330—Sarbyd *NE* **56**. PKS-2126-158—Davern *FN* **57**. PHL-5200—Tocx

Legend—Universal Territories

HD—Homeland / SC—Supercluster / AE—Andromeda Edge / OE—Outer Edge
BD—Boundary / OB—Outer Boundary / HZ—Horizon / OH—Outer Horizon
FR—Frontier / OF—Outer Frontier / FG—Fringe / OG—Outer Fringe
Territory Quadrants: NR—North / NW—Northwest / SW—Southwest / ST—South / FS—Far South / SE—Southeast / NE—Northeast / FN—Far North
Quadrant Sectors: W1-Northwest / W2-NorthwestSouth / W3-SouthwestNorth / W4-Southwest / E1-Northeast / E2-NortheastSouth / E3-SoutheastNorth / E4-Southeast

G-galaxy / CG-cluster of galaxies / SC-supercluster / QC-quasar cluster

Catalogues—3C-Third Cambridge Catalogue of Radio Sources
A-Abell Catalogue
BNC-Boreal National Catalogue of Stellar Objects and Spatial Properties
M-Messier Catalogue of Nebulae and Star Clusters /NGC-New General Catalogue of Nebulae and Clusters of Stars
QSO-Catalog of Quasi-Stellar Objects / PG-Principal Galaxies Catalogue

PHL-Palomar-Haro-Luyten Catalogue / PKS-Parkes Observatory Catalogue of Galactic Planetary Nebulae

TON-Tonantzintla Observatory

Φ—galaxy ⊙—cluster of galaxies—◇ supercluster of galaxies ✳—quasar cluster

Druid Dictionary

The *Druid Dictionary* serves to preserve the language used by the ancient hybrid species tree warriors. The dictionary has been accumulated, discerned and documented over several eons by the historical Druid species; one of the mortal cultures to come into contact with the original fibrous spiritual entities known as angels of the tree gods.

The ancient tree warrior language was essentially developed in four generational stages, beginning with the 'foundation words' used for basic communication among primitive species in the cosmos dating back almost ten billion years, or eight billion annua. Many of the foundation words typically use the phonetic pronunciation of 'ah' preceded by a consonant, which was and remains an easy sound to enunciate.

The second-generation words of the language were developed when mortal civilisations first came into contact with original fibrous angels and began to travel beyond their evolutionary homelands. These words augmented the rudimentary language mainly to enhance communication for the earliest tree warriors when venturing into heavily forested terrain; essentially constituting a trail guide lexicon.

A humble camp kitchen cook known as Johsep Kanuka, born of the early Nuuka mangrove tree warriors but transplanted into Druid tribes as a young orphan, is credited with formulating several second-generation words; initially for taste and different foods, and consequently for the organic senses. The ancient hybrid tree warrior Sarnah Makwha—a Druid by birth—was also at the leading edge of this new terminology, which she further developed in collaboration with Druid etymologists to produce a third generation of words: specifically conducive to logistics of the tree raids engaged by factions of variant warrior species.

Second generation words are known as 'trail guide terminology' and third generation words are known as 'tree raid terminology'.

The final stage of words was developed over several generations by the Druid semantic clan to complete the language and reflect some of the modern technological developments throughout interstellar cultures. These generational words delve to provide a comprehensive vocabulary for all of life's perceptions and nuance, but the language intentionally remains a modest expression of the semantics needed only for essential communication. This approach is regarded as an efficient methodology to provide effective linguistics that are easily comprehended and mastered. This final stage of the language is known as 'semantic generation' words.

The tree warrior language was first used in the unispheres of Plateau Grand Creation, but by the power of spiritual actuality Druid species evolved in all of the grand creations and the ancient dialect has become a truly universal language.

Abbreviations

FW—foundation word
SG—semantic generation word
TG—trail guide terminology
TR—tree raid terminology

adj—adjective	adv—adverb
int—interrogative	n—noun
pr—pronoun	v—verb

Word Count

Total Words—347 (including fifteen number words)
Foundation Words (FW)—47 **Semantic Generation Words (SG)**—61
Trail Guide Terminology (TG)—168
Tree Raid Terminology (TR)—71

Aa

ahskah (n, adj) TG—1. smoke; 2. smoky

annha (n) TR—1. the cosmos, including interstellar interactions as a whole; 2. the organic dimension; 3. the night time view of a planet's sky

ashah (n) TR—1. a spiritually enriched tree; 2. the spiritually enriched body of a tree warrior; 3. spiritual awareness

ashahssa (n, v, adj) SG—1. the brain of an individual creature; 2. an idea or thought; 3. to think or ponder; 4. attentive

ashak (n) TR—1. layers of planetary atmosphere; 2. daytime view of a planet's sky

ashee (n) SG—the genitals of a humanoid, male or female

ashum (n) SG—the abdomen of a humanoid

ashumee (n) SG—breasts of a female humanoid, or chest of a male

ashyb (n) TG—1. trees or bushes; 2. wood; 3. the colour green

Bb

bah (int) FW—to question who, which individual; or what, which thing

bahsygah (adj) SG—1. intense determination; 2. mentally tough and tenacious

beelah (n, adv) SG—1. respect; 2. to honour something or someone; 3. please

beez (adv, adj) TR—1. slow; 2. soft

bohko (v) TR—to prepare; something, or the act of an individual

bohtah (n) TR—the tree gods, or an individual tree god

bohtahna (n, v) SG—1. salvation for good deeds, derived from faith and confidence in peaceful existence; 2. a saviour; 3. to salvage someone or something

bohtrak (n, v) TR—1. an interstellar voyage; 2. any type of journey or quest; 3. to travel in the cosmos, or fly in planetary atmosphere

brak (n) TR—1. small arboretum interstellar flying ship; 2. tent or teepee

Cc

ceemah (n) SG—freedom and liberty

connah (v) SG—1. to lust for something or someone; 2. to kiss or show affection, including sexual intercourse; 3. to take off clothing

crah (int) FW—to question the reason, why; or the means for the reason, how

creeb (n) TG—1. outer layer of humanoid skin; 2. an animal hide; 3. hide or fabric used as a blanket; 4. a tarp or the covering for a tent or shelter

creebah (n) TG—a coat or robe garment of clothing worn over the upper body

creedak (n) SG—a tunic, shawl or sash garment of clothing worn over the upper body down to the waist, hips or knees, covering the arms or sleeveless

creedakee (n) SG—a loincloth garment of clothing worn at the hips, covering the genital area, including a breechcloth apron panel typically to the knees

creesha (n) SG—a hat or fabric covering for the head

creesum (n) SG—leg pants or some fabric covering for the legs

creesumah (n) SG—a belt or sash tied at the waist to fasten clothing

croon (n) TG—sound or noise

croonak (v, n) TG—1. to hear sound; 2. the audio sense; 3. the ears, or the anatomical feature that hears sound

croonlash (n, v) TR—1. music; 2. to make music; 3. to dance

croonsee (adj) TG—quiet, the absence of obvious noise

croontah (n) TG—the sound of thunder from lightning in the atmosphere

cyndah (n) TG—1. a mountainside; 2. an obstacle that impedes

Dd

dah (pr) FW—referring to oneself; I, me, my or mine

dahbid (v) FW—1. to have, possess, take or keep something; 2. (SG addition) to own something, including land or property

dahkee (n, adj) TR—hair, fur or feathers on a body; 2. naked, no clothing

dee (adj) FW—the front side of someone or something

deesah (n, adj) TG—1. a circle; 2. something that is round or curved

deewha (v, n) TG—1. to feel or touch something; 2. the sense of touch; 3. the hands of a humanoid; 4. to hold something or detain someone

deewhasee (v, adj) TR—1. to rub or polish; 2. something that is smooth or dull

dizz (adj, n) TG—1. something that is flat; 2. specifically, a flat plateau of land; 3. flat or calm water

dizzab (n) TG—forest floor vegetation such as grass, shrubs, moss or lichen

don (pr) FW—referring to the collective; we, us or ours

duk (n) TG—1. a ridge of land; 2. a wave of water

dukvahba (n) TG—a river waterway

dukwha (n) TG—rapids and fast-moving water

Ee

eefee (n) TR—sister; (also) **eemee**—brother

eesah (v, n) TR—1. to be, to exist; I am, we are, it is; 2. to be fertile and healthy; 3. to heal or mend; 4. all that is life

eesahnee (v) TR—to grow; including people, animals or plant life

eevah (n) TR—1. family bloodline, ancestors, descendants; 2. other people; 3. the birth of someone or something

eevah-fee (n) TR—mother; (also) **eevah-mee**—father

eevah-rygah-fee (n) TR—great grandmother; (also) **eevah-rygah-mee**—great grandfather

eevah-tah-fee (n) TR—grandmother; (also) **eevah-tah-mee**—grandfather

Ff

fah (adj) FW—1. small or short; 2. thin; 3. down or under

fahba (n) TR—a child

fahbee (adj) TG—1. to be inside a natural shelter or fabricated structure; 2. to be close in proximity; 3. to be here, indicating a time or position

fahsa (adj) SG—something that is new, or someone who is young

fahsak (v, adv) TR—1. to pull something or someone; 2. to be off, removed from a place or thing in question

fahsee (adj) SG—1. easy, not difficult; 2. weak, not strong

fee (n, pr) FW—1. a female; 2. referring to a female; she, her or hers

feesah (n) TR—daughter

Gg

gah (n) FW—anything eatable considered as food

gahdizz (n) TG—eatable organically grown grains, including beans

gahdizzab (n) TG—bread; any type of flour, cooked with moisture

gahdizzee (n) TG—eatable small plant life, commonly known as vegetables, herbs and spices, including eatable roots

gahnah (v) TG—to prepare and cook food

gahsum (n) TG—meat

gahsyb (n) TG—eatable fruit from plants and trees

gahtoo (v, n) TG—1. to eat or taste something; 2. the sense of flavour; 3. the mouth, or the anatomical feature that tastes

gahvab (n) TG—a soup or stew meal combination

gee (n) FW—an animal creature

geedak (n) TG—flying animals; bird species

geedee (n) SG—canine animals

geefah (n) SG—rodents and weasels, including arboreals

geesum (n) SG—ungulates; hooved land mammals

geeswee (n) SG—feline animals

geesygah (n) SG—reptile animals

geetah (n) SG—large dominant land mammals such as elephants, rhinoceros, bears and primates

geevab (n) SG—all marine animals

geevahba (n) SG—amphibian animals

goobah (v) TR—1. to throw; 2. to lift or carry; 3. to jump

goon (n) TG—a mountain, including its peak

goosyga (v) TR—1. to slip or fall; 2. to lay down

gootak (v) TR—1. to sweep; 2. to brush; 3. to stack or pile, accumulate; 4. to assemble something, or together as a group of people

gootakee (v) TR—to roll or tumble

goowha (v) TR—1. to kick; 2. to shake

Hh

hahnee (n) TG—1. a cave or den; 2. a hole or pit; 3. a hole in any object

hahsah (v) FW—to stop

hahsee (adj) TR—1. closed to deny access; 2. empty

hahseebee (adj) TR—1. open, accessible; 2. full

hudec (n) TG—1. welcome, greetings; 2. be brave and careful; 3. believe in yourself

Jj

jah (v, n) FW—1. to talk; 2. words; 3. the ancient Druid language

jahsygah (v) TG—to cough or sneeze

jahtah (v) TG—to yell or shout

jo (int) FW—to question for information; where, at which location

jobo (adv) TG—1. a location; 2. to be at a location; 3. to indicate a location; there

Kk

kahs (n, v) FW—a drink of any type; 2. to drink fluids

keeno (n, adj) TG—1. a friend; 2. trustworthy

klahsah (n, v) SG—1. truth; 2. knowledge; 3. vindication; 4. to learn

kohpah (n) TR—1. a tree raid commander; 2. a great tree warrior

kohroh (n) TR—fossil fuel, especially rock chlorophyll

Ll

laf (adj, adv) FW—1. a large number of things, many; 2. to emphasise a high degree or precise, very

lah (adv) FW—1. combining words, thoughts or things; and; 2. in combination; with, together; 3. positioned beside

lahtoo (n) TR—1. a mixture of things, or a collage; 2. everything and everyone

lap (adj, n) TG—1. light by which to see, the appearance of brightness; 2. light in weight; 3. specifically, sunlight and daytime

lapptak (n, adj) TG—1. a shadow or shade from sunlight; 2. heavy

lasha (n) TG—the spiritual power of the trees; an electromagnetic energy, both in its sporadic nature and in appearance

lashmuh (n) TG—1. a ceremony burning wood to acquire spiritual power; 2. a ritual to communicate with the tree gods; 3. generosity

lashyb (n) SG—the wood sacrifice squad of veteran tree warriors

leepash (n) TR—tree raid; (also) **leepash tahsak**—trunk thrust or takeover

leepkah (n) TR—any mode of planetary surface transportation

leepshah (n) SG—metaphysically teleporting into spiritual dimensions

loho (n) TR—1. victory, triumph; 2. a celebration or party

lohsee (v, adj) TR—1.to protect or defend; 2. conditions that are safe

Mm

maha (n, v) SG—1. the emotion of love and caring for someone or something; 2. the sentiment of happiness and enjoyment; 3. to help, assist or physically care for someone or something

massyb (n, v) TR—1. laughter; 2. to play games

mee (n, pr) FW—1. a male; 2. referring to a male; he, him or his

meelkah (v) TR—1. to infiltrate under disguise; 2. to deceive

meesah (n) TR—son

min (n) TG—a valley or canyon

minvab (n) TG—a lake or large open section of a river

minvahba (n) TG—an ocean, including ocean water

moobah (n) TR—1. manifesto hope for peaceful existence; 2. justice

muh (adj) FW—1. an affirmative response; yes, including with enthusiasm; definitely; 2. good; 3. beautiful

muzz (n) TG—1. a hill, including a hilltop; 2. a pile or stack of something

---

Nn

naga (v) FW—1. to do something; 2. to make something; 3. to want or need; 4. to get or retrieve something

nah (int, v) FW—a request for the will of someone to do something, or to inquire if someone did something; will you or did you; 2. expressing intention; I will, I do, you will, you do, it will be done

nahsah (v) TG—1. to give, especially a gift; 2. to bring or send

nahtoo (v) TR—1. to embrace, someone or something physically, or a concept philosophically; 2. to unite together; 3. to include

neewha (adj, n) TR—1. possible, maybe; 2. approximately; 3. opportunity

neewhasee (n, adv, pr) SG—1. something; 2. to identify something; that, this or it

---

Oo

oocree (v) TR—1. to hang something or someone; 2. to drop something or someone

oocreetak (n) TR—a rope or a line of some material

oonah (adj) TR—1. straight or dimensionally square; 2. across

oosah (adj, v) TR—1. a form of matter or energy that is flowing; 2. to pour

---

Pp

pah (int) FW—to question for information; when, at which time

pahva (adv) FW—1. an indication of time, later; 2. tomorrow

pin (adj, adv) TG—1. only a few, as opposed to many; 2. moderately

pinnah (adj) TG—1. to be alone, separated; 2. only, unique

po (adv) FW—1. an indication of time, now; 2. today or tonight

pohsah (pr) FW—1. an indication of time, before; 2. yesterday

poot (n) TG—a steep incline, ascent or descent, especially on land

Qq

quueesah (n) SG—a surprise

quueesum (adj, n) SG—1. necessary, required; must; 2. a task

Rr

rah (n) FW—1. expressing appreciation, thank you; 2. farewell

rahnee (n, adj) SG—1. thoughtful prudence; 2. good judgement

rushah (n) SG—wisdom that comes from the knowledge of truth

rygah (adj) TR—great in quality; impressive

Ss

sah (adj) FW—the back side of someone or something; the rear

sahba (adj) FW—1. a negative response, no; 2. bad; 3. ugly

sahzah (adj, v) SG—1. the quality of being lazy; sloth; 2. to steal

seebee (adj) TG—identical or similar; the same

seerah (n) TR—a vest, made with flexible inner bark-bast phloem fibre of a tree; made only with bark-bast, or sometimes with phloem fibre as a lining against the body, and smooth polished bark on the outer portion of the vest

seewha (adv) SG – always

shahmah (n) SG—the spiritual dimension, believed to contain tree gods

shahska (v, n) TG—1. to smell odour or fragrance; 2. the ole factory sense; 3. the nose, or the anatomical feature that smells

shahtee (n) TG—1. the visual sense; vision; 2. the eyes, or the anatomical feature that provides vision

shahtoo (v, n) TG—1. to see; 2. to understand; 3. realisation; 4. to describe; a description

shahtoonee (n) TR—1. a story; 2. a set of instructions; 3. an account

shahtum (n) SG—an individual's facial area, including the head and skull

snoh (n, v, adj) FW—1. fire; 2. the colour red; 3. to burn; 4. hot

snohssa (n) TG—1. summer season; 2. south

soonah (adj, n, v) TG—1. sad; 2. to be sorry; 3. pain; 4. fear; 5. to cry

soonahsee (adj, n) TG—1. sick, not well; 2. specifically, an infection

stah (n) TR—1. a warrior's wood instrument; 2. a fabricated weapon

suumwhah (pr) SG—sometimes, not always; somewhat in degree

sweesah (adv, adj) TR—1. fast; 2. soon

sygah (adj) TG—1. hard; 2. difficult; arduous; 3. tough, resilient, durable

sygahvee (adj, v) SG—1. broken, cracked, crushed or damaged; 2. rough, uneven, jagged; 3. defeated, failure; 4. to surrender

sygahzah (n, adj) SG—1. garbage; 2. wasteful

sylva (n) SG—a prophecy of unparalleled actuality in a tree warrior

---

Tt

tah (adj) FW—1. big or tall; 2. fat; 3. up or over; 4. stand upright

tahba (n) TR—an adult

tahbee (adj) TG—1. to be outside in nature; 2. far away in proximity

tahkah (n) TR—1. a planet; 2. solid rock, boulders or stones found on planets and stellar objects

tahkahfee (n) TR—an orbiting moon; also, asteroid or meteoroid

tahkahsoo (n) TR—small granular rock or organic matter forming soil, dirt or sand

tahkid (n) TR—1. an established camp for habitation; 2. a large arboretum interstellar flying ship

tahktigg (n) SG—steel or fabricated metal

tahktiggah (n) SG—precious metals and gemstones; also jewellery

tahsah (adj) SG—to be old; already existing

tahsak (v, adv) TR—1. to push something or someone; 2. to be on, in contact with a place or thing in question

tap (adj, v, n) FW—1. dark, darkness; 2. to sleep; 3. a bed or spot for sleeping; 4. night time

tappah (adj) TG—cold or frozen

tappahvee (n) TG—1. winter season; 2. north; 3. the colour white

tappvah (n) TG—ice

tee (pr) FW—referring to another person; you, yours

teelaf (pr) SG—referring to other people, including second person plural; they, them, theirs, you, yours

teesah (n) SG—1. arrogance and extravagance, pride and gluttony; 2. someone who is not intelligent, or foolish

teewha (adv) SG—never or nothing

tigg (n) TG—a fabricated structure; originally on a trail, such as steps, a boardwalk or bridge

tiggah (v, n) TR—1. to build something; 2. a building structure

tiggahsee (v, n, adj) TR—1. to cut or carve; 2. a cut in any material or matter; 3. something that is sharp; a knife; 4. someone who is smart

tiggat (n) TR—apparatus that functions as a container, such as pots, pans, bottles, fluid bags or baskets

tiggeet (n) TR—1. utensils for eating; 2. tools for wood working; 3. instruments or equipment for engineering and construction

tiggvab (n) SG—something that floats on water; specifically a boat

tonntah (n) SG—1. cosmic dust, gases, nebulae; 2. cosmic spiral corridors, thought to be occupied by wind warriors and vapour demons

tonntee (n) SG—cosmic stars, including galaxies and quasars

trak (n) SG—a mechanical interstellar spacecraft

traupah (n) TR—a spiritual tree warrior; (also) **bohtrak**—navigator; **gootak**—log splitter; **sweesah**—firewood harvester; **tah**—root thrasher; **tahkahsoo**—soil suck; **tahkid**—campfire maintainer; **tiggahsee**—bark shredder

traupek (n) TR—a mortal humanoid without spiritual powers

traushah (n) TG—a spiritual leader; shaman or spirit seeker

Vv

vabsoo (n) TG—precipitation, including rain, sleet and snow

vah (n) TG—the colour blue

vahba (n, adj) TG—1. water; 2. wet

vahbahsee (v) TR—to wash or clean

vahbahsnoh (n) TG—lightning in the atmosphere

vahbahsoo (n) TG—fog, mist or steam; also, clouds in the sky

vahbee (n) TG—shades of the colour grey in nature

vee (adv) FW—1. to repeat; again; 2. to replace

veebee (adj, adv) TG—1. different; opposite; or; 2. to contrast; however

veesak (n) TG—1. spring season; 2. east; 3. right hand direction

veesakah (n) SG—1. the quality of humility; 2. the colour yellow

veesoo (n) SG—fingers on a hand

veesum (n) SG—the arm portion of a body

vohko (adj) SG—1. strong; 2. courageous or brave

Ww

whaga (v) FW—1. to go; 2. to return; 3. to seek, investigate or survey

whagaswee (v) TG—to step; to walk or run

whaha (v, n) FW—1. to wait; 2. (SG addition) an era of time; **whaha wot**—eon, billion years or annua; **whaha lot**—millennium, one thousand; **whaha tot**—a century, one hundred

whasoo (n) SG—a foot, including toes

whasoolak (n) SG—sandals, shoes or boots; footwear

whasum (n) SG—the legs of a body

whassa (n, v) TG—1. the force of air currents; wind; 2. to take the lead, physically or emotionally

whassasee (n) TG—air to breathe

whasseeb (n) TG—1. autumn; 2. west; 3. left hand direction

Zz

za (n) TR—1. a coward; 2. a thief

zahka (n, v, adj) TR—1. war or battle; 2. to fight, or kill; 3. danger

zahkahsoo (n) TR—1. death; 2. an injury

zahnoosah (n) TR—1. the creed philosophy, expressing destruction and control; 2. evil intentions; 3. greed and desire

zeeb (adj, n) FW—1. disagree with complete defiance; strongly against, opposed; 2. (SG addition) anger and frustration

Gods / Original Angels (Warriors)—Tree Species

Crown Grand Creation
Var / Sinaitati (n) TG—bubinga trees

Idyp / Sar (n) TG—kurrajong trees

Verra / Peyote (n) TG—cactus trees

Lipna / Zadek (n) TG—mopani trees

Evbic / Marcynaki (n) TG—olive trees

Kwarg / Wabagoon (n) TG—alder trees

Cess / Nagawashi (n) TG—teak trees

Laavv / Atakeewan (n) TG—baobab trees

Nekrol / Prawda (n) TG—gum trees

Moht / Irbe (n) TG—rose trees

Maav / Yhar (n) TG—beech trees
Baf / Yabnas (n) TG—jute trees
Yanamea / Urbonas (n) TG—sassafras trees
Tyru / Wek (n) TG—kapok trees
Apar / Nuuka (n) TG—mangrove trees
Marn / Frev (n) TG—calabash trees
Rom / Avid (n) TG—rubber trees

Plateau Grand Creation
Wateko / Nycaa (n) TG—maple trees
Nybos / Syntra (n) TG—cedar trees
Svebb / Saleh (n) TG—ginkgo trees
Lirda / Talib (n) TG—elm trees
Gorb / Envrah (n) TG—aspen trees
Dkobi / Demkew (n) TG—poplar trees
Ardyk / Yndes (n) TG—tamarack trees
Quujj / Minga (n) TG—pine trees
Pefl / Dlailia (n) TG—willow trees
Sonus / Coulee (n) TG—birch trees
Zarkk / Naruka (n) TG—fir trees
Rulsp / Alka (n) TG—spruce trees
Fesso / Dewar (n) TG—oak trees

Summit Grand Creation
Jacobi / Haukna (n) TG—yew trees
Dwyi / Nylor (n) TG—jacaranda trees
Janale / Dovipan (n) TG—eucalyptus trees
Onu / Karv (n) TG—balsa trees
Kumi / Tusra (n) TG—greenheart trees
Eamaan / Wabeka (n) TG—ash trees
Rens / Kagiwosa (n) TG—tung trees
Palu / Zemder (n) TG—redwood trees
Forek / Swoon (n) TG—karri trees
Kymm / Suzhe (n) TG—ebony trees
Hume / Yonn (n) TG—incense trees
Yufe / Baltsa (n) TG—palm trees

Baqua / Sabaqua (n) TG—acacia trees

Yett / Pagron (n) TG—avocado trees

Kapid / Calli (n) TG—podocarpus trees

Cyte / Kuaandi (n) TG—mallee trees

Alsa / Drang (n) TG—mahogany trees

Numbers

FW—0 (zero)—**top** 1—**ap** 2—**ip** 3—**eep** 4—**at** 5—**it** 6—**eet** 7—**af** 8—**if** 9—
eef 10—**mot** 11—**mot ap** 20—**ip mot** 100 (hundred)—**tot** 200—**ip tot**
TG—1,000—**lot** 2,000—**ip lot** 1,000,000 (million)—**fot**
1,000,000,000 (billion)—**wot**

Ingram Content Group UK Ltd.
Milton Keynes UK
UKHW020626230423
420621UK00007B/1018